MY SONG'S CURSE

POPPY MINNIX

CITY OWL PRESS

This book is a work of fiction. Names, characters, places, and incidents either are products of the author's imagination or are used fictitiously. Any resemblance to actual events or locales or persons, living or dead, is entirely coincidental and not intended by the author.

MY SONG'S CURSE
Duet of the Gods, Book 1

CITY OWL PRESS
www.cityowlpress.com

All Rights reserved. Except as permitted under the U.S. Copyright Act of 1976, no part of this publication may be reproduced, distributed, or transmitted in any form or by any means, or stored in a database or retrieval system, without the prior consent and permission of the publisher.

Copyright © 2020 by Poppy Minnix.

Cover Design by Mibl Art. All stock photos licensed appropriately.

Edited by Tee Tate.

For information on subsidiary rights, please contact the publisher at info@cityowlpress.com.

Print Edition ISBN: 978-1-64898-005-3

Digital Edition ISBN: 978-1-64898-004-6

Printed in the United States of America

Praise for Poppy Minnix

"Poppy Minnix brings a fresh breath of air to Greek mythology in My Songs Curse. The characters jumped off the page and stole my heart."
– *Cassandra Kay, Host of Punchkeys Podcast*

"Putting a new twist on an old story, Poppy Minnix kept me on the edge of my seat."
– *Raisa Greywood, Bestselling Author of Demon Lust*

"From the steamy flirting to the classic lore, this story's magical from start to finish! Lula's fun voice will captivate you like it does all of humanity."
– *Jackie Norling, Author*

"Just like the myth, My Song's Curse will lure you in and captivate you. You won't want to stop turning the pages as you root for Alex and Lula's love to endure the odds in this steamy, fun, and flirty romance."
– *Lumen Ros, Paranormal and Dark Fantasy Author*

"A wonderful story, in which the paranormal aspect does not overshadow the plot and storytelling. It features compelling characters, lovely description, snappy dialogue, and melt-me steamy moments! A great read!"
– *Chloe Holiday, Author*

To John, who inspires the best qualities in my characters. Thank you for letting me be me.

Chapter One

LULA

Being a siren sucks.

Every customer stares at me in attentive silence as I sit at the least conspicuous table in the back corner of this mom-and-pop Italian restaurant.

Well, excuse me for clearing my throat.

Going out in public wasn't the best idea, but this afternoon, I held a heated conversation with the actors on my television. They apologized to each other with caresses and phrases of sweetness, but I ended up on the floor, hugging a pillow in the empty silence. When a show becomes my reality, it's time to leave the house.

Now, as usual, I've enthralled the humans. *Whoops*. They study me as if the next thing I do will make their lives complete. The attention is normal, but I'm the last being they should covet because there's much more to my species than being a lust magnet. A few more words from my hypnotic voice and they'd lick my shoes if I asked them to. Not that I would.

So now, it's time to return home. I push my chair back, but a shadow obscures the dim glow of overhead lights.

A man looms over me, dark and decadent, oozing charm with his confident smile. Well, hello, handsome. Other diners stand to follow him toward me.

"Stop," I tell them. "Return to your seats. If you work here, continue your duties." I bring my gaze to his. "You stay."

Even though our conversation will be as fake as the actors I argued with earlier today, my heart thumps an excited beat. It's been months since I've sat with someone.

I slide the empty chair out from under the table with my foot. "Sit." I keep my voice quiet and controlled, but it's a deep purr of promise.

He does what he's told, waiting with a familiar expression of hope mixed with dedication plus a dash of "do" me. Poor humans are so easy to captivate.

I let my fork drop against my bowl of pasta primavera, creating a loud clang that shatters through the room. "Name?"

"Jordan Oltier."

"Okay, Jordan." I draw circles on the checkered tablecloth with my fingertips. "Tell me three things about yourself."

He concentrates, lips pursed, and eyes to the ceiling. "I play basketball, own a dog named Maizy, and I'm a nurse at Grison General in the pediatrics department."

Wow. Mr. Oltier sounds perfect. I dig deeper just for giggles. "Do you have a wife, fiancée, or girlfriend?"

"No."

"Boyfriend?" I ask, taking another bite of pasta.

Unlike most humans, his focused pucker relaxes into a grin. "No."

His big hands rest against the cream-colored tablecloth. They'd unzip my dress and splay across my back, hot fingers digging into neglected skin. Eagerness flares in his eyes.

I haven't invited someone in for a long while. Each move we'd make would play out in a script with me as the director. Except I'd force my leading man to do whatever I wanted, unsure if he enjoyed himself or what he'd do if he had free will. After, he'd return to the humans, used for a night with fuzzy memories of me that would fade by the hour, while I'd hold on to every fake touch because it's the closest thing I have to a life in an empty room of endless time. I don't want that for either of us.

Still, what's the harm in talking about it?

I prop my elbow on the table, cupping my jaw. "What were your thoughts when you saw me? Before I spoke?"

"You were the most beautiful woman I'd ever seen. Confident and brave. Maybe a screamer." He lights up like the thought delights him.

He wouldn't enjoy my screams, but his comment makes me grin. I ask him my favorite question. "What do you wish to do with me?"

"Kiss you, then tie you up."

Yum. I didn't peg him as the type.

He shifts forward, his stare hard and unwavering. "And run a knife down your sternum thirty times, cutting deeper each time until I could touch your bones and play with your heart, the slickness of your blood—"

"Stop."

I hate it when this happens.

Chilled silence reigns in the restaurant, not because of creepy confessions but because my voice is a beacon to every creature that isn't a siren. They stare, not at this serial killer but at me. They should rage, call the police, or run for it. Instead, they wait for my attention, hanging on each sound. I wish they wouldn't.

"How many have you killed?" I ask.

"None," he replies.

Relief replaces the tight hold of terror in my chest. "Do you want to kill someone?"

"Yes."

His enthusiasm still simmers, but I don't appreciate this brand of passion. People tell me odd and honest things, but his confession is one of the more disturbing ones.

I lock onto his dark eyes, and my voice shifts into a deep and deliberate tone. "You will never kill. Think of how to help others instead of harming them. Pay for your dinner and leave."

Wannabe-serial-killer Jordan walks to an empty table near the front of the room, places bills down, and glances at me over his shoulder. He nods before exiting.

Odd. They rarely look back after I order them to go.

The room is so quiet, chills raise on my arms. I'm tempted to break a plate or turn over a chair to make a racket. Even the prep workers stare, frozen in the kitchen doorway.

A man and woman walk in, stopping short in confusion. The couple follows as each person's gaze is drawn to me. The man gives a low whistle, earning a smack on the chest from his companion. With a chuckle, he presses his lips to hers.

I want to sigh or say aw, but I bite my lip and keep quiet. I won't ruin meaningful kisses for those able to enjoy them.

His hand sneaks around her waist, and she melts into his embrace as the world shushes, leaving them alone to savor each other. He chooses her above others, even a siren, and his body language is a gift of insight into his mind.

Lucky humans.

Eyes follow my every move as I pin money under my plate and make my way to the exit.

Squeezing past the couple, I snatch a few buttermints from a dish on the hostess stand and call over my shoulder, "I was never here."

As I step into the warm night air, the chatter inside resumes. The customers and staff won't recall that I took over their dining experience, and those who see me around town will remember me, but I'll be nondescript. Forgettable. I'd love to understand why I'm this way, but even my most knowledgeable sisters tell me, "Just because, Lu." It's like they don't care to find out our history and where the three original siren mothers went.

Nonetheless, my ability is as frustrating as it is a comfort. I may not have friends besides my sisters, but I've altered wannabe-serial-killer Jordan's brain to a normal human mode...or he may go insane. He won't kill anyone, though. Win? I shrug to myself.

Not ready to return to my empty house, the endless downtown sidewalks beckon me. Couples file out of bars and head home or to the beds of others. They talk in loud laughing phrases about human world things—friends, politics, and pop culture until they notice me. Staring replaces the conversation. The urge to speak up is unmanageable; *I enjoyed that movie too. Yeah, the new governor is a douche, except he has good educational policies. Your girlfriend has princess syndrome.*

A hush falls over the city this time of night, leaving me to meander in relative peace. The rhythmic clack of my heels echoing off brick and concrete soothe me and send my thoughts wandering to the human culture I've experienced this evening.

My phone buzzes in my purse and I drag it out as I check if anyone is within earshot. Few people walk the streets. Smiling at Amah's name, I answer in a whisper. "Hello, Ma."

"You sound happy. Why are you whispering?"

I wince. I nicknamed my oldest siren sister 'Ma' for a reason, not just because it fits her real name or because she's the closest thing I have to a mother. Amah makes sure we take care of ourselves and behave. I'm one for two. "I'm walking downtown."

The tap of her nail clicks against metal. "Tell me about tonight's outfit," she says, toneless.

I glance at the sheath dress that clings to my every curve like a warm hug. "Sweats."

"Liar."

"Fine. My favorite green dress. I went to dinner, had primavera, stopped potential crime." Ma won't appreciate that. She takes a natural approach to the mortals. Farm what you need from them, then set them free.

"Oh, Lula. Only you. Let's see it's...my goodness, eleven where you are? Darklings and otherworldlings may be out. Please go home soon."

The memory of my first darkling encounter makes my steps slow. Lena's death was more than a century ago. It's over. I shove away sad thoughts. It's my night out on the town, my time to pretend I belong somewhere. I'll save heartbreak for when I'm alone again.

"The otherworldlings fit in with the humans," I say, clacking along the sidewalks. "They won't make a scene, and I can control them if they do. Plus, the streets are empty." Eerily so, even for the late hour on a weekday.

"I know. I just worry. Have you spoken to Gerty or Venora lately?"

"I spoke to Gerty last month, but Ven and I chatted two weeks ago."

"Gerty isn't returning calls. Ven's in love, again, and has been hard to catch. She tells me he's intense."

"Intense?" Venora's the romantic out of my seven sisters. I'm happy for her if she's found another to keep her warm and off the phone, but she holds onto her sweet, doting men and women a little too long before setting them free. "Not her typical choice of companion."

"No, he's not. He withstands her thrall well, but she claims he's human."

"You think he's an otherworldling?" The non-human species resist our ability better than humans, but they eventually succumb.

The chipped sidewalk catches my heel, and I stumble before a boarded-up building. I've wandered into an area of town that would terrify most people.

"I should go," I whisper.

"Let me know if you hear from them."

"I will. Love you, Ma."

"Love you, too." We hang up, and I pivot, put my phone away, and walk the direction I came.

"Mm, now there's a fine piece." A droning voice close behind me grabs my attention.

I spin and get a glimpse of green spiked hair before a fist rams into my midsection, and the air rushes from me in a harsh 'whoosh.'

Crumpling, I open my mouth to inhale, but can't get a breath.

Two pairs of scuffed boots and three sets of colorful kicks step closer. Straightening up shoots a pang through my gut. The five men circle—sharks scenting fresh blood. Each is menacing, with piercings, scars, and bared teeth. The same devil face tattoo marks their necks. Their sick laughter promises hate and pain, and I need to speak right now. A couple puff up, jerk toward me with aggressive movements, closing in to block my exit as I gasp to find my missing air. Nothing happens but a wheeze. Not good.

"On the corner tonight, sweetheart?" One harsh voice says. "I could use a good workout." As if I needed clarification, he steps closer to brush his hardness against my side. I move to hip check his crotch, but he hurries back, barking a laugh.

"Got a little fighter here," he says. "Fun, fun."

Balling my fists, I struggle to growl, but nothing comes out. I'd command them if I could only get a breath. These are the type of beings that need to be enthralled for good.

Someone jerks me upright as the man with hair like spring grass steps close, inches from my face, and shows off a cracked incisor. "What's a high-class bitch like you doing on our turf?"

His voice is a low growl. Demon? He'd be a runt if he were. My nose tingles with a lack of oxygen as I gulp at the night air that can't find room in my lungs yet.

"This is our street, Mama. Ain't nobody gonna save ya. Ready for me? Hmm?"

A man jogs out of the shadows. "Let her go." He strides forward into the dim light, his jaw clenched tight. He's wearing a plain gray tee, no tattoos cover his neck, and the ferocious scowl he wears tells me he doesn't belong to this group.

The man next to me gives a dark chuckle, reaching into his pocket for what I'm sure is a weapon. Finally, I inhale enough air to speak. "Step...back."

The three that haven't yet spoken walk backward in sync. My thrall and I have a rocky relationship. This is a proud, appreciative moment.

The one holding onto me releases my arm, but Grass-head in front of me only twitches. It's as if his body wants to move, but his mind fights it.

Coughing forces more air in, then out of my burning lungs. "Go home."

This time, four turn and walk away without another word. The stubborn fifth remains. Some humans have more resistance than others, and since otherworldling species hold out long enough to harm those around them, I always work fast.

I hum, though it's shaky. Three seconds of my note and he drops his proud stance. He swallows and blinks several times, then he raises his smitten gaze.

Placing my hands on my hips, I straighten so I'm as tall as he is. "Are you listening now?"

"Yes." He nods, a tapped bobble-head doll, and relief loosens the tension in my back. At least until I notice the onlooker still stands ten feet from us. My ability should have seeped through, even if he were deaf.

Witnesses are an issue, but sometimes life throws you gang

members and you have to make community servants. Or liquified bad guys. It can't come to that, though. Not here.

I'll handle the other man in a moment, but first, my focus falls on the enthralled asshole. I should make him jump in the sewers and let the wildlife deal with him. My sore stomach aches under my hand. "Treat women with respect. No punching, name-calling, and no grinding against unwilling participants, got it? That's just gross."

Past his shoulder, spray paint and neglect touch everything, but between two boarded-up buildings lies a big dirt lot under a streetlight. There's potential to give someone the purpose they need.

I point. "Start a community garden. Get your people involved and donate extra food. Go make plans."

He scurries away, leaving me with the stranger.

The streetlight illuminates him, a spotlight on a golden-haired movie star. Tonight must be tall and handsome night. This guy better be less psychotic than wannabe-serial-killer Jordan.

I ball my fists and shove my resurfacing libido aside. My body is so desperate, it has already forgotten the punch. "Did you not hear me? Go home."

He ambles toward me. Stubble lines his sculpted jaw. It's been far too long since I've experienced stubble burn. He halts a foot from me and stares with rare golden eyes. The color is inhuman. My hands fall from my hips, power stance forgotten.

"I heard you fine, Firecracker." His voice soothes, even though his powerful frame and towering height tempt me to step back. "Are you okay? I can't believe they punched you. That shouldn't have happened."

My eyes widen. No one resists my power except my species. There are no male sirens, right? I play over every detail of siren history. The three mothers exiled from Olympus only gave birth to females then disappeared. I'm the fourth generation from the line of Agalope, second youngest of eight sirens, so I'm aware that I don't know everything about our species like Amah does. I'm soulbound to my species though, I'd connect to this being, wouldn't I? I've learned much in my hundred and eighty-two years, but a resistant male is new. He appears concerned for me. Maybe he's slightly enthralled?

"I'm fine. Leave."

His furrowed brow smooths to an amused angle. "Care to explain how you turned a gang of felons into future gardeners?"

What? Wait. How? *Words, Lula, you can do this.* "Why aren't you headed home right now?"

"Because I'd rather be here, making sure you're safe. Are you okay?"

I should run. I have no weapons beyond my voice. Amah has warned me time and again that my curiosity will get me killed, but I have to figure him out. "What's your name?" He doesn't look like a Grizaldak the Torturer.

"Call me Alex."

That name works for him. I deepen my timbre, letting my vocal cords relax into each word. "Leave, Alex."

He tilts his head and perfect lips purse. "I'm not sold that you want me to."

This isn't right. I review my list of otherworldlings with the ability to disguise themselves as human and dismiss each species that doesn't match—no fangs, no fur, no tail. Tall, but not giant height. Two stunning gold eyes. I narrow the possibilities to a few choices. Shapeshifter, Nephilim, or incubus. Bad, worse, or worst.

I can't deal with this tonight. If I sing my siren song, even the saintliest among beings would murder for me, but after a verse, they become sleepy and unaware that their organs are dissolving. If I hit the chorus, there's not enough of them left to order around anymore. But releasing my power hurts even if the creature's evil. They scream in agony, and I have guilt-laced nightmares for months.

No, thank you.

This one tried to help me though and doesn't appear to be a danger to humans. I pivot, and the sidewalk leads me from the friendly enough bad guy.

"Hey, hold up," Alex calls.

"Go away." I break into a tiptoe run.

"Hey, wait." A hand snatches my forearm within a second, and Alex spins me. I slap at him, but he snags my wrist in mid-air and plants my hand against his chest, ducking his head, face level with mine. "I won't harm you."

"That's what incubi say before they suck out someone's life force."

The ancient song etched in my DNA spills from my lips in a rush of power. It's a cadence from celestial tongues, except the heavenly notes bring death.

Alex's eyes widen. Under my palm, his heart thuds a peaceful rhythm.

My voice carries with more strength, pulling deep from my soul. Releasing it makes my body hum, but my thoughts seize up as I wait for the disaster to come. When I get to the chorus, he bites his smiling lip, and the song dies in my throat.

"Beautiful. You're a siren."

He knows what I am. And he's still standing. How in the hell is he still standing? His face isn't showing pain. He's grinning like the guy at the restaurant did at his companion.

Oh, shit. Not good.

Fear sends tendrils of tightness to every muscle in my body. Black spots threaten my vision as my overwhelmed mind merry-go-rounds and the ground sways. Alex moves in, supporting me with a strong arm. "Hey, it's okay. I won't hurt you."

He must have calming pheromones because the heat of his skin calls to mine and I sink into his hold, breathing in his sweet citrus scent. Focus, Lula. Incubi are masters of seduction, but even an incubus wouldn't smile at my song. They wouldn't hold me as if I belonged in their arms, because they'd be busy on the ground, having their insides liquefied.

"What are you?" I ask.

Alex's amused expression falters, sending tightness through me again. I try to jerk away, but he clings and blurts out, "A demigod."

No way. A deity on earth? There's the slightest glow to him, a confident golden hue that draws me to him, telling me he's here to help. No otherworldling has that.

My palm lies over the heart of a god.

I've never met a deity. Amah says they abandoned the Earth long before I was born.

He—Alex—observes me, squinting. In the old days, people worshipped the gods that visited Earth in preposterous ways, right up to tossing themselves off cliffs to gain the divine's favor. Three decades ago, a nymph told me she came across two and tried to please them, but they wouldn't accept anything from her, only wanted to talk about humans and otherworldlings. Maybe this deity has questions too.

I breathe slowly, attempting to tame my speeding heart. "What's your real name?"

He leans forward, millimeters from my cheek, warm breath brushing my ear. "Alexiares."

I shudder, letting that information settle. I've studied him—the demigod who wards off wars. The son of Hercules and grandson of Zeus, the king of Olympus. Damn.

My eyes wander his features, searching for any clue to the phenomenon that is this deity. "I don't affect you?"

"Oh, you affect me."

Unable to keep the sarcasm at bay, I groan and step back from him. "My ability, I mean. Siren, remember?"

"Did you just eye-roll at a deity?"

I grin instead of performing the thousand apologies I'm sure he's expecting. My power doesn't work on him. I'm still wavering between belief and impossibility. It's a flaw, a dream, a crazy oasis mirage envisioned in a desert when I need it the most, except I'm not thirsty for water. I've never had an honest conversation with a male.

His full grin is disarming. "No, your ability doesn't affect me. You could ask me to kiss you and it would have no impact on me."

Intrigued, I eye his lips. "Really? Kiss me."

With a step forward, he cups the back of my head, fingers threading through my hair, and peruses my features with intent I've only seen in romance movies.

I'd contemplate that look, but he inches forward. Chills rise in response to the electricity shifting between us. I didn't believe he'd kiss me.

He's a deity.

He's also a stranger, and I should pull away.

"No impact, huh?" I whisper.

"Just a taste. Tell me to stop." His eyes search mine.

He radiates warmth, smells like my best dreams, and for one moment, I want someone to kiss me because they want to.

I relax into the hand cupping my head, tilt my chin up...

And wait.

Chapter Two

ALEX

Just a taste.
Bad idea, Alex.
Remaining in the shadows was the plan. I shouldn't have stepped in when I damn well knew Lula could handle things on her own.

For the first time in centuries, I didn't think things through.

I move to let her go, but her head fits perfectly in my hand, fusing my splayed fingers against her silky red curls. Imagining what touching her would be like couldn't capture the warmth of her or the impact when she's focused on me. I've watched her for a year, but unlike now, her gaze has never found me. The green is piercing, the exact shade of a chrysoprase stone. She stares up at me in a challenge that, were I a demon or a werewolf, would make my inner beast rage. I'm a god and should have better control, but still, all of me bends to her temptation.

I dip. My head spins with the faint, ghosting kiss I give her.

By the gods.

She's so soft.

Her scent recalls memories of picking berries after a rainstorm, and I'm unwilling to stop myself from pressing harder, teasing her lips to part. Lula grips my shirt with one delicate hand while wrapping her other fingers around my bicep and with the slightest exhalation, she opens to me.

She tastes of mint and garlic. An odd combination, but on her, it works. The temptation to cage her in and sample every flavor on her makes my head spin, but darkness shades the moment.

We shouldn't be this close. She stands on a path I'm not allowed to travel. My grandfather and his Council of old gods made sure of that long ago. Mingling with non-deities is illegal, and I can't give him an opportunity to strike out when my most-trusted friends and I are closing in on the changes the universe needs. I have to keep Lula safe and content. We need her.

I slow, kissing her with a few gentle teasing pulls. She nips my lip, stopping me from pulling away, making me smile.

She's not like other sirens. Despite the human world's rumors, most sirens are shy and kind for a race that could take anything they wanted and annihilate any Earth being with a song. Lula is kind, but there's an edge to her the others lack.

Her judgment is also better than mine because she flinches, and she gives me a last peck before she breaks away. I follow, but she keeps us separate with a hand on my chest, blinking at me with owlish eyes. "I took the bait there, didn't I?"

I cover her hand with mine. "You did, but I'm the one who's hooked."

I can't help playing with her. Rath explained the things she'd done with the humans. If they fell under her spell, she'd make them tell her a joke or ask them about the sweetest thing that ever happened to them. She doesn't use harsh commands unless needed, like this evening. Some people need a hard stop placed on their inner demons. Some demons need control too, and I believe she can do that as well. It's why I'm here.

I get an arched eyebrow response. "Nice one."

Her sassy smirk makes me want to kiss those perfect lips again. I've met few women who know what I am and haven't fallen over themselves attempting to impress me: bowing, speaking words of submission. Hell, they've even turned and lifted skirt, offering their body as worship.

Never an eye-roll.

In my younger days, I relished in their offerings, but the excitement wore off long ago when I realized the divine's gods-awful ways. Repairing this world takes precedence over play, even with a tempting green-eyed otherworldling.

A little growl of frustration escapes, and I clear my throat, attempting to disguise it. "Would you like to go somewhere?" Her eyebrows raise and I add, "To talk."

I can't tell her everything—that will come on a carefully-laid timeline—but I need to establish a relationship now that I've misstepped into the light.

Lula shifts on her feet. "It's late." Her expression doesn't match her deterring words. She catches the middle of her bottom lip under her teeth and lowers her gaze.

"You sure?"

Her curls shift, tempting me to touch them as she studies the streets and blows out a long breath. "Why?"

Because you're a piece of the plan. Because I'm intrigued for more. Because I'm dying for you to look at me as I've been looking at you.

"I've never had a conversation with a siren."

"I've never spoken to a deity."

Yes, she has.

I tilt my head. "That makes us a good match for a talk, yeah?"

Lula pivots. The clack of her shoes against pavement thumps through my chest. She blinks at me over her shoulder and my entire body shocks to attention. "Location will be an issue," she whispers. "If humans hear me, they will cause a scene."

"I have a place in mind." I pull my phone from my pocket and text Comus, *She saw me. We're going to the gastropub. Get a private alcove and tell Rath to take Zeph home.*

We can't have Lula believe we're associating with a human psycho.

"It's about a ten-minute walk. Are you okay in those?" I point to her heels.

"Yes. I like to walk."

"Me too." I sidle up next to her and head toward the restaurant.

"Is that why you're out here?" Her eyes flit around the night. Broken buildings and garbage laden streets make her lips tighten and her brows knit to a stressed concern.

"I needed to walk." I leave out the part where I needed to walk after her to see what she did after the restaurant. There could have been trauma from her encounter with Zeph. Instead, she met The Bringers and handled them too, after a strike to the gut. I could end Chaos right now for touching her. "Are you hurt? After that punch?"

She lifts one shoulder. "I'm fine. My name is Lula. You haven't asked."

"I was giving you your privacy." That one puts a sour taste in my mouth.

"But kissing me was—"

My phone buzzes. It's either Comus calling to get a full rundown or Rath calling to laugh at me. Rath's been pushing for contact with Lula for a while. He told me I'd crack one day, and I wasn't allowed to be an idiot around her. That conversation can wait.

"Kissing you was unexpected, and I'm not going to lie. It was decent. Nice meeting you, Lula."

A wave of emotions swims across her face: happy, amused, insulted, quickly followed by giddy. "Decent?" Then annoyance as the buzz sounds again. "Is that a phone?"

I wet my lips and drag my cell from my pocket. As soon as I answer, I blurt out, "You will not believe my night. I met a siren." Lula appears ready to bolt, and I take her hand and turn the phone to the side. "It's my friend Comus."

"Tell me I'm not on speaker," Comas says, his voice stifled against the music and hum of a crowd.

The God of Revelry can find the best locations and amplify the mood to an excited boiling point. Each visit here makes returning to Olympus more difficult for all of us. Humans are fun.

"No. We're headed to the gastropub. Meet us there?"

Lula's eyes widen and I squeeze her hand.

"Rath's already there," Comus says. "I'm on the way. Is she okay?"

"Excellent. See you in a few." I hang up and let go of Lula's hand. "Two of my friends are meeting us there if that's okay?"

Her lips part, but she says nothing.

I slide in front of her and walk backward. "They're also deities." Following, she nibbles on that lip again, and I halt. Stumbling, she almost runs into me, but I grab her waist and hold her close without a second thought.

She startles like a shocked cat and takes a step back. "I need time to...process."

"Sorry," I say. "I should have mentioned my friends first. The abilities of otherworldlings don't affect deities. I think we've proved that to be true today, yeah?" I tilt my head and give her a grin, hoping she won't run for it. "The gastropub is a public location, but there are private alcoves. It's quiet and you shouldn't have any issues speaking."

"I'm familiar with the gastropub. Why?" She crosses her arms. "Why are you here? Why me? What are deities doing on Earth? My sis—someone told me the gods disappeared. Sorry, I shouldn't be asking but—"

"You're curious. It's fine." I turn, signaling toward the path again. "We haven't had a presence here for a long while."

Rath is far too young to remember when humans worshipped our kind in person, but the older deities that remain crave to walk the Earth realm again. Humans' progressive minds flourish when they connect to our influence and attributes, and we benefit as well. It took several hundred years to convince my grandfather to allow us to travel for research. He hasn't yet realized that our findings will unseat him from his throne if all goes according to plan.

"And now..." Lula trails off as two men walk toward us.

They leer at her, ignoring me. I quicken my step and offer an elbow. The expression she aims at me is an awed shock. She slips her hand in the crook of my elbow and smiles.

Her siren call is stronger than my edge of divine influence, and the humans stop and stare. I'm not sure how each siren acts when mortals flock to them, only three. One of Lula's sisters basks in the attention, the other ignores it. Lula's mood about the attention changes, though I've only seen her out and about a few times. She respects the humans, staying silent and only demanding necessities. Even when her abilities frustrate her, and a group follows her, a flock of sheep to a shepherd, she stays patient and level-headed.

We stay silent, which I appreciate. A little information at a time is a better dose than feeding her from a firehose. It would scare her away. Comus will be better at a gentle introduction. By meeting her,

I've altered my plans. I should separate from her to think through the next steps before I accidentally blurt out everything.

The gastropub's old wooden door stands open under a green and white striped awning. I get another sweet waft of her scent as she moves by me into the lobby. Dark-stained wood covers every surface of the restaurant except for a stretch of a red brick wall and the leather seating. Amber tinted lights further warm the cozy ambiance. The bar is full of humans laughing and talking over one another as a TV blares a hockey game. I offer my arm again before the crowd notices Lula, and when she latches on, I walk her toward the back.

Rath sits on the edge of the private alcove's booth, shoulder brushing the tethered red privacy curtain. He tilts his head, piercing eyes squinted as he observes Lula. I glare at him as if any expression of mine would make his stubborn ass behave. Weathering his gibes for the next month will be hell, but I deserve it. I may as well have the words, 'doing what I shouldn't be,' written on my forehead.

As we approach, Comus leans forward, resting crossed arms on the table, not hiding his amused expression. "Having a nice night?" His attention falls to Lula's hand tucked against my arm. She leans into me.

"Yeah," I say. "This is Lula."

She untangles herself from me and sits when I signal to the U-shaped booth. Leather creaks as she slides toward Comus to make room for me.

Rath wears his usual brooding expression but, always the gentleman, Comus offers a hand to shake. "Good evening. I'm Comus."

Lula shakes his hand but says nothing.

"Having a nice time tonight?" Rath asks. His intense study of her makes me bristle. We may need to learn about her but that doesn't mean he needs a second by second observation of her reactions.

Shifting closer to Lula, I shake my head in a way that would appear to others that I'm moving my hair around, but Rath drops his eyes and takes a swig from his glass.

Lula opens her mouth, gives the faintest wince, and presses her lips together. Comus sends me a questioning glance, and I nudge Lula. "You can speak. You won't affect them, either."

Her wide-eyed expression makes me chuckle. Did she not believe me when I told her they were deities as well?

I lean to whisper in her ear. "And if you do, don't worry, I'll fight them off."

My jesting statement earns me an enticing smirk, which holds my attention until Comus clears his throat. The guys stare hard. They'll question my behavior later. We've discussed how this would go, and for once, I'm not following protocol. The closer I get to her, the harder it is to put her through tests. It's wrong and I don't want her hurt or scared, even if she may be able to save us all.

Rath taps a quick beat on the table, telling me in wordless reproach to get my shit together.

"Gentlemen, meet Lula. Lula...you met Comus. The other one is Rath."

Lula smiles and gives a wave.

Comus folds a beverage napkin. He'll make a throwing star or bird. "What's with the silent treatment, pretty lady?"

She tucks her hair and shifts, putting her an inch closer to me.

A waitress approaches, smiling wide and keeping her eyes on Rath. "How about another round?" She sets two waters on the table.

"Yes. Also, the same for my friend and a..." he eyes Lula. Rath told me she always orders Chianti, but he better not blurt that out and scare her. This fragile moment has no room for his antics. "Fruity rum drink?" His tone is one of distaste as if he's offering a moldy sandwich.

Lula shakes her head with a smile, and I release the breath I was holding.

"Maybe wine, then? They have a stellar Chianti, which appears to be the red of the year."

That makes her smile and nod, but the waitress only gawks at her, attention now off Rath. Lula shrinks back into the leather seat.

"Chianti and beer," I say, tapping the woman's hand to draw her attention from Lula. "Please."

She saunters off and Lula glances at me. She's as fluttery as a bird readying to take flight.

"She's a siren," I say before she can try to bolt.

Comus takes the last swig of his beer and sets the origami bird in front of Lula. "That's what you said on the phone, but I didn't believe it. What a rare find. Are the myths true?"

Lula purses her lips and pats the head of the paper figure with her finger.

This conversation isn't going anywhere if she won't speak.

Chapter Three

LULA

As if getting kissed stupid wasn't enough excitement for the night, I'm meeting Alex's friends—his god friends from Olympus—on the same night I run into a wannabe serial killer and a gang.

My evening makes no sense.

I've never spoken to a man before. Not really. Every conversation I've had was dragged from them by the force of my thrall. Now, one has treated me like we're dating, one gave me a present, and the other ordered me a drink. And I didn't request any of those things.

I'm far off-kilter, nervous, and leery because this can't be real. I need to calm down and get my brain working again because we're all staring at each other in this alcove of awkwardness. They've asked me questions and denying a deity anything isn't something you do, according to lore, but what if Alex is an anomaly and I enthrall his friends?

Alex runs a finger over my knuckles, and I latch onto his hand, embarrassed, but I can't let go. He's warm and real. He touched me on his own accord.

Rath's icy blue stare burns into me. Attractive is an understatement with those cheekbones, but there's darkness in him. He studies me like a tiny bug that he could squash flat at any moment. I shiver under his intense roving concentration until his gaze falls to my breasts, his lips forming a faint 'O.' Yep. Still a dude.

The waitress drops off drinks and asks about food, but my brain is still on the merry-go-round, so I ignore her. The Chianti is smooth and dry with a tart finish. It warms a path to my belly.

Rath refocuses on my face. "Got any sisters?"

I release Alex's hand to show seven fingers.

He makes an approving hum. "Big family for such a rare race."

A short, breathy snicker escapes me, and I glance past the table to make sure no mortals are within earshot.

Alex nudges me. "Not big then?" He raises his eyebrows, asking me to answer.

No humans are close by. I nibble my lip and take another sip of wine. "No. There are few of us in the world."

"What do you command, milady?" Comus asks, leaning forward. His intent, reverential expression reminds me of everyone I've ever spoken to besides Alex and my sisters. My stomach plummets before the corner of his mouth raises. "Too soon?"

"Ugh." I jab a finger in his direction. "That was not funny."

The tension around the table dissipates with the laughter of the gods, and I can't help joining. It's inconceivable that I'm not alone in the night. A little knot forms in my chest, and I take a deep breath, attempting to soothe it out.

"Tell me about these sisters, Lula," Rath says. "Are you close in age?"

Alex shifts and drops his arm on the top of the booth behind me.

"No," I say. "Hazel's the youngest. She turned fifty-one last month. My oldest sister, Amah, is over two thousand, but she stopped counting a while ago. Says it makes her feel old."

Everyone laughs, and for once I'm part of the group of friends I've observed in restaurants, bantering with each other. Unlike the humans, this group understands the longevity of ages. They're not bound by mortality. How old are they? Alexiares is mentioned in old tomes and I've heard the name Comus. A thousand years or more?

"Few sirens exist," Comus says. "The scarce information in our archives state that you call each other sisters, but cousins may be more suitable, I think?"

There are archives with siren lore? Do these deities know what happened to the first sirens? I shift forward. Maybe they understand how my species came about.

"Yes," I say and keep my eyes on Comus though I'm not sure what to look for. No one has ever lied or kept information from me. "The original three Mothers bore a daughter each before they disappeared. Their lines are separate, but we're as close as sisters. Only daughters are born, and it's a rare occurrence."

I scrunch my nose. I shouldn't have told them that. Since I was little, Amah has drilled in my head to keep siren facts in the family, but I want to share. It's new and irresistible. "Do you know where the Mothers are?"

"No," Comus says. "Until recently, I'd never met a siren." He smiles and signals at me.

I glance at Alex, but he gives a quick shake of his head. He takes a breath and opens his mouth—

"What does Hazel look like?" Rath asks, blue eyes burning.

I smirk. Hazel and I are from the same line of Aglaope as is Hazel's birth mother Venora. "Brunette with green eyes like mine. She's lovely."

"I bet. Would she like me?"

Rath's seeking stare sends a chill over my spine, but I refuse to turn away. "You may be too much for her. She's lighthearted...sensitive."

Comus waggles his eyebrows as he sips his beer. "Perhaps I should meet Hazel?"

Ignoring Rath's disapproving snort, I scrutinize Comus. Warm copper skin reminds me of late day sun peeking through fall leaves. Trimmed hair matches the shade of Hazel's. A toothy grin peeks out from his short beard, and intelligent acorn-brown eyes dart around, taking in everything as though he's envisioning how to use the world to his advantage. He's contemplative autumn to Rath's refreshing winter chill and Alex's passionate summer swelter. And here I am a fresh spring doe taking in a brand-new world.

"I believe Hazel would like you very much," I say, lifting my chin.

Though I doubt she'd speak at all in the presence of deities. Could this introduction lead to the sirens coming out of hiding? I hate that we all live so far away. The world has changed since Lena died, but Amah still insists that we spread ourselves across the globe to prevent our extinction and also to protect the humans.

Rath glances out of the alcove, then dissipates into a haze of gray mist before disappearing completely, and before I can question what the hell is going on, his face pops up inches from mine. "I'd be too much? How so?"

"Eep!" I slap his solidifying cheek and scramble back as far as possible in the booth. "Dammit! How about a warning before introducing a shade?" I clamp my palm over my mouth, and my face heats. These are not my sisters or humans. I'm talking to deities...Maybe. That makes little sense though. No otherworldling can resist my thrall, not that I've tested each one, but Amah probably has.

Alex pries off my hand and squeezes my fingers. "He isn't a shade, Firecracker. We don't get along well with any of the darkling species."

Rath reappears in his seat, rubbing his shocked face. "You slapped me."

"You deserved that," Alex says.

Rath's jaw is half dropped as he points to his red cheek. "She slapped me."

"Yeah, she did." Comus swishes his hand. "Nice shot, Lu. Had a cacophonous crack to it."

"Tell me what you are," I command Rath, then grimace. He's proven he's immune to me.

He remains silent in shock, according to his expression, so Alex answers for him. "He's the God of Shadows. Rath's attributes are different than most. One grants him the ability to slip between Earth and a shadow realm whenever he pleases."

That sounds important, as a god of the sun or tides. *Great job, Lula.* "Sorry, I didn't mean...I just, shades fade and..." My throat rasps. "I haven't heard of you."

Alex kisses my palm, laughing breaths tickling my skin. Silence pulls my attention. Comus eyes Alex with crinkled brows, and Rath's stare is blatant. Alex's actions toward me do not appear to be something he does regularly. That is a relief, yet not. If he doesn't wander the streets at night, kissing otherworldlings and taking them to meet his friends, then why am I here?

Alex lowers my tense hand to my lap, releasing his hold and picks up his glass. "Rath belongs to the new generation of divine beings which haven't been revealed to the humans. Our baby boy is three-hundred and twenty."

"Don't call me that," Rath grumbles.

"You're older than I am," I say.

He's on the border of amusement before catching himself and glowering again.

Alex lifts his mug, pausing before he drinks. "How old?"

"One-hundred and eighty-two. You?"

"A smidgen past three-thousand, but I was in a dormant child state for a third of those years."

Wow. A smidgen? In human years that would be like saying you're a smidgen past twenty-nine when you're thirty-three. What happens when you're three thousand? And he was stuck as a child? The information my sisters and I studied on the divine gave a bland description of the gods and their attributes. Two hundred questions lie on the tip of my tongue, but the waitress returns.

"We're closing up." She sets the check on the table and as I reach for my purse, Comus leans to set a credit card on top. With a grin, she picks it up and tucks a loose strand of hair behind her ear as she eyes Rath. "Thanks. Are you all going anywhere else tonight? Maybe…Um."

Now, *these* expressions I understand. It's irritating not being able to tell her to ask like I do to my television when a character wants something but is shy about it. *You clearly have a thing for the intense God of Shadows. Speak up so I can see what happens.*

Rath gives her a kind smile and leans forward, elbows on the table. "We have to go home. My goddess will miss me if I'm out too late."

Interesting. He sure is flirty to be going home to a goddess. Have I heard of her? Do they live in Olympus and where is that?

"Oh." The woman fiddles with a few pens poking out of the apron tied around her waist. "Goddess? That's sweet." The poor thing tugs at the black cloth as if it may grow enough to hide behind. "I'll be right back with this."

She skitters off and Alex squeezes my fingers. "Did you drive, or do you need a ride home?"

"I drove. I'm parked at Sal's Italian Bistro."

A jolt of disappointment flows through me and amplifies as Alex slides out and offers his hand. "That's only a block away. I'll walk you to your car."

Rath gives a grunt I believe means 'Bye', and Comus beams at me. "See you later, Lula."

See me later? We'll probably never meet again. I give a weak smile. "Thanks for the wine. It was nice meeting you."

Nice, is far underplaying the energy bursting from my chest. I haven't experienced a real conversation with a stranger ever, and here I am with three.

Alex leads me from the gastropub and across the street. "I want to see you again."

"Seriously? But—"

With a tug to my elbow, he turns me to him. "Why wouldn't I?"

"Because you're a deity and I'm a siren. Why are you here? On Earth, I mean."

Alex runs his knuckles against my cheek, golden eyes following the path of his fingers. The touch scatters my thoughts. He steps closer, and I lift my chin. Is this how it is for humans? I'm too warm, trembling with anticipation of another kiss.

A whoop makes us jerk our heads toward the interruption. A young couple laughs.

"Leave," I growl before thinking. *Oh, no.*

The man and woman bolt, as do a small group a few buildings down. I step away from Alex, a chill of regret replacing the previous heat. That was not the right thing to do. I press my fingers to my forehead and turn to walk toward my car.

Alex steps beside me. "You're powerful."

"That should not have happened. Sorry."

"It's fine, Lula."

"It's not. Do you know what happens to humans who fall under a siren's thrall?"

"No. Tell me."

Why would I offer to share this? No creature should be able to do what sirens can. It's not fair for anyone.

I wrap my arms around my waist as I slow to a halt. I can't face him, so instead I keep my eyes on a crack in the pathway. "The first time confuses them. Short term memories will blur, and they won't be able to grasp at distinct moments. It's like asking an elderly human to recall their prom; they'll get the gist but may forget their date's name or what restaurant they went to. If I were to continue, synapses would break. Their date would disappear completely, the songs they danced to… gone. More than a few days under my repeated thrall and their past would go. Then their present."

We are all different. Some sirens' abilities are stronger than others. For my victims, permanent dementia would take root after a couple of days, complete catatonia within a week, then seizures, and brain death. Venora can stay with a person for months and their mind will stay intact. That shouldn't make me jealous, we're all built to harm, but she can pretend with someone for a bit—form a shred of a bond that will last in her memories. I can have a scripted night.

Until today.

Alex tilts my chin up. His lips part to say something, but I turn my face. He'll either tell me something false, like what I do is no big deal, or he'll spout the truth. I don't want to hear that I'm a monster. Not tonight and not from him.

"Hey," he says. "Come on."

He brushes his fingers over my crossed arms and finds my hand. I've never held hands with someone. Not like this, when *his* grip is commanding. With a gentle tug, he leads me back into a walk. His unexpected thoughtfulness stabs my chest, tightening my throat and forcing me to swallow. Too soon we stand in front of my little convertible.

"Give me your phone," he says. "And I'll put in my number."

He would give me another night like this one? I drag my phone out of my small black bag and hand it over. "Is this a good idea?"

Is he crazy?

Are the legends Amah told me true, and the major gods would destroy or curse a non-deity for consorting with a deity? Something about the threat of mixed blood, I've been told. I'm one of the accursed and unable to ask the missing Mothers what they did to get my species cast out of Olympus, so I better not attempt a second strike against the sirens. *Just a taste.*

Alex taps on my phone and gives off an amused huff. "I'd like to get to know you better."

A ring sounds from his phone. He swipes mine off and returns it.

I click the locks open and turn, but Alex pulls me back and gives me a gentle kiss that melts the flutter in my belly. "It was the utmost pleasure to meet you, Lula."

I'll never see him again. I memorize the hue of his eyes, the slope of his nose, his scent of sun, and that sweet but unfamiliar citrus. If I ever come across the fruit, it will transport me to this exact moment. I smile and give a quiet, "Mmhmm," not trusting my voice to come out as strong as it should when speaking to a deity.

"I *will* call you." His eyes crinkle as if he wants to talk more or ask me something. Instead, he shoves his hands into his pockets and glances down the street.

"I'm so glad I met you, Alex," I blurt out in a pathetic rush.

He opens my door and lifts my hand, rubbing his thumb across my knuckles, sparking every nerve in my body to life. "Me too. I'll talk to you soon. Sleep well."

I step in, and with a sharp, echoing clunk of the shutting door, I'm alone again. Key in the ignition, my car purrs, and I steal one last glimpse at Alex before pulling away from the curb.

Best night ever.

Chapter Four

ALEX

This is a problem.

When Lula's car turns the corner, Rath appears beside me and Comus catches up with quick strides on the sidewalk. They stare at me with similar raised eyebrow expressions.

Comus speaks first. "Godsdamn, man. That was something."

Keeping my eyes on the street Lula took, I exhale a long breath and chuckle. "Yeah."

"What in Hades happened after Sal's?" Comus asks.

"He caved because he needed to kiss her hand," Rath says, turning to walk. "Then kiss her at her car."

"Voyeur." I stride on course with him and Comus. "Actually, the Warbringers surrounded her. Chaos punched her in the stomach, and she couldn't get a word out."

Rath huffs. "Ah, what an asshole. She went damsel-in-distress on you? Did you play Prince Charming well?"

"Not in the least. You should have seen her. Five Bringers ran up on her, stopped her power source, and she didn't panic. I approached, but she handled it before I could. She commanded Chaos like he wasn't walking death."

"Chaos?" Surprise lies over Rath's typical scowl. "She stood up to Chaos?"

"Yeah. Get this, Havoc pressed his dick against her while she's gasping for air, and she rolls her eyes. I thought she was going to rip it off."

Comus's shoulders relax and he beams. "She's perfect."

That she is.

She handled five of my biggest problems in this city without a mental breakdown. It was a better test than we could have set up for her. She's what we've been looking for but weren't sure existed. A group of humans staggers out of a bar, so I point to a side road and turn that direction. "Once she caught her breath, she told them to go home. Everyone but Chaos did."

Comus makes a note on his phone as we cross the street. "I told you he was part otherworldling. I wonder what though?"

"Later, brother." He will spend the next hour pondering otherworldling species if we veer down that path. "Anyway, she hummed for a few seconds, and he fell right in order. It was incredible to watch. She told him he'd do good from now on and to start a community garden. She's muddled my expectations with that group. We'll return soon to see what they do now."

"A garden?" Rath shoves his hands in his pockets as he steps back on the sidewalk. "Like growing tomatoes?"

"Yeah, tomatoes. Picture Chaos wearing overalls and holding a rake."

It is hard to imagine. Farming isn't something he would ever do without Lula's power. At least, I don't think so. The only reason I came across the gang is that Lula brought us here. Maybe once upon a time, he enjoyed getting his hands dirty in a more fruitful way. Could Lula sense that or was she focused on what the world needed instead of the individual? Maybe she will understand why we need her when we explain everything.

"That was unexpected," Comus says. "She's creative. And you're kissing her now? Did you manhandle her on a street corner before you decided to introduce us? You both seemed...pleasantly preoccupied." He clucks his tongue.

While his words are joking, his strides eat up distance on the sidewalk as if the fast pace will outrun past decisions. I'm not the only one who's been kissing sirens. This is different though.

"I was a gentleman," I say. That's a stretch. A gentleman wouldn't have kissed her the moment she came within reach. We pass a dark alley as we work our way around the block and toward the parking garage. A gentleman wouldn't even consider lurking in the shadows to study her.

"She's making you work for it." Rath shoves at my shoulder. "Didn't even invite you home with her. Are you losing your touch, old man?"

"My game is just fine, kiddo." *If 'fine' means dormant.*

Comus chides, "Before you two pull out the ruler, we should get the call to the dominant dumbasses over with."

"Yeah." I pull both phones out of my pocket. "I'll meet you at the garage. Are we still on the peace pitch?"

So many things are wrong in the divine realm, we don't know what to throw at the Council to make a change. They need to see the humans and realize they are having a bad effect on them. We show them examples of advanced humanity, and they scoff. We show them new methods of violence, and they don't flinch. Will anything make them leave?

"Yep, but adjust accordingly." Rath grabs Comus's arm and fades, dragging them both into the shadow realm with no warning. Comus will punch him when they get in the SUV.

The garage where we keep the SUV is only a block away, but this call won't take long.

I text Comus on the encrypted phone.

All set?

A call from the SUV comes through the phone the Council is monitoring.

Showtime.

"Greetings," I answer. "How did your research go?"

"Quite well," he says. "Rath spoke with two vampires."

"Good find. Did he see them feed?"

"No. They were older and slaked. Everything else was peaceful except for a political conversation and a small skirmish concerning a human relationship. Did you find the siren?"

I clench my jaw. We have to speak about Lula so the Council can overhear, but I don't like it. I recount the highlights again, referring to her only as "the siren," playing down her power and highlighting her calm. She has to seem harmless and common.

"Well, well," Comus says. "Here we thought sirens were pushovers or evil, but they're the opposite. There's much more to learn about them and the rest of the otherworldling species. They've all adapted to blend in with the humans."

Business as usual. Tout the harmlessness and intrigue of Earth species. If the Council doesn't see the non-divine beings as a threat, maybe they will visit, realize that humans are doing fine without them and how the otherworldlings follow our creation. Then they will either combine Olympus with Earth again and let us do our jobs, or leave, bored and ready for something new to work with and a new age will begin.

My encrypted phone buzzes. Rath texts, *Re-stoke interest. Darkling rumors.*

Already? He must have liked how the meeting went with Lula.

There have been more darkling rumors and that will be our tease of external violence and excuse to remain on Earth.

"Yes, the otherworldlings have accepted humans as a superpower. I caught wind of a darkling sighting but need more details. We should make a request with the Council to continue our research."

"I concur," Comus states, and I bite back a laugh, picturing his fake serious face as he firmly bobs his head once.

We hang up and a shred of relief relaxes my shoulders.

It's a dance with the old gods. Don't step on their toes. Let them think they lead, then convince them they own the ideas we put in their heads. Inflate their egos until they pop, and if all goes well, they'll walk away and let us roll into a new age with the gentle ease most humans now embrace, even if recent centuries were riddled with violence. It will take a long while to right the realm. Good thing we have eons of time.

The garage is a private double-decker block of concrete. It's boring and discrete. The stairs are rusted metal, and old chip bags and liquor bottles decorate the lower corner. Piss and stale cigarette smoke scent the air. If we can ever convince Zeus and the Council to visit the Earth realm, this won't be the first place we bring them.

I walk to the black SUV and slide into the back seat.

"Darklings, huh?" I ask Rath.

"You two drag your feet," he says. "If Lula can command them, we have ignition."

"To a war, young one," Comus says. "Tensions are high. If we move too fast, the Council will catch on, and no matter our intentions, they will see it as a declaration of mutiny. What would follow could rival the Titanomachy. We don't need to join the archives as the instigators of a divine war that would probably end the Earth as well. No. We have time and will use every minute."

"Ha," Rath says. "That may be the only way they'd write me into Olympian history."

I snort. "You have a better place in hist—"

The tone designated for Comus's father rings out. As Dionysus only uses the human device to summon us for Council needs, we groan in unison.

"Well, that didn't take long," I say.

Rath snatches the phone from Comus's hand and puts it on speaker.

"What do you need, Da?" Comus asks.

"Updates, news, evidence that the Earth beings are controllable," Dionysus's gravelly voice rolls through the SUV's speaker. "The King requests for Alexiares to arrive in haste." He hangs up without waiting for a response.

The warmth pulsing through me after my interaction with Lula turns to ice with the request. "The Council has no clue. They're completely out of touch with the beings of the Earth realm."

Dionysus is the easiest Council member to work with. He sees the problems created from the stale mindset of the old Gods, but he's also the closest thing to a friend my grandfather has. The staunch loyalty between them prevents us from using him to further our cause, even if Comus is his son. Our tiny army includes the three of us, a handful of other deities, some otherworldlings, and a few extraordinary humans. It's not enough.

"The mortal race has adapted and evolved in ways the Council doesn't have the capacity to imagine," Comus says, squeezing the steering wheel until the leather squeaks "They live in constant confusion and fear that they'll never acknowledge."

"If it confuses them, they kill it," Rath says. He slumps further into his seat and keeps his eyes out the window.

The brunt of the Council's fear fell on him long ago. His father is so ancient and evil, he's classified as a god, but his origin is unknown. He got a hold of Rath's mother and kept her locked away until she escaped during her labor. Zeus had declared a pause in breeding long before, a law that's still in play to 'calm the mortals', that is, try to stop evolution and not let anyone else take over. It's a shock that the Council let Rath live. Our guess is the scry from Pythia, plus petitions from Dionysus, Athena, Hades, and Hermes kept our friend alive, although, with the way other gods treat him, it's not a pleasured life. I try to squeeze the tension out of his shoulder, wishing he wasn't reminded of the past each time we discuss the wrongs of Olympus.

"Change will be hard," Comus says.

It's a long road that will unfold only if we succeed. Olympus hasn't changed since the ancient days of Greece.

"But that's why we're here, isn't it?" Rath shifts in his seat as though emerging from a cocoon created from the remaining tension. "The new divine generations, ready to allow the inhabitants of this realm see us as we are, gods in the flesh. Our humans are more open-minded now and it's our turn to follow. It's a big difference from the vicious actions of the dark ages."

"How do you know, baby boy?" Comus teases.

"Because I've studied *everything*." Rath's teeth show as he bares them in a smile of sarcasm. "I'm smart, remember?"

"How could I not, when you won't let me forget?"

I grip his shoulder now with a light, amused touch, and push him as I settle back in my seat. It's us who remind Rath of his creative thinking at every opportunity, but we enjoy the joke. Rath is more advanced than us. The new generation, though few in number, have minds more in position with human than god. They think beyond, *kill threatening things*. When they find a problematic root to age-old issues, they offer ways to dig it up. They are as different from our generation as we are from the ancients before us. Embracing that is how the universe should progress, but each generation's new ideas fall on the deaf ears before it... mostly.

We learn much from Rath. It took a while to be open to his

thoughts, but the Council will never acknowledge any word he speaks, no matter how brilliant or logical. And Olympus follows the old majors.

Comus and I have the ear of the Council. We're treated like royals, though we didn't pay attention to each other until eight hundred years ago. I kick his seat. "Remember when we met?"

"Yeah," Comus says. "I made Anice sneak our crew to the streets of England for a night of human debauchery. Your brother finally acknowledged your fascination with human culture and dragged you along for a crazy night."

"A night? Six hours into the time of our lives and Anice and his ilk bailed back to Olympus. They couldn't handle the 'boorishness' of humans, though I believe they couldn't relax from fear of being caught by the Council, but you and I were there for…"

"Three thrilling days," Comus finishes. "We explored everything they created. Drank and ate everything we came across, danced like flying-high fools. Humans out-party deities any day. My father threatened to come get us—by sending Anice back as the messenger."

"Who stayed another day getting hammered on mead and singing off-key pub songs."

We laugh at the recollection. Anice has always been the twin who followed the status quo. There was a time I did the same, but when we aged and Zeus's demands began, our paths separated. In that moment though, out of his elite Olympian group and among humans, we reconnected.

Comus rubs his face with both hands. "We came back and stood in front of the Council, forced to recount details of the expedition for six severe days of questioning."

"But they let us come back."

We thought they'd never let us leave. But when they did, we celebrated. We hadn't known that day that we'd walked away with a victory, but it changed our course, set us free. Well, freer than most.

"I'm thankful for that every damn day. Even if the Council's intention was to gain insight to control the beings of Earth." He lifts his chin toward Rath. "Then we adopted a twelve-year-old shit."

Rath puffs out his chest. "I was not."

"Uh-huh," I say, settling back into the seat. "But your reckless confidence drew us as did the discrimination against you. A full-blood child god more developed in mind than any other is treated as a dreg. Absolute bullshit."

"Wonder if they'll ever figure that out." Comus ruffles Rath's hair and dodges a slap. "Doubt it. You scare them. Damn, you were a reckless little shit, though. Still are, but you're our little shit."

Rath can pretend to sulk all he wants but I catch his smirk before he looks out the window. "Shall we reminisce into the morning hours or get your asses to Olympus?"

"I was letting Alex avoid. He needs time to adjust, you know."

The leather creaks as I sink further and drop my head back, closing my eyes. "There's no avoiding my grandfather. It's merely delaying another conversation about the evils of everything except deities."

"I've read up on siren lore in the human libraries, and Zeus will question you about Lula." Rath glances back at me with a determination that makes my stomach ball. "Do not bring up crossbreeding yet."

"Rath," Comus says with a groan.

"No?" I ask, feigning confusion with a dramatic head tilt. "I mean, I could spark a new age—combine species, blend into a super-species. Demis can be strong. Look at my father, Anice, and myself. Hybridization brings strength and fortitude, and mixed with a siren? Pssh."

"You'd get cursed or banished," Comus says. "But yeah, what would your descendants be like?" He squints at the ceiling, eyes unfocused.

"Hopefully more decisive, but that's not why he shouldn't bring it up." Rath faces me, demanding full attention. "If he doesn't kill her, Zeus will want first dibs."

His words douse any future banter. We understand the ways of my grandfather because he's proven himself repeatedly. Rath is right. If there were a break in law, Zeus would be the one to do it, except for one important detail—he treats me with near equality, and we haven't a clue why.

The Council put that law into place with the baby boom of demis and the few hybrids that were born, mainly stemming from Zeus.

"Unfortunately, that's true," Comus says. "He rid the realm of his powerful children—the ones who acted out. There has to be a line with you. Don't cross it. No fraternization with the siren."

"Um." Rath presses a finger over his lips, then points it at Comus. "You weren't fraternizing, huh?"

"I was careful, and I'm not Alex."

"Zeus lets me get away with way more than he would you. I'll keep Lula safe."

I hate it when they scrutinize me. It's not like I've gone that far off the plan, but they peer at me as if I've told them I've given up on saving the universe, and instead, I'm moving to the suburbs with her.

Rath studies me. "Could her ability have seeped through? She controlled Chaos." He looks to Comus, the oldest of our group. He's had the most time in the libraries before Zeus locked them down.

"Never happened before." For a split-second, pain coats Comus's features. "Just don't get wrapped up."

I'm not the only one who's acted out of sort these last few months. Maybe the sirens do have a certain hold on deities.

I will protect Lula from the spying eyes of gods though. As much as they act high and mighty on their golden streets and marble thrones, they're bored. Zeus waits for an excuse to curse someone as perfect as a siren. *Again*. It gives the bastard a sick power trip. He needs an occasional war to instill fear and keep a secure grasp on his title of king. Odd as he treats me with near-reverence, and my attribute is deterring one of his favorite pastimes.

"We're divine beings; wards of the realm," I say straightening up. "We can be better than this."

"We will be once everything lines up." Comus looks at me in the rear-view. "My father told me that Zeus wants to crack down on unauthorized human interaction. He's getting squirrely again." He pops his eyes wide, ping-ponging them in a zigzag. "All shifty, and chittering curses that blend into a nonsensical symphony of squeaks. Seriously though, be ready for him to discuss our meet and greets. Counter with the darkling bit. He should buy that we need time to question everyone possible."

For thousands of years, Zeus made it his job to create pure gods and goddesses. He pounced on any female he got within five feet of, expecting he'd get the wild mortal race to fall in line and return to worshipping us if he had enough of his bloodline populating Olympus. He couldn't have been more blind. His children weren't clones of himself, and they only helped the evolution of new ideas and technology in the Earth realm. He's continued his history of bad decisions since then.

"Let's get this over with," I say.

Then Lula and I can talk again.

Chapter Five

ALEX

Gold pavers gleam in the mid-morning light, leading the way to my grandfather's marble palace. The square buildings are similar, molded in white marble with columns and long corridors. While humans took artistic license once the break occurred, putting the city on clouds in the Heavens, the typical rendition of Olympus is accurate. It's a twin of Greece as it stood long ago, with flawless marble, and gold or flower-filled walkways instead of streets. The Olympian realm lays over the Earth realm like a shadow, our flora feeding from the rain and weather, though only sun shines in a flawless blue sky here.

The perfect appearance is a stark contrast to the broken system within.

I hope the new generation may see rain for the first time and react as Rath did. He fell to his knees, arms open wide. There may have been tears mixing with the water drips from the sky, but I'd never fault him for that. My throat tightened at his awe and when I exchanged a glance with Comus, it hit home that we all are missing so much life under the rule of the Council.

For two millennia, the deities stuck in Olympus haven't felt the electric connection when divine attributes are used as intended or how energies mingle when walking among humans as they pull from our divine influence. I hope one day they get to experience that relief.

Hair stands up on my neck, and my palms grow sweaty. Comus and Rath wear scowls. The Council allows us to walk the Earth for research but at any point could yank us out and imprison us in Olympus. If imprisonment meant you lived in a five-star resort twenty-four-seven where everyone waits on you, and never, ever talks back, because they're minor, shoved-down deities, or stolen otherworldlings, castrated and termed 'pets.'

Oh, and there's no human or otherworldling technology available. It's torture.

After a while, you want to go home, lie on an unmade bed with a half-rate beer and a slice. Try explaining to any servant in Olympus you want television to watch a comedy that makes you laugh so hard you shoot beer out of your nose, and they will stare at you as if you were an incubus requesting a couple of sacrificial virgins for an evening of "conversation."

As we ascend the staircase of Zeus's mansion, Rath stops at the white columns and sits.

"Later, brother," I say and follow the path of gray veined marble.

Giving his grunt of acknowledgment, Rath pulls out his phone to play some word game.

We'd have him slip into the shadows to listen in, but Ares and Deimos can sense him, and last time they caught him, Zeus threatened to zap him on the spot. I shielded Rath in a standoff I was sure would take us both from the universe, but with a jaw clenched so tight I swear he cracked teeth, Zeus backed down and told us there wouldn't be a second chance.

We may work against the King, but we understand our place. Rath doesn't enter shadows in Olympus anymore unless he's sure he won't be caught.

Comus and I walk the corridor toward the Council's main meeting room. Arches open to a tropical courtyard with a splendid array of bright flowers in beds of dark green leaves that have existed since the days of Eden.

Would Lula consider this place Heaven or the gold cage I do?

She's a puzzle I want to figure out. I rarely meet someone

unwilling to tell me everything from minute one. I need to talk to her, learn how she became courageous and feisty—such unusual traits for a siren.

Comus nudges me, signaling to the massive gilded doors. Two guards in golden armor and helmets with white plumes move aside, pulling their spears upright.

Ambrosia carries the scent of spun sugar blended with over-ripened fig and cinnamon through the air in the chamber as it does through most of Olympus.

"Alexiares." My grandfather's voice booms, bouncing off marble walls carved with battles of the ages. They love reminders of what they consider prime divine moments—bloodshed, power struggles, incestuous encounters that gave way to deities Zeus swears he planned. He wishes he had that ability.

Grandfather's massive marble throne sits center against the back wall. He rests his splayed hands on the two huge eagles carved in the front of the arms. A slight smile nestles in his dark beard, though his eyes hold irritation as he trails them over our clothing. He doesn't approve of human garb, though if we were to wander the Earth in himations, we'd get nothing out of the humans except selfies as they embraced the weirdos who were unaware that it wasn't Halloween.

Behind Zeus, purple velvet drapes from a golden cornice creating a royal backdrop in the white room. The Council members sit on the adjacent walls in intricate thrones, though my grandfather's dwarf the five on each side. Three seats out of the eleven remain empty.

Zeus's brothers, Hades and Poseidon, sat in the group before Zeus considered them a threat. Other majors had seats as well, though they left the universe in the exodus that set off the dark ages. I hope they kept their peaceful demeanors as they built their new universe.

Hera was once welcome at her husband's side, but I haven't seen my grandmother for centuries, and Zeus removed her throne, leaving his as the room's focal point. I'd consider her dead if she didn't pop up every once in awhile, as if she'd missed a mere day.

Tables sit in front of the Council, loaded with golden goblets, bejeweled carafes, piled fruit on platters, and is that a sucking pig? So typical.

We bow low as expected and only rise when Dionysus moves

forward, his cream robes swishing with each movement. He slaps Comus on the shoulder too hard. "My son. Glad you could grace us with your presence."

They exchange a silent father-son conversation—the kind I want to eavesdrop on because it's riddled with the child versus parent snark that's difficult to step away from no matter how old one becomes.

"Sit," Dionysus says, the command sharp.

We settle in the two ornate chairs that face the Council. Athena gives the slightest bow of her head when I meet her eyes, prompting me to do the same. She's tough but as fair as she can be under the thumb of a king who considers a goddess's purpose is best served on her back in his bed.

I glance down the line, acknowledging each; Apollo, Hermes, Dionysus, Zeus, Artemis, though she stares through me, lips clamped. For Rath's benefit only, I'd never out her to the others, but that doesn't make her any less ashamed at her relationship with someone she sees as far beneath her. I can't help but skip addressing Ares, who loves to get Zeus worked into a bloodlust, and Deimos. I'll never forgive Deimos no matter how many centuries pass.

While we all appear around the same age, frozen in our prime state of mid-twenties when we accept our attributes, there's pinched tiredness aging the Council members. They don't realize how stressed doing nothing makes them.

The Council stares at us, waiting for the King to begin. If they embraced the ways of the humans, they'd shine a spotlight in our faces for our interrogation.

I lean back in the chair and prop my ankle on my knee, then enjoy the slight wide-eyed shock of the surrounding deities. While the himations have their benefits, sitting comfortably isn't possible unless you care to show off what's under them. I smirk. I'd chose these jeans any day.

Zeus's dark gold eyes condemn us before the first word. "Let us commence."

We have a stare-off until the silence does me in. "Is there a specific topic you care to discuss?"

"Any new developments or interactions?"

Comus leans against the arm of his chair and spins the ring he wears on his left middle finger. "Typical human interactions. They are working on a new development in cancer research, and the support for those stricken by the disease is increasing with more empathetic members each day. In fact—"

Zeus waves a hand through the air. "Well enough. Any non-human interactions?"

Comus side-eyes me. "Do you mean *otherworldling* interactions?"

I bite back a grin. The humans are one headache, but the 'non-humans' stranded from the closing of the realms now blend in with the powerless mortals, accepting them as leaders in the world, an act that bewilders the Council.

I repeat verbatim the same conversation we performed on the phone. We want the Council to trust that what we say to each other, we'd say to them as well.

"At this point, they assimilate so well with the humans, we're unable to tell them apart until further investigation," I add to our story. "While Rath interacted with vampires this past evening, the three of us came upon a group at the bar last night." I lock onto my grandfather's disgusted face. "They were there to enjoy the company of mortals and dance. Did you know vampires love to dance?"

The old gods like to think there are huge differences between them and the Earth's inhabitants, but besides evolution, there's not. They eat, drink, dance, fuck, love, and fight too.

Comus bats my shoulder with the back of his hand. "Yeah, that one dude broke it down. He was a blast to watch. A savvy swinger for sure."

Council members shift and glance around. Though they refuse to acknowledge it, the language in Olympus has morphed through the years to match the Earth, separation or not. Olympians still don't understand slang because there is a lag in mystical energy, so Comus and I use it at every opportunity. The key is not pushing enough to get reprimanded, only enough to make them wonder if other Council members can decipher the phrasing. We're awaiting the day that one of them will ask to join us—to introduce them to humans. Then others will follow. One day they will see how the world has flourished, and sometimes faltered without them.

Zeus flexes his fingers against the eagles' carved feather heads. "What is the siren's name?"

The room heats with his question.

"Did you catch her name?" Comus asks.

"No. I didn't think it necessary."

There are occasional moments where I realize why an eagle is used to represent my grandfather. His gaze pierces as if I'm a fish in a shallow stream, and when I make a wrong turn, I'll fight a current I have no chance to overcome. He only needs to swoop, grasp, and rip me to shreds.

I drop my foot to the floor and straighten in my seat.

"Were there any other interactions?" he asks.

Comus and I respond in unison. "No."

Please, let this be done.

Leaning back, Dionysus taps a finger on the marble table and looks to Zeus. My grandfather strokes his dark beard before tenting his hands. "We require more interaction reports so we may determine how best to manage the non-deities."

We live to fight another day. "We will fulfill your needs."

"If we do not see progress or a way to rule them, you need not walk among them."

My stomach drops and I exchange an unsettled look with Comus. We need another alteration to our plan.

Zeus stands and navigates around the table. "Comus, I dismiss you. Alexiares, walk with me."

The prickling tension between my grandfather and me maintains a distance between us as we follow the marble path in silence.

"Why do you respect them?" he asks, voice quiet compared to his typical booming timbre.

"The humans?"

He nods, tired face seeking...understanding?

I blow out a breath, hoping for consideration this time. "We watch each generation learn, pass off knowledge, then die off to make way for another wave. The urgency of mortality makes them as reckless and violent as they are adaptable and inventive, yet they base their decisions on empathy for each other. It's... noble. They don't mind making mistakes, unlike us, which could be why they adapt to anything they come across." I study his profile as he stares ahead, unsure if I should push further. "So yes, I respect them."

"They are beasts in the realm, yet you interact with them as though they are divine." With a full turn of his face to mine, he bites out, "They are not."

If I play this right, perhaps my grandfather will give us something to work with and confess his secrets. "They are not divine, but we are linked, even after the break. You taught me as a child that we were symbiotic, yet this moment is the longest you've allowed me to speak candidly of them and the otherworldlings. They are not to be... feared."

"I fear nothing." Zeus flicks two fingers toward our path. "I listen to your words—your inflection. I wish to make sure they, and you, are on the divine path."

"Exactly. You remember I'm part human?"

"You are not one of them, Alexiares." His voice has the hard edge of irrational anger before softening. "You are special."

"Why?"

As usual, he ignores the question.

He's wrong. I'm not special or better. There are mortals who have more morality in one short human life than I had for a thousand years. I'm worse, because I followed my grandfather for centuries too long, and did things I'll never reconcile.

Fuck the divine path.

I shove my hands in my pockets to prevent him from seeing my clenched fists. "Human adaptability only goes so far, which puts me in the spotlight on Earth beyond research. I have animosity and power plays to monitor."

Unlike the Council, I work to keep the humans going in what I believe is the correct direction. Forward not backward, or worse, stagnant like the old gods. That means preventing wars, studying the beings of Earth, and trying to introduce new concepts like human technology into Olympus.

"It's not just humans waging war though is it, Alexiares?"

A chill travels my spine in an icy stab with his direct tone. He's suspicious. I've gone too far, and he wants more. More that will put me or others in deadly danger.

Recoil. "No, I suppose not." *Dodge.* "Some otherworldlings remember the days in their old realms and miss their own cultures. They want to fight to get back home, even after a thousand years. There have been renewed darkling sightings. So many, they may be breeding." His lips tighten, and it's time to divert. "Every species wants to carve a place out for themselves in the universe, even more since we shut the portals to other realms. If we opened the Earth as a hub again, there would be room."

"No." He's mastered putting a full threat into one tiny word. *You're an idiot if you believe I will let you do such a thing, and I will kill you if you defy me.* "You will come to my house in precisely a fortnight. Understood?"

Two weeks? "What's the occasion?"

He stops and slaps a hand on my shoulder, anger and threat washing away like blood down a shower drain. "For dinner, my boy. With your betrothed."

Chapter Six

LULA

I stare at the phone in my palm.

Don't do it, Lula. Do not be the first to call.

Still, my finger hovers above the new number in my phone. I have a direct link to a god. We had a real conversation, and he kissed me.

I want a repeat.

Nudging the phone across the marble counter of the kitchen island keeps me from pushing the button. It's been two days, not the preliminary three that human customs suggest. Not that Alex and I are dating. He probably won't call because he's a god and I'm a siren—a non-divine, plain old otherworldling.

"Why would he?" I ask my kitchen.

Our chance meeting was a one-time deal, and now disappointment reigns, because I understand the heart of my situation—Alex isn't coming back, and I have godlust.

That has to be a thing. They're the architects of our universe, the protectors, and influencers of the ages. When the gods walked among the Earth, they were rock stars. Were they worthy of the praise? Amah spoke of them in dark tales meant to warn children.

Now that I've had time to consider every word Amah told me about the gods, the research I've done, and the night I had with the deities, the truth is farther from my grasp than ever.

When I was a preteen, Amah gave me hypothetical situations where the gods were chaotic bad guys that would break a woman's body, then curse her to walk a hell realm, pass her around to other gods, enslaving the poor being, or giving her some terrible fate where a merciful death would be the ultimate reward. Amah acted as if they didn't exist, yet in the same breath, warned me to stay away from divine beings.

Now I've met them and the last thing I want is to stay away.

I suppose her stories were fairy tales after all because Alex isn't dark or dangerous. Comus seems kind, and even Rath, with his intense gaze, softened his features when he spoke of his goddess.

They are not bad gods.

Alex is beautiful and warm. His brain is full of astounding experiences I bet we could discuss for a decade and only touch on a slight part of his immortal life.

I'd love to talk to Grace again, but I don't want her depressed. After our conversation yesterday, we both gave a wistful exhale when I finished telling her every detail of my evening with the gods. The excitement through the phone was palpable. Until she told me she ended her fling with Liam the librarian a few weeks ago.

She should have told me sooner because she claimed she was fine, but she blew out a long breath three times as she explained in a shaky voice how she made him walk away, only to call him back again for a final ending kiss. Each of us has experienced the same.

Just a taste. I scratch at the tightness below my throat.

Beings under our control eventually show symptoms of our thrall —spacing out, anxiety, and acting odd. Grace's ability was too much for Liam to stay sane, so she cut ties. One boon of our species is when we tell someone the relationship's over, it's over. We only need to say, "Forget me, and move on," and they do. No messy breakups.

I grab a cloth from the sink cabinet and wipe down the counters again. My bright, quiet cottage is cleaner than ever thanks to my anxiety. My warm wood floors shine, and there's not a speck of dust on the cheery human decorations and artifacts of art I've found through the years.

The ceramic rooster on the cabinet shelf would stare at me if his wonky pupils didn't point in different directions. The man selling it said the statue came from an estate sale lot he purchased. A well-intentioned husband attempted a ceramic class to surprise his artist wife and created the purple monstrosity. It became one of her most cherished items and even after her husband died and she in her final hours, she demanded the rooster stay in the room to chaperone her back to her lost soulmate.

It's so ugly, but it's love actualized.

My phone rings and I launch myself toward the counter and snort at the name, Ma.

I toss the rag at the sink and answer. "I assume you heard?"

"I did," Amah says, in a sullen tone. "What are you going to do, dear one?"

"What's doing, Ma? He's a god."

"Are you sure?"

"We went out for drinks. I met his friends, and we had an hour-long talk that I didn't lead." I grin and bite my lip. "He walked me to my car and kissed me without my prompting. Yes, there's no other explanation."

"What do they look like?"

I explain the men—Alex's golden hue, Rath's iciness, and Comus's approachable, bearded face. The God of Revelry appears the most typical-looking divine being, but none of them are the hard, pupil-less statues of old, though I'm unsure of their chiseled states under jeans and shirts. My mind heads toward a shirtless Alex. He was thick, and I mapped the muscled ridges on his chest when he held my hand to him. Is there a statue of Alexiares? Are there… fig leaves or not?

"And if he wants to see you again?" Amah asks, interrupting my internet searching plans.

"If he calls, which he won't, I'd like to meet with him again." No way I'd reject Alex.

Amah's silence concerns me. It's a telltale sign she has a problem. We understand each other better than most because she raised me alongside Lena, treating me the same, even after her daughter's death. It would have been easy to cast me off, even though it was time for me to leave the nest and scatter into the world, but she didn't. She somehow forgave me for walking into that battle with Lena.

We don't speak of her or any of our other lost sisters—my mother, Petra, and the originals, Aglaope, Theixiope, and Peisinoe. Amah is like that. If something hurts, she sweeps the pain under the rug and never, ever, shakes it out.

"How are the gods not affected by us?" I ask. It's a mystery I ache to explore.

"They created the original three. They wouldn't make something that had control over them." There's a hard edge to her voice. I picture her tightened square jaw and wish this would have been a video call instead of just voice.

"That makes sense. Have you ever met a god?" I've asked when I was young. Her response was a hard, 'no,' clarifying that the divine was a limited discussion topic. I wish I could remember more from that moment.

"No." Her voice still carries that firm, drop-the-subject tone.

I bite my tongue, though I itch to press her. She's thousands of years old and told me that the gods disappeared from Earth over a millennia ago. She knows things. I grit my teeth, then take a cleansing breath. I will get this out of her. Once she realizes there's nothing to fear, she'll open up more.

"Ever dated someone from the other world?" I ask.

"I had a brief affair with an elf and a longer one with a demon." The way she intones 'demon' tells me he meant a lot to her. Unusual as she's always nervous about the otherworldlings. Some demons are better than others though, but she won't share much information about him.

"They were both affected by you?"

"Yes, but not like a human. They resisted for a while, but all succumb."

Except for deities. "Are you okay?" I ask, my tone soft.

Amah clears her throat. "Yes."

"Was it worth it?" I ask myself the same question with each forced relationship.

"Yes."

That must hurt. I've never had a definitive answer, except for the one time I went too far, held on too long. Nothing was worth that.

Since then, relationships with humans are fleeting moments to fill a need—not good, not bad.

"I'm sorry." I'm surprised by her confession, but her openness creates more questions. Have any other sisters dated otherworldlings? They haven't spoken of it. What if? "Has any siren been through a heat cycle with an otherworldling?"

"No. Not an otherworldling."

Only humans then. Amah's strained voice makes a knot form in my throat. Something's off. "Amah?"

"Any word from Gerty or Venora?"

"You know I'd tell you if I had. Ma, what's wrong?"

"Nothing, dear one, just…be careful."

I cannot remember having a tenser conversation with her. "You're worried about me?"

"You're acting like Ven. It's been a while since I've heard you excited. Gerty's missing, Grace split from Liam, and now deities spoke to you."

"Meeting the gods was random and they probably won't contact me again. And Gerty's almost your age, she's gone long spans without contact before."

Another long pause. What is happening?

Before I jump in again, Amah speaks up. "She's never disappeared like this in the technology age. I'm worried. You understand the vulnerabilities our abilities create. If we pull too much attention at once, we could create chaos. Humans are smarter now. They could force us into a situation where we would need to… harm. Or wouldn't be able to speak."

I rub my stomach where I was punched, though it's not sore. "What does that have to do with gods and breakups. Do you have a theory on Gerty's silence? Do you think humans have her?"

"No, but even Guene hasn't spoken to her in months. I'm considering traveling to her house."

Gerty wouldn't take off without contacting her daughter. I trace a light vein in the black marble counter. "Humans do have technology now. Maybe there are recordings near her house. It's a long shot, but we can check feeds. I'll do some searching. Anything else I can do?"

"Just be safe. I don't know what we would do." She falls silent, and I grip the edge of the counter, holding my breath. If I keep quiet, maybe she will continue her thought. "Please, dear one."

I'm so tired of the secrets. "What we would do if what, Ma?" What is she thinking? I press. "Amah."

"Lula, I can't lose you."

Me? "Hey, we aren't losing any siren sister." Never again. "We're fine. Let's find Gerty and tell Ven to answer her damn calls because it's freaking you out." I blow out an exasperated breath.

The line is so silent, I'm afraid she hung up, but then she sniffs. "Be cautious around gods, Lula. The deities' intentions are unclear, and it's impossible to make them tell you the truth. Do not share our information with them and don't get yourself cursed because of some man. Even if that man is a god."

"Is that a possibility?" I recoil. She's right. The inability to control him is appealing, but also terrifying.

"Yes. Be cautious."

"I promise to be careful. We'll talk more soon."

"Hooroo, dear one."

"Until next time."

Nibbling a finger, I call both Gerty and Venora. I call Gerty's county in California and ask about video feeds. The man says he will search a mile radius around the property and send me everything he can find. I make him give me his cell in case my thrall wears off before the job is done.

The silence in my home sends a chill through me, even though the temperature's too warm with late summer sun blazing through the huge kitchen window.

I glance at the grandfather clock in the foyer. Mid-afternoon. The farmer's market is still open.

In shorts and a hoodie, I head out the door. I doubt if Alex would fit into my convertible and smile as I picture his long legs scrunched against the dash. It's a gorgeous day—blue skies with puffy clouds. In the sunlight, I bet Alex's dirty blonde hair has highlights of gold that match his eyes.

The drive through town is a blip with my distracted thoughts involving the deities. How would I say 'no' to Alex if he contacts me again? He's the first man I can talk to. Plus, staring at him for a solid decade seems like a delightful way to pass some years. Each movement of his lips against mine was an unexpected delight, creating the most thrilling interaction I've ever experienced.

I park the car in the public parking lot and rest my head against the window while I get my thoughts in order. The crowd mills around the stalls. Adults hold hands, interact with smiling strangers, and hug friends. Kids sprint over dirt and grass, playing hide and seek between parents' legs. Such a simple and beautiful existence.

Amah didn't need to remind me of Alex's divine status for me to understand his place is among the divine, not with a siren. By continuing this godlust state I'm in, I'm setting myself up for disappointment that will require many bubble baths and chocolate. I enjoyed the conversation we had, the kisses he gave me, the night of fitting in that deities gifted me. Now, I'll reinforce the wall around my heart and prepare to not see him again, but if I do...

Don't trust and don't share.

But I want to.

Before today, 'scared' was not a word I'd have used to describe Amah. I thought she'd seen too much to embrace fear anymore, but her voice on the phone made my heart-rate skyrocket. After Lena's death, we haven't been the same. Immortals don't expect to die, especially not young ones. Hazel, Grace, and I are third-generation sirens from the three original Mothers and the only ones besides Lena born in the last millennium. She shouldn't have died.

The Mothers have long parted from the Earth, and I'm unsure if they met their demise or found the alleged realm portal. Why will our eldest sisters not speak of them? It's frustrating as hell. Why are we not privy to information we should have received in the first twenty years of our life? If we're trustworthy enough to fit in with the humans without the tantrums and drama of youth, we should be able to handle our own history.

Why were we cursed? What happened to my mother? How old was she when she died and what are the exact ages of Gerty and Amah? Why is Amah so distrusting of Alex? If I understood more, it would settle my mind or give me a rational reason to steer clear of him.

When I step out of the car, the warm sunshine disrupts the moody cloud I'm stuck under. The fifteen pop-up canopied stalls are busy with a decent crowd as humans meander under banners or posters displaying the names of local businesses or farms.

The grass in late summer is dark green and tickles my ankles as I make my way to the vendors. Bins with every color of fruit and vegetable surround me in an edible rainbow. Smells of each harvested crop blend with beeswax candles and herb-scented soaps.

I close my eyes, imagining the garden the produce came from, the hands picking each item, or working with raw materials. Sometimes immortals lose sight of the simplicity of making something with our hands, especially in the modern world, where we no longer have to do manual labor to live. We remember the days of candlelight and washboards and have grown lazy with new, simplifying inventions.

These folk take pride in something as simple as growing tomatoes or making a candle with the products of the Earth. They have it right. Humans are on a limited timeline and use their years to the fullest extent of their abilities. Though bound to end, they find joy in simple tasks and caring for each other. I'm charmed by them.

Studious gazes follow my path. I should make this a short trip.

I head to a farm stall and collect vegetables, deciding on dinner with the available harvest. The man behind a table loaded with zucchini and peppers stays quiet as I hand him money. His gaze tingles the back of my neck as I exit the white canopy.

"Are you a movie star?" a teenager blurts out as his friend shoves him toward me.

Smiling, I shake my head and continue walking, but the boys keep pace a few feet behind me. Past them, an adorable little girl with wild brown curls pulls on her mother's hand. She breaks free and speeds my way on tiny, agile feet. I throw my arms out in warning, but little ones are chaos incarnate, and she doesn't even slow before she attaches herself to my leg.

I set my bag on the ground and scoop her into my arms. Tears well and my chest tightens as she wraps her soft arms around my neck, nuzzling into me as if she loves me with every ounce of her being.

Her mother sprints through the crowd to get to us but slows as she meets my eyes. Panic drains from her face. She acts as though a stranger holding her child is the most natural thing in the world. I resist the temptation to tell her I will keep her sweet daughter and raise her as my own.

The girl grows heavy in my arms and people stare, but it's not every day I get hugged. "Go to your mother, little one," I whisper.

She releases her grip on my neck and leans away from me. The woman scoops her into her arms and smiles at me. "Thank you."

I stumble toward the next stall, heart overjoyed and breaking. The different scents of soaps and lotions calm the cold ache. I thought I'd like to have a child. Having someone I could live with for a while, raise and care for was the ideal plan for a siren. My heat won't occur for another hundred years, which still isn't enough time for me to adjust to what it will do to my mates. A child would be the best thing to come from that terrible time, but it's unlikely, and I'm not sure I'd want this existence for another. Whether the divine or nature created us, we're not meant to reproduce well. Maybe there's a reason for that.

At the fourth market stall, I stop dead in my tracks. A tall, broad-shouldered man stands with his back to me. He has dirty blonde hair and—yep, a super nice ass. For a moment, my hopeful mind sees Alex, but even though I didn't get to check out Alex's backside, it's not him.

The man turns, and he's beautiful. Breathtaking for a human. He looks at me, his expression turning to lust in a second.

He would go home with me.

I could pretend he's Alex and use him to fulfill my needs. Stepping closer, I inhale his scent. He smells of pine and musk. It's okay, but not right. His eyes are blue, not gold. He treks my arm with his hand, and the touch doesn't make me burn. It creeps me out.

When I back away, he moves forward, but I whisper, "Don't follow," and turn to leave. His brows curve into a puppy-eyed expression.

It's better for both of us. Trust me.

Working my way to the car is difficult with humans wandering into my path and trying to touch me. Each interruption makes my irritation grow until it's a snarling entity.

Once I'm settled into my car, I gawk at my phone. I consider deleting Alex's number before I shove the device in my purse. A second later, it's back in my hand. It was two kisses and conversation. Let him go.

The ringer goes off, making me jump. 'Alex' is blinking. No way. My insides settle into a tiny ball as if trying to hide. Did I dial him?

It rings again. I answer. "Hello?"

"Lula," he says, a smile in his voice. "What are you up to today?"

"You're calling me?" I cover my eyes with my hand.

Alex's laughter rolls through the line. "Lula, you trust me so little."

"It's not that. It's just…I…" My face heats. "I'm surprised."

"I'd have called yesterday but got wrapped up in meetings."

"It's fine. I've been busy too."

Meetings? I picture a board room of deities in suits. Are the others like Alex, Comus, and Rath?

"Find any adventures today?" He sounds like he's walking.

"I'm visiting the farmers' market to get dinner supplies." A small group still stands on the grass, staring at me.

"Seriously?" He sounds surprised. "The one off of Jefferson?"

"Yes. You've been before?" I can't imagine a deity at a farmers' market.

He chuckles. "A time or two. You sound surprised again."

I am surprised. A little flicker of hope lights a torch in my chest, but I tamp it out before I get too excited. "Just taking it all in, Alex."

"Are you there now?" he asks in a cheerful voice.

"I am. Well, I'm in my car getting ready to leave."

The world stops on the other line. No Alex, no wind over the speaker, no birds.

"What are you making for dinner?" he asks, startling a jerk out of me. The sounds return—he's walking again.

"Stuffed squash with a side of dragon beans."

"You cook?"

I scoff. "Is that hard to believe? I've picked up a few recipes in my two-century existence."

"There are millennium-old deities who'd struggle to boil an egg. If they ever had to boil an egg."

"That's crazy. It's boiling water, how hard—"

A knock on my window makes me yip.

Eyes, crinkled at the corners, are even more golden in the light of day. Hair with 24-karat highlights shine and a perfect, godly smile drags a trill, squeaking sound from my throat.

Chapter Seven

LULA

Alex opens my car door and extends a hand. "Lula. It's nice to see you again."

Slipping my hand into his, I let him pull me from my seat and blink. I hope I'm not blinking Morse code for, 'I'm a moron around you.'

Alex is striking in the light of day, with a perfect nose and sculpted lips. The same golden hue of his eyes and hair tints his skin, and I bet he tastes like the sun. He's magnificent, and I'm staring hard. "You're here?"

Not even attempting subtlety, his gaze traverses my bare legs. "I am."

My hand's still in his, and I stare at it, amazed he's touching me. He drops his hold and runs the back of his fingers against his scruffy chin. I want to inspect that scruff.

"What's going on in the farmer's market today?" he asks, then tilts his head as his perusal of the market lands on the few people staring.

I point to the line of canopies. "Want to see?"

"Yeah, I'd like that."

Before we reach the humans, I quiet my voice. "Were you in the area?"

"I was close. I'm glad you're here."

"Why? Did you need help picking out a handmade doily?"

Even his grin is divine. "No. I just wanted to see you."

Really? I bite my smile into submission. The whole market population will follow us as if on a leash if I giggle.

Alex scrunches his face. "I forgot you can't talk."

Every eye follows us as the crowd parts for us. I shrug, pointing to a stall with homemade beeswax candles I hadn't visited because there were too many people following me. They're leaving me be now though, eyes still on us, but the air is calmer, the tension dispersed. It would be incredible if Alex's presence dulled my ability.

The heavenly scent of the lemon cookie jarred candle makes my eyes close in olfactory bliss. I hold it out to Alex. He inhales and closes his eyes before he takes it from me, tucking it under his arm. Lifting another to his nose, he pushes his lips out, contemplating, and holds the candle out. Blackberry jam. I nod and smile.

We go back and forth in silence until everything smells the same and my nose itches in a near-sneeze. I rub at it with the knuckle of my forefinger and scoot out of the tent.

Alex pays for two candles, with difficulty, as the older woman working the booth keeps rambling about the candles, bees, and weather. She even fans herself at one point.

Don't worry, lady. I get it.

We head to the vegetable stand, and I pick up a bunch of carrots.

"Better cooked than raw," Alex says, then points to a purple, striped eggplant. "Originally, these were white and small. Demeter created them right before I was born, but centuries later Dionysus was having an..." His eyes crinkle. "...event and he bit into one, thinking it was a boiled egg. He wasn't pleased because the original, raw eggplant was a work in progress. He splashed wine on them, streaking them with purple so they would stand out and he'd never make that mistake again."

I beam at him. An event, huh? Probably an orgy with nymphs feeding deities grapes. Does that happen? I lift my eyebrows in question and point to the eggplant.

Alex considers, then ducks, coming close to me. "I love it fried. Any other method of cooking is useless."

Eggplant parmesan may be my favorite dish. I pat his chest before filling my palm with a perfect heirloom tomato. He snatches the dark red fruit and grips the prized possession to his chest. That's a favorite. Maybe I'll make bruschetta… not that I'd be making it for him. I drop my smile. I can't believe he's here. Why?

"What's wrong?" Alex lifts my chin.

It's tough to toss on a fake smile, shake my head, 'no,' and turn to pick out more tomatoes. Maybe he has questions about my kind that I can't answer. This may be a problem. Amah will not be happy. I'll just have to avoid siren talk.

He nudges me, displaying a huge cucumber. I raise my eyebrows, tilting my head. I could make a vinegar salad with tomatoes and spices or throw it in a salad. Possibly both—it's a huge cucumber. He furrows his eyebrows as he looks between me and the cucumber before he drops the produce back in the bin like it's on fire. He gives me a pointed, yet teasing, look. "Dirty girl."

I widen my eyes, and my cheeks blaze. "No, no, that's *not* what I was thinking about." I giggle against my palm. "I was planning dinner and—"

The world halts at my outburst. Everyone within hearing distance stares at me frozen in place, holding goods, paused mid-step. *Dammit.*

Alex's attention darts over the crowd. "That's some powerful mojo, Firecracker."

Wincing, I peek up at him. *You have no idea.*

He surrenders the tomato, unloads my armful, and leads me from the stall.

As we pass through the parting crowd in silence, our entwined hands hold my attention. Is this what it's like for the humans? A warm tingle spreads up my arm.

We stop in the parking lot. I pull from Alex's grasp and confront the crowd following us. "Continue your tasks and do not remember us."

As I duck behind a minivan and lean against the blue metal, the crowd shuffles away.

I cover my hot face with both hands. I don't want this. The control I possess hangs its heavy weight around my neck, threatening to strangle, and I can't shrug it off and walk away. Amah is grateful for our ability, as is Grace. I'm the siren who struggles most in my skin even when I wield my power for good. It's not right, and it mocks my difference—displays it for all to see. This time, though, someone will remember.

Warm fingers pry my fingers away. Alex strokes my cheek. I lean into his touch, and an approving sound comes from his throat. "This blush."

"Come to my house for dinner." What am I doing? After that public display of power I offer—no, command to cook for a god? But I can't be alone right now. He's given me something too addictive to walk away from. "I mean—"

"I'd like that."

"Really?"

Alex tugs my hand until I take a step closer. "Always so surprised. Yeah, I'd love to."

Moving closer, I think he may kiss me, but he signals to my car, parked a few spaces away. "Can I ride with you?"

"Of course." Mischief is a little nymph on my shoulder whispering that Alex squeezing into my car will be the entertainment of the century. The nerves I've been swallowing down dissipate.

He folds himself into the coupe. "This is a tiny car. Too tiny."

"My car is perfectly sized. Perhaps you're too big?" I nibble my lip and click my seatbelt.

He searches for, then presses the button on the side of the seat. It glides back with a quiet whir. "No one's ever said that to me."

"There's a first time for everything."

"Not when you're two thousand years old. Tends to be, same shit, different decade."

Warmth bubbles out of me in a laugh, and Alex's sharp interest reminds me I shouldn't be doing this. Too much, too risky. I focus on driving instead of this relationship that'll never flourish. People walk the streets, unaware that I'm chaperoning a literal god past them.

"You okay?"

I bob my head. "We'll be at my house in five." Alex skims my upper arm with his knuckles, sparking antsy energy through the fabric. "Do you like squash?" I ask, trying to keep my attention off his mesmerizing touch.

"I do."

I cut my eyes to his concerned expression, then fixate on the road. "Good. That's good." With so many things I want to ask him, I'm not sure where to start. "Um, why are you on Earth? From my understanding, your type doesn't come down from the clouds."

Alex shifts in the cabriolet's small seat. "With permission, several of us study humans. We report back disease control, invention progress, and religious news."

"That's a good thing; learning about humans."

"Yeah, I suppose." His harsh tone is a surprise. He shrugs, brows relaxing. "The older gods don't see our studies in a positive light, but as a necessity. Some believe we should stay in Olympus."

The road forks and I follow the right tine. The city tumbles into a forest with houses tucked between trees and balanced on rocky hills. "Maybe you should take humans or otherworldlings up to Olympus to study the gods. The information we have on deities is outdated."

His fingers fist, before he splays them wide and eases them back to cup his knee. "It's the same as it was five centuries ago, but with a couple of new deities in the mix."

My house comes into sight, with my little red mailbox mounted on a wood post surrounded by a rainbow of zinnias. I'm glad Alex can see them in full bloom and drive slowly by them as I turn into the driveway. "The same?"

Alex keeps his attention out the window, scanning the wild yard, brick path, and red door. I try to see it as he would. My little beige craftsman crouched in the middle of an acre of wooded property, far enough away from neighbors so I can sing and not worry too much about the repercussions.

"Yeah,' he says. "It's um—I'll explain later. It's complicated." Looping the bags on one arm, he follows me up the cobbled path and waits while I fumble with the keys to the front door.

A warm hand alights on my spine. "You sure you're okay?"

Don't get yourself cursed.

The lock clicks, and I put my hand on the doorknob, but pause and face Alex. I'm not okay. The electricity between us arcs out, wanting to wrap him up and pull him closer. "My sister told me that Olympians can't consort with mortals and otherworldlings. Is that true?"

Unnamed emotion passes over his features. Determination, maybe? Irritation? He steps forward and ducks his head. My fingers twitch to reach out and bury themselves in his thick hair, but I clench harder on the doorknob and ball my other fist.

Keeping my hands off him shouldn't be difficult, but with him towering over me and moving in, my logic skitters away.

He stops inches from my face. "We'll talk about it." His hand covers mine on the doorknob and twists, then we back into my house until the door hits the foyer wall.

"Welcome to my home." I wave a grandiose gesture to my foyer with my unpinned digits, then rub my forehead to hide my wince.

Alex drags his eyes from me and takes in the staircase to the right, the arched doorway to the living room on the left, then the short hallway lined with original human art leading to the kitchen. The intensity lessens and I'm ashamed that I want it back. He's overwhelming. An unexpected and unexplored entity.

Though I shouldn't, I pull my hand from under his and trail my fingers over the strong, veined back of his hand. Light, golden hair peppers his arm, but no freckles or scars. I appreciate the hard muscles of his shoulder, his sharp collarbone under his shirt, and walk him back a few steps.

He moves my palm with the rise and fall of his chest, and his eyes devour me. "We definitely need to talk about it."

Amah was right then. I drop my hand and walk to the kitchen. "May I get you a drink?" The fridge creaks and pelts me with cool air. It's not a cold shower, but still effective. I smile at the six-pack of microbrews I picked up yesterday for no apparent reason. I like wine and cider better. "Beer?"

"Please." His voice is husky as he studies the art on the wall.

"Those are from local artists." Popping the lids on two bottles, I beckon him by waggling the beer in front of me.

The corner of his mouth twitches and he closes in with three strides. He takes up the room and not only with his size. The afternoon light brightens, and the air warms.

After a sip, he runs his tongue across his bottom lip and sensation ghosts over mine. "Delicious. It has a hint of berry."

He steps past me to place the bags on the island.

I face the fridge and pull out ingredients. With Alex behind me, I bend at the waist to get the cheese in the bottom drawer. He groans and tries to hide the sound with a cough. It activates repressed sensuality I haven't been able to explore. He makes me want to play, to tease him into a frenzy so I can study his expressions, and more of his sounds. I've never needed to flirt or try, and the challenge is too tempting to resist.

"Can I help?" he asks, so close that heat radiates from his body.

I stand and grip the handle of the refrigerator. I could lean back, brush my backside against him, and tilt my head back to gaze at him with half-lidded eyes. Lick my lips. Tremble for him. What would he do?

Wait. No.

The gods cursed the original three. Was it because of something like this?

"Yes. Here." I shove a container of ricotta cheese into the hands that I'd rather have on my body. "Tell me another story, Alex. One about what we need to talk about."

The lust he exudes simmers, and he steps away. "Myths are true, at least partially. Zeus is the king, and he consorted with many beings besides the divine. Gods and humans produced Demigods and we maintained or even exceeded the strength of pure gods."

"Is your father truly Hercules?"

He gathers the zucchinis I set on the counter and leans close. "Have you studied me, Lula?"

"Only a little and it was long ago. I studied other gods too." His cocky pursed-lip smirk falters. It reminds me that he is a deity and is used to worshippers and control. Powers I can't fathom. I keep on. He knows so much, and I want a taste of truth in the myths. "Well… is it true?"

"Yes," he says. "And Zeus is my grandfather." Now, he appears irritated. He rinses the vegetables in the sink, comfortable in my space. "And before you ask, the legend of him being a womanizing asshat is true. He tested out the otherworldling species and when a few gave birth, the children were more powerful than the rest of us."

"Powerful how?"

"They had odd attributes—rare, amplified ones that could do

remarkable things. One hybrid could create flora that could move and reroot itself."

"Oh, wow. Is that on Earth?" I picture a fantasy Ent lumbering its way on trunk legs across miles of forests, head of leaves bumping amongst the treetops.

"No. They were destroyed, as was their maker."

I stare at him in shock. He couldn't mean... "They killed him? Why?"

"Where do you want these?" He lifts the handful of wet zucchinis.

I pull a wooden cutting board from the cabinet. When Alex sets them down, I nudge his arm with my shoulder. He bites his lip. Having someone not tell me what I want to know is odd. I'm tingling with anticipation, and it's so quiet, my ears ache.

"He was stronger than me, stronger than my father, and grandfather. Zeus killed him because he thought the hybrids may take over Olympus and unseat him. He doesn't handle threats to the throne well." Alex gives off a huff. "Not that there was a threat."

Stretching over the island, I run my fingers along his clean-shaven, flexing jaw. This conversation hurts him, or is he angry? Every confession I drag from humans and otherworldlings is an uncaring, blank-eyed blurt. I can recognize emotion, but the options swirling in his golden gaze are too many.

He turns his head to kiss my palm, sending a flurry of warmth up my arm. "He and the Council decided the threat was too great and banned divine from crossbreeding with non-divine."

I drop my hand and take a step back. I understand his expression now—indignation.

There's no reason to be upset. I didn't expect a relationship or anything, even though he kissed me and is now standing in my kitchen, helping prepare dinner. He winces, wipes his hands off on a dishtowel, and approaches me as if I may run for it. I take a step back and he drops his extended hand.

"Lula, I—"

"What would happen?" I wrap my arms around my waist. "If a divine being were caught with an otherworldling... or a human."

His chest rises and falls in a heavy breath and he leans back against the island, crossing his arms. "It depends. Comus, Rath, and I have permission to interact and the older gods won't come to Earth, but—"

"But." I unwrap my arms from around my waist and walk to the counter, grabbing a knife to cut the zucchini with the precision of a pissed-off short-order cook. "Let me guess, if they found out, there would be cursing and death." Always with the cursing and death.

He plants his palms on each side of the island and grips the marble edge. "No. Not unless things progressed further than they should. And they won't." His determined eyes are believable.

"What's further?" I pause chopping and tilt my head. "You kissed me."

"I did." His tone makes my stomach flutter, and he eyes my lips. I'm not the only one who wants to revisit that little slip-up. "No sex. Nothing that could cause reproduction."

I grab a spoon and tunnel through the soft inside of the zucchini halves. Ripping into something helps soothe my mind. "Are they… watching?" Ew. The back of my neck itches with the thought. "How would they know?"

"They're not watching." He glances around checking for something—not an assuring movement. "They could do a scry with oracles. Check on past chastity if they cared to."

I assemble the stuffed zucchini dish. "So they don't scry for kisses then?"

"No." The amusement in his voice is clear.

"Good." I take a deep breath and put the dish in the oven. I pull more food out—salad supplies—because I'm not sure what to do with my hands. I'm not sure what I expected from him, we don't have a definitive path. We can kiss but no sex, and he's still hanging out here. Well, his appearance today isn't about getting in my pants, but I won't talk about me and my sisters. Even if I have questions too.

Alex steers clear while helping me prep dinner. He gives me a nudge here, a lingering gaze there. A roving hand before turning away. It tempts me to poke at him. The brush of his knuckle down my arm sets my nerves on fire even through a layer of cotton, but then he walks to peek in my fridge. I throw a carrot at his backside. His sharp gaze makes my heart pump overtime. What will he do? I want to test every angle until I understand each expression. He grabs the carrot, tossing it in the trash, and asks me about food I like.

It's easy to be around him.

We fall into the give and take of conversations about humans and unusual human activities like tetherball and bungee jumping. He asks softball questions about my family and I change the subject, which he easily navigates seemingly unoffended. I wish I could peek into his mind because the moments of thoughtful silence, where he taps the table with his forefinger and stares at me as if he wants to ask me deep, life things about myself, makes me want him to ask, then I feel guilty. I can't give him more.

Dinner is quiet. The lemon candle sits between us on the table in the kitchen nook. The windows surrounding us let in the dimming sunlight, the warm glow bathes us in golden luminosity like a deep, comfortable dream.

I have questions, but my throat goes dry each time and any conversation about Olympus pulls my thoughts to the original mothers. Without blurting out topics that will lead to the things we cannot talk about, I can't grasp a cohesive topic beyond the weather and the wallpaper in the kitchen.

"I like how you decorate," he says. "It's…human."

"I'll take that as a compliment."

"You should," His fork clinks against his plate. "Olympus is white marble and gold. The carvings are wars and death, the tapestries display blood and pestilence."

And here I am with my purple rooster, old photos of beaming humans riding the first bicycles, and an impressionistic canvas of a pregnant woman gathering fruit in an orchard, surrounded by her family.

"I guess it's easy to obsess over death when you don't have to face it." I stand and gather plates. "More?"

He watches me for so long, I nearly ask him if I have cheese stuck on my face, but then he cups his chin and leans forward. "No. Thank you."

I collect plates and walk them to the sink, but before I turn on the water, he's behind me. Hands encircle my waist, and the dishes fall with a clank against stainless steel. Alex's rumbling chest presses against my back. "Butterfingers."

I tilt my head back to rest on his shoulder. "My fingers are not buttery."

"Oh yeah?" he says low and breathy as he turns me in his arms, encircling my wrist with fingers that may as well be perfect bathwater with the ease he engulfs me in. I'm going under, sinking in with a resounding sigh.

Alex sucks my finger, sending a slew of heated sensation bouncing around my body. He gazes at me. "Nope. No butter. Raspberries."

I touch his face, delighting at the sharp sensation of scruff, then run my fingers through his hair. I'm not surprised at the softness. His eyes flutter closed, hands tightening around my waist. I move to my tiptoes, pressing against his warmth, but a nettling thought breaks through. "We can't," I whisper.

Gold eyes open and Alex dips his head. His lips brush mine, spurring a hot sensation in my belly before it travels lower. This is not smart, but the lust rolling through my body shoves aside rationality.

One hand threads through my hair again. I never knew the back of my head could be an erogenous zone, but sure enough.

His soft kiss intensifies, and he moves his hands up my back.

I cling to him and try to memorize everything: his smell, the shape of his lips, and the scruff that will leave a red flush on my skin. I'll be so glad for that mark because it will mean this happened.

This is real.

Chapter Eight

ALEX

Kissing Lula was not the plan.

Without a doubt, she is the best and worst dilemma I've ever encountered. At least we talked about Olympus. I'm easing her into my world, starting to share the horrors of divine life, hoping she will embrace the outrage my group does. Then we can really talk.

We head into dangerous territory, careening along a forbidden path. My muscles tense in preparation to step away, but Lula must want me as well because she kneads my hips and bites my lip, sending a spike of heat down my spine. I tilt her head and lick her tongue.

She slips her fingers under my shirt, grazing my stomach, and moans a breathy sound. I reciprocate with a short growl.

She is not obtainable. Not yet. Still.

Her hair is soft in my clenching fingers, and she claws the ridges of my muscles with biting pressure. I swing us around, lifting her to sit on the kitchen island, bringing her up to my height.

I expect her to freeze, panic at my eagerness. She should. *Push me away, Lula. Be stronger than I am and tell me what a fucking terrible idea this is.*

She cups my face while I ravage her mouth. When I step closer, she wraps her legs around my waist, and yanks me where I belong, right against her heat. My mind wanders into a blank fog, where her scent drifts over me, intoxicating when paired with the taste of her lips. Her whimper heats my nerves with a fiery blend of demand and serenity—ratcheting up the tension in my muscles but calming my thoughts. I give her the slightest direction. She gives no resistance, only a throaty moan. There is only this moment. May it last for eternity.

She turns, breaking our kiss, and I growl at her like a beast.

Unyielding lust wars with reason, and it's winning. I crave to be against her, on top of her, inside her, and I'm losing my calm. This is not me.

"Are you going to answer that?" she asks.

What? She's squirming against my front, and I'm groping the most perfect legs I've ever touched. Soft and tan curves with muscle from walking in nature. With her lips out of reach, I nibble her neck. The fringe on the tiny shorts is soft under my thumbs. I want dessert.

"Alex." She moans a melody that rings in my ears. "Your phone."

There is another sound that's not as demanding as her heat or her clutching fingers. Her lips are parted and wet.

"It'll stop."

The ringing phone ceases. I crash against her, savoring every sweet inch I can reach. A ring pierces the quiet again.

Lula smiles, licks the center of my top lip, and retreats. Grumbling a curse, I fish for the interruption from my pocket, refusing to put an inch of space between us. I fumble with the answer button.

"Alex," Comus asks. "Alex?"

"What?" My gravel voice is reminiscent of times awoken after one of my friend's gatherings.

Lula lifts her chin, soft hands exploring my shoulders. I lean in, inhaling her neck. There's vanilla and a spice I can't place, then her—raspberries and rain.

Comus's voice is a ramble of words that are not lining up, but one crucial phrase grabs my attention. "Council's calling. We've got to go."

I stiffen, and not in a pleasant way. "What?"

"What in the hell are you doing? Drinking and drugging without me, brother? Unacceptable."

The curved junction of Lula's neck and shoulder lures me to

nuzzle against it. "No, but I'm busy." She strokes my sides like a sculptor, and I'm twitchy to pull off my shirt to give her better access.

"It's important."

Lula's bottom lip sends tingles over the pad of my finger. "Can you give me..." What movies does she have? Exploring the rest of her home and kissing her in every room will take a while.

"A decade," Lula says as I ask, "Until tomorrow?"

I lift my eyebrows, and her face hits a fresh shade of red. By her shifting glance and flinch, she'd run and hide if I didn't have her trapped against me. My gaze follows the flush covering her neck. I hook a finger onto the collar of her hooded sweatshirt and tug to view the crimson hue below her collarbone. Sucking in a sharp breath, my fingers flinch to drop the phone to unzip—rip off anything else keeping me from her skin.

"No," Comus says. "Your father wants to know if you're receiving your attributes. Something's happening."

Ugh. "Hang on." I set the phone down and kiss Lula with urgent need. One more taste to keep me sane or lose me further.

Her protesting groan as I step away from her doesn't ease my displeasure.

I rub my face and adjust my jean-crowding erection. Lula covers her smile with her hand. She's the most delightful mix of sex kitten and blushing flower I've ever met.

With deep breaths, I focus, pulling forth the attribute that's always buzzing in the back of my brain. Small skirmishes are so constant they're background noise, but once I'm under control, an overpowering chill shocks me to attention.

Fuck me. She's a top-echelon distracter.

I grab my phone. "Yes. Did Anice alert the Council?"

Through the line, a car's engine sparks alive. "He did. Do you prefer to go direct or ride with us?"

The guys should witness what's going on firsthand, and I keep my method of travel as secretive as possible. "Ride."

"Did you make it to her house?"

Lula smiles when I turn my attention on her. Sirens don't have enhanced hearing. Test complete.

"Texting the address." I hang up and text him, *Yes, and nothing more yet.*

All I need is for Rath to walk in and blurt out, "So are you joining our war against the Council?" I shove my phone into my pocket and face Lula.

"Everything okay?" she asks.

The buzz is now a low roar, sending me flashes of sand and fire. "I have some Olympus things to settle. Comus and Rath are on their way."

Her green eyes, full of concern, blink. "Did another statue lose its arms?"

Keeping a straight face is an epic accomplishment. "No. Pan acquired a new flute. They have summoned an investigation."

The mischief disappears as her eyes widen and the laughter tingling in my lungs gets the best of me.

She covers her heart and releases a lengthy breath. "Pan didn't make someone into his flute, did he? Tell me the legend's an exaggeration."

"It was. Mostly." Eh, she will need more time before I spill the old truths. I ball my fists, setting them on the counter next to her hips. I can't touch her, or I won't stop.

She leans in and kisses my cheek. "I got carried away. Sorry."

"So did I." I huff a laugh and lean, settling my forehead against hers. I want to tug her close, taste more of her. My control is out to lunch around her. With a kiss to her nose, I step back, offering a hand. "I'll help you clean up." I wave a hand at the scattered dishes.

"Don't worry about it." She takes my hand and slides from the counter, then squirms and blushes again. We did get carried away, didn't we? "You shouldn't have to help."

"Why? Because I'm a demigod?" I grab the cutting board, now angled halfway off of the island. The discarded lettuce ends are on the floor.

Lula considers a moment, but what? I'm intrigued. She doesn't know the gods yet but being placed in the same category sends tension into my shoulders.

"Because you're a guest," she says, but she's holding back.

"Well, you cooked for me and I'm going to help." I gather

displaced vegetable bits and trash them, then bring the leftovers from the table. I'm tempted to dive into the dish again. What else does she cook?

I reach to return a glass to the cabinet Lula indicated when my phone dings.

Here, Comus texted.

Lula stands still, one hand on the counter. Her glassy eyes give me pause.

"They're here." I stroke her cheek. "Are you okay?"

A high-pitched cackle comes from her before she clamps teeth on her lip, silencing the sound. "Yes. I'm great."

She's a dreadful liar. A forced smile lights her face as she shakes herself, rattling off whatever dark thoughts plague her mind. As she walks past me, I snag her hand to halt her. "Tell me."

Patting my chest, she laughs again, artificial and tinny. "I'm fine. Why wouldn't I be?"

Because you don't want me to go.

But I have to go. One day, if everything goes as planned, I'll be here with her. I'll carry her upstairs, lay her on what I'm sure is a fluffy comforter that smells almost as good as she does, peel those shorts off, and slide into heaven.

I bet being deep inside her would be a highly memorable moment in my eternity.

She escapes as soon as I let her go, then hands over the bag with the berry candle. "The other isn't safe for travel until it cools." The lit lemon candle remains on the table.

"I'll come back to visit the candle." I poke her side in a gentle taunt.

"It will be waiting." Doubt shades her words, making the banter of goodbyes less playful and more...permanent. I can't have that. She turns and walks to the foyer, opening the door, peeking out to wave at the guys. "Thanks for joining me for dinner. It was a pleasure, Alex."

Comus waves at Lula then gives me hurry-the-fuck-up eyes from the driver's window.

I direct my attention back to Lula. "I'd like to see you again."

"What happened was, um..." She tucks her hair behind her ear and won't meet my eyes. "We shouldn't."

"We should."

She turns a fierce gaze on me, surprising me so much, I shrink back.

"Alex, whatever this is between us isn't possible because keeping control around you is…" She brushes fingers through the air. "I'm glad I saw you again but—"

Cupping her face, I kiss her. Melting into me, she grips my forearms, clamping on as if hoping our skin will fuse together. I'll do better next time I see her. I have to.

How could the Council forbid this? The excitement swirling through me, lighting up bleak areas, could never be wrong.

This time, I'm the one to pull away. "I enjoy being around you. We can have another conversation." I tilt my head and smile at her.

She grins back. "Okay. Goodnight, Alex."

"Night, Firecracker."

I walk the brick path to the car, aching to veer and go back inside. Her face lights up when I tell her Olympian stories, and the art on her walls is an eclectic mix that requires discussion. I didn't even ask how long she'd been there. It's been fourteen years but would have been a good conversation point to get her sharing. How sloppy of me.

The door clicks closed and with her out of sight, my attribute roars through me.

Striding fast, I get to the car. Comus glances at the door. "Get info?"

"Not yet. I shared why it's illegal to crossbreed."

"That's what you led with?" Rath asks with a glare.

"No, we explored the farmer's market, but it's a sore point…" I wave toward the porch where we kissed. "Clearly."

"For who?"

Comus drums on the steering wheel at Rath's jab.

"Yes, it's a sore point because she likes me, and since Zeus is the reason we can't go beyond making out in her kitchen, it was an excellent introduction."

I run my hands through my hair and try to calm my body. Tension and dread flood through me. I'm jittery with pent-up energy. This isn't right, and it's not only my active attributes. I'm not myself since getting a taste of Lula.

"Attribute firing off?" Comus asks as he drives toward town.

"It's coming in."

"Just now? Anice reported an hour ago."

I clench my teeth and meet his seeking stare in the rearview mirror. "I was… distracted."

"Told you," Rath says, nudging Comus with his elbow. "How quickly do you think you can unveil the plan to Lula? Do you trust her?"

Not yet. In minutes, she could ruin what we've been assembling for a century. "She deterred any discussion about sirens. She doesn't trust me yet."

Rolling mountains of sand flash in my vision, but no people crash together, no weapons fire. Then, a grassy hill. Back to the desert. Smoke. Are there multiple locations?

Comus turns on the main road toward the garage. We park the car, and the tingling sensation subsides. I signal the guys to wait. The strong perception highlighting an impending war trickles away like the last heat of a sunset as it dips into the horizon.

I'm left colder, yet at peace. "I'm losing the location. Let's go."

Sparse, lifeless land greets us with miles of sandy dunes on one side and flat scrub everywhere else. The sun beams overhead, making the region hot as the hell realm. Eerie air, thick with soundproofing tension, makes the hair on my body rise. It's like standing in falling snow, except instead of chilled flakes, I'm pelted with gravel of doom.

The only signs of life are sparse bushes and a scavenger bird on a scraggly, dead tree. With two flaps, it leaves the brittle branch bouncing and flies toward the west before a sharp dip to the south. I jog in the direction the bird avoided. Rath and Comus follow behind me without question, even though my attribute now lays quiet. We pass scraggly bushes and rock.

"There," Comus says, pointing to the faintest line of gray smoke billowing from past a dune.

We slow when we breach the top of the sandy hill. Engulfed in flames is a mound of bodies, and ten feet from the burning pile stands my spitting image except for a short, neat haircut.

At least Anice isn't in a himation, though his outfit belongs back in nineteen-fifty. He only wears human clothes when his attributes call.

His confused expression deepens when he notices our approach. "Alexiares?"

The smell of charred flesh surrounds me. "What happened, Anicetus?"

He rubs his neck, features strained. I haven't seen him this agitated since we forced Moros, the God of Doom, into a hell realm. Then again, I haven't seen him much since then. He's usually composed, and concern for my twin sends a dropping sensation to my stomach.

His hand falls to his side. "I do not understand. Though weakening, I followed the call. Arrived and again, nothing. I walked until I came upon this." Signaling to the pile of bodies. "What could this mean?"

"Again? How many calls have you followed?" We have similar attributes, though sometimes they call out for separate reasons. Mine wards off wars, Anice follows the call to conquer. Our attributes usually overlap, but unless Lula's even more distracting than I thought, something is out there that I can't avert.

"Two others, but the call was weak, and when I arrived on Earth, there was nothing."

"That's not good," Rath says, running a hand through his hair.

"Other areas have not attracted you?" Anice turns toward me and tilts his head.

"No. Small visions here and there, but this has to link to something big." The burning pile reminds me of the old days—dark times with dark wars, where body counts were too high to bother with graves. Where are these people from and who do they belong to?

"I concur," Anicetus says, scrutinizing me for the first time in ages. He takes three steps closer to reach out and grasp my shoulder. "Too much time has passed, brother."

I clasp his opposite shoulder and bump his forehead with mine. "It has."

We survey the pile, then search the ground for evidence of the mystery people, but there's not a trace. No items, or clothing, and the sand has covered any footprints there may have been. Identifying the bodies enough to determine if they were male or female, much less human or otherworldling is impossible. The humans will panic over this.

Kneeling, Comus throws sand by the handful on the burning mass. The rest of us follow suit until the flames settle. We reconvene in a huddle, and Comus wipes his hands on his pants. "The Council will want a report so they can decide if it's worth the gods' attention or whether to leave it to the humans to sort."

"I will inform them." Uncharacteristic irritation radiates from my twin.

"How's the divine life?" I try not to put too much bite into my words, but he reads me well.

His shoulders slump. Interesting. Anicetus always takes the side of the divine, defending, excusing, and lessening the Council's constant poor decisions. He's irritatingly loyal.

Though a long while passed since I've considered us close, he catches the implied question. His eyes are tired, resigned, and he looks older than his comparable thirty-year-old human appearance. "We should speak. Where is your next destination?"

Expressions of curiosity from Comus and Rath ask me what the plan is. Despite the guilt and despair tugging in my chest at the harm these beings underwent, Lula claims my thoughts. The sand's tone mimics the color of her skin. The sound of her moans spirals in my ears to the point of madness.

Something is off in me, and I need an oracle to confirm or deny my suspicions. Perhaps prolonged exposure to a siren affects a deity, and that's why they were cast out of Olympus.

"I have an errand to run on Earth. Need anything?"

Besides the few of us who enjoy walking among them, deities do not need human things. Even when deities use a human invention, they claim the influence of the gods made the discovery divine.

Anicetus bobs his head once. "Actually, yes. Bring me back a souvenir. One of their clever inventions."

Leaning in, I tap my ear. "I'm sorry, did you say you wanted something made from an unintelligent, unimpressive, non-deity?"

"I never believed humans were useless. Yes. Please bring me

something human-made. Something I have not seen before." He hasn't visited the Earth outside of attribute calls in decades, and human technology moves fast. He strikes a serious tone. "We need to speak soon."

"We will." I grasp his shoulder before he shakes hands with Comus and Rath and turns to leave. He didn't even bow or use formal, divine farewells. My friends' wide-eyed expressions match mine. The most loyal are deviating from divine tradition.

It's happening.

When Anice leaves the plane, Rath turns to me. "Returning to your siren?"

"Not yet. Something's so off that I should visit an oracle."

Rath leans back, tucking his chin. "I know you're not talking about heading to Pythia?"

"Hell no, not Pythia. Anything she read, she'd tell Zeus. I need to confirm."

"Confirm..." Rath rolls his hand through the air, an impatient signal for me to explain.

They won't let me get away with radio silence. The guys are too perceptive. We carry the knowledge of each other that comes with hundreds of years of growing as friends—heartbreak, mindset, every nuance memorized out of the sheer volume of time together. "She's the only thing on my mind. She distracted me from my attribute which had to be calling strong with this going on." I signal to the smoldering pile.

Rath leans forward to poke me in the forehead. "Yeah, and?"

I should've expected their indifference. My time studying sirens and Lula in particular has taken my mind from other things. When we met, she had me wrapped around her dainty, raspberry-tasting finger. "It's not right. I'm not right."

"You believe she affects you? She can't." Rath crosses his arms but asks Comus, "Can she?"

"Well, that's why he needs an oracle." Comus looks to the bright sky while he considers. "I know someone."

He always knows someone. People and parties are his job. "Of course, you do."

Chapter Nine

LULA

No word from Alex for a week.

Asshole.

I take it back, he's not an asshole. He's wonderful—his stories, his kisses… yes, wonderful. Except now he's gone, leaving my house and me quiet and cold. Who knew one deity could take up so much space in my house, only by being in my kitchen for a couple of hours.

I vacillate between appreciation at meeting Alex, and disappointment that something so amazing isn't possible. For a moment, I received a glimpse of how a normal relationship starts, and now that's gone.

It was incredible, though. Eye-opening and powerful, licentious and thrilling, overwhelming and…gone.

Just gone.

I breathe deep to soothe the tightness in my chest. Dammit.

My phone rings and I dart to the kitchen island to answer. It's Amah.

"Did you find Gerty?" I ask.

"No," she says, voice tight. "She hasn't been here for a while. There's rotting food in the refrigerator, and two cups of molding tea on the counter. Lula, what do we do?"

A sob sounds across the line, making me flinch. I don't want to put the idea in her head, but the truth will help. "She's not dead."

"I know that!" Amah blows a breath across the microphone of the phone, making a static wind. "Where would she be? Gerty's never gone this long without talking to us. It looks like she walked out the door and didn't come home. This is bad."

I plop myself on the floor and lean against the island. She's right. Gerty's quiet, but she wouldn't want us to worry. "Did you call the phone company to check her recent calls?"

"I didn't consider doing so. I'll call right now and keep searching. If you find anything, call me. Be careful, Lula."

"You, too, Ma." I hang up and am left alone once again.

After dressing in jeans and my favorite gray tee, I drive to the grocery store, the quiet one a few minutes farther than the fancy one everyone visits. The old store smells of disinfectant, and aged vinyl floors, but it's never crowded. I gather what I need for the week and a little extra.

A tiny hope lingers, though it shouldn't. Maybe when I get back, I'll pull into the driveway, and Alex will be on my porch with his disheveled hair and a kissable smile on his handsome face.

Driving home, I ignore the sunset, and the humans interacting with each other. Instead, I replay the gastropub and dinner with Alex. The comforting memories are hard to suppress.

A white, upright creature runs in front of my car, and I swerve to the side of the road.

Though I've never seen one in the flesh, I've studied it. The wendigo emits an ear-piercing scream and glares at me with glimmering, pink-tinged eyes. What is a darkling doing here? Long pale arms hang to its knees, and blood drips from long talons. It was in one hell of a fight. One of its antlers is broken, only adding to the terror of this feral creature caught in the evolution between man and beast. What did it battle? A car maybe? Hopefully, no one saw it. Humans can't handle the truth of darklings—not mentally.

Emitting a snarl from a fang-filled, drooling maw, it lopes across the road toward a grouping of tall condos.

I step out of the car and cross the street before I consider the danger. I haven't seen a darkling for a century. They shouldn't be in this realm. It should be in a hell plane eating other darklings, not here, threatening humans.

In the fading light, I follow the loping beast, chastising myself. "Why couldn't I be endowed with a cool superpower? No, I get to control everyone to an annoying degree."

I was born the wrong otherworldling. Wouldn't want to be a vampire, though. I enjoy the sun too much. A shapeshifter would be fun, as I've always wanted to fly. If you're a shapeshifter and the skies are calling? Boom, be a bird. Awesome. Too bad they're unpredictable and murdery. I've never experienced a friendly encounter with one, but I've never needed to sing around one either.

I hurdle a trench of water while keeping an eye on the limping creature. "You should be in your hell realm, Wendi. Not here."

It snarls and pauses as though it's using its brain for more than destroying, though I'm not sure darklings grasp more than kill, eat, mate. They're as skilled as otherworldlings, but with a wild lion's brain. It's a dangerous blend.

The beast's eyes glint in the light as it eyes me, a snarl on its lopsided face. Is its jaw broken? I bite my lip to keep from convincing myself to run back to the car. *Get your head on straight and find your missing spine. You are a siren.*

I'm not strong, not fast, but I melt my enemies. It's a last resort I've only put into play a few times, but I'll use it if I must. This creature will kill anything it comes across. I'm surprised it's avoiding me, but maybe it recognizes imminent death when it sees it.

The wendigo lowers its head. A chill runs up my spine. It steps out of the brush, glaring at me and licking its fang-filled mouth. Stepping forward, I begin my song. The last beams of daylight dapple through a line of trees, bathing the secluded area in an orange glow. The humans should be safe from my voice.

I let the words flow from my throat with intent and power. The creature stops short, mouth opening in a soft yip, then lopes forward. I halt and hold my ground. My song breaks forth, delivered from my soul—a complex cadence of primal, deep notes I hate more than anything ever.

Its shoulder hits the ground, and it hacks sharp coughs, then staggers up to unsteady feet again. The emotions running through me turn to pity. Collapsing once more, it stays, gaping muzzle to the mud, and legs flailing.

Why is it here? Has it been here since the portals closed? Wendigos are cruel killers. It would leave a trail of parts in its path. What if it's not? What if the lore is incorrect and it's harmless? No, the snarl and death glare doesn't belong to a gentle species. It's injured, which is why it didn't attack from the start.

It gurgles a whine and skin rips over ribs. I focus on the orange-tinged clouds, continuing my song. It's still a creature, alive with blood and bone. It suffers.

I close my eyes and cover my ears with shaking hands when its whining gasps increase and turn to gargled screeches. The acrid scent of death makes me swallow a gag.

I'm sorry.

When its death sounds fade into silence, I stop my song, drop my hands from my ears, and observe the remaining disaster of the creature. In a second, I'm back on that battlefield.

Lena tied off her fourth arm-tourniquet as they carried a screaming soldier missing both legs into the medical tent. She turned with a concerned expression I knew well. Something wasn't right, even for a battle. We passed off our medical supplies to a young, nervous-looking woman and hurried out the tent door.

Unseated riders called for help from the field, wild-eyed horses galloped in every direction, and stationed in the middle of it, working his way toward us, was the most massive man I'd ever seen. Holding a rudimentary machete, he slashed his way through a line of infantry, scattering men like chess pieces swiped by a defeated opponent.

Lena lifted her sharp chin. I understood her intention—to use our ability to calm this foe. He wasn't human, and the immense bloodshed needed to end. Continuing, we stepped over bodies, making our way to the action.

Hands grasped at my legs, holding tight. The man's face was so pallid, I blinked in surprise that he was strong enough to halt me. "Please. Please help," his weak voice pleaded with such agony.

I knelt beside him. "Everything's fine." His face relaxed, and I told him, "Release my leg."

The tight restraint loosened and fell away.

"Stand down," Lena commanded, yards away.

The beast tilted his head, assessing her. She drew the attention of everyone. Even the nearly dead calmed and rolled until she was in their sights. On hulking legs thicker than Lena's waist, the monster approached. She spoke louder, confusion lacing her words.

"I said, stand down. Halt!"

Dropping his weapon, he lunged with unforeseen speed, biting her, ripping her clothing, thrusting against her as she cried out in terror, uselessly fighting. Lena's bones crunched and popped. I screamed for him to stop. Our ancient song fell from my lips without thought as I stumbled over bodies. Everyone's rapt attention deflected to me as I ran toward my sister.

Though panicking, I lowered my voice, aware of the imminent outcome of my song. The monster slowed its assault, turned his black eyes to me, and arose from my sister.

Wet warbling sounds came from Lena. I choked on my words, repressed a scream, and fought to stay on task, holding onto the fact that she was immortal. She could recover. With time, she'd be perfect again. Balling my fists, I sang, infusing every bit of my power into my words.

When it took a few lumbering steps toward me, I stepped backward. The air left my lungs in a rush with the realization. The seven-foot-tall creature, wearing animal and human skin as rudimentary clothing, was a berserker creature. A darkling.

I thought a crazed otherworldling demon fought among the humans, not a primitive, recalcitrant species ruled by fundamental needs. Power surged through me, and I increased the volume of my song. Those falling around me would die anyway if the beast lived. I became a weapon of necessary evil.

The berserker snarled and licked Lena's blood from its lips. It came closer, and I stumbled through my words. I was young and had never sung before. A thousand doubts made me wince with each heavy footstep. I sang louder, my fists clenched so tight, I drew blood from my palms.

Ten feet away, it slowed, staggered, growled, and stumbled to its knees. I hit my chorus, the peak of bodily destruction, and it collapsed to its elbows on the ground. Each melodic note became stronger until it fell forward, convulsing. Even as skin darkened to purple from internal bleeding and ruptured, I sang. I sang until there was no chance this monster would ever rise again. When the blood-slickened heap lying before me was no longer recognizable, I quieted with a choking sob and took in the stillness of the gruesome destruction.

The silence in the field was the loneliest I'd ever heard.

I rushed to Lena. Bones protruded from multiple places on her previously flawless skin and her throat was open, leading a red river to the crimson ocean covering the ground. She stared at me with the faintest glimmer of life in her brown eyes. I had to try something, anything to save her, but she was so broken. Before this moment, I could have done anything—conquered the world with my ability, but in the most critical moment of my life, I was useless.

I needed something to help my sister. The medical tent was a green island among the sea of death. If anyone lived, I'd command their help. I told Lena to hang on. Before my muscles flexed into action, her chilly hand alighted on my arm. Her chest moved once more with a squeaky whisper, and eyes unfocused and stared through me.

It was too late.

I whispered her name. Shook her lifeless body. Yelled at her to wake.

Standing, I screamed furious, unintelligible words to the surrounding dead, to the gray sky, and to the gods. It should have been me. I was the brave and reckless one, except for this one time she led the way.

Mindless with anger and unimaginable loss, I couldn't process anything besides broken rage until the link of her life severed from my soul.

Searing pain wracked my body, the pull of energy tangible before it left me cold, and less a being, a piece of me lost to the wind. The agony silenced my ranting and brought me to my knees. My sisters suffered the break as well—one of the many curses of the siren.

I shake my tight fists out. Over a hundred and fifty years and the habit remains. With blurry vision, I glance at the dents in my palms from my nails.

Covering the mess as well as possible with sticks and leaves, I try to ignore the recollection of Lena's terrible last moments, her relaxed, gray face. Sometimes, I wish I could mimic Amah and push some memories so deep that they're forced into silence.

Without pausing my steps, I command, "Go home," to the two gentlemen who stopped to see why I parked on the side of the road. They pull away from the curb when I do.

My phone rings, startling me. Swallowing, I try to loosen my tight throat. "Amah?"

"She was seeing someone." Her voice sounds tight as mine, but with panic.

Gerty's the shyest of us. She doesn't date or interact much with anyone. If she did, it's possible we wouldn't be aware. "How do you know?"

"Plates are in the sink, doubles of things. Two wine glasses, two juice glasses."

"Maybe she doesn't do her dishes every day?"

"Possibly. The phone company gave me records. A number called Gerty every day, and she called the number as well. It's been going on since late June, and now, no outgoing calls for three weeks. I dialed the number. No answer, no voicemail. I don't like this, Lula."

That doesn't sit well with me either. "Where are you now?"

"At a hotel, thirty minutes away from Gerty's house." She pauses, blowing out a lengthy breath. "Have you seen Alex again?"

I cringe at the sudden subject change. "Yes. He met me at a farmer's market, and we had dinner." I squeeze the wheel.

"Did anything happen?" Amah's disappointed tone makes me cringe.

For the first time, I don't want to share with her. After our last phone call, I'm not sure I want more doubt or truth. I'm an emotional mess, and after I get home, I want to reevaluate life for a moment and then dive into figuring out where Gerty is hiding and why.

Then again, my faux pas should be out loud, so I remember his divine status and my lack of divinity, the impossibility of a relationship. "He kissed me but was called away."

"Lula." A stern tone replaces the disappointed one. "You didn't—"

"No, no, nothing more happened. Just kissing."

"Is he familiar with our heat cycle?" She blurts out.

"I don't believe so. Why?"

"Curiosity," she says in a light tone, but I'm not buying her passing interest.

"Is that the only reason?"

"I'm wondering how perceptive the gods are of us—our physiology, our whereabouts." Her firm tone flags my interest, and I question how much this involves history, possibly back to the Original Three.

"When I spoke to them, they knew our numbers were few but said the archives didn't contain much of our lore. What things do you want to know? I'll ask Alex if I see him again."

"Lula, you cannot speak of us to the divine."

"Yes, but we could learn from them. Maybe they could help us find out—"

"The less others know about us, the better. We need to stay hidden and find our sister. How are your funds?"

Amah's never changed subjects so bluntly.

She's nervous. Then again, we've never had a missing sister this long, at least not in my lifetime. Maybe she will be more open to sharing when we find Gerty. "I have plenty of money."

"Alright. If you need more, let me know."

Guene is our money keeper and has taught her daughter about how money makes money through the years—gold, bonds, and now Grace has taken over the stocks. I'd contact them if I blew through my bloated allowance.

"Anything from Venora?" I ask.

"No. Hazel is traveling to her home tomorrow."

"Can anything else be done?" I'm tempted to go myself. While Amah is stringent on visiting each other, this is a new age with airplanes, fast cars, and phones. Meeting up more often isn't a crazy idea and would help us all.

"No. I do not believe so."

When was the last time Amah saw a darkling? My hands tremble on the wheel. "I killed a wendigo."

"What?"

"It ran in front of my car, and I followed."

"Lula!"

"It would have killed people, Amah!"

"Okay," she says, tapping her finger on the phone. Clearly, not okay. "I understand. You're okay?"

"Yes. Just shaken. I keep remembering. Sorry." I shouldn't bring Lena to mind. We're all close, but Amah lost her birth daughter. There could be no greater pain.

"I'm sorry, dear one. It's never easy to end a threat, and I know each time triggers her memory."

"I miss her. I miss our heart to hearts. How she silently loathed hateful people—glared them to death while she simmered." I swallow hard and swipe at an escaped tear.

"She disliked mean people."

"I loved playing with her hair. Pitch black, like you and Nysa."

Amah clears her throat. "Yes. The daughters from the line of Peisinoe."

"I loved making her laugh until she snorted and then poking the sensitive spot above her hip, making her squeal an off-the-charts note. She'd chase me around attempting retribution." The farmhouses we lived in didn't have the amenities like my cottage, but we were happy.

"Her laugh was so beautiful, and no one could get her going like you could." Amah gives a chuckle sob. "She made up the silliest games. Both of you did."

My breath staggers. My sister was a beautiful soul.

"Lula, we need to keep each other safe now more than ever. Need to stick with what and who we know. Do you understand what I'm asking?"

My chest is caving in. She's right. I put myself and my sisters in danger by meeting with three deities I had no control over, then invited Alex, a stranger, into my house. "I do." My weak voice shakes.

"Consider moving. You've been in that location too long."

"I-I won't. I'm fine." My sisters may move frequently but I need stability.

"I'm sorry. Until we find Gerty and Ven, we must protect ourselves. We cannot protect ourselves from gods."

"I get it. I do." My driveway never looked so welcoming—my

home a comfortable sweater to slip into after a chilly situation. "Please call me if you hear anything, okay?"

"Oh, Lula."

"I'm okay. I am." I will be.

After farewells, I sit in the car. The last reserves of energy drain out of me with the streams on my cheeks. Contributing to Amah's terror and endangering my sisters was never my intention. I glance at my unoccupied porch. As expected—the best scenario. Still, disappointment simmers.

I'm so selfish.

Inside my home, I'll put away my groceries, pour a glass of wine, and continue scouring the videos near Gerty's home that the detective sent. I'd love to compel more officers to help, but we don't exist to humans. We're alone in our search, and it's an enormous world.

Tomorrow, I'll wake and go for a hike. I'll take a bath—wash Alex out of my system.

I'll find my sister.

With one more glance at his number, I press 'delete.'

Goodbye, Alex.

Chapter Ten

ALEX

The halls of my grandfather's immense, godly mansion are gold, with a hammered damask pattern. I bet I've traced each one I could reach.

I cherished learning about my lineage in this place that embodies pomp and circumstance to the thousandth degree. Servants and pets delivered the best wine from golden cups and served me delicacies ninety-nine percent of the non-deity population have never tasted.

Over a thousand years Anicetus and I roamed between our parents' house and our grandfather's, locked in children's bodies, learning expectations, history, and the way things were and would always be.

The musty aroma of ancient tomes wafts through the open door of Zeus's library, spurring pleasant memories of a million hours spent among the stacks. Corridors lead to lush, unused rooms and spill out into exotic gardens, our playground for long games of hide-and-seek. At four-hundred-years-old, I discovered a hidden study behind a private sitting room tapestry and realized many things had been kept from us. The small, dim area contained books filled with fantastical creatures, other realms, and humans. Anice and I sat each day studying the unsacred.

I'd tell him, "I want to meet them."

He'd respond, "But they are non-deities."

When someone emptied the space without a word, I sought loose-lipped deities who took pity on an innocent, curious child and shared information beyond the books. Anice spent time with a different crowd, practicing divine expectation.

We reached nine-hundred and requested liberation from our prepubescent entrapment, claiming we wanted to experience the full spectrum of godhood.

Our mother, the goddess of youth, balked. She attempted to shield us from everything, including accepting our attributes and achieving our god state. The oracles scried that my powers would aid warfare, while Anice wouldn't be defeated. We were ready to fulfill our duties to Olympus.

Mother was unprepared for our request, hadn't even considered that eventually, her children needed to grow up. After a hundred years of attempting rational discussion with her, I lost my temper and, though unsure of the possibility, threatened to accept my attributes with no guidance and leave Olympus.

My grandfather approved of my obstinance. "He will be my supreme commander," he announced, chin held high as he sat on his throne. "His brother, my unconquerable general."

My father was reluctant, done with the war and bloodshed he'd waded knee-deep in for centuries, making the name, "Hercules," a standard on Earth, but the king had spoken. Mother cried for a half a year, then released us from our young state.

While we waited for growth so we could accept our attributes, Anice and I practiced with our new bodies in sports, then fighting, then sex. My twin took the goddess Zeus arranged for him without a fight. Similar to our grandfather, Anice may not realize how many children he has.

Compared to the prolonged time I'd spent locked in a child's body, growth to maturity came in a blink, equivalent to fifteen human years. Accepting my godhood was slipping on a pair of well-worn jeans. I hadn't realized how off-kilter I'd been until I was whole. My blossomed ability showed that my involvement in war was to stave it off, disappointing Zeus. Even today, he still holds hope that I'll fill the role he's imagined for me and lead the army, though there's nothing to fight.

At the throne room door, I draw a cleansing breath and tug at my himation. The loose linen swatch of clothing may as well be a straitjacket. The guards bow and step aside.

I haven't appreciated one of Zeus's conversations for a thousand years, but once this little meeting of the minds concludes, I'm finally on my way to Lula.

Sing found that Lula has no hold on me. Well, her ability doesn't enthrall me, which was both a relief and a surprise. The quirky witch that Comus has been hiding on Earth, instead of dragging her to Olympus when he discovered her oracle abilities, was a joy. She's the most talented and exuberant human I've met, though I'd like to have known about her previously. Comus is my best friend but he remains mysterious sometimes, only giving up secrets when we need them most.

The reading relieved Comus, and Rath shrugged. Nothing surprises him except getting slapped by Lula. She surprised the hell out of him—out of all of us—with that move.

The need to hear her voice has called to me over the past week, but Zeus's lackeys have followed me around Olympus and three days ago, when I thought I had the chance to reach out, I walked into my room, encrypted phone in hand, to discover a nymph pet in my bed, courtesy of my grandfather. Her relief and happiness when I told her, "no thanks," and snuck her to the North Forest to visit her coven sisters was another reminder that what we're working toward is important.

But it confirmed that I can't contact Lula from Olympus. It's too risky. Plus, she distracts me, and focusing on this meeting is the top priority so I don't do something stupid like give into Grandfather's demands.

With a deep breath, I step forward.

"Alexiares," my grandfather says, voice booming through the vast room.

He stands from his ornate throne, a mimic of the one in the Council's chambers, and crosses to me, cream robes swishing. He gathers me in a powerful hug. Remnant emotions from my youth invade my mind, and a place in me warms. I steady my aim.

"When will you give me great-grandchildren?" he asks, a smile in his words.

He outlawed divine births as well as non-divine, forcing enchanted ambrosia upon us to prevent reproduction, but told me upon my betrothal that Naea and I weren't to drink it like the others. Besides the few deities that forwent the concoction and now live their days locked away after their unlawful births, we are the exception. I thought at first it was just another move to get me to do what he wants, but he has offered more frequently over the last decade to host the wedding of the ages.

"When you release me from my betrothal and let me choose my path," I answer with indifference. I may get a lightning bolt for such a bold statement. My skin crawls at the memory.

He pushes my shoulders back. "Alexiares." His tone shifts to a warning. "You have avoided your divine duties too long."

"I'd be less reluctant if I could choose my bride." Which will take me a millennium, or until we've repaired the universe.

With his contemplative silence, I chance to hope. Then, he slaps my shoulder. "No. Ichnaea is a splendid match. She has waited for you."

No, she hasn't.

Through much practice with conversations such as this, I stay expressionless. "Others have chosen their own partners, why am I bound to her?" He's never explained his reasoning for the match, but he does nothing without deliberation.

"You will choose Ichnaea."

"I'm not ready." If we stall long enough, maybe he'll move from whatever plan he has for us. Then, Ichnaea can marry Plutus instead. They've been together since before the betrothal.

Zeus lowers his chin, his gold eyes piercing. He's impatient to win this battle, and I'm toeing the line. "Do you wish for another? Another goddess?"

"I wish for the choice."

He taps his bare foot against the marble floor. "In a few minutes, you shall dine with Ichnaea and join her for the evening." The smug grin he wears reeks of scheming.

"I don't understand." If this hoopla is one of his surprise galas with the couple of hundred Olympians left—

"You understand. Your betrothed will be at your service for your… needs." He grins as if there's a joke between us. "She is lovely, yes? I have arranged the royal guest chambers in the left-wing."

Sick bastard. I pull in a long breath, preparing to spout my thoughts of his asinine plan when a maid rounds the corner and dips into a bow. "The Goddess of Tracking has arrived, Sire."

"Splendid." Zeus slaps his hands together. "Inform the kitchen to serve dinner."

The woman speeds away, and I'm left glaring at the man I used to revere. We could be mistaken for siblings except for his bagged, ancient gold eyes that saw humanity begin, though Zeus wasn't scheming his way to the throne yet. Earlier divine entities handled cosmic formulation and begot older gods such as my grandfather, who, with violent bloodshed, booted them from the realm.

Our purpose is to oversee life—to inspire growth and change, but the Council lost sight of that when the humans evolved to the state of the gods, then surpassed us. Other realms are more advanced, and some are early in their development, but this one is in danger of breaking apart at the seams if the Council continues to push its agenda of fear and struggle.

"Will you ever stop?" I ask.

His grin sinks to a firm line. "You were always such an obedient boy. If I requested anything, you would skitter away, honored to serve the realm." He straightens in front of me. "Perhaps I should have kept you as a child."

"I wish you would have," I whisper. Then I wouldn't have ruined the universe.

He slaps my back, ignoring my murmurs, and shoves me toward the door. "Go greet your bride. Take her to the dining hall and feed her well."

My anger has morphed with passing time, though Zeus can send me into a rage like no one else. A healthy dose of pity now blends with fury and disgust. Battling for power takes a toll, and he's tired.

This realm's inhabitants have evolved beyond his mental capacity, even altering their response to his fear tactics. They no longer run from the natural disasters he throws at them. They face his wrath, help each other, invent devices to study storms, and build better structures to protect themselves.

If we succeed, the realm will never be his perfect place of cowering masses that bend to his every sick whim. He refuses to see how far they've come. We're symbiotic with our beings, we must unite again, combine so we can surge into a better age.

The words, 'Not in your eternal life, you sick bastard,' lay on the tip of my tongue but I swallow them down. He'd take out his frustration on someone—the humans, a pet, or perhaps another deity would go missing. There's no contentment in Zeus's heart unless he's a hundred percent in control and that's not possible.

That was proven when the birth of Anice and I spurred openings in the veil between the realms that touch Earth. Other worlds began to explore our creation. For a blip, Zeus thought it was a boon, but a round of breeding to otherworldlings led to powerful hybrids, then humans documented and worshipped the gods of the otherworlds. Zeus panicked, outlawed non-divine breeding, had us shut down the realm borders, then broke us away from Earth.

Until now, I've helped him every step of the way.

I understood what I was doing, but just like every other good Olympian, I followed orders and trusted an untrustworthy king.

What he's doing with my betrothal, this demand of sex, is odd. Why me and why now?

I storm through the throne room's door. *Let's get this shit show on the road.*

Around the corner in the small greeting chamber, situated before the dining hall, Ichnaea stands with her attending maid placed one step behind her, to the left. Keena styled Naea's dark blonde hair in formal braids. Blue eyes meet mine for a fraction of a second before Naea drops them to the floor, as any minor goddess would do.

She's so good at her job.

"Hello, Ichnaea. Keena."

Naea's eyes go wide at my casual greeting, and both women jump into action, performing curtsies, bowing heads in submission.

"Greetings to thee, my lord," Ichnaea says in a small, mousy voice.

If Lula stood beside me, she'd shake her head, green eyes wide. She's well versed in divine lore, but she doesn't realize how fucked the godly lifestyle is.

Not yet.

If Lula and Naea's roles were reversed, Lula would greet me with her deep purring tone and a crimson blush, an invitation designed to drag me in as if she were a high-powered magnet. I need to push Lu from my mind, though. Otherwise, Naea and her maid may get the wrong idea with how my body responds to my thoughts. Himations don't hide much.

Not for you, Naea.

"Let's eat." Turning a heel, I stride out of the greeting chamber. When the women jog to catch me, I slow. I'm angry at Zeus, not Naea, and displaying rage would get back to the King. Naea's had a much worse time than I, and we need to talk alone. That hasn't happened in our two-hundred-year betrothal, even when requested.

In the extravagant dining hall, a dozen servants, watered-down demis that weren't lucky enough to be produced by major gods, stand in perfect placement for our arrival, and a harpist blends into the corner, quietly strumming. Historical tapestries depicting divine revelries throughout history hang in the room. The table is wooden and decorated with sprays of wildflowers and ferns. This is Hera's comfortable design.

I hold Naea's chair for her while she sits. The servants, prepared for our gathering, snap to updated locations when I disregard protocol and sit across from Naea instead of next to her. A gold plate containing a jumble of tentacles marinated in thick black sauce lowers in front of me. *Gods are so weird.* The servants stand in rows, close behind us in case we need our faces wiped or another fork. Because the four perfectly placed ones just won't suffice.

Naea waits, hands clasped in her lap. I spin a small tentacle and pop it in my mouth. Well-prepared squid, flavored with clean brine squishes between my teeth. Once I swallow, Naea eats with refined finesse. After two courses, the quiet tinkling harp in a room full of silent deities sets my teeth on edge.

"Why are you here today?" My voice blares, and everyone jerks to attention.

We can stroke another thread of discord in Olympus, though I'm not comfortable pushing too much without preparation. Everything rides on the line, and we could put too many in danger with words that Zeus may consider a threat.

Naea sneaks a glance at Keena, and the woman blots Naea's lips with a cream-colored cloth.

"I." She takes a deep breath and leans forward, keeping her voice hushed. "I was told we would commune on this eve."

My snort echoes through the room. "You agreed to this? You want to commune?" That ought to give an impactful impression to the servants. *See everyone? Not either of our decision.*

She tilts her head and her arched eyebrows furrow. "The King summoned me to do so." Her actions and words are perfect from years of honing the art of fitting in.

I could start an argument, yell about the unjustness my grandfather has forced us into, and how Olympus is on the verge of falling apart because of the unnatural separation from our humans, but that wouldn't help at this time.

It's best to keep our slow, steady pace. We've started the flow of information—all is not perfect in this false paradise. The servants deliver the main course. On a bed of purple and cream-colored leaves lies a mystery foie gras. Probably the rarest swan on the planet. The brown glop fills me with disdain.

I want a burger. A delightful human invention.

Irrational anger heats my face.

Naea takes her last bite, setting down her fork to signal her completion.

"You done?" I ask, curt and informal. The guards and servants will think the worst of me, that I am a product of Zeus and mean to strip Naea of her flowing chiton and her rights. That is until the rumors spread, and they will, because we're under a spotlight, and I won't do what my grandfather wants. Not now. Not ever.

Naea's eyebrows furrow, but she nods. She understands me, but this push from me is out of character. As the diplomat of our bunch, I'm never impatient, but growing resentment overflows and it's time to move forward. I must remain in control though, reign myself in for all of our sakes. If I yell that I'm sick of the injustice, we're working to bring down the Council, and everyone should join us now, I'll ruin our progress and any chance of a peaceful outcome.

I stand, attempting a kind expression, but my lips are firm and uncurling. "Come with me."

When she hesitates, I offer my arm, and she accepts, giving me a subtle squeeze. I'm unable to remember the last time we touched. A decade? Two? We've maintained distance, not wanting to give the impression that we're content with this path.

Once she stands, I lead her to the guarded bedroom my grandfather ordered us to stay in for the night. Her servant tries to follow, but I stop and raise a hand. "We've got this."

Keena shakes her head and mumbles, "But I am required to prepare her for you."

"We're good. Thanks. Bye."

She squeezes through before I shut the door and rushes to Naea. It doesn't matter anyway because two guards stand on either side of the bed. Not sure why that should turn my stomach—my grandfather would want a play-by-play—but it does and also adds rage in my jaw. Naea trembles, giving me a nervous side-eye as if I'm going to pounce on her. She always was a talented actress.

"Look Naea—" Her maid jumps at my words, undoing the pins of Naea's draping chiton. I step forward to steady her hand. "No, no, no, wait."

The woman blinks at me before averting her gaze. "My humble apologies, my lord. You must prefer to undress her. Please continue."

Naea's eyes widen, and I step back. "Ichnaea. Is this what you want?"

Now we dance.

"It is what the king summoned me for."

I may as well try again. "Please leave us."

The guards stay still as statues and Keena only stares and falls in line behind Naea. The demigoddess has stood next to Naea for decades. Maids are an invaluable source of information and getting gossip spread.

I take Naea's hand. "Does Plutus know you're here?"

Her face pales, and she covers her mouth, dropping her eyes to the ground. "My lord, I—I."

It's an appropriate reaction. She's kept her relationship under wraps. If we play this right, we'll gain sympathy, and if there's any blame, it will fall on me for not marrying her yet, not her.

"Hey, it's fine."

Keena releases a quiet gasp, and Naea wraps an arm around her waist in a self-hug. Her maid steps closer, laying a gentle hand on her shoulder.

"You mock me." Her head snaps up, and for the first time, she holds my gaze. "You cannot possibly approve of my indiscretions."

Never would I have believed that virginal chambers, where young goddesses have their virginity negotiated among gods and taken with no concern or consent, would help our cause. Naea hasn't needed to stay chaste, thank goodness, only unbred, and two-hundred-years is a long time to go without sex.

"You and Plutus fit. He's a gentleman to stand beside you, understanding your betrothment. I hope he treats you well."

"He is kind to me." Her voice is a shaky whimper. She loves him still. Her desire to break our betrothal remains strong.

We can work with this and hit the sympathies of the younger gods from both directions. Followers of the Council use goddesses as they see fit and approve or deny marriages to create pacts for Olympian space or allowance to crossover studies. We're pawns on their decaying chessboard.

"I'm glad for that. Are there others?"

"No," Naea says and sniffles. "Only him."

Hell, even my chest clenches at the longing emotion in her voice.

Another one of Zeus's gems is a law that states deities may only learn about other deities' attributes and abilities from the source. No discussing how other divine beings work and no studying them in the ancient, locked-up libraries, unless you're the King and the Council. They understand how every divine being's powers work in detail and could use that knowledge to curse the deities or kill them. Deities of my generation and younger have created Olympus's favorite pastime —pillow talk. Burn away boredom and energy, then connect with a conversation about how someone ticks.

I'm slowly introducing the indiscretions happening under the Council's nose, hoping they will discourage communing but not outright outlaw it. It's not sex they'd be angry about, but the way their law is being interpreted. The Council has taken rights from Olympians one by one until there's not much left, though they've done it at an unobtrusive pace, so everything appears normal. If they push too hard, like outlawing sex, Olympus may burn to the ground instead of getting hot enough to make the old gods leave. We want angst, not aggression.

"You will not be communing with me this evening, will you?" Naea discretely winks at me while wiping a tear. Her view of the guards behind me must show her something good. They'll report this back to Zeus and how they spin our conversation could help us, especially after I walk out.

"No, Ichnaea. I'll never force another to join with me. Without love or acceptance between us, communing would be wrong."

Keena bites her lip, eyes angled in a way that makes me think the word, "aww," must float through her mind.

So few understand love in Olympus. The relationship between my parents has been my only guide. They fought to be together until Zeus and Hera left them alone. The king can be swayed with careful, intelligent guidance, even if he only understands need, obsession, and greed.

Naea blinks at me under worried brows.

I gather her in my arms. "He's placed us in unacceptable circumstances, hasn't he?" We haven't hugged since Zeus announced our betrothal and altered our friendship. It's not a common action for Olympians.

Sniffling, Naea wraps her arms around my waist and squeezes. "I trust Zeus's reasons, whatever they may be."

Dammit. She still doesn't understand why he's forcing us together.

"Reasons he refuses to share with anyone," I say, giving her my information. "I for one, am exhausted by the demands thrust upon us with no discussion."

Keena looks as though she wants to take notes as a thousand thoughts glint in her eyes. This conversation will hit Olympus like a plague. *Perfect.*

I rub a circle on Naea's back. "Do you love Plutus?"

She pulls away, scared. With the appalling treatment of the lesser deities, her response is perfect. "I—"

"Do you want to be with him?" I ask, lowering my chin and staring hard. *Come on, Naea, admit your true wishes. They need to hear this.*

Zeus won't lash out at them, because love doesn't mean squat to him. Marriage is a business deal; children are a transaction. As long as Naea remains subservient, she will fall below Zeus's radar.

She puts her hand over her mouth and sobs, bobbing her head. I give her an honest grimace. They should be together. I've learned much from humans and they wouldn't stand for this treatment. We won't either.

Keena wipes at her face. Naea is a brilliant secret keeper, the best partner I could have imagined on the inside of Zeus's circle, and she trusts few—another testament to her intelligence. I don't want to marry her, but if I have to be trapped in a betrothal, I'm glad it's with her.

If I could, I'd turn to see the guards' reaction to Naea's breakdown, but that would be obvious. If anyone got the notion that Ichnaea and I were working together to unravel my grandfather's system, Zeus would have the archivists document the torture we'd both receive in order to strike fear in future generations.

"Is there another you want?" she asks, sniffling.

"Yes." I flinch at my confession. I'm intrigued by Lula, even a smidgen enamored. Wait, enamored? No, that's not right.

A lone tear spills onto Naea's cheek. "I wish you luck with your goddess."

I work my jaw. Her eyes widen, and she ducks her head, swiping at her eyes. Well, that's out now—not a goddess. A sharp streak of fear pierces my chest. If Zeus finds out, he'll question me, and the threat he likes to throw at us about benching us from the Earth realm will become reality.

Keena's expression morphs from concern to furrowed brow anger as she watches Ichnaea and me. Hopefully, she isn't as attuned to Naea and my expressions as we've learned to be.

"Good luck with your god, and Ichnaea?" I wait until she brings her eyes back to mine. "I won't commune with you until both of us are ready." Which will be never.

"It's the way of the divine, Alexiares." Her voice carries a weak shake.

"Not all divine. It's time we reconsidered our ways." Before opening the door, I smile at my friend.

Most assume I'll cave to my grandfather's will and settle with Naea. She's a perfect vision—beautiful face and lithe body. In Olympus, she'd keep a quiet, organized house and bear meek, lovely children for me, though her heart longs for exploration. We'd live a facade neither of us wants, forever or until we left this universe.

I miss how she used to be—the person she's forced to hide—and though she's perfect, she's not Lula.

My heart pounds in my chest. *She's not Lula.*

I want Lula's purring voice whispering in my ear, telling me each minute of her life before I walked into it. Visions of my fingertips trailing her flushed cheek flash into my mind. Her silky hair against my palm makes my fingers clench, and I inhale as though I'm breathing in her skin.

My senses fire alive with her memory. Her laughter and moans ring a phantom cadence in my ears, a siren's song enthralling every inch of me except my free will. My choice is my own.

The corner of her mouth twitches and her fingers flutter a secret farewell by her side.

Until next time, Naea.

Hurrying from the room, I cannot get out of my grandfather's house fast enough and am glad the guards don't follow. It surprises me that there's no clank of armor behind me, even the guard on the door stays put. They haven't considered that I'd dare to go against Zeus's wishes.

That's all I've been doing lately.

Chapter Eleven

ALEX

The midday sun is bright in Belize and I'm tempted to walk the beach instead of sitting around the driftwood kitchen table. This is my favorite of our secret safe houses. We've decorated it in a minimalist way in navy and cream with mocha-colored woods except for the light gray driftwood table in the kitchen.

It's not cozy like Lula's home, but it's comfortable and not Olympus—we have technology, high-speed internet, and lots of human gadgets like ice that comes right from the refrigerator door and keypad entry. We figure if any Olympian ever discovers this place, we could escape while they're distracted by the wooden deck, grill, and lighting. It's a whole new world down here.

Comus exhales and passes a joint. "He wanted you to what?"

"*Commune* with Naea. He prepared a room. Brought her to his godsdamn home and stationed guards by the bed." Smoke wraps my tongue until it relaxes.

He pours three shots. Amber bourbon swirls into each glass while the bottle laps in the air to replace its lost liquid. "To fucked situations."

Rath pops in and winces as he sits. Without a word, he snatches a shot glass. With a clink of our glasses, we shoot. Impatience tenses my muscles, makes my foot bounce, makes me squirm. "I have to call her."

Comus snatches my cell phone out of my hand. "Gods' awful idea."

"Give it back," I growl and lunge for him, but he tosses the phone to Rath, and the bastard dissipates as I move to tackle him.

"Rath! Get back here, or I'll tell everyone you fade into Artemis' chamber and watch her sleep."

Rath limps around the hallway corner. "She'd take my balls." He adjusts himself as if trying to make sure they're still safe.

I tilt my head at him. Is that blood on his forearm? What did he get himself into? *Eye on the prize, Alex.* "Phone. Now."

Instead of my phone, another shot lands in my hand, courtesy of Comus. "Let's get gloriously jagged. Shall we, gentlemen?" There's a tension to him, uncommon, and he won't meet my eyes.

"Patience, Alex," Rath growls. "She's safe and you can't mess around with her. Stick to the plan. Otherwise, no one will get what they need."

He's right. My head's fogged. Not from either of the inebriating substances we partake in, but because of Lula. Comus tinks his glass against mine. "To women who are far too perfect for the likes of us."

Grunting in agreement, I slam the shot.

Rath slips into the leather seat next to me. "You fell for her. Fucking terrible idea."

"Gods, I know," I admit, then rephrase. "I'm intrigued, not falling."

"Mmhmm," he grunts, pursing his lips.

"You're lusting after her," Comus says. "Hard."

Rath flexes his fingers, the shakes his hands out. A jagged but healing rip follows the indent of muscle in leading to his wrist "So. Damn. Hard." I release an exasperated breath with a laugh. "Lula's different. Facing pure evil? She fights, and she has her own agenda. Not like a siren, but exactly what we needed." I slam back another shot. "And her face. That hair."

"Mmm. Red." Rath scratches at his chest, then winces.

Comus sucks his cheeks in and pours again. "The unmistakable, illuminating, impossible-to-resist call of the siren."

"Yeah." I point at Rath. "And don't look at me like that. We're going on forty years of you chasing Artemis."

Rath holds his hands up in surrender. "Understood."

His relationship with the major goddess of the hunt and chastity has been a best friend's nightmare. Comus and I stand by and watch him torn down, trampled, and pulled back in because she loves and hates him. She can't step away from the old Olympian mindset, and that gives her more hang-ups than a coat rack store. She's a high and mighty major goddess and Council member, so Rath is and will remain her dirty little secret. I have zero respect for her and navigating that with my friend is a tension point that's boiled over more than once.

Comus blows smoke rings across the circular table. He puffs out a spear through them. "We get it, brother, but you're bordering on obsession over there." He gestures, circling his pointing finger in my direction. "And we have too much to do. We cannot screw this up because we won't have another chance. Lust is a powerful thing, and I'd say do her and get it out of your system, but you'll fuck everything to hell if you do." His expression hardens, and he leans forward. "He's watching you, probably scrying your chastity monthly with Pythia, and he'll kill any non-deity."

My fingers tingle with stress. Zeus wouldn't pause unless it was to fantasize about her perfection before he unleashed his green-tinged death bolt. "Both of us."

Comus pours and hands out shot number...no idea at this point. "Not you. He needs you for something. Naea didn't give any hints as to the purpose of your betrothal and exalted rank equivalent to major god?"

"Nope."

"Damn. I was hoping she'd have found something out by now," Rath complains. "How did you two get out of communing, anyway?"

I recount the whole crazy-ass story. Rath snorts, and Comus's lips twitch. I give him a shove. "What's on your mind?"

"Ahh, Naea's ovulating. As soon as I heard I tried to warn you, but you were already in the building and the guards wouldn't let me pass. Zeus hasn't forced you two together in a while, so I knew it had to be something big, but a move that desperate? Damn."

"Bastard means to trap me after he commands that no one breed?" I scratch my chin. "Hey, how in the hell do you know Naea's ovulating?"

Comus's face pinches. *He doesn't want to tell me?* "Are you having sex with my betrothed?"

"No! No." Comus's hands fly up in defense. "Um. How was Keena?"

"Naea's maid?" I remember her flushed cheeks and messy braid. "How long has that been going on?"

"A month. Right after 'the breakup.'" He uses air quotes and pours again. "Keena's full of good info."

Rath snatches a shot. "And you."

Chuckling, I smack his chest, making him grunt and lean forward. Did he come across Ares or Deimos again? "Alright, what happened to you?"

"Just get it over with," Comus says and wanders over to stand beside Rath.

Get what over with?

"It worked out fine… enough," Rath says. "It's not the outcome I wanted, but she's a powerhouse."

Why is no one looking at me? The walls are holding their attention better. "Who?"

Rath runs a finger along the rim of his shot glass. He's weighing the pros and cons of something and I ball my fists. There's not a lot my friends will withhold from me. They only clam up when Rath is in danger of getting punched, and there's only one thing lately that can get my fists flying.

"Lula?" I ask. They exchange a glance, sending a ball of ice straight to my gut. "What happened? Outcome?"

"Uh." Rath shadows across the room. "First, she's fine. Sad for some reason, but the damned thing didn't touch her."

My chair crashes to the floor with the force I put into standing. "What damned thing?"

"Eh, the wendigo." He disappears and I crash into the wall, leaving a shoulder sized dent in the drywall. He appears behind the kitchen island. "I'd heard a rumor about it wandering around Thailand, and I caught it."

"A fucking wendigo?" I roar.

"Don't stand so close to the walls this time," Comus says with an inflection of boredom as I sprint past him.

Rath's face appears on the ceiling.

"Get your ass down here and talk."

He can't speak without his lungs and he can't float in the shadow realm when more than small portions of his body are solid on Earth. Remembering him dropping flat on his face several times when he was testing his abilities takes the slightest edge off my anger.

"You did not sic a wendigo on her." That restores the fire in my spine.

His lips part, then slam tight together. He appears next to the dent and sucks in a breath. "We needed to test her abilities with darklings. I couldn't pass up that opportunity."

"Test her once she knew what the hell was going on, Rath! Dammit. It's a darkling. You should have told us. We should have been there."

"That is true," Comus agrees, back in his seat and smoking.

Rath raises his arms wide in the air. "You can't hide in the shadows and watch, nor can you find a darkling, and transport it through the shadow realm to the location of your choice. And that bitch could bite."

"Not helping," Comus singsongs. "Just let him do it."

"Fine!" Rath gives that universal signal of 'come at me.' "But you get—"

I connect my fist to his jaw with a sharp crack. My knuckles pop, and his head leaves a dent above the one my shoulder made. Our way of punishment for when we do stupid shit is a tradition we started when Rath accepted his attributes. We heal in hours, but the brief pain and embarrassment remind us that we may be gods, but still chase perfection, which is faster and always changing directions.

I shake my hand out. "She better be okay. We do not fuck with darklings without backup in a safe environment."

I'm three seconds from ringing her doorbell.

"Ow," Rath says and drags his ass off the floor. A red welt paints his jaw. "You don't give her enough credit. She melted the beast. I wish she would have commanded it, she didn't even try, but hey, she can take out darklings with ease, and that's something."

"She was upset?"

Rath's wince shows even through his newest injury and he crosses the room to grab an icepack from the freezer. "Yeah. Killed it then stood there for a while, trembling. Didn't say anything but—" He points at me. "No more hitting. There were tears. Not sobbing or anything, but it hurt her, I think. Not physically."

My phone rings from somewhere, and I swivel my head, trying to pinpoint where the sound is coming from. What if it's Lula?

Rath shoves me into my chair as he passes by and heads toward the bedrooms. He returns with my phone in hand and his brows knit. "It's Anice."

When was the last time I received a phone call from my brother? Years, and only because I convinced him to have an emergency phone.

"Where are you?" he asks before I can greet him.

He doesn't know about any of our Earth homes and can't without us risking the Council finding out. "What's going on?"

Fast footsteps sound from the line. "Greetings to thee," someone calls out in the formal way of Olympus.

"And to thee," Anice responds before whispering with a harsh rasp, "I need to speak with you."

Something is way off. Anice doesn't sneak around Olympus and he certainly doesn't get mad. He's unconquerable—that comes with a heavy dose of confidence. "Everything all right?"

"No. Praxis is joining me."

Oh, hell. Ice is a permanent fixture in my stomach today.

Comus reaches and taps my hand.

"Hang on." I shield the phone. "Anice needs to talk. He's with Prax. We need to get them out."

"You trust him here?" Rath whirls his finger, signaling to the room.

If Anice comes here and tells Zeus about this house, we'll have to get rid of it, and our new home will be the marble cells in the Olympian barracks.

"Pass me to Praxis," I tell Anice.

A shuffle and Prax jumps right in. "I wasn't seen, but Anice is in deep. We need to be where you are."

I keep my eyes on Rath and flip the phone to speaker. "Where?"

"Two steps into the west entrance of the North Forest."

Rath disappears.

"On it." I hang up and put the phone on the table. "Anice isn't one to flee."

"I've stationed Prax in Zeus's house as counsel. They must be coming from there. This should be interesting."

Our plan is altering by the minute. Strange for something that's been in play for a hundred years.

Rath drops next to the hallway and releases Anice and Prax's hands.

"Marvelous job rearranging Rath's face," Prax says from behind my twin. He resembles a huge bodyguard at a toga party, his square jaw flexing, challenging Rath's typical scowl. "You okay?"

"Is he okay?" Rath asks with spit and signals to the mess I made of his jaw, though the swelling is already going down.

"I'm not okay, yet." I have to check on Lula first.

My brother is frazzled with messy hair and wild eyes. Our conversation in the desert was a reminder of how much I miss him—miss the times we were close. There wasn't a break or fight, we just wanted different things. Still do. I enjoy Earth, and he likes his place in Olympus. However, here he stands like a cornered lion, flexing his claws. The divine life isn't treating him well right now.

I wave them over. Prax grabs a substantial armchair as if it's a barstool and huddles in around the table. Anice isn't distracted by decor or lights, but he's traveled to Earth because of his attributes. Rath offers him the joint, and Anice takes the offering and drags long.

Comus leans forward and wraps his fists against driftwood. "Oh, this is going to be glorious."

Prax snorts as my brother's golden eyes meet mine. Anice blows smoke into the air. "Why does our grandfather want me to commune with your betrothed?"

What. The. Hell?

Both Rath and Comus lean back in their seats with wide eyes and

I huff out a sarcastic laugh. "He's fucking lost it." I snatch the joint from my brother's fingers.

Comus stands and walks to the kitchen, returning a moment later with a couple more shot glasses.

Pour and shoot. Twice.

My stomach warms, loosening that damn ball of stress. Bourbon isn't ambrosia, but it does the job, for a few. Deities burn off the effects quickly.

I pass to Prax. "I assume you eavesdropped?"

"Oh, yes," he rubs a big hand over his mouth as he levels a glare at his empty shot glass. "Zeus was unaware, but I was in a hallway behind him and heard it all. When Anice escaped the building, I told him he needed to talk to you."

"You were right." I run both hands through my hair. If Anice disobeyed Zeus's orders, we're either screwed or our cause may be ignited. It depends on my brother's friends. They're the upper crust of fusty elite and have sway, *if* they use it. Against the King though? Doubtful.

Comus eyes the ceiling, lips pursed. He's considering the same, I'd bet. I clap Anice on the shoulder. "He wants Naea pregnant so I'll marry her. He demanded that I spend the evening in the guest room with her *communing*."

"You have displeased him, but he wouldn't explain why. He told me to find you and threaten to commune with her myself if you didn't return. Then follow through but—" He makes a face as if he may be sick. "But not to eject into her. He described how to go about that, including offering a pet to join us. Then he wanted me to tell you about it after, saying I also do not drink the elixir, and the guards would come to fetch you to be sure you returned to perform your duties. If you didn't, to repeat until you did."

Fire sears through my veins. Ichnaea better be okay.

"What an asshole." Comus pours again. "He knows how to push Alex's buttons, but that's one hell of a desperation tactic. Why? What changed?"

The question of the hour. "Did he say anything about why he's forcing Ichnaea and me together?"

"No," Anice says, rubbing his chin. "But Alex. He has lost it. I have not witnessed his anger for a long while. You should—" He stares at the table and worries his lip. "Why don't you want to?"

"I don't love her. Not like that."

"You need not love her to marry her," he states.

Rath pipes in before I can. "That what you did?"

I shift in my seat, to block my brother from tearing into Rath. Anice glares at him a moment, leans back, and squeezes his eyes shut. "I don't love Iaso, and she doesn't love me. Not like… we do what we must." Blinking, he chews his lip. This has bothered him a long while.

"Everything he's put you through and you still support his tyrannical reign." Comus's tone shocks me cold. He and Anice have been friends for more than a millennium. Comus separated from most of Olympus after his sister's time in the virginal chamber and my punishment—we both did—but he's usually an expert at emotional restraint.

"It's the way," Anice growls then amends, "Even if it shouldn't be." Worry etches his face, aging him.

I raise my shot glass, pausing it inches from my lips. "Shit needs to change. It's not right."

Anice observes me a moment, tilting his head. "Have you found love?"

There is no point in denying, and he needs to understand. "No. Not yet. I've found someone I want, though. It's a chance I'm not allowed to explore. But my distaste for the Council's demands has nothing to do with that. They've gone from influencing the realms to locking down and dominating the lives of the gods. How much farther will they take control? The older gods are wrong and you know it, but those that oppose disappear. Have you noticed?"

"Where's the line between what we will accept and what we won't?" Rath adds, twirling his shot glass. "And can we live with ourselves for allowing the continuation of abuse?"

"Yes, but it's the way. If you married Ichnaea, you'd still—"

No. I slap my hand on the table to stop his words. "Is that what you do, brother? Enjoy your harem on the side? Do you care for any of them? Love another?"

My brother's eyes glisten with emotion. "I do not know love with a woman."

"Ceraon?" Comus inquires.

When my brother's eyes widen before closing in defeat, I understand.

The room is silent as we mill over that. Rath and I look at Comus, both of us wearing a slight glare. He doesn't lie to us, but he withholds like a pro. He keeps his eyes on Anice.

I had my suspicions, but Anice never talked to me about his close friendship with the Demigod of the Meal, and I never pressed. Ceraon is shorter than most goddesses, but his exuberance and quick wit hold a joyful audience. I'm not sure anyone could dislike him, which probably makes hiding their relationship easier.

Still, Comus should have shared. Careful conversation is crucial and I'd have liked to have processed this information.

"You love him?" I ask. Love is uncommon in Olympus. Saying it is not taken lightly.

His, "Yes," is a whimpered proclamation. It tells me he's scared, unsure of the future, and yes... deeply in love.

"You don't mind leaving his bed to go back home to your wife?" I need to ask but keep my voice gentle. I don't like hurting him, but we need him on our side, especially after that revelation. He loves someone, and he's married to another. "That's not a fair living. Still believe the Council keeps our best interests in mind?"

His eyes open, pain shimmering. "I hate it. She hates it. He hates it."

"How long have you been with Ceraon?" I ask.

Anice glances around the table and withdraws, folding into himself as if struck.

Comus lifts his chin at me, approving of my question, egging me to continue. He must already know.

"Anice." I lean forward and squeeze his shoulder. "There's a reason you're here." He disobeyed our grandfather. I'm not sure that has ever happened.

"You made a choice," Comus says.

My twin runs a hand down his face, shakes his head, opens his mouth then closes it. Finally, he flops back in the seat. Relief spreads over his features, a lightbulb blazing his thoughts to life at the same time a window to escape opens. I've seen this expression on him a couple of times, most obvious when I explained how we could demand to grow up.

"I did, didn't, I?" He huffs a laugh. "I was not jesting about needing to speak with you." He points to the hallway. "May we?"

Rath stands and takes the icepack back to the freezer. "Are your wife and boyfriend in danger?"

Distrust still peeks out of his eyes. "I'm not entirely sure," Anice says, worry in his voice. "Are they?"

"Your relationship with Ceraon is mostly unknown," Comus says. "Your wife will remain safe as long as she's not in on your falling out with his majesty."

Anice's tight jaw and clenched fists don't relax.

"Prax?" I ask. "Would you mind keeping an eye on Iaso?"

He winces. "I need an injury, don't I?"

"It would be weird to go to a healing deity without a reason," Rath says, leaning against the kitchen counter. "Besides, the minotaur hasn't sparred in a while. Not after it broke the demigod guard. It's probably itching for exercise."

Prax stretches and puts the chair back. "I could use some exercise myself, just in case. Who do you want on Ceraon?"

Just in case. We're trying to stay peaceful, hoping the older gods will realize the new age doesn't need their violence, we should prepare for when they treat us like they do every threat. Now, for the first moment of trust. "Have Eos keep an ear out and step in if needed."

"Excellent choice. That will thrill her." Prax offers his arm.

"I'll be back in five," Rath says, grabs Prax's wrist and disappears.

The Goddess of the Dawn is also in the inner circles and itching for change. Eos and her siblings are of the age of titans though they didn't leave in the first or second exodus. She and Helios embrace progress and the humans, but her sister, Selene, is more along with Zeus's mindset.

Eos longs for the connection we lost in the separation. She's as impatient as Rath but has had millennia to harness her actions, unlike my friend who jumps first and thinks later like when dropping off a wendigo to test a siren who may save us all. *Seriously, Rath?*

"Eos?" Anice asks, wide-eyed.

The best time to temper my twin to see reason is while Rath is playing taxi.

"Yes. She also believes things should change."

"Tell us about your children." Comus wears his this-is-old-information expression. That's three things I'm learning about today that he's kept from me. He's on deck for a conversation after this.

It crossed my mind that I can't remember Anice every being without Ceraon, why does he have such a big brood? Anice's last child was born on the cusp of the break.

Panic lies over his features. "If this gets out..."

"I swear it will not," I say. "Anything you say is safe here."

Anice bites his lip and runs a hand through his short hair. "They're not mine," he says in a rush as if the dam holding in his thoughts just crumbled. "Some are grandfathers from when Hera last threatened his manhood. Several I named to save the goddesses from telling the true fathers."

"Holy shit," Comus says. At least I'm not the only one surprised at this bomb-drop.

"Anice," I breathe out. I cannot believe he's been living this life.

Anice's fists ball. "I don't want to live the way we do. I'm so tired, Alexiares."

Finally. "Brother, are you ready for what needs to be heard? It will change everything."

He considers it, brows tugged together in concentration. He should weigh his options. The knowledge we hold, the plans we follow, will thrust him into a rabbit hole he won't be able to ignore. He steadies his gaze, sits straight, and reaches an open palm toward me.

It's now or never. Anice holds power in the hierarchy. He could be a significant player.

I grip his hand. "We need a new Council."

I pace the dark floor of the bedroom and dial Lula.

We've made more progress in one night than we have in the last decade. My twin is on board. Once we stoked the fire, Anice let his guard down. He's pissed, zealous, and blessedly agreeable to our ideas, especially with the goal of no violence. Even with everything Zeus has done, killing him turns my stomach. How many others hold back for fear of having to fight and murder?

Deities are a small group considering we've been locked in the same area for a thousand years. We're a small town of a few hundred, and while we haven't had a death in several centuries, we've had a couple of disappearances, which means the same thing.

Sharing everything, even a business-like description of Lula, lifted a burden from my shoulders. Everything is going in the right direction.

Now, I need Lula to be okay.

On the third ring, the line clicks alive, but no voice joins the connection.

"Hey," I say. "Are you there?"

Continued silence through the line makes my face pinch. I expected a sultry greeting or at least a giggle. Is Rath wrong, and she's hurt?

"What do you need?"

Where's the warmth? She melted against me days ago, but now? Arctic blast. I need to see her.

"I apologize for not calling you sooner. I was tied up."

"No problem. I'm in the middle of something."

I stop pacing as tendrils of concern slide over my skin. Something is wrong and I can't have that. "Hey, what's going on?"

"Nothing. I'm just busy. Thanks for calling."

"Lula, what—" The line goes dead. I stare at the screen and blink. What the fuck was that?

She doesn't answer when I dial her again. It goes straight to voicemail the third time.

I take the stairs two at a time.

Rath snaps his fingers, bringing my attention away from the phone in my palm. "Headed out?" He and Anice lounge on the gray mudroom couches. Anice looks as out of place in our space as a peacock in a broom closet. We need to get him some updated clothes.

"Lula hung up on me," I murmur.

Rath's head tilts. "Like, pushed the end call button out of excitement from hearing your godly voice?"

"No. She said she had something going on and hung up. Are you sure she wasn't hurt?"

"It didn't touch her."

My brother tilts his head as he watches me. *Dammit, Anice, don't analyze me just yet.*

Comus rounds the corner with a mug that says, *If nobody pukes, it's not a party.* "Lu hung up on you?"

"Yeah."

Comus glances at Rath with raised brows, and Rath mirrors him.

"What?" I ask.

Rath drops his legs from the table. "She's banging someone."

No. She hasn't taken a lover since I've known her. There were many times I was away, I didn't watch her constantly, but I'd know, right?

"Banging?" Anice asks.

"Communing, joining, sex, fucking." Comus sips his coffee, with a careless slurp.

"Oh." His surprised expression turns into a wince.

I stomp toward the door.

"And where are you off to looking so indignant?" Comus asks.

"Where do you think?"

Chapter Twelve

LULA

Cucumber slices lie warm against my eyelids. This super long bath in lavender-scented bathwater is helping. When I sip my glass of Chianti, the clay mask covering my face tightens. I should wash it off.

Every detail of the minutes spent with Alex repeat on an eternal loop. It's a beautiful curse. I even liked his friends. Comus was clever and sweet, and I bet there's more to Rath under all that sullenness.

Alex's lips were both soft and firm, plus demanding. That was new. What would've occurred if he could have stayed?

Oh yeah. Death.

I've never hated what I was. At times I'm dissatisfied, but you get what you get, and it could be worse. My mind wanders back to the golden god. Fantasies of a world where the two of us meet like humans run rampant. They blend with memories of reality. He smelled of grapefruit touched with the sun and sugar; he tasted of warmth and life. The way he fit against me—sheer bliss. My heart rate elevates, skin flushes, and tight sensation twinges below.

Ringing interrupts my daydreams. With a growl, I blindly slap around the small table beside the tub until my fingers find the phone. My muscle memory of the answer button location works just fine. "Yeah?"

"Lula?"

My eyes spring open, sending the cucumbers plopping into the bath. Why in the hell is Alex calling me back? Didn't I reject him?

When it comes to him, words elude me. "Um. Hi. Again." *Brilliant work, Lula.* I slap a wet hand over my face.

"You hung up on me."

I scrunch my nose and keep quiet.

His voice lowers. "Are you distracted? There's music. French?"

"Yes. I'm busy. Now, if you'll excuse—"

"Are you okay?" he interrupts.

Not really. "Yes. Fine."

"Hurt?"

I reposition in the tub. The water has cooled, sending a shiver through me. "Why would I be hurt?"

"Was that water? What are you doing?"

His tone slides from concern to irritation. The hard mud mask cracks at my furrowed brow, and I rub at it with soaked fingertips. "Why do you care?"

"Lula."

He's angry. Why? I'm the one who has to cut ties with his perfect ass because of his stupid divine status and my stupid otherworldling species. "I'm taking a bath. Gotta go."

"Alone?"

Is that what his harsh voice is all about? The mud mask tightens around my mouth as I grin. I shouldn't smile. I'll tell him I'm not alone. Quick and clean. There's wine and a book here somewhere—those count as companions, right? Still, the words won't come out. "I have to go." I smash at the end call button.

The phone rings one second later.

Why is he making this difficult? "What?"

"Open your door."

My heart leaps, and I fumble the phone before bringing it back to my ear. "You're here?"

"Open up, Lula. I need to see you."

Him disrupting my solo get-over-Alex party is not in the plan.

Go for a hike. Check.

Take a soothing bath. Check.

My Song's Curse

Add wine. Check plus.

Tell Alex it's over if he calls. Well, I thought I'd conquered that task, but he didn't catch my meaning. Did I say it wrong?

I leap from the bathtub, end call, and fling my phone onto the counter. My face is brownish-green. *Well, that won't do.* Swiping at it with a washcloth, I pull the plug on the tub, throw my robe on without drying off, and storm out the bathroom door.

How dare he show up after I—alright, I didn't tell him to leave me alone, I hung up on him. *I hung up on a god. Thrice.* Doesn't matter. Nothing will happen between us, and he needs to go.

Tearing down the stairs, I mumble a script of what I'll say. *I can't hang out with you because we always end up kissing.* Then our lips would meet, and then other parts... Ugh. *I can't tell you anything personal, but I want you to share every detail of yourself.* That will go over well. *Hey, do you think one night in each other's arms is worth painful, definitive, immortal death?* Actually, that may be a good one to ask.

I struggle with the front door before realizing it's locked. Flipping the latch, I fling it open.

Alex stands on my sidewalk, arms crossed over a shirt that strains against his taut muscles. He drops them to his sides and his gold eyes trail from my bare feet to the damp bun on my head. The beauty of him makes my breath catch and fizzle in my lungs.

No! Save yourself. Save your sisters.

I cross my arms. "You're here."

He approaches with a forceful, sexy stroll. "I am."

"Please leave." My voice deepens as it does with an influx of stress and adrenaline.

His gaze still wanders, but it's clinical, touching my body without heat. "Are you okay?"

"Why wouldn't I be okay? I'm fine."

"Lula, I—" His firm jaw hardens further, and he stabs his hair with his fingers. Why is he so stressed? He's probably never had a woman hang up on him. "Are you alone?"

My stomach balls. Of course, I'm alone. I'm always alone. *Lie. Do it. Tell him you don't want him because someone else is here and we're doing... things.* The words are on the tip of my tongue, but they hold fast when my lips part to spit them out.

His eyes narrow, and he charges past me into the house.

"What in the hell are you doing?" I follow.

He turns and walks backward, eyes trailing me again. He shoves his brows together, making two wrinkles between them. He spins, stomping away from me. Power rolls off him in waves as he tramps around my house. His shaven jaw grinds so tight, I'm concerned that he's cracking teeth. He stomps into my kitchen, hair flopping left and right as his head swivels; then he turns and storms toward the staircase.

"Stop! Dammit, Alex!" No reaction. It's like he doesn't even hear me.

I've spent most of my life wishing I couldn't control everyone. Now someone fits the bill, and I just want him to follow my orders. It's ironic in the most frustrating way imaginable.

He conquers the stairs two at a time, and I scramble to keep up. "What are you doing? Maybe you don't know human courtesy, but you can't barge into someone's house."

Glancing into my study, he pauses, then moves to the bedroom, fingers gripping the doorframe. My bunched duvet is messy, and the strap of a black bra hangs out of my chest of drawers.

I duck under his arm and punch his chest, though I may as well punch marble. "What in the hell are you doing?"

He stares through my open bathroom door. There's a splash of red in the wineglass perched on the tub's edge, the base surrounded by bubbles. Powerful French verse still radiates through the tense air.

Alex's glare melts away. "I thought—you're alone."

"Yes. Would you like to check the closet?" He glances in that direction as if he's actually considering. "Don't you dare. Look, I'm alone. Well, I was. Now leave!"

He tries to reach out to me, but I back away. I want to lay a thousand kisses on his face without being reminded of his warm skin and electrifying touch. His palms turn up in offering to me. "What happened?"

"You stormed into my house like a jealous boyfriend."

"No, not that. You hung up on me. Wouldn't tell me what happened." He dares to look put out, as he stands in my bedroom, uninvited. "Why?"

I press my fingertips to my temples to massage out the ache of irritation. I can't even tell him why. It bugs the hell out of me. If I tell him we can't hang out because he can't know anything about me, the first thing he'll want is more, personal information. That's what I'd do. I'd ask, "why not," and poke and pry until he revealed whatever he was keeping a secret.

"Go!" I point toward the stairs.

He glances around my room, pausing at the framed 1920s Vogue magazine covers and the pink floral curtains taken from the 1940s governor's house. My bedroom is an eclectic mix of the decades, and if I wasn't so angry, I'd ask Alex what he thought.

"Come downstairs," he says, now calm but firm. "We need to talk."

I open my mouth to explain that the only talk we will be having is *none*, but he's already gone.

I tail him. "We don't need to talk. You need to go. You can't be here." Why is this so hard? When I tell someone I'm done with a relationship, they leave. Easy.

He walks into my kitchen and faces me so suddenly, I nearly slam into him. "Explain what I did. Why the sudden change?"

I swallow the lump in my throat and glare. "We can't be together. You're putting me and my species in danger. I don't trust you." I want to, though. Every thought could be his, every touch, all of me, but it's impossible.

The situation is hopeless, but he's in front of me, golden gaze assessing me for answers I don't have. Unable to keep the pressure inside, I shove him. He moves maybe an inch, but his eyes widen, and I believe he finally understands I mean business. I take a deep breath, ball my fists tight, and put every ounce of strength into my voice, hoping some control will get through. "Leave. Now."

He doesn't budge. "Firecracker, what happened between the last time I was here and now? You were sad when I left, but *this*?" He signals to me in my robe. When I don't respond, he takes a few steps backward to lean against the kitchen island. He glances at the sink area. When he runs his hand across the surface of the counter as if reliving our intimacy from a week ago, his phantom touch slides over me. "What happened in this room—"

"Will never happen again." The tingle of tears is an uncommon annoyance.

He's against me in a blink, one hand splayed across my spine, the other on the back of my head. Inches from me, my favorite scent overwhelms my senses. "Tell me what happened." His warm breath crosses my lips, making me quake.

My bottom lip trembles and I bite it to keep it still. The fears about my missing sisters itch to escape, the wendigo encounter longs to be shared to ease my mind, but Amah's right. We don't trust those we cannot control, and this god has proven my thrall does squat. I ball my fists against his chest, though I'd rather clutch his shirt and drag him closer. "Leave." Shit, I didn't even convince myself with that whine. "Please."

His warmth parts from me, leaving me a confused blend of sad-relieved.

His fingers twitch at his sides, and gold eyes pierce into me to give him something, anything to work with. *I can't.*

"Fine," he says. "But we're going to speak about this soon. I'm here if you need me. I mean it, Lu. Anything at all."

A landslide of thoughts careens toward my mouth but then bottlenecks, stuck in silence. He should know my regrets, and that I can't speak to him ever again. Someone like him deserves everything he wants but I'm not the person able to give it to him, but then, he's out of the house, leaving my front door open. He walks from the porch and glances back over his shoulder, wearing a somber expression that makes my heart skip. I want nothing more than to run into his arms, but my intelligent feet stay frozen to the hardwood.

"Soon," he says as he raises a hand and slices downward. Like sharp scissors through fabric, the air parts and warm-hued light peeks through the chasm.

I tilt my head. *No way.* The line shimmers, a clear break in reality. Alex slowly steps through the rip.

Did he just open a portal?

The descriptions in books don't touch on how portals are created. They just existed and now they don't. Amah used them a few times, though she wouldn't say why. My guess is she was seeking the original three because if I'm correct, I'm looking at an actual shroud between realms, Earth locations, otherworldling realms, and maybe even Olympus.

According to Amah, they became less frequent, then disappeared when I was a baby. We didn't understand how they worked, but otherworldlings could travel between Earth and their home realms until one day they couldn't.

While I watch, staring at him like he made gravity in front of me, which isn't all that unrealistic, he edges further into the chasm. He's leaving. He listened. This is good. Exactly what should happen.

Facing me through the veil, he gives me one more glance, then runs his hand from the top of the rip down, sealing it like he has all the time in the world.

Where is he now? Olympus? Some other world? *Quit it, Lula, and stay inside.*

How does he do it? Is this an attribute? Can all the gods— I have to stop. It doesn't matter. What matters is he's going away, and I'm not in danger. This is for the best.

Holy hell, Alex is a portal keeper.

With inches left in the rip, I step onto my porch. "Alex?"

Chapter Thirteen

ALEX

Lula's sweet voice stays my hand at the last inches of the portal opening, and I release the breath I was holding tight in my lungs. This was risky. Comus is going to yell. The last thing I should do is show off my greatest attribute to an otherworldling that's pissed at me.

I'm one of three beings in the universe who can open portals: my brother, my father, and me. Two of us have to work together to open world portals like the elven, demon, and archaic hell realm, but individually we have free range in Olympus and on Earth as long as we've been to the location before or our attribute calls us somewhere. I'm infinitely more traveled than my family members. Hercules knows Greece and Europe. Anice the same unless his attribute pulls him elsewhere as it did the other day.

Older otherworldlings remember the portals, and if rumors start that there's an open one, every species will flood here in a tsunami of hopeful creatures, wanting to return to their homeland. The gods would hear of a modern migration, and I'd be the only suspect.

Yep, showing off was a gamble, but Lula is worth the risk.

I bite back a smile and reopen the closure. Bright green eyes are wide and sideways because her head's tilted. I step through the veil and close it behind me. "Yes, Lula?"

She blinks, and I cross the distance, fixated on her perfect lips. She's not injured, and she's angry, not sad. I can work with this. I reach her, grab her face in both hands and dip, but before I connect, her fingers lock around my wrists and she gives the littlest whimpering, "Please don't."

Why won't she talk to me? What in the hell happened? Concern rolls through me like a raging beast. I touch my forehead to hers. "Lula, tell me what happened."

She bites her lip, blinking back tears. "Alex. I'm so sca—" Her lips clamp together hard, and I pull away to get a better look at her expression. She gulps. "Sorry. I'm so sorry."

"That's not what you were going to say. You were going to say scared." Rage grows as too many scenarios reel through my mind as to why she'd be scared. Did another deity find her? That shouldn't be possible unless Zeus somehow got Pythia to pinpoint those I've been in contact with. That doesn't make sense, though. Pythia is powerful, but she's not that powerful.

"Is someone threatening you?" I ask. "Who?"

She slaps my chest. "Alex." Shoving herself away from me, she crosses her arms. "I'm fine, I'm..." She growls—an actual rumbling, teeth-clenched growl that makes me want to nibble her. She stares at me for a long moment, worrying her lip, then takes a deep breath. "Rules. Are you ready?"

There are rules? "Okay?"

"Don't kiss me, and don't ask me personal questions."

"Why not?"

She rubs her forehead, glancing toward her neighbor's house through the wide tree trunks. The porch light twinkles through leaves, but otherwise, the cottage is dark. She scans the yard and the empty road. Anywhere but on me. Has she seen something out of place? Is someone following her, besides me and sometimes Rath?

"Because I won't answer them."

Not what I meant. She will tell me everything. "I was talking about the kissing."

An exasperated sound falls from her lips as she turns and storms inside. "Get in here before we cause a scene."

Biting back a smile, I follow. Crisis averted. Lula walks around the kitchen island before facing me with her hands on her hips. "You opened a portal."

"I did."

"You're a—"

"A portal keeper. Yes, I am." Placing my elbows on the counter surface across from Lula, I prop my chin in my hand. I cannot stop myself from eyeing her curves wrapped in a fluffy white robe plucked out of a high-end spa. Maybe it was. My gaze returns to her face to find pink-tinted cheeks. "If you don't want me leaping this blockade and discarding that tiny piece of fabric for you, I'd suggest you change." Her lips part in a sharp inhale, so I continue, curious about her reaction. "I've wanted to explore your blush since the night we met."

Lula rushes toward the stairs, fists clenched and mumbling curses.

"A turtleneck sweater may do the trick," I call after her. A nun's habit if you own one?"

"Asshole," she whispers under her breath.

My jaw drops. "I heard that, Firecracker."

A muffled growl accompanies stomping. *Sassy little minx.*

I snort and drop into a kitchen chair, the Queen Anne with arms and a floral striped cushion. The jarred candle from the farmers' market sits in the center of the oak table, and I spin it with one hand. Lula has burnt it at least once since then, maybe more.

It's time for a game plan. She's pissed, frightened even, but she let me in. I bet she has so many questions. I do too, but I'll be cautious in my approach because I need to understand what the hell happened after I nearly dry-humped her on her counter. A surge of lust flows through me at the thought, but now's not the time. My need to reestablish our connection goes deeper than needing her for our plans, and I try to shove that thought down a bit. She needs me to be professional, though at this stage, new in our budding relationship, the best way to reconnect is with our bodies, melting together and pushing against that stringent line the Council set. But no kissing... apparently.

She'd knee me if I tried anything other than banter anyway. She shoved me. Well, if you could call that breezy push a shove. Sirens do not have super strength. Test complete.

Soft footsteps bring my attention to the perfect specimen sashaying through the kitchen. Lula's in shorts again, and a tank top underneath a flowy, diaphanous shirt. I bite my lip to keep from telling her I want to bend her over the table, yank her scrap of denim off—

"It's summer. Control yourself." Lula glares before I further contemplate what we can't do. "You really did open a portal?" I nod at her question, and she continues. "Can all of you, the gods, do that?"

"No. Very few of us and we're all related." There's so much I need to share. Not everything though. Not yet. However, the more information I give, the more she will speak. "What do you know about the portals and our realm?"

With mousy caution, she gravitates to the table, dropping into the seat across from me. "Portals are a travel point between realms like here and Olympus. They can lead to other planets?" She squints her eyes but continues when I smile. "Some places are similar to Earth but hold different species—otherworldlings. Some are like the fairytale Hell. They contain a variety of evil creatures—darklings."

Leaning back, I cross my arms over my chest, and her attention drops to my biceps and pecs. I ignore the stare she's giving me because this conversation is important. "Close. Our universe holds a series of realms. They shadow around Earth, tightly fitting in bubbles that overlap other realms, so sometimes the species there share traits like magic, or mating habits with the worlds beside them, even if they're unaware of each other's existence."

"Wow." She leans as though this is the best story she's ever heard. "Around Earth? Like we're the center?"

Head of the class. "Yes. It's the main hub if you will." Eventually, I'll explain that Zeus made us close the portals with no warnings to the other gods or the otherworldlings and they became trapped on Earth. Then Olympus used to be Greece until he broke the connection between us and cause the separation. That will open too many other questions that will lead to the role we'd like her to take. "The realms evolve at different rates, house different gods, but we're all connected, even with the realm portals closed. The hell realm lives in the only untouched band on the outskirts and because of the distance, and the disconnection, it is unevolved, godless, and houses primal species."

"Darklings. They're godless?"

This is good. We need to be talking about the darklings and Lula's role. If she can direct them, she can bring them here, control them, and force the gods to come to Earth to prevent the destruction of the human race. Chaos yes, but with Lula, controlled. The Council needs to see how independent the mortals are, and how they work with the otherworldlings. They need to see that the beings in need of the old gods' heavy-handed rule are the darklings.

All in time. I'll ease Lula into this, just as we're doing with the humans.

"Yes," I say. "The hell realm and its inhabitants live in a state of chaos, destined to evolve with no direction. They could use a divine system, like Earth has, to nourish their mottled minds. Other realms, even if they lack strong divine influence, will progress, but if it involves deities, evolution occurs at an expedited rate, and can take beautiful creative turns."

"Like with the humans." She smiles when I nod. That's a big thing that Lu and I have in common—we respect mortals. Her knee bounces the table, and she leans forward. "Are there deities in other realms?"

"There are. Advanced, peaceful places have a group of gods' influences to push them along." I've met some, and I'd like to see them again one day.

"How does that work? Influencing?"

I stand and stretch. I need a second to gather my thoughts. "Can I have water?"

Lula hops up but I wave her away and open the glass-paned cabinet full of glassware. She has enough cups for a party of twenty. They're heavy and don't look used. It makes me frown. How many people have been here beside me? Her refrigerator is like the one in Belize, ice and water stationed in the front panel.

"When a deity reaches the human equivalent of mid-twenties, an oracle reads them for the powers they possess," I say, walking back to the table while draining half the glass. "If the Council deems them worthy, they're allowed to accept and become a full god or goddess."

"They can do that? Not let someone..." She worries her lip as she searches for the word.

"It's called reaching zenith. And, no, not really. A god can accept their attributes at maturity whether or not someone gives them permission if they can figure it out. It's easier with a guide. Claiming they can prevent a divine being from accepting their attributes is a power play the Council uses against young deities. Oracles and archivists train those approaching zenith on how to accept and use their new attributes and after that, influence the world by injecting their will to the inhabitants of the realm. Some attributes are even pinpointing in nature—able to affect an individual instead of an entire population. Some are more personal abilities, though each is unique and affect the realm in some way."

"Like when you open portals?"

"Yeah."

She tilts her head again. "Did you shut the portals down?" *Curious kitten.*

"Yes, but—" I mill over her words, weighing how much I'm ready for her to hear. I didn't think things through back then, just followed. Now, otherworldlings are shut out of their original realms, away from their families and friends for two-thousand-years. I'll have to fight to keep the shame from entering my tone.

She flinches before I continue. "Alex, why are you telling me any of this?"

"Because I trust you and want you to trust me too." I keep my voice strong and shift forward to display an open palm in front of her. "Trust me, Lula."

Swallowing hard, she lifts a hand from her lap, brushing her fingertips against mine in a sweet kiss as they slide into my palm. I enclose my fingers around hers in a light, hopefully comforting squeeze. She gives the slightest tug, but I'm not relinquishing the physical connection between us.

I follow each of her knuckles with the pad of my thumb. "My brother and I were ordered to shut them down to…" I tilt my head back and forth. "Protect the species of Earth and Olympians. Some otherworldlings and darklings became stuck. Have you ever encountered one?"

She clears her throat and studies her lap. "Would they harm you for sharing this information with me?"

"You're well versed on the gods. With everything you know, you tell me."

"Yes."

The word is too trembly for my liking and my heart rate increases at her distress. The optimist in me hopes this is an insight into her affection for me, that she wouldn't want to see me punished. Realistically, she's been through too much. She's stressed, and something caused her fragile state of mind—something I will discover.

"Are you listening?" I ask.

Her head pops up to meet my gaze, and I squeeze her hand. "I trust you not to discuss our conversation with others. Just as I'd never share what you tell me with anyone that would harm you." I move our discussion forward before she overthinks. "Have you ever encountered a darkling?"

She purses her lips and as the temptation to lean in and nip that pout grows out of control, she nods and her fingers tremble. Maybe it was the wendigo that frightened her. I trace a light circle on the back of her hand. Her tight fingers relax.

"Were you able to control them?" I ask.

She bites her lip, her attention falling to her lap. My thumb stops its rotation. She pulls from my grip, and I fear I've lost her, but she walks to the fridge and retrieves two microbrews. Her home is silent, making the pop of the caps loud. Her bare feet steer her back to the table. Holding out a beer to me, she takes a swig of the other. "What do you want for dinner?"

Fake bravado is an acceptable response for now. "You."

How Will Lula React? It's my new favorite game.

She scowls. Called that one. I shouldn't provoke my sweet little beast, but the need to get her riled up is strong. How many secrets would she yell at me if she wasn't calm and collected?

My fingers itch to grab her hips and tug her to my lap. My arms flex to wrap around her, tease out her words with light kisses to the back of her neck, but she's not ready. I need to ease her mind.

Pivoting, she stomps to the fridge and pulls colorful items from the depths. As I approach, her green eyes glance at me from the side, but she won't look at me. She places a cutting board on the counter and vigorously chops carrots. I'll make this right for her, on the timeline

I've got in place, though I've jumped the gun by several months when I made contact.

Back to it though; get to know her and her powers, stoke a fire of rage about Olympus, introduce the plan, let her insert herself into the plan, and carry it out. *We've got this.*

I lean against the island. "Are you ready to tell me what happened after I left?"

She surprises me by slamming the knife on the wooden surface sending a few carrot slices rolling. "Personal question, Alex."

"Fine. What did I do?" I waggle a finger to shush whatever sassy response is about to cross her pretty lips. "Not personal. It's about me, not you."

The anger radiating off her rushes away in a wave and she studies the countertop. "It's not you. Well, it is, but it's not your fault."

"Tell me."

She glimpses at me, fists tight against the countertop, and blows out a lengthy breath. "Alex, I don't trust myself around you. You're a danger to me."

I consider her words. She's not incorrect. "Lula, I'm not willing to give the Council the power to keep me from talking to people."

Heat dashes through my veins as I step closer to her, placing a hand on her hip, and tug her toward me. Danger here but shouldn't be. Why have we let them rule this long? Lula doesn't fight but doesn't melt against me as she did before. I angle her head with fingers on her chin, and get so close to her lips, it pains me not to move the final few inches to connect, but that's not my purpose.

"They don't understand captivating, entrancing emotions," I say. Her berry scent is heady, and energy rotates between us, growing stronger with the seconds of closeness. "Are you able to ignore this connection?"

She blinks, brow furrowed. "No."

I move forward the slightest bit until the warmth of her breath brushes a sweet breeze across my lips. I wait, staring into her bright, green gaze, frustration mounting. "The deities that created such a restrictive law will never experience this."

I'm confident she'll push up on her tiptoes and kiss me, breaking her own rule, and just when another second of torture would madden me, Lula drops her head and rests her forehead against me, palms on my chest. "They may not comprehend, but it won't stop them from harming anyone defying their law. Are the legends true—the murder and punishment?"

Her words are heavy in my chest. The lava in my veins from her closeness cools with her question. "Yeah, but that was long ago."

She steps away. "I'm right."

"For now."

"Meaning I'm right. Is there some easy fix to ancient, divine law?" I move forward, wanting her body where it belongs—against mine—but she takes another step back, and thrusts her palm between us. "Are you trying to get me killed?"

I grin. "Kissing me won't get you killed."

I could tell her. Lay it all out like ripping off a bandage. We'd either heal or gush, go septic, and die. I can't risk it and I'm not ready. I don't know her well enough yet. While I love her reactions, the one where she throws me out and bans me from her house isn't what I want to see.

"Then what will, Alex? Touching?" Her eyebrows lift. "Oral?"

"No, Lu." I move closer, breath quickening in response to the crystal-clear visuals, and her increasing passions. Yeah, she's angry. I am too. We can use this to fuel our cause.

She glares up at me. "If I went down on you, tasted you, what curse would I earn? Maybe instead of getting dropped out of Olympus this time, I'd get my species thrown into a hell realm. I could visit the berserkers. Haven't done that since I was in my twenties."

My sex-focused brain swerves at her words. Yeah, getting her riled is the path to information. "You've met berserkers? Could you control them?"

Pain radiates from her and her voice wavers. "Didn't have the chance to find out. Had to sing before it killed me, too." She twists away from me and moves to cut vegetables again.

Shit. Too far. Still, this is progress. I should have been gentler though. I wrap my arms around Lula's waist, burying my face in her hair. "Sorry. Tell me about it." She shakes her head. This is a sensitive subject to press. "What do you want me to do besides leave you alone? I'm not sure that is within reason."

She stops cutting. "When you were here last time, we got... carried away. We were interrupted. Would you have stopped without receiving the phone call? Where is the line, Alex?" My silence is all she needs. Not much would have pulled me from her, and I would have taken it farther. "So, don't kiss me. Please."

My arms drop away, and I recline against the counter behind her, gripping the edge, to keep from touching her as I let her words sink in.

Lula goes back to slicing carrots.

She's right. Impatience is for the young, but I'm over three thousand years old. The next decade will be as short as minutes in the long run. Once we get a handle on our plan and Olympus changes for the better, I'll explore this thing with Lula, thoroughly and with leisure.

"Alright," I say. "You're correct. We will be friends."

Lula peeks over her shoulder, confusion in her eyes. "Really?"

"Yeah. Let's talk like friends. What do you want to know?"

Her eyebrows skyrocket and she turns, crossing her arms. "Oh Alex, don't tempt me. I will take advantage."

"Ask away. But first..." I point to the purple sculpture of what resembles a lopsided chicken. "You have to tell me about that monstrosity."

The smile on her face could light up the darkest hell realm. It warms me from the inside out. She could ask me for anything. *It's hers.*

THE MORNING LIGHT MOVES UP THE BED AND TOUCHES LULA'S BARE arm. Without thought, I trace the line between shadow and light lying across her shoulder and back. Though it pains me, I retract my fingers. This moment's too beautiful for me to interrupt. Her little home is tranquil. Motes float through the stream of sunshine, diffusing the glow into a surreal scene that comforts and terrifies me in equal measure. I want this too much.

Why don't I have the attribute of freezing time and stopping the inevitable conversation that will yank me from this heaven? I shut the Olympus phone off last night after receiving several calls and messages from my father. My grandfather's in a rage and demanding my return.

Good.

All of Olympus will hear of his tantrum and my obstinance. I only hope the conversation between Naea and me spreads enough to build sympathy from most Olympians. Zeus wants me to finish what he attempted to start, but it's not going to happen. We are not breeders forced to couple at a madman's whim. Naea will be fertile for another day or so, then I'll return to face the music.

I'm glad my brother is with me on this matter and tucked away in Belize, becoming familiar with the new human. Another point for Olympians to ponder. Comus tells me that my twin has taken over my room and indulged in an hour-long shower, emerging twice, buck naked to talk about the showerhead, glass door, and plumbing. We may have to drag him back to Olympus for once.

I've missed Anice and part of me has settled in warm comfort with him on our side. We have work to do but if he realizes the corrupted, archaic practices our grandfather and the Council perform need to change, others will follow. We're that much closer. I can't tell him everything yet, but I'm glad I introduced the idea of Lula.

Last night over dinner, wine, and a conversation spanning into the morning hours, I learned a lot about her, even with her graceful avoidance of siren-talk. She ducked and weaved, cleverly dodging my pointed questions by offering fewer personal details or general information on otherworldlings instead.

When I asked about her mother and father, she withdrew like a mouse racing to a hidey-hole at the sight of an owl. I caught her in the kitchen and dragged her into my arms, promising not to ask her again—though I hope she'll eventually tell me—then moved along to easy topics: art, music, television.

I shift, careful not to jounce the bed, and inhale her shoulder before writing invisible letters across the softness. *B* then *E*, *A*, and *U*. *T* and *Y*. I continue, penning truths and hopes, a perfect canvas highlighted by the rising sun. Chill bumps rise on the soft skin my finger touches, and I smile, leaning to place a kiss on her spine before she becomes coherent enough to realize how much she let me in. I'm not sure which version of Lula I'll meet when she awakens.

I'll behave and play by her rules for now. Get so entangled in her world she won't be willing to push me away again. Friends until we make this realm right. Then constraints won't bind us to separate worlds.

We will be free.

All of us.

Chapter Fourteen

LULA

A sensation on my arm coaxes me from the sleepy depths consuming me. Alex's scent lingers in my mind—a warm dream draped in sweet citrus. It's as if he's beside me, a godly cocoon of comfort that escorts me deeper into slumber. Something touches the center of my back, followed by a heated exhale.

I open my eyes, then squint at the brightness. Consciousness attempts to elude me, and I grasp at the thought. The warmth leaves my skin, and I freeze as if I'm not lying here dead-still.

The sensation starts again on my arm. I vault off the bed and flip around, my back smashing into the wall. Alex stares back at me. Dropping my eyes from his, I take in the shorts and tank top I wore last night—not naked. I'd have remembered that, though I don't recall falling asleep. Alex came here, opened a portal, we talked, there was wine, then...

Alex tilts his head, sending a golden wave of hair over his eyebrow. "Good morning?"

I want to throw something at his perfect, amused face. He's wearing the same shirt, but his jeans are draped over the armchair. He must have brought me up to bed. "You're still here," I say, voice sleep rough.

He props up on a pillow and lays an open palm on my bed, beckoning me with his forefinger. "I am. Is that okay?"

"What? Yes? No, I…" I clench my fist to keep from fanning my hot cheeks. "We didn't—you didn't?"

The haze of morning scatters my thoughts to the wind, but Alex chuckles in response. "Nope. We were as chaste as two school kids. Now, get back here."

Two school kids who want to bang under the bleachers, but instead of getting detention, we'd get the guillotine. "Bed? Not with you and your…" I flip my hand at him. "You."

Alex slides from sheets with a graceful quickness more suitable to a vampire. He scoops me up and plops back to the sheets, pulling me to him despite my uncoordinated struggling. "Settle down, Firecracker. It's early. Cuddle with me."

He squishes me to his hard chest before a protest forms, and warm comfort lulls my body to stop fighting. I whisper, "Do friends cuddle?"

"Yes. Definitely."

His fingers brush through my hair, and I close my eyes, settling into him, tracing the bulge of his bicep with my fingertips. "In bed?"

"Absolutely," he says with no hesitation.

I grin and bite my lip. "I don't remember falling asleep."

"Yeah, because we were talking, and you just conked out."

"Oh yeah? What were we talking about?"

Alex's chest shakes, jostling me. "I asked you to tell me a secret. Instead, you fell asleep. It was a ruse. You faked it, didn't you?"

"I never fake it." The words come out in a near purr and I grimace, lifting my head to peek at him. My face heats. "I mean. Um." That slipped out. I shouldn't be this comfortable, and he shouldn't be here. I can't ask him to go though. My mornings have never been like this. They're silent and lacking life except for singing birds or an occasional bug launching a war against the window. There's no conversation, no banter or flirting. No warm, hard-bodied deity that inserted himself into my empty routine.

With raised eyebrows, he waits for me to spit out my words.

I bury my face against his massive chest. "Shut up, Alex."

He shifts, slipping his arm around my waist and pinches my ass.

"Hey!"

I reach for a pillow, but he flips me under him and pins my hands. "No weapons!"

"Weapons?" I kick him with an unpinned leg. "A pillow is hardly a weapon!" I could nip him. His neck is there and smelling like it would be the best taste first thing in the morning.

"In your hands, it would be." He gathers my wrists in one hand and grabs above my thrashing knee, stilling my leg against his hip.

We've positioned ourselves for a superb time, and my eyes widen. Alex glances at my lips, gathers his lower lip between his teeth, stays long enough for me to understand what I'm missing, and rolls off me. I lie there, stunned.

I want his weight on me, connected with an intensity I'm positive I've never and would never experience again, even if I lived a millennium.

"Breakfast?" I ask. Food is a good distraction, and we can talk some more. He's given me a taste of Olympian lore and now I need to feast.

His fingers skim my belly, and I close my eyes at the inviting sensation. A big hand spreads over my hip and tugs, dragging me closer to the danger zone. Alex nuzzles his mouth and nose against my bare shoulder. "Five more minutes."

The warmth of his skin tempts me, draws me close. I'm not sure Alex understands the extent of my frostbite, or how I want to melt into his heat, how hard he is to resist.

A final exhale and then, I stop fighting.

"You ate all the melon." I fake-glare at Alex over the refrigerator door.

"Because it was delicious," he says with a heart-stopping smile.

"Why in the hell haven't I kicked you out yet?" *Please don't leave.*

He tilts his head. "Why *haven't* you kicked me out yet?"

I snatch an orange from the crisper drawer and throw it at him. He plucks it out of the air with the skill of a professional baseball player. I go back to rummaging through the fridge to hide my grin. "Because you amuse me."

Alex leaps to sit on the kitchen island and starts peeling the orange. "Mmhmm because I amuse you. Fine. I'll take it. You never answered my question."

I pull out an orange as well and hold it over the trash can, glancing between Alex and his pile of rinds. "Oh yeah? Which one?"

He grabs the pile of peelings on the counter next to him, stretching to drop them into the open garbage bin while raising one eyebrow at me. The back of his hand slides over my arm as he retreats, leaving me shivering. "Tell me a secret."

My grin slips into a frown. Remaining silent, he tosses an orange segment in his mouth and stares at me.

What to say? So many secrets. I could sneak my way out of it by telling him about the art I have in the house or that I tried to attend college once and didn't tell my sisters. He'd expect something like that though. Good things. Easy things. What I've done while trying to find my way through this life isn't all honorable and maybe—as Alex stares at me as if I'm this fascinating gift—maybe, he should know more. Not too much, but something real.

My mouth goes dry and I rub my throat. "I used my ability on a bully."

His grin is impish. "They deserved it, didn't they?"

"It wasn't right," I say, reaching to rub my forehead before remembering my sticky fingers and using the back of my hand. "He was sixteen, maybe. I should have been an adult about it."

"What was he doing?"

"Beating a kid half his size. Then he messed with the kid's sister."

I trail off, not wanting to recount the details. Regret is consuming and I'm immortal. I'll never forget how I stooped to the level of a bully and became the bad guy. I nibble on an orange slice in the silence. When I peek up, he's staring at me with narrow eyes. My face heats. "What?"

"What else happened?"

Damn his observant ass.

"He dragged the girl away from the crowd, held a pocketknife at her throat. He said he was going to give her a taste of a real man. She was screaming, and not one kid moved to help."

"He sounds like a psychopath. What did you do?"

"Hm." I eat another slice in silence, not even tasting it.

Alex reaches to trace a line from my forehead to the tip of my nose. "It's okay. Tell me."

"I'm ashamed."

"I could never think badly of you. Not ever." He strokes my cheek with a thumb.

An opportunity to share hard topics isn't something that happens every day. Not like I have to be perfect in front of him, anyway. "I sent the other kids away, then commanded him to cut his testicles off." Alex fumbles his orange, and I focus on my fidgeting fingers. "When he was, um... freed of one, I realized how cruel it was. I stopped him and told him to remember what he did to deserve the punishment. I left a boy mutilated and screaming for help." My voice wavers. I lied to myself. Even if it doesn't matter, I never want to see disgust or disappointment in his eyes. "What do you think of me now?"

He detaches an orange segment. "You'd fit right in with the gods."

"What? You're not serious."

"Oh, I am. There's truth in the lore, Lula. I've seen worse but doling out that punishment took balls. Well, one ball."

I groan, "Alex," and fling fruit at him, which he catches and eats with a smile.

We're silent for a long moment, letting the words settle. Alex speaks first. "I once replaced the educational books in the virginal learning chamber with satirical sexual fiction and historical accounts of the first communions."

"I don't understand what that means, but it sounds titillating."

Alex's expression is an odd mix of relief and anguish. His shoulders sink and his face relaxes except for the wrinkle of worry between his brows.

"Olympus houses young goddesses in a building called the virginal chamber when they come of age," he says. "They're separated from the rest of the population to keep them chaste. Gods then choose to commune with them—" His nose wrinkles in a sneer.

"Commune?" I ask.

"Sex. They take the young goddesses virginity, sometimes bidding against each other, or trading items for the opportunity." His fingers clench the marble counter. *Oh whoa.* "Afterwards, the goddess is free to choose—though she's more likely to be chosen—as a lover or spouse. She can join the various divine guilds or become a servant. The goddesses with the most affluent potential are educated more liberally and have more choice in their lovers and lifestyle."

This is so much information. Terrible information. "I assume the gods don't have to go through what the goddesses do?"

"Not even close. Still, we're bound to rules, but the goddesses…being unlocked is just the beginning."

"Unlocked?" I massage my temples. "That is so screwed up."

"Oh, it's royally fucked. They're fed this tradition like it's a beautiful rite of passage. Some are so misled, when the actual event happens, they become inconsolable because it didn't live up to their expectation. If the wrong god chooses them, the results can be devastating."

"Really?" I've studied the divine, but this is all new. Getting it from the source is captivating.

Alex's irritated expression further piques my curiosity. "There have been a few dramatic shows of discontent. After a bad communion with a complete asshole, one demi-goddess threw herself off a cliff."

"Oh, that's awful."

"Absolutely. She didn't die, but her injuries were enough to gain the Council's attention. Still didn't change anything. Made it worse for a while."

"How?"

"The Council frowned upon her 'show of defiance'. They reward subservience. She disappeared. Rumor has it they cursed her though she's probably dead. They destroyed the record of her unlocking, and the god—a Council member—didn't even get a wrist slap that I'm aware of."

I press my lips together so tightly, my jaw hurts. "You're right. That's terrible. Have you ever…" I trail off because it's none of my business. My comfort around him makes me forget he's a deity.

"I used to." Alex stares at the counter, lips pursed. "Not often and only if they showed interest."

I focus my attention on the drawer in the kitchen island to hold back my curious questions, making sure measuring cups and spoons are stacked and not creeping into the serving spoons, not that I use serving spoons. I want to know everything about this divine being, but it's not my business.

"Ask me," he says. "Whatever you're thinking, ask me."

"I don't want to offend you."

His laugh is a tight huff. He sits straight, rapping a beat on the marble. "Not possible, Firecracker."

Oh, I'm sure if I tried… "You are a deity, Alex. That alone demands respect. I shouldn't ask you personal questions."

It's the first time he's directed a scowl at me. "We'll address that later. Ask your question."

"Give me a warning if you're going to curse me or something, okay?"

He reaches over to tweak my nose with orange-scented fingers.

"Why'd you stop?"

He raises his eyebrows, "I didn't expect you to ask that."

"You don't have to—"

Waving me off, he slides from the island. "We had some adjustments in Olympus for a while, and there was a time that the virginal chambers were closed and goddesses had to wait for their communion. It gave me time to think. The goddesses too. They decided that they would like to forgo their communion and start their lives. The Council put them back in the virginal chambers and the same god that unlocked the cliff-jumping demi-goddess had Comus's sister in his sights. Deimos is a psycho. He and Comus had a legendary rivalry going on, and Deimos told Comus that he'd unlock Dalia and wreck her for anyone else. Comus has a lot of half brothers and sisters, but Dalia is the youngest. They were close, had a good relationship. They're related by their father, Dionysus. Dalia's mother is Lyssa, the spirit of madness, but Dalia grew to be sweet and meek, even after being shunned for who her mother is. The Oracles couldn't get a solid read on her potential attributes, so she had zero say in her upbringing and unlocking. Comus always protected her as much as possible, and when the new date of her communion approached, he broke and begged me to protect her in the only way we could."

It dawns on me. "You communed with her?"

His pained expression makes me take his hand from across the counter. He stares at our entwined fingers. "I did. We tried to find another, but no one else would consider crossing Deimos or consorting with a shunned goddess. The keeper of the virginal chamber knew I'd take care of her and arranged it before there was a chance for him to cause a problem."

I squeeze his hand. "Did she get in trouble for that?" If they treat goddesses like that, and Deimos was a major, she was taking a serious risk. They both were.

"There was a kickback, yes. It mainly fell on me, because as little rights as goddesses have, the chamber maiden has rule within those walls, leaving the goddesses under her care untouchable. The whole situation was so screwed up. Dalia knew me as Comus's best friend. I cared for her like a brother, so it was...awkward. Comus blames himself." He squeezes my hand. "I tried to help but made a terrible situation worse. I alienated Dalia, who has yet to accept her unknown attributes. On a larger scale, I ended up supporting a sick system I'd hoped had died off."

I brush his hair back from his eyebrow. "You helped her."

"She won't speak to me or Comus."

Regret etches his features, and I wish I could ease his pain. "Even if she doesn't talk about it, she appreciates what you did."

"What if I screwed her up more than Deimos would have done?"

"Alex," I say, low and with warning. "One goddess Deimos *unlocked* threw herself off a cliff. Can't get much worse than that. Besides, you're sweet. You took care of her."

He tightens the hold on my hand and with the other, traces an unknown pattern on the sensitive inside of my wrist and forearm. "Oh yeah? How do you know?"

"I believe it's who you are. You're a good man. <u>D</u>eity, I mean."

"You don't consider me evil for taking part in such a tradition?"

"It's a tradition you were raised with. You were trying to help."

Eyebrows raise in question. "You're not jealous?"

Oh, I'm jealous. It's a good thing I'll never meet Dalia, or the other women Alex has slept with because I don't want to hate them for experiencing what I never will. I lie, "Unlocking, are you kidding me? Nothing to be jealous of there. Besides, friends, right? You're not mine to lay claim to."

"What if I were?" Intense golden eyes wait for my stalled answer. "What if I were, Lula?"

Fighting back hope is difficult. How could he ask me such a thing when it's not feasible? "Don't toy with me, Alexiares. You belong with the divine. Not me."

He's silent for a long moment before saying, "I won't ask you about your past lovers because I just..." His jaw clenches, head shaking back and forth as if he's telling the thought to get lost.

"I'm no saint." Charged from his reaction, I need to get this out in the open, tense air. I pull my hand from his grasp. "There have been so many I've lost count. All humans, all consensual, however not as well. I stole their free will. My first time..."

He storms to me in a flash, cupping my head in one hand, the other pinning me against the counter. "I will kiss you quiet, Lula."

I challenge his glare with my own. "No, you won't."

He needs a reminder of what I am. This odd friendship is all we'll ever be. "I commanded every movement, every thought, and had to give step by step instructions because he kept asking. Each time has been that way. I've never been with someone who wanted me for me. Do you have any idea what it's like to always be unsure of someone's affection?"

Fingers clutch my hair, and his eyes are wild with emotion. His thumb spurs a sensation on my hip that is somehow both numbing and searing. "I'm starting to."

The silence is thick as if the world around us is holding its breath, but Alex remains still and staring.

"That's my life, what I am." I whisper, "I'm not one of you. Don't treat me like I am."

He releases my hair and strokes my cheeks with both thumbs.

"This is different. *You* are different."

"You're different for me, too." I push his chest. "Let's enjoy this...friendship while we can. Please."

Instead of letting go, he wraps powerful arms around me. "We are more than this."

"More than what?"

For the first time, his cheeks darken. He steps away from me, looking at the wall with a tense jaw. "You're right. Let's just enjoy this friendship."

"Okay." With a pivot, I shuffle toward the stairs. I never want him to leave, but he will. He must.

On autopilot, I grab clothes to sleep in and walk into the bathroom, turn on the shower. Undress and step inside. While I wash, I stare at the white curtain as if I can see beyond.

It hurts to be apart for mere minutes. What if I step out of the shower to an empty house, and return to my normal, silent routine? I'm not sure I could. A full day of him, and I only want more. Conversation has filled dulled hours and made time blink by. I've skirted talking about my mom and sisters. I promised Amah I wouldn't, but the words are there, and they want out. Alex is already woven too deep into my heart, and if I keep sharing, there will be nothing left of me when he's gone. When he leaves me, I can tell myself, 'at least I didn't tell him our siren secrets,' though I don't know all our secrets.

He fills my house as though he's always been here. When I do something mundane, like loading the dishwasher, he gives me these meaningful stares. I stare right back. He makes me want everything I cannot have. He's more dangerous to me than a damn incubus.

I should let him kiss me, be with me. Then the gods will put me out of my misery because with him following my every movement, touching me as if I were the one for him, and sharing so much, he makes me feel wanted and equal to him. It makes me hope, which then squashes me with crushing disappointment. I could handle this better if it were only an obsessive attraction, but it's not.

He's right, dammit. We are more.

I shut off the water, dry off in the silence, and dress. Follow my day's end routine and slide into bed. A minute later, footsteps sound. I close my eyes. After the best day, the bed dips, and a hand slides under my hip to rotate me.

Curling against a solid mass of warmth, I allow myself to pretend this could be my life and drift to the rhythm of Alex's steady heartbeat beating in time with mine.

Chapter Fifteen

ALEX

I SWEAR, THE KITCHEN ISLAND IS THE KEYSTONE TO THIS HOUSE. It's our meeting place, conversation, and flirting spot. It stands between us, a stoic referee that reminds us of the rules by its presence, keeping us safe and rational.

"Lu, it's lunchtime. We're hungry and out of food. Seriously, this is insane." I lean, elbows to the marble, fingers on my phone to call for delivery. "How can you love olives, but not want them on pizza? You make no sense."

Lula glares hard from across the kitchen island. "No. Olives."

"An everything pizza is not complete without olives." This ridiculous conversation shouldn't provoke rage, but my fists clench, and Lula burns a hole through me with her glare.

She stalks to the pantry, pivots, and a can of olives soars through the air at me. "There are your fucking olives. Happy now?"

The can slaps into my palm, but I keep my eyes on her. Sharp green eyes punch into mine like a physical assault. Her hair cascades in wild curves, the color matching the tint to her lips, firm and tempting.

I want to tackle her. Take her to the ground. Bite those lips until they're red and swollen. Kiss her with the pent-up passion these last two days of being around her has incited.

I'm furious for her. Livid at the godsdamn Council. If I wouldn't get dead, I'd portal to Olympus and kick every one of the old fogeys' asses, come back here and take this woman the way I need. *Am I happy now?* "Yeah, I am."

She must read my ravenous expression because her eyes widen and she tears off into the living room. I'm on her heels. A dodge, a spin, and a spry leap gets her out of my grip but only for a moment. I snag her around the waist and toss her on the couch. She squeals and blinks at me, a rabbit facing a wolf, but instead of following her down and devouring her, I turn and head back to the kitchen. "I'm going to order the pizza. Extra olives."

A quick growl sounds from behind me before Lula leaps on my back, and I'm in a headlock. I laugh, tug her arms from around my neck, and reach to tickle her side.

A melodious giggle erupts before morphing into another growl. She drops to the floor. "Quit, you bastard!"

I grab her waist, lifting her against the wall, pressing myself between her kicking legs and pin her arms as well. "You sassy minx. Did you just call me a bastard?"

Her legs find their way around my waist, her chest rising and falling in quick succession. She blows a stray curl away from her eye. It drops back, inhibiting her vision. I lean in, nudging the red lock aside with my nose, skimming her skin in the process, breathing her in.

A short gasp sounds, alerting me to the dangerous game I'm playing, but after two days of pre-foreplay torture, I'm losing it. My lips trail to her ear, grazing the edge. She moans. Thank gods I'm not the only one affected.

She's a tough one to figure out. Once we spoke of behaving, being friends, it's like a switch flipped. I should have known better.

I drag my lips from her jaw to her chin—not kissing, behaving. I speak to the hollow in her throat. "One day, Firecracker. Just like this."

I press impatient hardness into a perfect nook, prompting a sweet whimper from her.

No. I can't.

Stepping back, I set her on her feet and study the fire in her eyes.

"I have ingredients for a quiche," Lula purrs as if her words were actually, *take me hard against this wall, then over the couch, and also on the floor.*

I open my mouth, but she points and glares, breaking the spell. "Not with olives." She stamps toward the kitchen.

Not what I was going to say but it's a welcomed subject change.

Once she's out of sight, I turn and lean against the wall, running my hands through my hair. This is hard. Harder than expected.

Once I have my mind and body under control, I stroll to the kitchen. Lula's standing at the fridge, forehead resting against it.

"Lu?"

Her vacant eyes make my stomach drop, and I cross the room to pull her into my arms. Thankfully, she doesn't resist. I tell her the truth. "I'm going to fix it." *With your help.*

"Shut up, Alex."

I rub circles on her back. "I am."

She pushes away from me. "How?"

I part my lips to explain everything, but nothing comes out. The need to do right and confess all is heavy in my chest, but the stakes are too high. I can't lose her and I can't put our plan in danger. We're making progress. She's thoroughly repulsed at Olympian traditions and I haven't yet told her how I was punished. She almost asked when we spoke of the virginal chambers, but she held back. One day she won't and we'll take another step forward, together.

I thumb her cheek. She goes back to the fridge, opening it this time and taking out a carton of eggs.

"You can kiss me. Lula, we'll make this work."

Shaking her head, she places items on the counter and preps food. "No. No, I can't. Rules still apply. No kissing."

"How about licking?"

The exasperated breath she expels makes me crack up because sometimes situations suck so bad there's nothing left to do but laugh. Her whisk pauses as she dips her finger into the bowl and touches my nose. "There's egg on your face, Mr. Deity."

Swiping a towel, I wipe away the offending substance. "Did you just put egg on my face?" I ask, slow and dramatic. I eye a canister on the counter and move toward it.

Lula brings out a playful side I haven't had since I was a kid. Well, at least in the first decade of being a kid. When I moved on to my adult state, there wasn't much play left. Lula comes along with her spark and makes me feel like a human starting out in life. There's a need to make her laugh, to bring her guard down further so she'll share more about herself.

"Don't do it," she says.

I lift the ceramic lid. She growls, "Alex," in a tone mothers use when reprimanding their children as I dip my hand into the fluffy substance.

She lunges for me too late and gets a face and chest full of flour. Screeching, she catches what she can of the falling clumps of white powder, then dusts more off her skin and into her palm. Eyes blazing with intent, she approaches, sending poofs of flour into the air from her stalking movement and quickened breaths. Now here's a worthy adversary ready for battle.

I dip my fingers into the canister again. "Lula, don't do it."

Flour flies. From her, then me, and me again. She battles me for the arsenal, trapping both our hands in the canister. I drag her away, a tight grip against her stomach, but she relaxes every muscle in a surprising defensive move because she slips right out of my arms and cackles from the floor. A powdery cloud thwacks me in the face when I follow, and we wrestle on the ground, white as snowmen, breathless at how ridiculous we are.

I roll, and she straddles me, holding my wrists as if she could overpower me. I grin at her smugness. "Kiss me, Firecracker."

"No. You're covered in flour."

Her grip falls away as I move to wipe my face with my flour-covered sleeve, though it's a hopeless effort. I wrench my shirt up over my head and rub my face with the inside. "There. Kiss me."

Lula's expression is taut and contemplating. Her gaze wanders over my shoulders, then chest, stomach, before returning to my face. My hands twitch to pull her to me, but the fact that she's even considering keeps me at bay. If I push, she'll run.

"Are you married?" she asks, a puff of flour hitting the air with her exhale.

What? Does this woman do anything normally? She fidgets with the powder on her arm, scratching at then, then sweeping it away.

I dust her off. "No."

"You made a face."

"I'm…" Not ready for this. This wasn't part of the rollout of information. It's out of order but I can't lie. "Um. This isn't going to sound good."

Face contorted to a pained mask I never want to see again, she twitches to stand, but I flip her under me. She doesn't fight but won't touch me either. If I kiss her, nuzzle her, would it make this better? "I'm betrothed." Green eyes divulge panic and she struggles against me. "I have been for a couple of hundred years. I won't marry her. I won't."

"A couple of hundred years? Your betrothal is older than I am." She puts her floured hands over her eyes. "Alex. Why are you here? We can't, I'm not—"

"Because I enjoy being around you." I didn't even need to think to spit that out.

"We can't—"

"We can't have sex."

She bites back a tight smile, jaw clenching.

I bring my hand from her hip to spin through the air. "Just say it."

"Say what?"

"Whatever it is you're biting your lip to hold back. Tell me."

She shakes her head, and I nod mine. After a minute of signaling at each other, she says, "It's difficult not having sex with you."

"Thank gods. Yes, so tough." Rolling, I take her with me, and she straddles me again. "Now aren't you proud of me for not jumping you and getting us both killed?"

"They'd kill you?"

Her concerned expression brings me up on my elbows to get closer. "I'm not sure what they would do." And that's the truth. They could lock me up, curse me into shackles at the bottom of the ocean where I'd die death after death just to rise again, or Zeus could fry me again, and this time, not stop.

Fingertips walk my chest. "You're betrothed?"

"Yeah. We were friends, and one day, my grandfather gathered us together and told us we were to be married. I stormed out and have avoided the situation ever since."

"Do you see her often?" Lula swallows hard, and her tightened lips twitch.

She maintains impressive control of her voice, but her face—the downward curve of her lip, and the angle of her eyes shows much. There's… disappointment? Maybe a touch of fear. I want to understand all Lula expressions. Just download her personal encyclopedia into my brain so I can understand every nuance of this intriguing woman.

"No, I don't. We're occasionally forced together at parties, dinners, and such."

"That's all?"

Nerves hit my stomach for a moment. She couldn't know about my grandfather's demands, right? "What else would there be?" Her snarky expression is one I am familiar with. "You mean, am I *doing* her?" I pause for dramatic effect. "No. I'm not, and do not plan to ever *do* her."

"Okay." Her thighs relax against my hips, putting hot pressure exactly where I want, and swiping away remaining playfulness.

Her cheek is smooth as I brush away flour, revealing the pink of her blush. "Kiss me, Lula."

She leans forward and my heart speeds. Her fingers stretch, pressing a palm to my bare chest. I hold back a moan because I don't want to interrupt wherever her thoughts are leading. She grazes my forehead with her lips and trails my temple. I dig my fingers into her hips to keep from grabbing her face and taking over.

She gives my nose a tiny peck, sweet breath tantalizing my heightened senses. "No, Alex. It's impossible to stop with you."

I cup her neck, but don't drag her to me. "We'll make this work."

"How? Can you say you're happy to only hang out with me? That you won't need sex?"

Hell no. "I want to take you in this floury mess we made. One day I will, but for now, we'll be good." It's a surprise to find myself inches from her face. We've gravitated toward each other again without realizing it. She grinds against my hips so faintly, I'm not sure she even notices. Our bodies are clearly on board with the thing that cannot happen.

Her voice is quiet and breathy as I inch forward. "We can't."

"I know. Kiss me, Lu."

After a kiss to my nose again, she stands. She offers a hand, and I take it, dragging her to me. She yips at the startling movement. I roll on top of her and cradle her face in my hands. "Hey, this is all going to work out."

"I hope you're right," she says, eyes locked on my lips.

"Because you want to have sex with me?"

"Shut up, Alex."

"I'm joking." I'm not. "Look at me."

When her inquisitive green gaze is back on me, I tell her, "We'll behave until I get shit sorted in Olympus but, Lula, I want to continue this. These have been two great days for me."

"Me too." Her expression morphs to downtrodden, and I'm positive my expression follows. "I've enjoyed having you here," she whispers

I move to kneel and pull her into my arms, holding her for a few minutes while our words settle. Her soft curves hug my body as if created by measurement. We're two beings never able to be close enough. Her touch and closeness comfort and frustrate me. It's not enough. I want everything. Releasing her, I help her to her feet. "We should clean up."

She peruses the mess, then me. "Are you out of clean clothes?"

I portaled to the Alpine safehouse to grab an emergency bag—something each of us keeps in the closets of our secret houses, but this was my last clean shirt. "I am. You get me naked from now on."

She pushes my shoulder, then tilts her head and with gentle fingers, squeezes my bicep instead, brow furrowed. "I'll do laundry. After showers."

I give her a playful pout. "Don't you mean, 'shower'?"

"God, Alex." She shakes off flour and pivots.

"Demigod, actually," I call after her, eyes honed on the natural, sexy swagger she owns so well.

The air in my lungs exits in a drawn-out exhale.

LULA'S IN *THE ROBE* PUTTING QUICHE IN THE OVEN WHEN THERE'S A knock on the door. My protective instincts flare, and I step forward intending to answer, but she moves in front of me and points at the peach towel wrapped around my waist. "If that's Ms. Frances from next door, you'll be responsible for killing an old lady." Turning the knob, she says under her breath, "But what a way to go."

"Hi," she says, a smile in her voice.

"Is Alex here?"

Comus. I relax and walk around the corner.

"Fuck," Comus says with wide eyes.

I approach with a smile. "Relax, we're still lawful citizens."

He tilts his head and points at my waist. "Nice towel."

Lula steps back to let him in. "Thank you."

Comus gives her an inquisitive look as if trying to figure her out and receives a grin in response.

"There was a baking incident," I say with a shrug.

He snorts. "And you had to get naked."

"How else were we supposed to wash his clothes?" Lula walks over to the bi-fold door of the laundry closet situated in a nook under the stairs, opens it, and pulls warm clothes from the dryer. Delivering them to my open arms, she heads to the kitchen and winks over her shoulder.

Smiling at Comus's shocked face, I tug on my laundered shirt, then pull on my pants before removing the towel from my waist. "Is it bad?"

When he twists his lips and tugs on his right ear, I have my answer. "Hercules called me. On the phone. Yeah, it's ghastly. Zeus has something on the Council's agenda and is sending your father to rein you in." He ducks his head, lowering his voice. "Progress?"

"Some," I whisper and walk to the kitchen. "What's the main topic?"

He frowns and glances at Lula.

"She stays."

Lula shuts the oven. "I'm going to get dressed. When the timer goes off, pull the quiche out of the oven. Oh, and use the mitt because it's hot." She gives Comus a quick smile as she exits.

"I'm a demigod, Lula, not an idiot," I yell after her.

"Are there oven mitts in Olympus?" she asks from the stairwell.

She's got me there. "I have no idea."

"Mmhmm."

Comus blinks at me as if my face is no longer familiar.

I turn the oven light on to view the egg masterpiece Lula threw together. "Don't say it."

"I was going to tell you that I get it."

"You do?"

He wanders around the kitchen, eyeing the art on the wall and the round, blue rugs. "Yeah. She's lovely. It smells like lemon cake in here." He points to Weirdo Rooster. "What the fuck is that?"

I smile. "That's love. I'll let Lula tell you the story."

"Alright? Are you two having a nice time ensconced from the evils of the world?"

"Yeah. How much trouble am I in?"

"Quite a bit. The Council wants to meet with us."

That's a surprise. "Both of us?"

He purses his lips as he opens the utensil drawer on the kitchen island and brings out a whisk to inspect. "Nope, just you, but I'm going with you."

"No. You're not getting caught in the crossfire, brother. Besides, if I get banished, we'll need you on the inside, feeding us info."

Comus points at me with a purple spatula as if it's a sword and he, a talented fencer. "Pissed as he is, your grandfather won't banish you. My father already told me that. For whatever reason, you're Zeus's golden boy, and he'll do whatever possible to get you on his side. He's calmed down, and Olympus has stopped rumbling… the thunder, not the gossip. That's been a rampant righteous rager."

A little chill goes through me. Yeah, I wanted gossip, but by being involved with Lula, I'm putting her in danger. If my grandfather decides I've shirked Naea because of another woman, he'll find Lu and use her as leverage to keep me in his control. I need to be more careful.

"He doesn't have any suspicions, does he?" I ask.

The timer goes off. I grab the oven mitt and pull out one delicious-looking quiche. The top is slightly brown, cheese bubbling, and the smell of peppers smacks me in the face, making my mouth water.

"No," Comus responds, practically drooling on my shoulder.

"Haven't heard a peep about that. He believes you are petulant because you were a kid for so long. I can eat that, yeah?"

Lula yells from the top of the stairs, "Is it ready?"

"Yep. Looks amazing. Come down here before Comus eats it all."

She arrives in tight-fitting jeans and a loose t-shirt. Her bare feet pad across the hardwood and she wrinkles her nose. "Sorry I don't have more variety. *Someone* eats like a bear."

She sends a glare my way, but I stare in response, frozen in place. Her hair's in a messy mass on top of her head, and I want to untie it and wrap the length of her mane around my fist while I kiss the hell out of those lips.

Her eyes widen, and she checks her outfit. "What?"

"You're gorgeous, that's what," Comus blurts out.

She blushes, and I snap at him. "Hey now, you're making me look bad." I turn to Lula. "You're gorgeous, that's what."

Narrowing her eyes, she grabs plates. *Hey, where's my blush?*

Comus grabs a pinch of the quiche and pops it in his mouth. He groans. "Gods, no wonder you haven't left."

She raises an eyebrow. "Aww, and here I thought it was my titillating conversation skills keeping Alex around."

I take the plates from her and nuzzle her cheek. "It's everything about you, Lula."

She freezes, stiff as a board.

Comus's eyes are wide, and he smiles but gapes as well. It's an odd expression on his typically carefree face. "Well, I figured you might have Alex under your seductive siren spell."

Lula's tight shoulder eases, shifting down a few inches against my chest. "My ability doesn't work on you all, remember?" I yearn to lick her grinning lips. She's radiant. "Besides, I've done a fine job resisting this charming tempter. I've even banned kissing."

"She did," I grumble, and peck her cheek, then dodge a half-assed slap. *Firecracker.* I bump her hip with mine, sending her a step toward the table. "Go sit."

She sashays to the table, and Comus releases a sharp laugh. I can't remember ever being this content. Going back to Olympus and confronting the Council will be hell after these perfect days.

After we devour the quiche and Comus has charmed Lula with

stories of epic parties, he goes to the SUV and leaves me standing on the porch, staring at Lula. Her eyes are teary, and there's a weird knot in my chest. It's so tangible, I rub the area with my palm, but it's inside, itchy and tugging at everything around it, like an emotional vortex inside my body. "Kiss me, Lula."

Her frown morphs into a smile, and she shakes her head. I thread fingers through her hair, and I touch my forehead to hers. She clears her throat and straightens up, pressing harder into our point of contact. "Um. I'll be here if you want to come back to visit."

I pull her tight against me, nudge my face against her neck, and inhale her berry scent. "Like I could stay away."

There's so much I need to tell her going beyond the things we've already discussed, but not yet. I trace her jaw with my lips. "Soon."

Pulling away, I stride to the SUV in a cloud of irritation. I'd stay here all day, forever, but the faster we accomplish what we need to, the quicker I return. With a last glance at Lula, I hop into the passenger seat.

Comus reverses out of the driveway as Lula shuts her door. "Define 'some' progress."

"Goddess treatment, an introduction to Olympian politics, and Council members." I gave her all the names so that if they ever found her and introduced themselves, she'd know them and hopefully get away.

"Did you bring up Dalia?" Comus squeezes the leather wheel. Regret and grief still burn. Since then, nothing has been the same. They forced us into action with no possible positive outcome.

"Yeah." I squeeze his shoulder. "She was thoroughly outraged."

He huffs. "Not mad at you then? Did you tell her what happened after?"

"No. That would have been too much. She may like me and want me around but she has to want to help Olympus." Telling her that my brethren stood by while my grandfather struck me with bolt after bolt until the tips of my fingers and toes burned off and my hair singed away isn't the way to get her on the side of deities. She'd make plans to send the darklings to Olympus instead of endangering the humans. All that would do is paint Olympus in blood and plant the Council's asses more firmly in their thrones. And everything depends on *if* she can control the dark species.

"Are you going to?"

"Eventually."

His eyebrows raise. "And nothing happened between you two that Pythia will catch?"

"No. We slept in the same bed both nights though. That was…"

"Hard?" He finishes for me with a wry smile.

"Yes—So. Very. Hard." I grin. "Where is Rath, by the way?"

"He's on gossip patrol. I told him that would work better in beds instead of hiding in the shadows but that led to an argument. He's going to face some tough choices as we edge closer."

"Artemis won't side with him no matter what. She's proven her loyalty, and it's not to him. Never will be."

"He needs to get laid."

"Well, that's not happening, unless Selene somehow digs her claws back into him." The tree line slips away to brick and concrete buildings. "His taste in women is epically dreadful."

Comus gives me a side glance. "They're majors… not a siren."

A line of energy simmers over my arms until my fingers ball. "Lula is kind, and she doesn't manipulate. She cares. Do not compare her to either of them." She'd make a better goddess. Her loyalty lies with the right things, not power and greed, horrid traditions, and discrimination. "She'd do the right thing." Artemis would do what Zeus told her to, and Selene would sit on the sidelines while the world burned around her.

"That's fair. Her knowing our plan will change everything and put her in even more danger. You shouldn't tell her until necessary."

"By our timeline, that could be a year."

"Longer. Up to a decade."

My fists clench. *Too long.* "We need to speed up the plan."

Comus laughs, sarcastic and tight. "You're serious?" When I don't respond, he smooths his already-in-place hair. "I never thought you'd be the one to get irrationally impatient. Rath is going to…actually, he always surprises me. Not sure what he'll do."

"He'll do what I ask him to." Rath is loyal too, and he

understands that I'd never ask him to do something against Artemis. We'd never ask him to harm.

Comus glances at me with raised eyebrows. "Well, aren't we just blazing for battle."

"We need to be. Maybe it's time I asserted myself into the role my grandfather wants me to take. Be what he's positive I am."

"I like it. It's time we started challenging the Council and commanding conversation."

Zeus has no idea what he's up against. It will shock him more than any lightning bolt he could conjure. I hope he doesn't burn us to cinders in the process.

Chapter Sixteen

LULA

My bed's cold, and my house is too quiet. I flip around for the thousandth time, my limbs too free. How quickly I adjusted to having Alex next to me. My mind will not settle and replays a highlight reel of my days with him. After he and Comus left, I fought hard, but still sank to the floor in a puddle of tears. Then I called Grace.

She's worried about me. I'm worried about me, too. Alex isn't mine, can't be mine, and the sooner I believe the truth, the better off I'll be. Rational thought doesn't keep my brain from reliving every minute of our three days together, and I alternate between crying and smiling. I'm losing it.

Tomorrow, I'll go out into the fascinating human world and pretend I belong. I'll try to push Alex from my mind, though I'm well-acquainted with the impossibility of such a task. I have no clue when I'll see him again.

Clinging to my pillow, I seek comfort in the dark when my phone dings.

My heart staggers at Alex's words. *Sleeping yet, Firecracker?*

Not yet, I reply and stare at the screen until the chime sounds again.

Sleep isn't possible without you against me.

The sigh I let out is so loud in my quiet room, that a giggle chases after it. *I'm pretending my pillow is you.*

His response is immediate. *Is that working out for you?*

Not well. It doesn't flop around as much and smother me with muscles.

And here I thought you enjoyed the muscles, he replies.

Oh, I do. It's easier to talk to him in text messages. I'm not peppered with guilt for wanting him and for keeping my secrets my own when I don't have to gaze into his golden eyes.

Good, Alex texts. *I'll call you tomorrow. Dream of me.*

Not going to be a problem.

Holding my phone to my chest, I caress it, and whisper in the dark, "I can't get more hung up than I am."

I'm not sure if I'm warning myself or stating a fact.

I wake late, having had no problems dreaming of Alex's touch. As I join the conscious world, the empty space beside me chills my warm waking. I scrounge for breakfast, but there are only crumbs after our days together. My home is different without Alex in it. He doubled the comfort and then took it all with him when he left.

I head to the grocery store. Why did I plan to take Alex here? How could I have considered that he'd be happy with mundane human tasks? He's a divine being with servants and fancy food every meal.

I speed through the aisles on autopilot, not even sure what items I'm shoving in my cart. How stupid could I be? Attachment to a divine being is like searching for a pony, finding a unicorn, and thinking, *this is my new steed.* Why would a rare creature exchange a magical existence for plain wood fences and a drafty barn?

Thoughts of the virginal chambers, the violence of the old ages, and the tone Alex uses when speaking of Olympus crosses my mind, but I swish them away. He's a god with mystic, incredible powers. What the hell could he see in me?

Not to mention, I threw out keeping my sisters and myself safe. Alex overruled my caution with his sweet words and perfect, divine body. How could he promise to fix things and give me hope when he shouldn't? He can't change a millennium-old law. No one can.

The scowl I wear makes my face sore as I drive. He's a drug, and I'm in withdrawal. Is this phenomenon a trait specific to gods? Maybe Earth beings worshipped deities because of supernatural reasons, similar to how my voice enthralls. If I spent an evening with Comus or Rath, would the same thing occur? Nothing more than warm friendliness bubbles through me toward them, but I didn't spend a lot of time with them either. They didn't touch me beyond a handshake. I was riding on a cloud after the gastropub, though. It felt real, but…

It's the only logical explanation for the way I'm acting towards Alex. He must release a bonding pheromone when he's around me, and now I'm addicted. I bet people under my ability's spell struggle like this after I leave. Serves me right.

After I arrive home and put everything away, I call Grace. "Have you read anything about deities being addictive if you're near them?" I ask when she answers.

Amah's the most knowledgeable about this subject, but I'm not comfortable telling her how I spent the last few days. *Great, now I'm sad and guilt-ridden.*

Grace sings across the line. "Lula's in love, Lula's in love."

"I am not, jerk. I'm addicted, that's all. Crashing after a three-day divine bender. Deity withdrawal." I slide down the kitchen island. I do my best brooding from the floor.

The line goes silent for a long second. "Three *days*?"

I rub my forehead with my palm and tell her the story—sleeping wrapped in his arms, keeping information about us from him, and how he made me tour him around my house and explain each piece of art. I go light on the details of what he told me. It's too… new. Too personal.

"Oh, Lula." Her voice rings all-knowing and pitying. "You feel for him."

"I don't. He has special addicting pheromones. It's all over him, on his fingertips when he talks, in his…stuff."

"Um," she says, and I picture her angles brows pinched tight in thought. I would have made this a video call except I don't want her to see me in this frazzled, withdrawn state. "There was *stuff* involved?"

"No. But I'm sure it's like that." She cackles at my words, and my giggles break free in a burst from stress and ridiculous notions. "I'm not joking!" I yell. "Research needs to be done." I'm insane. All of this is a weird dream.

She heaves her breaths. "In. His. Stuff?"

"Yes, in his stuff! It's a thing. We'll do research, and it will prove I love him because of his mystical juju."

Her laughter hiccups into silence. "You're in love with him then."

Shit. "I'm not. He's a god with luring pheromones. This is just, companionship, sorta. Friends are all we'll ever be."

"Are you friends, Lu?"

I smile. "I believe so."

"Are you happy?"

"I am," I say with no hesitation.

"Then have fun. Be friends. Enjoy every ounce of his bond-producing *stuff*. You know, without cursing and killing us all." I scoff, and she snickers again and adds, "But, don't let him break you. Don't pull a Venora, alright? The rest of us couldn't handle seeing you in that state."

Right now, the similarities between Ven's typical reaction to her crushes and my own are uncanny and unexpected. Now, all I need to do is fall into a two-month depression, complete with drowning in gin and romance movie binges. Icy chills travel my spine and spread to my limbs. I've been neglecting the search for my sisters. That's a big reason to step back from Alex.

I have to move and push off the kitchen island to stand. "Still no word?" The thinking path travels from the kitchen to the living room, then the foyer, and back to the kitchen. It's my anxiety circuit.

"No. Everyone's just sick about it. I hope they're being reckless. Having a midlife crisis or something like humans do. Although we aren't the reckless kind. Well, except you."

"I'm not reckless."

"Uh, okay. Says she who invited a strange deity over to her house for dinner and a petting party right after she met him."

"It didn't go that far, Grace."

"Yeah, okay, Miss in-love-with-a-deity."

"That's enough about me today. Are we tracing calls on their cell phones?"

"We tried but—oh, hey, that's Ma on the other line. I gotta go."

"Call me later, alright?"

"Will do. Bye, god-lover."

"Bye, jerk."

After getting Nysa to send me phone and utility records, I pin down when Gerty went missing—two months and ten days—then call to check on more video surveillance around the area she disappeared. My contact had a lead, but faulty technology snuffed out that trail. Dead end. Hazel's on her way to her mother's home and maybe that will give us information on Venora's whereabouts.

As I make dinner, my phone rings. It's Alex. I can't talk to him right now. I'm still in the spiraling depression brought on by the lack of contact with him, and if I hear his voice, I'm positive the cycle will repeat. When the worst part of this Alex detox is over, I'll be strong enough to speak to him and resist his charm. Right now, I have to focus on my sisters.

The second time he calls, my finger lingers, itching to press the button. He could help. *Do not trust those we cannot control.* I should call Amah and have her talk more sense into me.

Leaving my phone on the counter, I walk the neighborhood. Squirrels chase each other, diving branch to branch in the woods beside the road, making a racket of crunching brush and chittering that shouldn't be so loud for such tiny creatures. Late summer blooms and long grass wave in the warm breeze. The evening sky darkens, purple and red overtaking blue in a bright farewell to the day. I turn when the pavement turns to gravel, and head back to my house. By the time I reach my driveway, it's dark.

"Are you okay?"

I screech, jump back from the voice in the dark, and slap a hand over my mouth. Alex stands from my porch and reaches out to wrap his arms around me. He cups the back of my head in his hand and presses his nose against my neck. I relax against him. Damn those magical pheromones.

"Are you okay?" he repeats.

"Yes. I'm fine." I'm standing in the dark, but with him so close, it's brighter and warmer than the afternoon of sunshine.

He rests his forehead to mine. "I was worried."

"You shouldn't be. I can handle myself." My words would be more convincing had I not startled like a mortal five seconds ago. I push against him, but his hold is borderline crushing, yet solid and comforting. I shouldn't, but I'm glad I'm not the only one who's world isn't stable without us breathing the same air.

"You didn't answer my calls or texts."

His messy hair and tired eyes in the dim light make guilt surge through me in a sickening wave. The ache for him that's been building all day overrides my hesitation, and I wrap my arms around his neck and slip my fingers into his soft locks. I shouldn't be this close to him but I've never come home to someone waiting for me.

"I was trying to give us space," I whisper. The sweet smell that was faint on his skin before is stronger, taking his scent from sugared grapefruit to citrus taffy. How odd.

"For what reason?" My mouth opens, but nothing comes out as my thoughts tangle. He grabs my chin and lifts my face, gaining my full attention. "You need space?"

When I don't answer, his lips tighten. Releasing me, he tries to step back, but I catch his shirt. "You're a deity, Alex."

"Established information. What does it have to do with needing space?" He widens his arms like an offering. I can't tell him about the pheromone thing—I'd either be right or he'd think I was crazy and both roads lead to goodbye, which is what I should want, but I don't. He's too encompassing to walk away from. Not yet. "Lula, do you need space?"

"Why do you want me, Alex?" Something isn't adding up for him to attach to me. He's millennia-old and a divine being with a positive influence on the world. Is it intrigue with my species or me? A rebellion against Olympus because he's not allowed to be with me? "I'm not like you. You can't—"

He cuts off my words with a crash of lips that tilts my world. My mind tells me to run, but instead, I plunge my fingers back into his hair and whimper into his kiss. His growls in response, a quick rumble that tightens my inner muscles and raises chills on my skin, even in the warm outdoors. I bet the magic he possesses over me is on his tongue because the link I was attempting to sever grows stronger with each lapping lick and every devoured breath.

He breaks away and I follow until I catch the warning in his eyes.

"Do you want me, Lula?"

My head bobs without consulting my brain, and he's on me again, tongue stroking mine, consuming me with a coursing power. "Yes," I hum, and swoon into him, reveling in the warmth and hardness of him—holding on with clutching hands. We battle kiss-for-drugging-kiss.

He pulls back too quickly. *No, come back.* I clutch at his neck and he runs his hand over me—my hips and up to stroke my shoulder. He thumbs my lip.

"I have to leave," he whispers. "But I needed to see you, and make sure you were safe." He steals a few more light kisses. "Stop running from this, and *do not* doubt my desire for you. If you glimpsed inside my mind right now." He takes a laden breath.

Lingering, I meditate on our foreheads touching together and his hand on the back of my head. Slowly, he steps away.

"I'm not sorry I kissed you." Walking a few steps away, he slices his fingers through the air. "Answer my calls please, so I know you're safe."

Speechless, I stroke my tingling lower lip and nod. Within seconds, I'm alone again, trembling in the dark.

Chapter Seventeen

ALEX

"Reckless," Comus criticizes, stroking his beard and pacing in front of me in the mudroom.

"I know." I pinch the bridge of my nose. "Gods, I know."

He slaps my shoulder. "What's happening in that mind of yours, Alex?"

"You need to ask?"

I now have personal stakes to change this world. I've wanted it for others—for Rath and Dahlia to be respected, freedom for the otherworldling slaves Olympus stole, castrated, and termed 'pets.' The virginal chambers will never open again, even if more goddesses are born. The pressure to fight for the rights of others has hung around my neck since I closed the portals, but the weight doubles each time I touch Lula.

I want her.

I want to be able to have her—to walk up to her like I just did, kiss the hell out of her, and take her inside. Cook dinner together, then have wine and talk. Watch a movie during which I get distracted by her curves and manhandle her to bed while she curses me between kisses because I made her miss the end... again.

"You've never acted this way, so yes, I need to ask," Comus says as I try to shift by him. Staring me down, he blocks my path. "Be careful. If not for you, for her." Does he think I'm unaware of the danger? The risk? "You can't get her hooked on you and traipse away."

"I have no intention of walking away from her. Besides, she's not hooked. I am. Sometimes, we're on the same page, but I can't get into her head. She's cryptic—holds back. Every time I think we get each other, she does something unexpected, and I'm lost again. She didn't answer my calls today. No one has done that to me. The woman is a dark forest with no trails."

Comus pats my chest and lets me pass. "Then you need to protect yourself and us. We need her and with the way women act with you, if she isn't following you around like a puppy after your little retreat, then rein it in."

I grab a container of leftover fried rice from the fridge and snag a fork from the drawer. "You act like I'm stalking her."

"Brother, you portaled in front of her house because she wouldn't accept the multiple phone calls and text messages you sent her. You glance at your phone every few minutes and keep your hand on it in your pocket in case she contacts you. You're one step away from studying her sleeping habits."

The image of her slumbering face hijacks my thoughts. "Whatever." *Just call me Alexiares, king of comebacks.*

I am a stalker. I wish I knew what she did all day—what she's doing right now. Thoughts of her intermingle with another growing awareness getting stronger by the minute. I pause chewing and close my eyes.

"Your attribute calls?" Comus asks.

I stretch my neck, allowing the call to permeate my mind. The vision is fuzzy, the location a needle in a haystack. "Yeah. Something's building."

My phone buzzes in my pocket at the same time Comus's rings out loud. We exchange a glance of confusion and tug our phones out of our pockets. It's my father. Comus takes a step back and turns to answer. "Yeah, Da, what's going on?"

I click the answer button. "Hello?"

My father's gruff voice is rapid. "We need your guidance on information on the humans. Are your attributes active?"

I throw the box back in the fridge and walk toward Comus. "Yes. What's going on?"

"Come to the main hall." With a series of beeps from pushing the phone's buttons, my father hangs up before saying anything further. He's still getting used to the human invention. Most of the Council wouldn't acknowledge the mortal device if it weren't the only way to monitor us. Zeus believes all deities should use a divine messenger servant, but that doesn't work when so few of us are allowed on the Earth realm. If Zeus could bend an inch, he could have every Olympian at his fingertips in seconds. The signal is strong even in Olympus, as the realm lies over the Earth like a shadow. Next, we'll bring in more generators, then wait until everyone demands electricity and forces Zeus to share how he broke us away from Earth. The key to reconnecting may be unlocked by human ingenuity.

I open a portal and we slip through to Comus's Olympian living room, rush to the door and out into the pink light of sunrise. As we approach the boxy building lined with columns, arguing voices are a jumble of noise.

Zeus's voice booms above all others, echoing off the marble. "How could you not envision this occurrence? An oracle should have been aware of the situation."

"Sire," Pythia's deep timbre says in a plea. "My prophetic attributes do not relate to this event. They were humans, and I require a starting point."

Shit. Pythia's here, the entire Council, servants, and more. It's too early for this many to gather. Comus glances at me with wide eyes, and I mimic his surprised face. We both speed up until we spot our fathers side-by-side. Hercules does not get involved. He dwarfs Dionysus, thick arms crossed and head bent as he listens to Comus's father. The muscles honed long ago still bulge and ripple under a tawny himation, tied with a braided blue cord. Well, isn't he feeling rebellious?

"Alexiares, perhaps you will explain." My grandfather storms forward and the crowd parts for him, creating perfectly straight lines around him as if they'd rehearsed for this moment.

My gaze lands on my twin's downtrodden face. Something big happened. I nearly balk, wondering if I'm in for another round with

Zeus. I spoke to him. Well, stood by as he berated me for disappointing him, then told me he understood, berated me again for letting down Olympus, and dismissed me. I didn't apologize. The *conversation* seemed conclusive to me.

By the shifting bodies and clenched jaws, everyone's nervous, but it's unclear if the reason for their distress is because of what's occurred or because my grandfather is on the rampage.

I clear my throat. "What may I assist you with?"

"The event involving the humans," he states, rolling his hand through the air as if this information should have already reached me.

My blood runs cold. "What type of event?"

"You did not bear witness?" He tugs on his beard, something he only does when irritated and in the company of those he trusts most. "It must not be war related. That is somewhat of a comfort." He turns to Apollo. "Send out seekers to gather knowledge."

"What type of event?" I ask again.

My grandfather turns back to me. "A group of humans perished by an unsanctioned act."

If that news hit Olympus, it was big. "When? Where?"

He glances to the clouds. "There was an occurrence in a discreet location in the northeast map a day ago. An entire village decimated. A smaller event occurred a week ago. Fifty humans or so, however, it is within foot proximity to this one."

Comus runs a hand through his hair. "We need details."

My grandfather turns a steely gaze to him, but Comus's father approaches setting a hand on Zeus's shoulder. "I will update the lads if it pleases you. You should not be bothered by such matters."

"Fine," Zeus says but keeps his gold eyes on me. He steps forward, leaning close. "I have not and will not forget your disobedience," he whispers in my ear. "We will speak more of it."

The Council stands by, watching our exchange. Deimos lifts his lip in a sneering smile. Athena's gaze holds pity but her stance, tall and unmovable, is stoic as usual. Artemis hides behind her brother Apollo, keeping her focus on the dark green grass.

"Perhaps after we correct the wrongs in the realm," I say, lifting my chin. He doesn't know what that fully means yet, but he will. They all will.

His eyes narrow and he turns. "Inform me if anything of use comes of your discussion," he yells over his shoulder and storms away.

Dionysus claps Comus on the back and signals to the breezeway that leads to the Great Hall's inner corridors.

My father approaches, grasps my neck, and touches his forehead to mine. "Son."

"Father." I squeeze his shoulder. "How's Mother?"

"She misses you. Come visit soon, yes?"

"Of, course."

Our mother will want to know everything I've done on Earth in the past few months, and I have a hard time lying to her. Hebe misses the humans, longs to see the interaction between them, and visit the vast amount of children running amok. It's been a long while since we've had a birth in Olympus, and the goddess of youth is bored, her attributes unused. She would like Lula's nature, and how she treats mortals.

Anice sidles up beside me and we follow inside and to the nearest room on the left. The room is small, the only furniture is a small pulpit stationed center on the back wall. The doors close behind us with an ominous *whomp*. Dionysus crosses his arms. "It's bad."

WE BEELINE BACK TO COMUS'S PLACE THROUGH A THICK FOG OF perplexity. Rath will arrive soon. We need to regroup after the bomb that was just dropped on us.

I must call Lula.

No, I need to go to Lula, but the Council wants another meeting, another conversation. We need to work together for once if that's possible.

Without a word between us, Comus and I walk down the hall. He's been here since the separation, but the decor hasn't changed since the Iron Age. He's had a few goddesses stay for a while and put their touch on his place with a few carvings and tapestries, but this isn't a home. He turns into his room and I settle into a guest suite, the one with the carved canopy bed. The feather-filled linen mattress sinks as I lean back, dialing Lula's number.

She answers on the second ring. "Alex?" The timbre of her voice runs warm through my body and I close my eyes to shut off everything that's not Lula.

"Hi, Firecracker."

"You sound sad." Her concern is touching, and I wish she was draped over my arm, flush against me.

"It was a rough day."

"What's going on?" she asks with a sincerity that makes me want to tell her everything— even the gruesome details to get it off my chest, but I won't upset her when I'm not standing there with her in my arms. She'll need comfort. "Sorry," she says. "I shouldn't ask. It's none of my business."

Oh, it is though. "It was just tedious Council stuff. How was your day?"

She's quiet for a long moment and I picture her, leaning on the kitchen island, nibbling her lip. "Well, this super handsome guy kissed me, even though he shouldn't have."

"You better mean me," I growl, adding a smirk.

"Was that you?" She laughs a tinkling note, making me grin from ear to ear. "You're a hell of a kisser, Alex. Made my head spin."

"And forgot it was me kissing you."

"I forget lots of things when your lips are on mine," she says, no longer jesting. "But I could never forget you, Alex."

The world stops, her vulnerable tone expressing more than words and my heart swells in my chest. "I could never forget you either, Lula. Not in a million years."

"I should go." Her voice is thick, and she sniffles.

I sit up and run my hand through my hair. I'm one second from portalling, Council meetings be damned. "Lula, talk to me, please."

She clears her throat, takes a breath. "What do you want to talk about?"

I go through the extensive list of things I want to say to her; how I need her for more than personal reasons, and that we're going to fix this world together. I could demand she tell me what I mean to her and hope it matches what I'm feeling for her. It's too new, and what we need to discuss—the real stuff—will lead me to the same place. Shut out.

No. We need a derail. Something easy and fun. "Do you like pets?" I ask.

"Pets?"

"Yes, pets. Dogs, cats, rats."

"Goats," she says. "Baby goats."

"You're joking?"

"No, I'm not *kid*-ding at all." There's a smile in her words. "See what I did there? A baby goat is called a kid."

I cover my eyes with my hand. "I figured that out. Why baby goats?"

"Have you ever seen a baby goat? They're so adorable, it's ridiculous. Evolution made them so cute, they're irresistible to any species." Her melodic voice grows fast with her excitement.

"A wolf somewhere has eaten a baby goat."

She gasps. "You take that back. There will be no speaking of eating baby goats."

I won't tell her about some divine dishes served in Olympus then. "You're right. Nothing's ever eaten an adorable, baby goat." *Lies.* I'm positive baby goats get eaten every day, but if Lula wants to put blinders on, blinders it is. "Is it just their cuteness that makes them deserving of your affections?"

"No. They're playful and intelligent. They make up elaborate games to interact with their environment and other goat friends."

"Have you spent a lot of time with baby goats?"

"Only a few times. The farmer's market brought one in last spring. Other than that, sometimes I watch videos of them online. Thank goodness for humans and their creation of the internet. Love baby goats," she says, more to herself.

"You stole the baby goat, didn't you?"

"I did not!"

She did. The tight inflection in her voice gives her away.

"Lu."

"Fine, I did, but only for a while. I took him back after a couple of hours. He was calling for his mom."

"We'll visit baby goats in the spring." Before she objects, because she rejects all things past one week in the future, I blurt out, "You have a small garden—what's your favorite flower?"

For a half-hour, Lula and I talk about the mundane. She's more open with me over the phone. I don't ask her about family, us, or anything she could take too personally, and now, I have an arsenal of information.

There is a light knock on the door, and Comus pokes his head in the room. He mouths, *Rath's here. More details.* He winces.

I rub my face. What could be worse than a siren killing humans?

"Hey, Comus is calling for me. I have to go."

"Oh, okay." The disappointment in her voice both thrills and saddens me. "Tell him I said 'hello.' Rath as well."

I've never had someone ask after Rath. She's such a sweetheart. "I will. I'll call you soon, alright?"

"I'll talk to you later then."

She sounds more hopeful that I'll call. As soon as this mess is figured out, I'll sneak away and go to her. We hang up, and I hold my phone to my chest and lie on the bed for another minute, lingering in the warmth ignited from our conversation.

Chapter Eighteen

LULA

I roll to my side, and my hand alights on a warm, hard shoulder. Smiling, I shift closer. A defined bicep is too tempting not to sample with my lips, and I inhale. Deeper under his god-spell I go.

Alex has frequented my house more often than not over the last week and a half. I've woken in his arms, or he shows up at sunset with takeout he picked up in Venice or Beijing. I haven't seen him for two days, but when I came downstairs yesterday, I found my fridge full of exotic fruit and vegetables from who knows where. The pantry had six new cans of olives. I spent the afternoon internet-searching and tasting the mystery produce, and after a walk, I fell asleep smiling.

I've come close to asking him to take me somewhere, but the portals scare me and the only place I need to visit is my sisters' homes. That won't work because we don't talk about them, even though I want to. They've been the only people in my life for a hundred and eighty-two years. Now I have someone I can honestly talk to, but I can't tell him how much I love them or why I'm increasingly worried —but he's noticed—because now Hazel has gone silent. Maybe she's out of cell range and with Venora.

I won't talk to him about it though because…I'm being safe. Amah's still not thrilled about me spending time with him.

Whatever's going on between Alex and me is temporary, but the divine juju in his skin has me hooked. When he leaves for good, his parting will leave a gaping chasm in my heart, but I don't care, as long as it doesn't endanger him or my sisters. He's worth the fall and I'll keep the memories. I'll be like Amah and her demon.

He stopped pushing for deep personal information and questions about what we are. Our future holds nothing positive, and I appreciate the reprieve. He lets us be us, and us just being, is the most beautiful thing I've ever experienced.

I run a finger over hard triceps. His body is a work of art. I can imagine him in marble, standing tall, ridged abs of rock and lower to—

Strong muscles tense and Alex moves so fast he's a blur. He flips me to my stomach, spreads me with a knee between my thighs, and loops his arm under my waist, dragging up my hips. He presses against me, hard. I moan and panic at the same time, heart racing for flight. I'm not even sure if he's awake.

"Alex?"

Instead of words, he growls, and the sound reverberates through me, creating an electrical tingle everywhere. He flips my hair aside, lips crashing into the back of my neck. He sucks my skin, and I arch, hips lifting on their own accord.

"Shit," I say, the fog in my mind only clearing a little. "Alex. We can't."

"We won't." His raspy voice is fierce.

He shifts his hand from my hip and slips it under my shorts and panties.

"Alex," I say, but it's a weak, mumbling plea instead of a reprimand.

"I won't fuck you. I swear it, but…" His finger slides into me with ease. He groans, and I whimper. "But I want to. It's unbearable, Lu. I want you too much."

He shifts behind me, fabric rustling, and the length of him brushes my backside over thin cotton shorts. I gasp, but steady myself, dropping my forehead onto the pillow. If I look, there's a zero-point-zero percent chance I won't have him in my mouth and then inside me right after. Another finger joins the first between my legs, and his palm presses against me.

I buck against him. "Oh, fuck."

He smiles against my neck. "How's that, *my* Firecracker?"

My mind stutters over the pointed way he growls *My*. It's possessive, and a thrill travels my skin, igniting me. I'd respond with some snarky comment to remind him what this is, but he nips a sensitive place on my shoulder and lust dissipates whatever I was considering. I grip the sheets and focus on the fullness of his fingers, the kiss of his palm.

My thighs shake, and my hips have a mind of their own. As thrusting fingers keep a steady, entrancing pace, Alex whispers between kisses to my neck, "I would rip off the clothing between us, sink in, torture us both even more. Do you feel me?"

He presses deep.

"Y-yes," I cry out and reach back with one hand to clutch his hip, his backside.

He's pure muscle, thick and solid over me. The stance he's taken behind me gives me space, but there's no doubt that while I'm under him unpinned, going anywhere else isn't an option. Not that I would. I should, but I can't. He feels too good. I want him too much as well.

"I'd move in you until you were a writhing, stuttering, ball of fury in my hands." The heat of his words against my ear has me raising my hips, widening my stance.

I push myself up until I'm kneeling, leaning back against Alex's chest. No longer having to hold himself over me, he slips his free hand under my shirt. *Yes, please. Up. Touch me.* He takes his time, caressing his way up, tracing my sides. It's maddening in an impatient but worthwhile way. It's waiting for the curtains to open for a show, or for a perfect sunrise to light the skies.

It's coming, and it will be glorious.

I run my fingers through his hair and wedge my other hand between us to grasp his hard length. His breath leaves in a rush, and the touch brushing the underside of my breast leaves. I open my mouth to yell, but Alex grabs my chin, tilting my head so he has better access to the muscle running from my neck to shoulder. The pad of his forefinger touches my lips, lighting up the nerves. He nudges a finger into my mouth, and I eagerly suck on his digit, teasing it with my tongue.

"Godsdammit, Lula, you're my perfect torture," he says, breathless. He takes his digit away from me to grip my breast over my shirt and traces my ear with his teeth.

I arch for him, squeeze in rhythm to his pumping fingers.

More. Closer. "Please, Alex, please—"

With a snarl, his fingers drive deeper, palm pressing hard, making me pitch forward with the rapid tightening of my core. I place my hand over his on my chest. My breath comes in quick gasps.

"Just touching," he whispers. "Like this. When I finally sink into you, and we're connected—fuck, Lu. We'll rival the heat of the sun." He turns my head so I'm staring into pools of gold. "Sing for me."

Blazing electricity sears through me in pulses. My head falls back on his shoulder and I cry out as I ride wave after wave of intensity. Alex holds me upright to thrust into my palm. My blissed-out mind clears with his panting breaths, and I try to twist.

He holds firm. "Wait, Lula." His words are ragged, intoxicated with lust.

"I need..." He scrambled my brain and thoughts won't assemble into a coherent request. "Alex, let go."

He groans in distress and releases me enough so I can turn. My hands are everywhere—in his hair, caressing his chest to his waist. Tugging at his tank, I kiss, lick, and nip every reachable location in a frenzy. I need his skin, his cock, him. I need the mystery of his touch and his sounds—everything.

He tries to back away but I re-grip, and he groans. I dip, lips teasing the hard ridges of his stomach on my way down. He half-heartedly protests, "Lula, we can't."

"Just a taste." I try to push him down, putting my shoulder into it, but he doesn't budge. "Lie back. Now."

He drags his shirt off and lowers to the mattress with a moan. Even the skin of his glorious length is golden, but I don't have time to explore further because I need it more than anything. I take him between my lips.

Alex lets out this sexy stuttering grunt and a string of incoherent words I've never heard before, but they sound old—original language old. *Faster. Deeper.* His hard body is so tense he could break me if he wanted to, but his shaking fingers thread through my hair with delicate care. It's a heady power he's given me as he stares down, heated gaze making my stomach flip.

"Lu?" he asks as if I'm not attuned to every breath and twitch he makes. "Lu, move, baby."

He tries to guide me away with a hand on my face, but I brush it off, humming a dissenting moan. He arches back, grit teeth, fingers burrowing in my hair. With a grunt, he erupts. I close my eyes, smiling as I savor him—his heat and passion. As the tension leaves his body, I release him with panting breath, placing a soft kiss on him before sitting up.

Golden skin now carries a flush of coral and a sheen of sweat. His chest rises and falls like he battled an ancient foe. My blissed-out mind snaps to reality. This shouldn't have happened. Did I just get us cursed? We're too close—dangerous to each other. Even bombarded with concern and regret, my greedy body throbs for him to fill me. I'd think I was going into heat if I didn't know how painful that would be, not that I've ever experienced it. No, this is purely need and godly pheromones.

It's only a matter of time before we get too wrapped up to stop. Hell, if he wasn't spent, I'm not sure I'd have the resistance not to climb him. *Closer.* The echoing word sends my adrenaline racing. I flinch to leap off the bed for the safety of both of us, but he tackles me, pinning me to the sheets, his lips on my neck and trailing down. Chaotic hands slide under my shirt and tug at my shorts and panties.

"Alex," I say, squirming under him. I have to be the voice of reason. "This is bad. We—I… what if— "

"Shh, it's okay," he coos while removing the clothing between us. He settles wide shoulders between my legs. "We're okay,"

"But Alex—"

He dips to taste me, and my words turn into a moan. He mumbles, "Raspberries," and goes to work, making brand new sounds fly from my mouth. Every move is a shock of pure bliss, an unexpected gift. At one point, he groans, and the vibrations travel right to my heart. I shatter again, sharper pulses surging through me, a keening cry dragged up from deep inside—the kind that would kill anything other than a divine being. When I melt into the mattress, he kisses up my body, completely removing my shirt, which is bunched to my neck. I wrap my arms around him, welcoming his weight against me, the slide of his skin with nothing between us except laws promising death.

He kisses the top of my breasts, my neck, my chin, my nose and looks at me with a staggering tenderness.

"May I kiss you?" he whispers, playing with a curl of my hair.

I eye his lips. "Alex, you just tasted me. Down there. And now you ask?"

"Is that a yes? I don't want to break your rules."

That makes me laugh. "Have you ever followed the rules?"

His lips tease mine three times as he shakes his head, then connects. The intense lust simmers, leaving behind gooey warmth. Toying kisses flutter over me while we lie skin to skin, his heart thumping against mine, my legs around his waist.

We roll, so I'm on top, leading our movements while his hands light up paths along my bare body. We turn to our sides, staring into each other's eyes, continuing to kiss. My lips grow sore. *I don't care.*

His final peck melts me before he moves out of lip range. I'm nervous without the distraction, impending doom entering my mind.

"Am I going to get cursed?" I ask.

His arms tighten around me, his hesitation bringing my anxiety to an overwhelming level.

"No," he says, though his tone isn't confident.

"We can't do that again, can we?"

He moves closer to thumb my cheek. "We shouldn't."

"Okay."

He stares at me and smirks. "You taste like raspberries and rain everywhere."

My face heats. "You taste...right. Like Earth and sea and probably Heaven."

His gaze travels me, slow and attentive. "I love your taste." He kisses me hard, scrambling any response I form. I settle in, appreciating his bare skin as it radiates heat. Being near him is like sunbathing. The thought brings the temperature down. Is that a side effect of our closeness? How could anyone emulate the sun like this?

He nips my ear and I moan. I'll ponder more later.

Alex's phone rings from the side table, but he doesn't move to get it. His heart thumps a steady beat, and I'm perfectly content to leave my leg wrapped over his bare hip. He cups my backside with one hand and strokes my arm with the other.

After a brief pause, another ring interrupts the silence. He has to leave. He crinkles his eyes at the screen, then softens them. It's getting harder to let him go, and after today, my emotions dip further into unknown territory. I could stay in bed, inhaling his skin, basking in his warmth for the rest of eternity. My eyes stings, and muscles in my jaw tighten. I nuzzle against his collarbone to distract me from the inevitable.

He reaches and brings the phone to his ear. "I'll call you right back."

He'll walk away in a few minutes, and I'm not sure when I'll see him again, or if I should. Sure, I'm basking in the best afterglow of my life and we didn't even fully come together, but he's a deity and doesn't trust that Olympus won't discover what happened. What if they find us, right here in my home, and then the sirens, who fell once from divine status are back in the spotlight.

I have to say goodbye.

Alex holds me tight to him as if he knows. I bite my lip to keep the sob at bay.

"I need to call Comus back," he says and kisses my head.

Lifting my chin to give him a quick kiss, I slide off the bed. "I'm going to shower."

He rolls off as well, and hugs me to him, nose burrowing into my neck. "I'd join you, but I want your scent on my skin all day."

I lean away and smile, hoping he misses the uncomfortable tightness in my face. "You're sweet."

"Am I?"

I pull away, grab clothes, and head to the bathroom while giving a little hum of affirmation. He watches my bare ass. Good, he won't see the clouds of dismay in my eyes.

"You okay?" he says right before I shut the door.

Biting my lip, I nod and close him out.

Chapter Nineteen

LULA

Alex paces while he talks to Comus. To my relief and dismay, he put on jeans and a tee while I showered. It's for the better. Focusing is hard enough without him walking around my bedroom like a living, nude statue of the perfect male form.

He pauses and runs tense fingers through his hair. I'm worried about him. His agitation has escalated, his nervous energy makes me edgy. I want to soothe him, hold him as I explain the joy and excitement he's brought to my life, but it's not my place to do so. It will make things worse before we part.

I text Grace, *I wish I could come see you.* More than ever, I need my sisters.

"Is there any further information on the state of the bodies?" Alex whispers into the phone.

A chill runs up my spine.

"I'll be there in five," Alex says, now determined. His shoulders drop as he glances at me. "That's the plan. Bye, brother."

I try to sneak by him to the door, but he snags my hand and pulls me to his chest. He drops the phone into his pocket and cups my face in his hands. He kisses me with a need that makes my throat tighten, then rests his forehead against mine. "I wish I could stay."

Biting my lip again, hard, I try to keep my tears at bay. I'm afraid to even breathe for fear of shattering. "You're busy," I say with as much nonchalance as I'm able to muster. "I should get some things done as well."

He holds onto my face, the bullshit meter firing off in his eyes, but he doesn't call me out. Instead, his thumbs stroke my cheeks. "I'll miss you," he whispers.

I'm going to sob. It struggles to break from my chest. I jerk away as if Alex's fingers have burned me and walk out the bedroom door, but he swings me around again to face him.

"Dammit. Lula, talk to me. After all of that, tell me what you're thinking."

My throat constricts, blocking speech. My lip will bleed if I don't let up, but it's keeping me from turning into a sobbing puddle of siren. 'Goodbye' is such a simple word. I say it to my sisters all the time. The meaning here is different. It's heavy and final. The thoughts swirling inside me are conflicting tornados, a steady one built of reality, and a dangerous one structured of hope. They shred my heart as they battle each other for more space.

Alex releases me, fisting his hands at his sides as he takes a deep breath. "I wish I could get inside that head of yours. I have to go."

There's a coldness to him I haven't seen before. I'm responsible for that, but we're not meant to be, no matter how much I want him. He storms from the room, leaving a wall of tension behind. Each stomp away reverberates through me like an electric shock. As soon the front door squeaks open, I panic.

Even if we have to part, I owe him as much of an explanation as I can give. If he never comes back—

I can't get down the stairs fast enough. "Alex, wait!" I throw the door open and sprint onto my front lawn.

He's gone. Too late.

I cover my sob and walk inside, wandering in a fog to the kitchen. Breathing is hard with the tight itch in my chest and throat. What if he deletes me like I did him? Blocks me and disappears back to Olympus. I should regret letting him into my house after I tried to push him away, but it would be a lie. I'd let him in over and over no matter how much this hurts. Something is wrong with me. I need to clear my system of him. I grab a cup of water.

Some things cannot be. I'll never have him or any real relationship. It's the way of the siren.

After taking a sip from the glass, I throw it against the wall, the spot between pictures and cabinets. It shatters with a rejuvenating crash, sending water and shards flying. I drop to the floor in a pile, curl on my side, and let the tears fall.

This is for the better. I've been alone most of my life, and because of that I now depend on Alex. It isn't fair for either of us. If he doesn't come back, the mystic force binding me to him will lessen. I'll get over him.

That's a lie. There's no getting over my golden god.

A faint knock on the door sounds miles away. If it's Alex, he shouldn't see me like this. I try to calm, but my breath comes in pants and my eyes won't stop leaking. I cover my mouth to quiet myself. *Just go, whoever you are.*

A dark mist forms in my foyer. *Oh shit.*

Rath exudes anger as he spins around. His fierce expression melts to confusion, complete with a head tilt.

"Go, please." I turn from my side to my back and hide my face with both hands.

Heavy boot steps sound on the hardwood. "What the hell happened?"

Deities need to work on their listening skills.

"Why are you here?" I say, not even sure my words are coherent.

He takes my wrists and uncovers my face. Confusion slides right into piteous pinched-face concern. "Because you're jerking my friend around and he won't talk about it, but now I'm not sure what's happening." Sitting on the floor next to me, he tugs at my hand until I sit up, then loops an arm around me and holds me against his side. He smells like warm amber and cinnamon sugar. I hug his bicep and wheeze snotty breaths. Fading would be a good ability. I could use that at the moment. "Talk to me," he says in a gentle whisper. The last being I expected comfort from was Rath. He's an odd creature, a predator that cuddles instead of biting an arm off like he's expected to.

I take a few choppy gasps to find my voice. "What do you want me to say? Alex's mystical juju has me acting like a crazy person? Just go while this wears off."

I try to push away from him, but he only allows me far enough to give me a *Lula's nuts* expression. "What in the hell are you talking about?"

"It's a deity thing, right? You get someone hooked on you. Pheromones. They're probably in your fluids. Your saliva, blood, other...stuff."

"What? No." His eyes dart around the room. "Did you take something? Drugs of some kind?"

I bark a laugh. "No. The only drug I'm taking is an almost daily dose of Alex. Get my fix every time I'm near him. Then today..." My face heats with a flush and I lean back into his arm, so I don't have to look at him.

He squeezes me, then scoots away a foot. He's crossed-legged and facing me, somehow folding his tall frame into something smaller and less intimidating. "Wait. You believe there's a substance in Alex that's like a drug? Addictive?"

"Of course I do. When he leaves, I crash—go through withdrawal. There's no other explanation." He stares at me until I grow uncomfortable. "I'm not kidding, Rath. You get someone hooked, so they'll worship you. Hell, it's probably a physiological evolution you have no control over. Alex told me that gods and humans are symbiotic. This pheromone attachment is an adaptation to keep the connection, right? You come in contact, and the bond gets stronger. If I got close to you as I do with Alex, I bet the same thing would happen."

He leans closer to me. "Wanna test that theory?"

"No, you ass." I shove his shoulder and glare. "Gross."

"Gross?" He gasps in shock. "Getting close to me would be gross? Wait. What did you two do?" He raises an eyebrow.

"None of your business. Not sex." I mean... so yeah, in a way it was, but it wasn't *the sex* or anything. I bring my gaze down from contemplating the ceiling to Rath's beaming blues and wince. "Shut up."

"Oh, wow." He chuckles, then clears his throat. "I have bad news." My stomach drops to the floor at his serious expression. Is

Alex in danger? "We don't exude any mystical bonding pheromones."

No, that can't be right. "You have to. This..." I wave my hand at the disaster that is myself. "Is not me. I don't do this. I'm an addict."

"Do you think you may just love him?"

That's not possible for us. He's said it. Amah has said it. "No. It's pheromones."

"Lula, I swear upon the realm that there's no mystic *juju* tying you to Alex. Do you like spending time with him?"

I shift and hug my knees to my chest. "Yes."

"And you like who he is as a person."

He's wonderful. As perfect as they come. "I think he's a good person—deity. He's kind and makes me laugh."

"Yeah, he is." Turning his head, he looks at the floor. "It's tough, isn't it? Every time they leave, you're ripped apart from the inside out." His voice grows low and scratchy. "And when they're out of your sight, part of you is missing." He's experienced this before.

"It's a pain you'd do over and over again." I would too if it weren't so dangerous.

"For millennia if need be."

Tears springing to my eyes again, I touch Rath's arm, and he straightens, intensity returning.

"I never thought—" Rath rubs a palm over his mouth then drops it to his thigh. "You need to tell him."

"I can't." My words come out in spurts of excuses. "He's a divine being. Thousands of years old. I'm a siren. A young one. Being with him is impossible, so there's no point in telling him how I feel. Whatever that is. His grandfather is freaking Zeus. He's betrothed."

"He told you about Ichnaea?"

Ah, getting a name is a different experience than, *The Betrothed*. I ball my fists and close my eyes. "He didn't tell me her name."

"He doesn't love her like that, and she's..." Rath trails off, lips pursed in thought.

"She's?" I ask. My stomach rolls knowing Alex may be with her one day. He has talked about the Council and their demands of gods and goddesses. What if that's a requirement? Oh, and *love her like that*? What does that—

"She's not interested in him."

Sure, she's not. If I had the opportunity to marry Alex I certainly wouldn't wait two hundred years. Especially if other gods like Deimos and Ares are taking or bidding on goddesses. Hell with that. Take me to the altar with a sweet, honest golden god.

"That doesn't mean they won't end up together, Rath. I've studied the lore of the divine, the culture. My place isn't with Alex."

Rath takes my hand and unfurls my clenched fist. "What are you going to do?" He sounds so kind as he massages my tight fingers.

"There's nothing to do," I say, choking on the truth. "The way is unchangeable."

He looks like he's battling with words—pursing his lips again and bobbing his head side to side as if weighing his thoughts before the moment stops and his eyes find mine again. "I'm sorry, Lula."

"Then you understand it's better if I break from him." I sob, pulling from his grip to cover my mouth.

Rath stands and offers a hand to me. "You know, definitive timeframes are a mortal trait. We have time on our hands." He pulls me up, surprising me with a hug, resting his chin on the top of my head. He doesn't rub my back or seem like he has ulterior motives to the touch—only holds me in calm silence until the tears slow and I can breathe again. He steps away and gives my fingers a squeeze. "I'm happy he met you, Lu. You've given him a taste of heaven far beyond Olympus."

His body fades to shadow and I wipe my face. I'm glad I met Alex too, but we're unable to stay around each other. I'd never forgive myself if something happened to him or my sisters because I can't keep my hands off a deity, and I'm not convinced there's no mystical influence reigning over my emotions.

I take a deep breath. Instead of a depressed Venora in times of breakups, I'm going to pull a fun Grace. I drag my phone from my back pocket. She texted me, but I had silenced my calls. *Oh how I'd love to see you in person, but you know what Mamma Amah says. One day. You okay?*

Not really, I write. *Want to do a virtual out-on-the-town night?*

Her response is immediate. *What happened? Alex?*

She knows me well.

Chapter Twenty

ALEX

"Share time," Rath says, sipping a mug of coffee. He crosses his arms and studies me. "We won't live through another day of your brooding. Spill it."

That's a turnaround, though everything's been upside down lately. The meeting with the Council lasted long past sundown. They dragged us in as if we were part of them, and Zeus even dismissed Ares when he suggested we start a war in retaliation to the human murders. *Fight death with more death to show it's not getting to us.* Only Ares. As much as the Council wants to deny it, the divine have a strong bond with the mortals, and losing them hurts us all.

I rub my face, working out the grogginess of a brief night, tossing and turning, head full of unwanted knowledge, and my arms empty. The time zone switch from Lula's place to Olympus is getting to me. "I shouldn't see Lula anymore," I tell the guys. "Leaving her is...too much. She's made me into the weak link and literal lives are riding on the line. I can't screw this up."

"Yeah, but she's an imperative link in our grand scheme," Comus says, tapping his thumb against the marble kitchen table in his Olympus home. We've been at the Council's beck and call and he's been holding everything together while I've been either with or thinking about Lula.

"Like he could stay away." Rath blows a double smoke ring.

I set my elbows on the table and glare at him. "This coming from the guy who told me a few days ago that I should take some repair time because she's sucking all my brain cells out through my cock. When she wasn't." They don't need to know more.

Leaning forward, Rath raises an eyebrow, then smirks that teasing smile of his. "Oh, it's like that, huh?"

I ball my fists.

"Wow, Alex" He chuckles. "I haven't seen your battle face in a long time. You should head back to Lu's. Work out more of that pent-up energy."

Now is not the time to push my buttons. He knows better than anyone how worked up she gets me and what can't happen between us. Artemis isn't receptive to Rath like Lula is to me. She teeters back and forth, too sick in the head with Olympian expectation and guilt to let things progress between them. Lula wants me as much as I want her. That's clear now.

Has Rath changed his stance? Does he want me to skirt town, get lost with Lula, and abandon everything we've worked for? Even then, the Council would find us and probably sooner than later.

No, he's just being an ass, as usual.

But his poking makes the part of me that wants Lula—wants the ability to choose to be with her—stand up and shove the side of me that says, *give up hope*. I run my hands over my face and growl into my palms before slapping them against the table. "Shit, who am I kidding? Jackass is right. Staying away from her is impossible. I have to break the betrothal. We have to make the Council see their wrongdoing and tempt them out of this realm."

Comus's lips tighten. "Not yet."

Rath approaches and sits but scoots his chair out of punching proximity. "The most high-power human-made microscope wouldn't help their vision."

"Are you losing hope, brother?" Comus leans and squeezes Rath's shoulder. "It's a daunting task but someone's got to tackle the tornado. For the sake of humanity and all."

"And so Alex can ride off into the sunset with Lula riding him."

My attributes buzz for attention. The tug to an impending event is getting stronger. With a deep breath, I close my eyes and let the mystic force run over me in waves of tingling, warm power. Visions of a grassy field on a cloudy day pop in flashes through my mind, but the crowd is blurred, the players unfaced. It's closer though. Any minute.

We've been waiting for another event, hoping to stop one and find out more. Are the human deaths occurring from the sirens or is there a new siren-otherworldling hybrid?

I tried to bring Lula's sister up again, but she still avoids the conversation. Then, after what happened between us, there was something wrong, and she won't talk to me about it. She's pulling away and I need to think. The only thing left to do is to tell her everything and hope she doesn't banish me from her life. She may.

A blotchy mountain range behind a line of deciduous trees circles a group. It's an impressionistic watercolor painting in my mind. The picture wavers, sharp to blurry, a camera trying to find the focal point. A crowd bigger than the scope I'm given walks in lines on a dusty road—an army, except in plain modern clothes. No weapons as far as I can tell. Mostly golden hair, some dark, a few silver. A mix of skin color. A child.

The slide of a chair across marble makes me open my eyes.

"Your attribute?" Comus asks.

"Yeah." I focus, grasping at a location. *Where are you? America? Europe?* Little skirmishes are everywhere, always have been, but something big is brewing—something that could lead to a world war or, for all I know, universal conflict. The field keeps coming back to the forefront of my vision.

My forehead dapples with sweat. The blurry apparition clears enough for me to hone in on the place. It's not a name. I couldn't say the latitude and longitude. We link as if both the event and I were swirling through space and our orbits finally spun into the same location at the same time. My palm itches to open a portal.

I stumble to stand with a jolt of impatience surging through me. "It's time."

"We're coming," Rath says, getting to his feet.

Why bother deterring them? They should get a first-hand view, and I don't want to be alone in this. I have an overwhelming sense that darkness is tied to this, whether it's because of the link to Lula or something else. There's only one way to find out.

I walk to an open area of the room. Closing my eyes, I concentrate on the spot my attribute is showing me and seek a clear drop-in point. The trick to Earth portal travel is not landing in the middle of a crowd of humans. They tend to frown on people popping out of thin air. However, with the invention of television and special effects, if I land amongst them, they think they're imagining things and usually give me an odd once over, then disperse.

Pinpointing a spot masked with trees, I raise my hand. Current runs from my mind to my palm, and the air ripples around my fingers. I push it aside like a curtain and step through with Comus and Rath on my heels.

"When we get back, we need to talk about Lula," Rath tells me.

I glance at him in question, but as we walk between a sparse patch of scraggly pines, a feminine voice pulls my attention. My chest seizes tight.

"Oh, shit," Comus says because he understands as well.

Rath shadows out and re-emerges in another grouping of trees a hundred feet away. He's next to a rocky cliff, looks down, then back at us with a pained expression. He pivots to the action and links his fingers behind his neck. Comus and I rush to Rath's position, halting right at the edge, which turns out to be a steep hill.

I've heard the song before, but in a different voice. It's a mesmerizing cadence of ancient words so beautiful it's easy to forget its devastating effect. A hundred feet away, a mass of humans writhes on the ground. Their last breaths morph to wet, liquid wheezes. Crimson overtakes the shades of skin and clothing colors.

My stomach lurches. I scan the mess for my brother but he's not nearby. Either I pinpointed the spot first, or he's informing the Council.

Comus kneels and tents his hands over his mouth. "There are hundreds."

In the center of the crowd, a red-headed man cups the face of a stunning blonde woman. His features are blocked from the ways he's turned, but the pair resembles lovers as he strokes her cheeks. The siren is no hybrid monster, but not a sister we've met. Her pained expression reminds me of Lula's when she sang at me. As though the song is pure torture to the one singing it.

The man is the problem. He's controlling her and isn't affected. A deity? Maybe a hybrid that somehow escaped Zeus's wrath?

The song halts with a sob. Wrapping her arms around her thin waist, she crumples forward, but he holds her firmly in place.

In the utter silence of the field, her whimper reaches me. "Please, don't make me sing again."

"I have not yet received my wants. You hath—have," he says, annunciating the *V*. "—failed to help me and therefore my hand has been forced again." The man's voice is familiar, the accent unique and old, but I can't grasp where I've heard it. He releases her face. "However, with our new arrival, the time to retire you is near."

Her wet eyes contort to terrified as he grasps her wrist and weaves his way through the gruesome slurry of bodies, dragging her along.

Comus and I launch ourselves down the steep hill, sliding and leaping to reach the bottom. We both pause at the edge of the carnage. The siren struggles to keep up through the grime when Rath arrives in front of the two, bunched fists eager for a fight.

Laughter laced with malice makes my skin crawl and my hair stand on end. An enemy of old stands on Earth again, and there's no way this could be. Comus's wide eyes tell me I didn't imagine that familiar laugh.

Rath steps toward them, but as I shout, "Wait!" the man—god grabs Rath by the neck and throws him twenty feet to the left like he weighs nothing. Rath lands with a grunt and rolls on grass, flopping over a rock, as he grasps at his throat.

Moros turns and his black eyes narrow as they meet mine.

My blood seems to slow, though my heart speeds as surrealness engulfs me. It's been almost two-hundred-years, and our parting wasn't pleasant. The God of Doom is the last person I expected to see since Anice and I trapped him in the hell realm and two of us must work together to open a universe portal. Unless my father and Anice have been sneaking around, which they wouldn't, there's no explanation as to why he's here.

Moros flashes a wicked grin and grips the siren's arm with his deadly hand as he backs them away. "You are who they send to welcome me home? Oh, and the child. How disappointing. Attend to your comrade, Alexiares, and do not follow unless you wish to join him. I will see you again soon enough." He continues his path through the sludge with the siren dragging behind, staring at us pleadingly.

Comus runs toward Rath. "Let her go, Moros," I yell, following. That's Lula's sister.

Moros doesn't slow but calls over his shoulder, "Not until I have what I want."

"And what's that?" Taking him on by myself is suicide. I need Anice, and as much as I hate to admit it, the Council too. He's unkillable—a primordial fate that refused to exit when the others of his age set out for new universes, understanding that their span here was complete when the Olympians defeated them.

He laughs his deep, cawing cackles. "The realm at my feet."

Comus calls for me. "Alex, we need a portal."

"Ah, ah, Alexiares," Moros says with a grin as I take another step forward. "In the name of warfare, we call a truce for now."

"Release her." I eye the siren. She has blonde hair and pleading blue eyes. She trembles and shakes her head at me in warning. Does she want to stay with him? "Moros, let her go."

"Your boy is dying. He doesn't have long. Tick-tock, child." He clucks his tongue in a clock sound. He joggles the siren. "This one will be taken care of until we meet again. Go. I don't care to kill you just yet." His smile turns to a firm scowl.

"Alex!" Comus's voice holds a desperation I've never heard.

I growl and run toward Rath. He seizes among what's left of the bodies, struggling to breathe, his throat black from Moros' deadly touch. Comus picks up Rath's flailing body and positions him on his shoulder. "Portal now. To the healers."

Moros shoves the siren into a blue car parked behind a tree and glares at me before getting into the driver's seat. As soon as the portal is open, Comus sprints through. With a knot in my throat, I take one last look at the carnage seeping into the ground, and the plume of dust from Moros's exit before stepping through.

I have to get to Lula before someone else does.

As I close the portal, separating the event from the healer's temple,

Anice's wife, Iaso, already works on Rath. An umber curl bounces in her face, escaped from under a gauzy cloth ribbon. She can lift men, reset bones, or tug spears from flesh, but her hands waltz over Rath in delicate patterns, exploring the extent of his injuries.

He lies on a white cushioned cot, pallid, with a look of terror I know too well in his eyes. I swallow back my worry for him while he gasps for air. My panic is the last thing he needs to see. A gray-tinged mark spreads outward across his fair skin from the contact site.

"It's okay," Comus says, struggling to hold him down while Iaso works her attributes. "You're in the hands of the healers."

Iaso glances at me with an expression of pure terror. Her fear is warranted. She's familiar with Moros's devastating touch. I nod at her. *Yeah, it's him.* The flicker of hope, as if this was a mistake she misread, snuffs out of her chestnut eyes.

She calls an awaiting servant. "Travel to Asclepius and tell him we have a wound of Moros. Find my husband, then our king. Go in haste." She wants Anice over the king. That is daring and will give them a moment to regroup before Zeus arrives.

The servant speeds away through the open archway and Iaso focuses on Rath while addressing us. "How?" She lights a bundle of herbs, running her fingers through the smoke before settling them on Rath's neck.

"He's back," I say, pinning Rath's forehead with my fingers to hold him still. He relaxes with a grunt and I pull my attention to Iaso. "He's back and conducting the mass deaths of humans."

Comus faces me with wild, wet eyes. "Go." He mouths, *South.*

Lu should be safe at the Belize house, at least for a while. We'll move her around if we have to. What in the hell is Moros doing with a siren? The species is an otherworldling created in Olympus, like the nymphs and legendary half creatures; centaurs, minotaurs, and satyrs, but the sirens were the only ones cursed and sent to Earth. Does Moros know why?

I stroke Rath's sweaty forehead with my thumb, unsure if he's even aware of it. His skin is a pale gray and his eyes close. What would I do if this were to be the last time I saw him? *My brother.* My beastly, brilliant, reckless brother.

"He'll make it, Alex," Comus whispers.

The knot in my throat is painful. I try to swallow it down but it sticks and makes my jaw tight. I bend to touch my forehead to Rath's. I don't like the chill of his skin. "You will get through this. You can't let one primordial being take you out. Don't be that guy."

Comus gives a watery chuckle. "Yeah, that's too easy a demise for you, brother. You need flames and bountiful women clutching their pearls."

"That's right," I say. Rath's lips twitch into a pained grin. Good, he hears. "Fight hard, asshole, and come back to us soon." I stand and squeeze Comus's shoulder. "Call me if anything changes."

"Anice will find you," Iaso says, peeking at me from under her lashes. How much has my brother told her since he came home?

"Thank you," I tell her and mean it. She is a talented medic. A bored one as we have few injuries, but she's quick-thinking and empathetic. I see her in a new light now that I understand more about her and my brother's situation. If Anice has entrusted her with our plan, she's with us.

Down the hall is an empty room. I portal to a remote location in France just to have a buffer, then to Lula's yard.

After closing the shroud between realms, I bang on the front door. It's dark with no lights on in her home. Pulling my phone out, I dial her, then knock again as I wait through the rings. No answer. My muscles threaten to shatter with the tension coursing through me.

The evening is silent, highlighted by a full moon high in the sky. I open a portal and step into the kitchen. "Lula?" Turning on a light, I search each room as I consider the situation.

Moros, the bringer of destined doom, has returned. Anice and I threw him into the hell realm hundreds of years ago. How in the hell did he find his way back? This does not bode well. Did the break between Olympus and Earth cause a weak point somewhere else?

I text Lula, fumbling with what to say to make her contact me. I'm still irritated that she wouldn't tell me what was wrong when something so clearly was, but that doesn't matter anymore. It seems silly now.

After three attempts I settle on a generic plea. *Please call me and let me know you're safe.*

If anything happens to her. Tendrils of insanity touch my mind, ripping out any trace of rational behavior.

I run my hands through my hair and open a portal to Comus's living room. Zeus will hit the roof with the news that Moros has returned and is using a siren as a murder weapon. I should be there so he doesn't get suspicious. He knows we've been in contact with the otherworldling species, and he's impatient for answers. Moros is a deadly wrench we do not need to be thrown into our plans.

After what will probably be another Council meeting or four, I'll grab Lula, hide her away, and somehow explain that she should be on our side when this crashes down. I should have told her everything before now. Sharing the plan while telling her that her sister is responsible for the deaths of at least a thousand people over the last two weeks isn't going to be easy.

Chapter Twenty-One

LULA

On stilettos, I stagger to my hotel room and pause at the door. The trio of brutes behind me halts. They approached me at the bar where I took care of their tab and whispered my demands. They danced with me and Grace via a muted video conference all night and kept everyone else at bay. My battery died hours ago, and I wonder if Grace is just as tanked as I am. I bite my lips together to keep from cackling and only make a nasally, unflattering snort.

Swinging around, I give a pout lip and wave. "Go home," I whisper-slur. Well, it's whisperish. It's definitely slurish.

My three devoted bodyguards turn and walk toward the elevator. They were helpful this evening—a safe distraction. After Rath left, I pulled myself together, cleaned my house, packed a bag, and drove to the city. Then I got drunk and danced all night. Only two fights broke out over me this time, so I call that a win.

I burst out in giggles, slap my hand over my mouth, and slide the key card in the lock slot. I slap the handle and nearly face plant when the door swings open, only catching myself by grabbing the doorframe of the bathroom door. The door slams behind me, thank goodness. Keeping my lips covered, I peek out the peephole. It's hard to see through it with my body swaying, but I manage to catch a glimpse of several people wandering the hallway searching for the source of the giggle.

"It was me!" I whisper into my hand.

I bite my lip to shush myself and dance through the hotel room. Alex would love my dance. It's all hips and wiggles, and there's a spin in it. Snagging the bottom of my dress, I tug while continuing to gyrate. He'd think my sexy dance is the greatest. I kick off a shoe. He wouldn't like me taking off these gemmy, thick-heeled sandals though. They're all sparkles and a little extra height so I can reach his lips better. He loves it when I wear heels. Well, when I show off my legs, which I do often because it's summer. That gleam of want in his eye the first night I met him as he looked me over. Mmm. And then at the farmers' mark—

Dammit.

Apparently, getting out of town and shitfaced is not a cure for my Alex addiction. I'll keep dancing, though. At least I'm not crying anymore. Lacing my hands over my head, I twerk my ass.

I guard my giggling mouth with my hand again. I need to shut the hell up, or I'm going to have a lot of unwanted company.

Showering is a struggle. Everything is slippery, from the little bottle of shampoo to the temperature handle. I waver on my feet and accidentally flip it to ice-cold for the second time, then cover my mouth to keep from screaming at the jets of ice pelting me. But I'm soapy, and I spend a good couple of minutes sputtering suds while adjusting the handle and dunking my face in the now too-warm water. There's nothing sexy about me at the moment. This is what Alex should see. Then he'd realize there's no reason to want a creature such as myself. Not that he wants me anymore after the way I acted.

Keeping a hand on the tiles for stability, I focus on the near-scalding water and try to push the thoughts of him away, but it's useless. I need sleep.

I plug in my phone, toss it in the bedside drawer, then flop into bed, hoping to pass out so I don't spend the rest of the night—morning—conjuring up Alex. Would he have danced with me tonight? Spun me around and growled at my bodyguards? Taken me in his warm arms and cupped the back of my head, directing my gaze to his? I'd have slipped my fingers in his hair, rolled against him, and nibbled those biceps all night. No, blacking out is what—

My stomach lurches me into consciousness, and I launch myself out from underneath inferno-hot covers. I stand still in the spinning hotel room, arms out for balance. My heart is beating a hyper pace, so fast, it hurts. I'm going to barf.

Sprinting for the bathroom, I crash in front of the toilet in time to spew the remains of a night well spent. My head throbs, and my mind races as if trying to outrun an unseen, unfightable danger. I'm chased, trapped, and dead all in a millisecond. *Slow down, Please.*

Something's wrong.

I throw up again, spit, and try to get a handle on the panic coursing through me. It's not my stomach that's upset. It's everything.

Scooping water from the faucet with my hands, I swish out my mouth, then splash my face. There's only one of me in the mirror. A pale, wild-eyed me, but the room doesn't spin. I'm sober.

Icy dread replaces nausea in my gut and spreads through my body until it envelops my limbs, leaving my fingers tingling. No, this cannot be happening. *Not this.* My heartbeat pounds in my ears until it blocks out all other sounds.

"No, no, no," I whimper, over and over again as I clutch at my chest. It hurts. No, the pain is more than that. It's agony—a living fire ripping through me and burning away a piece of my soul. I've experienced this one other, dread-filled time in my life. Part of me is missing. *My sister.* One of my sisters is dead.

Choking on tears, I stumble around the room to find my phone and push the button to start it. The moment it's up and running, it rings. When I answer, Amah sobs, "Thank the gods. Call Hazel and Grace."

"I love you, Amah." I hope she understands my words.

"And I, you, Lula my dearest."

We hang up, and I dial Grace. She answers with a gasping sob.

"I love you, Grace, my sister."

"And I, you, my sister."

With blurred vision, I dial Hazel. One, two, three rings. *No.* Four, five, and six. *Please, no.* When her voicemail picks up, I end the call and text Amah, *Grace is okay.*

I try Hazel once more. A loud sob breaks free from my throat on ring four. I hang up and stare at my phone. I want Alex. He needs to tell me this will be okay. Leaning with my forehead against the wall, I dial Hazel again and once more after that.

A text message pops on the screen from Amah, *Guene, and Nysa are fine. Hazel?*

A slew of other past messages floods my phone now that it's on.

She's not picking up, I type back with shaking fingers. Cold loss is settling in, sending me into teeth-chattering tremors.

Gerty is still unreachable as is Venora, Amah writes.

Redialing Hazel, I curl up on the bed as it goes to voicemail. I sniffle in the silence. "Please call me. I love you, Hazel."

I check my other messages. There are eleven unread texts from Alex. In the first few, he wants to be sure I'm safe. Then they become more desperate. *I just need to talk. I'm sorry I upset you. Forgive me and let me know you're okay.*

I stop reading at seven and open his contact. The pain in my chest is excruciating, and I try to calm myself to no avail. It doesn't matter. I need his voice to know he's out there, alive and strong. I press the button and hold my breath.

In the middle of one ring, Alex answers. "Lula, where are you?"

Hearing his voice speeds up my world's tailspin. I need his arms around me more than anything I've ever wanted. Forming words through tear-laden gasps is impossible. It's just wet garble.

"What happened?" he asks with a panicked tone, making me cry even harder. "Are you hurt?"

My throat seizes up, and I choke out the words, "My...sister."

Alex breathes like he's trying to calm down but fails and grows frantic. "Are you back home?"

"Nnn-no." I take in deep breaths, hoping to become capable of speech.

"Baby, where are you?" His words come faster. "Tell me, please."

I blow out a lengthy breath but it doesn't do much to calm me. I rub at my chest, right over my heart. "Hotel on Eighth. Downtown."

I stumble through the words and my teeth chatter, but they make sense.

"Okay, listen. Lula, are you listening?"

I mumble a hum of affirmation.

"Can you get outside and stand in a dark, open space? A courtyard?"

"Y-Yes."

"Go there, now. I'm going to hang up. If another number calls you, it's Comus. You can trust him. Are you walking?"

I start for the door. "Mmhm."

The line clicks off, and I'm left alone again with a burning hole in my chest. I glance down the tee I'm wearing to be sure there isn't a gaping hollow, but my skin is fine. Was it this bad when Lena died? It was a hundred-and-sixty-years ago but that kind of pain is memorable. It burned for days. Being in it is different though. Who was it this time? Why is this happening?

I clutch my phone and keycard in my hand and walk into the hall on shaky legs. The lights are too bright, and nausea returns.

A woman steps out into the hallway with an ice bucket and freezes at the sight of me.

"You don't need ice," I command through sobbing. "Go back inside."

She must understand because she walks backward, and the door shuts.

I make it to the elevator and smack the first-floor button with my palm. My face is soaked, and I cover it with both hands and lean against the cold wall, allowing more tears to escape in sobbing gasps. When the ding sounds on the first floor, my wails won't cease. I stumble into the lobby where two attendants check in three men in suits. All eyes widen, and they move toward me in unison.

Walking backward, I trying to tell them to forget me, but they don't understand. As one reaches for me, my back hits a wall. "Go to sleep!"

All five of them lie on the ground and close their eyes. That will draw attention, but I can't do anything to fix it now.

I bite my lip, cover my mouth, and hold my breath to remain in control of my voice as I sneak down the hall. My lungs itch and burn, twitch like inflated balloons that landed in a briar bush, but the thorns aren't sharp enough to puncture, just enough to make me wish they would. I stumble out of a back door, gasp for air, and walk barefoot on grass. Two brick walls and a line of trees surround the courtyard.

    The bright glow from an overhead streetlamp hits me like a spotlight in the night. I clutch at the hem of the shirt I'm wearing, tugging it further down my bare legs. I've never been more on display, yet frightfully alone.

Chapter Twenty-Two

ALEX

"Don't try this, Alex." Comus grabs my arm and swings me to face him. "Who knows where the hell you'll end up."

Shoving him off of me, I concentrate. Panic is an overwhelming undertow that's drowning me with its strength. She's so upset she can't speak. She was missing for hours. Every twisted scenario imaginable has slithered through my brain in that time—Moros's hand around her throat, Zeus lighting her up over and over again until she's a complacent shell, duct tape over her mouth at the whim of a group of humans who realize what she is.

She's immortal but not invincible. I need her in my arms before I lose my mind.

As Comus grips my shoulder, I stare him down, daring him to continue deterring me. His jaw clenches tight and lifts. "I'm right."

"Lula's in danger. Something happened and she's so upset, she can't even tell me. If I portal to one of the places I've been before, it will take too long to reach her."

"Your attribute doesn't work this way. If you end up at the bottom of the ocean, it will take you a lot longer." I scowl, and Comus sighs. "You need a point, brother. Whether it be your pull to war or a familiar location. Attempt this, and you could wind up anywhere."

I open my arms to him. "I know *her*. She'll be my point."

"Consider what you are doing, Alex. You've known her a mere two moons."

"That's not quite true, is it?" It may be almost two months since I kissed her, but I've known her heart for much longer.

Comus studies me a moment, then takes a step back. "Okay. I hope to gods this works."

"It will." *It has to.*

I focus on Lula. Her hair, her smell, every inch of her curves from each angle. I envision her smile and picture myself a few feet from her to view her body. The veil is there, a tingling sheet in front of my face. I swipe my hand through it, and it parts with silken ease. Breath held, I push the rip aside. I brace for the worst and step on the lawn of a dark courtyard, hoping like hell I'm where I need to be.

A choking sob from behind spins me around.

Lula.

She's in my blue t-shirt. The one I left at her house accidentally on purpose. It hangs off her shoulder and falls mid-thigh, looking a thousand times better than it ever has on me. Seeing her in it makes a place deep inside me roar with satisfaction, but the pride is short-lived. Her face is blotchy, eyes puffed and red. The tear tracks down her cheeks make my heart seize. What hell has she been through?

As she locks her gaze with mine, what's left of her thin composure crumbles. Her face pinches tight and each pained gasp makes my skin flinch. The ten feet between us spans a mile.

The moment I embrace her, she buckles. I lift her against me, and she wraps her arms around my neck, holding on to the point of pain as if she could never get close enough—clinging to me like I'm a raft in her sea of dismay.

This shouldn't make me happy. Not when she's breaking in front of me, but I can't help it. I want to be this for her—the one she comes to for comfort. It's an honor to be her chosen protector and I'm more than willing to own that role.

I hold her tight and make quiet shushing sounds. "It's okay, Firecracker. I've got you."

Comus approaches, glancing around the tree line of the

courtyard, then up the brick walls to the lines of dark windows. He locks eyes with me. "All clear." I crinkle my nose, glad we don't have an audience, but disappointed in myself that I'd been too preoccupied to notice. "Close the portal," he says.

I take a few steps back, shift Lula enough to hold her with one arm, and swish the opening closed. I massage her wild curls and she sobs in shaking hiccups against my neck. We need to get out of here before someone notices us.

Comus reads my mind. "Get her inside."

I duck my head to whisper against her ear. "What room?"

"Two-oh-seven," she whimpers. Rage and concern flood through me. Whatever did this to her will pay, but I'll exact my revenge with her in my arms because I'm never letting her go.

After Comus pulls a key card and phone from Lula's tight grip, he squeezes her empty hand in his. She latches on, and I share a pained look with my friend. I'm not sure how she knows her sister is with Moros, but there's no way we're getting anything out of her until she rides this breakdown out.

Comus opens doors, and we travel to the elevator. Humans lie on the floor of the lobby, curled up or sprawled, eyes closed. There's no blood.

Lula lifts her head off my shoulder. "Wake and resume your business." Her voice is shaky, but her words are clear now.

The people open their eyes and stand, walking to the desk.

"Whoa," Comus says as we board the elevator.

Once in Lula's hotel room, I sit on the bed, refusing to relinquish my hold. She takes in sharp sucking breaths. I kiss her forehead, then her temple and cheek. "I've got you."

Her buzzing phone in Comus's hand brings her head off my shoulder.

Comus looks at the device. "Amah says 'Still no word from Gerty or Venora. Hazel?'"

She crumples again and reaches out for the phone. When Comus hands it over, she dials and lifts it to her ear. After the fourth faint ring, she's back to sobbing.

As Comus takes the phone, he glares at it like it's the source of the agony plaguing Lula. "Want me to respond?"

She nods. "No w-word from Hazel."

He types, and I tilt her trembling chin up. "What happened?"

"One of my sisters died tonight." Her voice wavers, but her words are painfully clear.

I shoot a glance at Comus who closes his eyes, shoulders dropping in a heavy exhale. It couldn't have been the siren Moros had, right? I shouldn't have left her. I should have called in my brother and Olympus as I followed them everywhere. Then Rath would have died. He nearly did.

"Hazel?" I ask.

The shrug she makes is a tense body jerk. "We can't get a hold of Hazel, Gerty, or Venora."

"How do you know one died?"

She clutches the shirt over her heart. "Because we're connected. A soul left mine. It...hurts."

Damn, that's rough. What asshole deity cursed the sirens with that gem? I rock us back and forth, nuzzling her cheek with my nose, inhaling her.

Comus leans and pushes her hair out of her face. "I'm so sorry, Lu. We're getting you out of here, okay?"

She sniffles. "Where are we going?"

"Somewhere safe and warm," Comus says. Belize will be good. The seclusion will help ease my mind. There are too many people here.

"I can go home."

His mouth settles into a tight line. "No. Not tonight."

She sits up in my arms. "Why? What's wrong?"

I pull her close again, hand splayed over her back. "I'll explain in a bit. Let's get you out of here first."

Lula stiffens, pushes away, and turns her piercing green eyes on me. Even in heartbreak, her fiery side makes itself known. "Tell me," she says, her tone firm.

I tuck a wayward strand of red behind her ear. "You may be in danger. I swear we'll explain, but we need to take you to a safe place first. Will you trust us to do that?"

She bites her lip and nods.

"Okay. Let's get you packed."

Lula stands and grabs folded black cloth from an open bag on the dresser, then zips it closed. Glancing at Comus, she spins her hand in the air, signaling him to turn around. He does. I'd been right about the lack of shorts underneath the t-shirt.

After slipping into the pants, Lula walks across the room and picks up a shoe by a heel covered in crystals, searches, then beelines the way she came to grab the other. She returns to the bag, stuffs the heels in a side pocket, and turns to me.

"Okay. Let's go."

"That's it?" A goddess would have three servants packing up a wardrobe of fabric, makeup, hair bobbles, and jewels.

"I travel light."

There's no amusement in her tone, and I long for it. She's been through so much already, more bad news is the last thing she needs.

I take Lula's hand and open a portal to the kitchen in Belize.

Comus turns on a few lights. "I'll do a sweep." He goes through the archway toward the stairs. The maid service we use has been by recently for the once a month rounds. Pineapple air freshener scents the house—not my favorite, but there are worse things. It will clear out with new activity and smell like sand and salt again. I love it here.

"Where are we?" she asks.

"Belize."

She glances around, then steps forward to study the abandoned oars Rath collected from all over the world and mounted on the wall between the kitchen and hallway to the mudroom. Which of the fifteen will be her favorite? Mine is the one Rath brought back from Greenland. It's not Viking-ship big, but the pitted, petrified oak has to be from that era.

I wish we were here in a happier situation. Does she like the beach? The property is beachfront on a secluded peninsula. The closest neighbor is a half-mile away and separated by palms and scrub bushes. The only thing we can see outside at the moment though is dark water, the silhouette of the covered dock, and sand highlighted by a crescent moon.

"What can I do for you?" I ask, wanting to make this better for her somehow.

"Why am I here?" she asks. "Was it because of what happened? With us?" Her eyes widen and tear up again. "Is my sister—" She swallows and tugs at her hair. "Dead because of—"

"No, Lu. No." I wrap her up in my arms. Her breaths come in erratic gasps. My lips part to speak again, then close. I don't want to be responsible for more of her heartbreak.

"All clear." Comus heads behind the kitchen counter. "Take her to the mudroom. I'll get drinks. Lu, do you like wine?"

"Chianti if we have it," I answer for Lula and lead her down the corridor to the side of the house. The name *mudroom* is deceiving in this case. It's a sunken, cozy solarium with a glass door leading out to the beach. The gray leather couches hug you when you sit in them. If there's an ideal place to receive shitty news, this is it.

When I motion for her to have a seat, she stalls and steps closer to me, placing her shaking palms on my chest and rising on her tiptoes to kiss me. She's gentle and exudes vulnerability. Relaxing into me, she exhales like she's been holding her breath for too long and I'm the one who owns the air. Her taste on my lips, the heat of her, is exactly what I need. I cup her face with both hands and thumb away warm tears, thankful she's here, protected. While chaste, it may be the most intense kiss we've shared yet.

Comus comes in and mutters an apology. Lula meets my gaze, and lowers her heels to the floor, dropping her forehead against my chest. I hold her tight and kiss her tresses until she pulls away to take her glass from Comus.

The three of us settle on the couches with wine in hand and stare at each other. Lula closes her eyes and breaks the silence with a long exhale. "Just tell me."

I clear my throat. "Something involving a potential war is setting off my attribute. It's big."

Her brows furrow. "That's why you've been agitated?" Her expression is chastising—a silent, 'why didn't you tell me?' *Because that's just the tip of the iceberg, Firecracker.*

"One of the reasons, yes." Now's not the time to discuss us. I continue before she questions me further. "Yesterday, I was able to pinpoint the event. We followed it to a location…"

I pause because this will hurt her and that's the last thing I want.

Comus leans forward, elbows on his knees. "Lu, we should do this quick—like ripping off a bandage. It must be discussed, but it won't be pleasant."

Her glassy eyes threaten to spill. I take her wine glass and set it with mine on an end table, link our fingers, and kiss her hand.

"We found a deity named Moros," Comus says. "He's from the first generation after the primordials."

Lula nudges my arm until I loop it over the top of the couch. "I've heard the name, though I didn't study him."

The tension drifts out of Comus as he watches her snuggle against me, molding her body to mine. He settles back in the cushions. "He's dreadful, to say the least—the bringer of doom. Alex and Anice worked with the Council to close Moros out of this plane, but somehow he found a way back. Lula." Comus swallows. "He had one of your sisters with him."

Lula grips my hand tightly and drops my arm from the couch to encase her against me. "He was forcing her to sing to a group of humans. It's not her fault, okay?"

She rubs her temples with her fingertips, rocking in distress. "Did she… kill?" A sob escapes and my chest tightens. She must read me because she asks, "How many?"

I hesitate, working my jaw. "A lot."

She puts her head in her hands and lets the tears fall. I rub her back until she calms. After a moment, she wipes her cheeks and sniffles. "None of us would harm without being forced. We wouldn't."

"We know," I say.

"What did she look like?" She holds her phone at the ready. "Did she have green eyes like mine?"

Comus swipes his fingers across his mouth. "Maybe blue? Ah, a lot was happening. Rath may..." He grimaces.

I think it was blue, but I'm not certain now. I should have paid better attention.

"Rath was there too?" she asks, tilting her head. "Where is he?"

Both Comus and I are silent for a second too long, and Lula's eyes fly wide with panic. "Is he okay? She didn't affect him, did she?"

I squeeze her hip. "No, but Moros deals out death with a touch and he grabbed Rath. He's recovering. It was a warning."

"So he's okay?"

"He's..." Comus tips his head back and forth. "Healing."

It's going to take some time and Rath may wear that black mark as a reminder for eternity. Deities are invincible, unless at the hands of another deity. It's a system the primordials probably set up to keep us humble. Piss off enough gods and you'll die like a mortal. I doubt if they considered the divine beings from the odd age between primordials and gods who don't fall under that rule. Moros is the only one of his kind—the personified concepts—who stayed in this universe instead of leaving with the titanomachy exodus. Now we're dealing with an unkillable psycho.

"Okay, that's good," she says, shoulders sinking before her features pinch again. "Was my sister blonde?"

Comus and I both answer, "Yes."

With a hard swallow and a sniffle, she dials and lifts the phone to her ear. "Ma, I think it was Gerty."

Lula relays to Amah what we told her with barely an interruption from the other line, then stands. She points at the wine glass on the table, prompting me to hand it to her with a quickness. She takes a long swig. "Leave your home for a while. Go off-grid. Somewhere like the cabin you stayed at in Montana except don't tell anyone where it is; not humans, not the sisters, not me. We all need to do this until we figure out what's going on and how this asshole is finding us."

I glance at Comus, who raises his eyebrows. "She's right," he whispers and counts on his fingers, no doubt tallying the safe locations we can hide them. We have a small house in Switzerland, a flat in Hong Kong, though that's certainly not off-grid, a cabin in Ontario that would be fine until winter came. I'm not sure Lula would entrust us with her sisters yet.

Lula wears a trail in the rug. There are pauses that she breaks up with, "I know." She motions around the room as if her sister is here, wagging a finger, and tapping her foot. Lu and I have spoken on the phone often, did she do the same with me? "You think Gerty would just off and kill people if a deity told her to?" She tosses up a hand. "No." Slices the air. "I bet he was holding Ven and Hazel's safety over her head for... whatever reason." Ticks each finger off then swishes the thoughts away.

I gather those knocked-around ideas. Why is Moros using more than one siren? They're not bloodthirsty, bold, or resilient, even with their power. Lula makes a furious grunt from across the room, pivots, and stamps the other direction. *Most* sirens.

We've met Lula, Grace, and Nysa only because of heavy research of unexplained events and scrying from Sing. We haven't a clue where the others are though. Nysa made the mistake of accidentally enthralling a concert hall in Italy and we found her because of the news. With a little information from Nysa, Sing found Grace for us, and Grace told Comus so much, thinking he was human and wouldn't remember. She loves Lula—refers to her as the courageous one. They're all loyal to each other and respectful to humans. Drawing attention is the last thing the sirens want. They wouldn't do it unless forced for extreme reasons.

"Look Ma," Lula says, coming to a halt. "We're past the point of keeping this to ourselves. I get that you're comfortable at your house, but if Moros can control one of us enough to kill and possibly tell him where our other sisters are, you need to pack for several weeks and get the hell out of Dodge. All of us do."

I glance at Comus, who blinks and shakes his head in incredulity. I tip up my chin in agreement. *My Firecracker is strong.*

She takes another swig. "I know—Dammit, I know, but with Ven and Hazel missing, do you want to take that chance? We need th—" She winces. "Shit. You've got to be kidding me. Fabulous timing. Okay, I'll call her and figure out something."

How long have they been missing? I mouth to Comus. She's as good at keeping secrets as I am.

She puts her hand over the phone's receiver and looks at me. "Would you happen to have a secret location available?" She looks around the room as if questioning if this house meets the criteria, then starts walking again. "It would have to be far away from people."

I glance at Comus as he says, "The Swiss house?"

"We have a house in the Alps," I tell Lula.

"It can't be near any humans—" She grimaces. "Or anyone for that matter."

I open my mouth to question her, but she stops me with a finger in the air. "Ma, I have to go. Please, make the calls. I'm working on a place for Grace." All her jittery, pacing movements come to a sudden halt. "Okay. Why?" She closes her eyes, and her jaw clenches. "Ma, this isn't the time for secret-speak." After a long pause, Lula growls. "Ma, I...I got it but...Amah! We need to talk about this. It's time." She rubs her forehead. "I'm not promising that. Not after all of this. Look, I love you, but I've got to go."

When she hangs up, she stares at her phone, holding it in her palm as though it's fragile. I stand, and the motion pulls her attention. She sniffs and clears her throat. "One of my sisters is going into her heat phase. Do either of you know anything about siren heat cycles?" We both shake our heads. Lula takes a swig of wine and sighs. "This is secret siren stuff, so be quiet about it. During that time, Sirens emit pheromones. It's irresistible to any human male capable of reproduction, no speaking necessary. It attracts them from up to a few miles away. That's how the cycle begins. It escalates as the fertile cycle goes into full phase. We take any men seeking us and destroy them in the, um, process."

She winces, and so do I.

"Have you..?" I ask.

"No. Not yet. We go into heat every three-hundred years-ish."

I don't have time to dwell on my relief before Comus says in a rush, "Miles? The Punic War." He claps his hands on his knees and stands. "A crashed fleet of ships, a hundred thousand deaths but no one could figure it out. The goddesses started a rumor about sirens luring men into the sea, and in a way, they were right, but not how some believe. Geez, I've been wondering about that for ages. It's one of the few things I've been able to read about siren lore."

Lula's eyes narrow. "How long ago?"

Comus studies the ceiling. "Um, about twenty-two hundred years or so."

"The mothers. That would explain so much. My oldest sisters won't tell us anything about their births or where the original three went. The first generations are all around that age." Lula studies her wine, seeming deep in thought.

Comus has a gleam in his eye. He's been studying lore forever and loves a good mystery. The missing tomes of the sirens are a huge mystery. Lula's unknowingly given him a mission, and he's going into fact-finder mode. "I have to talk to a couple of people, but if I remember correctly, three sirens were involved, and human lore points to them as well. It may have been the falling." His excited expression falls and he stares at Lula, who's clutching the t-shirt over her chest again. "Sorry. This is not the time. Let's get your sisters squared away."

Lula sighs. "Is the safe place you have completely secluded? We don't want to draw attention to us or you all."

She's pale and dead on her feet. I pull her close. "It is. Probably five miles from anyone."

"And you would take Grace there?"

"A portal would be the most efficient way to travel."

Her expression hardens. "You shouldn't be around her."

I raise an eyebrow. "No? She may affect me?"

"I don't know. Neither of us has been through a heat, and this hanging-out-with-deities thing is new." Lula pulls out her phone. She types a text message then dials a number and relays the plan to her sister. I catch the concern in her voice, and the lines hardening her face. She wants to know if anything can offset the symptoms. Comus's brows furrow.

When Lula hangs up, he asks, "Is the cycle difficult? How will she take it?"

Lula nibbles her lip. "Not well, considering she's choosing not to give in to it, but she'd rather not hurt anyone. She'll survive."

"But your race may not," Comus says.

Lula's eyes harden as she studies his face a moment. "So?"

I squeeze her hand. "Lula."

"We won't kill. Being with deities is outlawed. There are no options here. Besides, a siren's life isn't easy. You don't understand that not being able to affect any of you has been the highlight of the last century. I'm not exaggerating either. I wouldn't wish my existence on anyone." A tear escapes and I snatch it with my thumb. Her glittering green eyes turn their fire on me, then soften.

"The night I met you," I tell her. "I watched you enthrall an incredibly dangerous man to make him do good, and he has ever since. In seconds, you solved a problem I'd been trying to fix for years. You and your kind are far more important than you believe. There's more to you than you even know."

Comus clears his throat.

He's right. Now's not the time for a conversation about our plans. Lula needs to grieve first and be in a better mindset before I drop that bomb.

Chapter Twenty-Three

LULA

I take a sip of wine as I hang up with Nysa and find only a remaining drop in my glass. Pivoting on the path I've paced for the last hour, I collide with Alex's chest. He plucks the empty goblet from my fingers and hands me his half-full one as he presses his lips against my forehead and inhales against my hair. My eyes flutter closed. I'm not alone. I couldn't be more appreciative he's in my life than this very moment.

And, despite Ma's warnings, he *is* in my life. He's my first thought of the day, my last waking vision. Though I understand her trepidation, she doesn't know him. I trust him. He won't betray us. We may not be suitable for each other in the eyes of deities, but he cares for me, and I'm falling hard for him.

"What do you need?" Alex asks against my hair.

My sisters are fleeing into hiding, and I'm bone-deep exhausted—empty and torn apart. Leaning into my anchor, I rub my hand on his hard chest. His steady heartbeat under my palm calms me. "This."

Comus approaches from another room. "I need to check on Rath."

Alex withdraws his nose from my curls. "Quick walk to the water before you go?"

"Most definitely."

"Want to stay here?" Alex asks me, kicking off his shoes.

"No." I thread my fingers in his. "I'd like to come. I haven't been on a beach in a long while." Also, I'm not willing to be by myself with my body and mind stinging from loss. My poor sister. The other sirens are alone with their grief and I nearly curse Amah for convincing me that we needed to separate and scatter all over the world. Maybe the eight of us could have fought Moros, escaped, or at least been together during this. We don't even know where she was when she died, or if it was Gerty.

We walk out the glass door and onto a wrap-around deck with wide pale planks and ten steps on the left that lead to the sandy yard. The sky shimmers with an early purple glow. The still beauty of the morning is a stark contrast to the previous anguish. Cool sand is as soothing as Alex's warm hand in mine. Gulls swoop and caw, and sandpipers skitter along the shoreline, chasing the tide. We follow the line between dry and wet sand in silence. The sparkling sea ebbs and flows, creating a lulling symphony of waves along with the water lapping against the poles of the long dock.

Comus and Alex stop in sync at an invisible point, as if their minds are fused. It's difficult to imagine walking with someone so often your bodies understand each other without words. I could explain Grace's exact mood by the inflection of her voice, but standing face-to-face, I'd be lost. I haven't been near her in sixty years.

"Tell Rath to quit milking his injuries for attention and get his ass over here," Alex says in a thin, tight voice. "Alert Prax and..." he trails off and gives Comus a pointed glance. I furrow my eyebrow as I try to discern what he could mean.

Comus nods, apparently understanding. He seems worried and tired with lightly bagged, pinched eyes and slumped shoulders. "Will do. I'll send up the flares when Rath can travel."

Alex lets go of my hand and raises his palm to open the portal. I approach Comus and hug him. "Thank you," I whisper.

When he releases me, his eyes are glassy, but he turns too fast for me to question, and steps through the curtain between realms. Alex waves it closed behind him.

The Belize house is beautiful—a three-story cottage in a light gray-green shade with windows everywhere. The lower and upper decks overlook the ocean and are an ideal spot for morning coffee and reading. There are even loungers with thick, navy cushions. Is this Alex's regular home? Was he in my area for business? He must have been visiting the gang guys and we were in the right place at the right time. How lucky.

I sidle closer to him, wrapping myself around his arm. I'm not sure what happens now. My sisters are scattering to the wind, except for Grace. There's an evil deity on the loose, and he injured one of Alex's best friends.

"Do you need to check on Rath?" I ask.

"I'm staying here with you."

Warmth thaws out the pain in my chest as we walk up the stairs. He's going to stay with me? There must be so much to do. "I'd be okay."

"I wouldn't." His words are curt and he squeezes my hand as if in apology but doesn't look at me.

Oh.

I grip Alex's fingers, and he pauses to turn toward the sunrise. The pink and coral sky is as brightly colored as fruit sorbet. His arms engulf me, and I settle into them, holding onto strong forearms. Who knows what the future will bring. I'll soak up this moment and allow myself a flicker of hope.

When the bottom of the sun parts from the horizon, I turn to rest against Alex, listening to the rhythm of his ancient heartbeat. How many sunrises has he witnessed and with how many other people? I'd ask, but words would interrupt the peace so I keep quiet while his fingers thrum through my hair in a caress so sweet, it's as if I'm the only one who has received this type of treatment. He tempts me to think everything will be alright.

Unfortunately, it won't, and my comfort is short-lived. I shimmy my phone out of my pocket and dial Hazel once more, but again, there's no answer. As I disconnect, I hide my face against Alex's chest.

"You're exhausted," he whispers. Instead of leading me into the house, he lifts and cradles me to him.

"I have legs," I say in a half-hearted protest.

"And they're the most beautiful legs in the realm."

I smile against Alex's neck as we ascend a staircase and pass into a mostly white bedroom. The deep brown wood floors make a stunning contrast against pale fabrics and walls. Instead of stopping at the bed, he continues walking to a bathroom as dark as the bedroom is light.

Alex sets me on my wobbly feet and reaches into the glass-walled shower to turn on the water. Once steam turns the clear door opaque, he pulls his shirt over his head, then drags mine off. "I like this on you." Going back and forth between us, he removes each garment until we stand naked before each other. He's statue-worthy, and my gaze settles on his growing arousal. He gathers me to him and backs into the shower "I think we both know how much I desire you, Firecracker. Just ignore that."

Once the door closes, and the steam encompasses us, Alex washes my hair and body like he was created for this task alone. Hands slide over every inch of me, warming me more than the hot jets. His touch isn't like before—the desperate need to touch, to grab, and light each other up is now a gentle check-over meant to soothe.

Cherished.

That's what this is. Not something I thought I'd experience. I'll accept his comfort and, for once, won't worry about the consequences. After rinsing me, he quickly cleans himself and shuts off the water, then wraps me in the fluffiest towel ever made.

"For guys, your taste is lush," I jest, too drained to say anything of importance but not wanting to stay in silence.

The corner of his mouth rises as he crouches to dry my legs. "Were you expecting a barebones frat house like in the movies?"

I was. I don't have a lot of experience with men's houses. "No, just more bachelor pad and less modern resort. Did you date a designer?" Did some goddess of domestic decor stay in this place?

He looks up at me with a mischievous expression, and rises, coming so close my nose nearly taps his chest but he lifts my chin. "Are you fishing for information about my past love life?"

A little cringe goes through me at the words *love life*, and his smile grows. "Forget I asked," I mumble.

"No," he says, towel-drying my hair. He tugs my locks, tipping my head back to kiss a path from my neck to ear. "But that conversation is for another day." He takes my hand and leads me from the bathroom. "We'll talk about it soon, though, alright?"

"We don't need to—"

He pivots and cuts me off with a kiss. "Yeah, we do. But not today. Today I hold you while you sleep. Got it?"

"Alright." I swallow the lump in my throat before the back of my legs hit the bed, and he follows me down, tucking me into his body. I sigh, my heavy eyelids are unable to stay open.

I wake, wrapped in warmth. Bliss lasts a split second before reality crushes me. I'm no longer whole from the loss of Gerty. Curling into a ball, I let the tears fall. Alex shifts me to face him, thumbs the wetness from my cheeks, and drags me on top of him. He holds me in silence until I calm and drift back asleep.

My eyes open as I rouse again. I'm wrapped in sheets, but not Alex. I rise and stretch. Soft light peeks through drawn, beige curtains, and my empty bag rests on a leather wing chair. Opening the drawers of a massive walnut armoire, I find my clothing folded inside and smile. I dress, needing to see Alex.

The rich aroma of spices leads me to the kitchen where Alex unboxes food on a long peninsula countertop. He looks up when I approach and winces. "Sorry. I wanted to be there when you woke, but lunch came."

He drops what he's working on, strides over, and embraces me. I'll never tire of his hand on the back of my head. "Let me get you fed. Want something to drink?"

"Just water. I'll help."

He points to a round, driftwood table. "Sit. Let me serve you, and before you deny me, I have an unrelenting need to take care of you at the moment. Please, just let me." He winks and refocuses on his task.

I bite my smiling lip and cross the room. The cream-colored fabric chairs are plush. He sets a plate filled with rice, beans, a tamale, and thick stewed meat in front of me. The scent of spices makes my stomach rumble, and he hands me a fork along with a kiss.

We spend the day in relative silence as we walk the beach, sit on the deck with wine, and order a pizza for dinner. I didn't even have to say, *no olives*. We do every task with few words. I'm numb, and Alex allows me to be distant while I absorb everything that's happened. It's tough. My brain doesn't want to explore details or what needs to be done. It wants to live in a fuzzy gray space of numbness and for my golden god to be touching me so I can cling to his aliveness.

From the lounger, he passes me a glass of water and shifts me onto his lap as my phone rings. Amah's name flashes on the screen. I'm still angry with her and uninterested in another lecture, even if she's right about some deities. Moros is bad. Alex is not, and I'm not giving him up just because I can't control him. I don't need to control him nor do I want to. She'll text if it's important. I press the ignore button.

Alex's pinched expression tells me he disapproves. He wouldn't if he knew how much she hated me being here with him. She doesn't want me relying on or talking to him. Told me to stay away from all deities and my sisters. As if I could stand to be alone right now. I'm half tempted to see if Alex would allow all the sirens to come here. We could throw a family reunion on this secluded slice of paradise and mourn together. Have a memorial for Gerty like the humans do. We will once Venora and Hazel are found and safe with us again.

Alex slips his warm hand under my shirt and rests his fingers on my side. "Want to talk about it?"

"No."

He hugs me closer, supporting my secretive thoughts with a soft kiss on my neck and roving fingertips. I rest my head against his strong shoulder. Our hands entwine, and he brings them to his mouth, sparking tendrils of joy through me as he tastes each digit. Heat floods through me, and I lean to lick his bottom lip. His eyes study mine before he cups my face and kisses me. We part for a moment, and Alex stares at me with intensity and question. "Lula. I..."

My phone buzzes against my thigh, sending my heart skyrocketing into my throat. "Grace." I peck Alex's pouty lips and answer. "How are you feeling?"

"Restless," she says. "Achy. I'm probably still a week away from the peak." Her words jostle at a rhythm. She's pacing.

"Are you packing?"

"Yes. According to Amah, the heat will last longer with no available men, so I packed for a month. A taxi is arriving any minute."

"Okay." I run my fingers through Alex's hair, and the tension leaves my shoulders. "You have the location Alex provided?"

Grace titters. "Yes, Momma Lula. It takes about five minutes to get there from my house."

"Oh, wow, that's close."

Alex shifts and he purses his lips as he looks out at the ocean. I hope she's headed to the correct place.

"I'm glad we're speeding this up," Grace continues. "We could wait a few days, but with the unknown effect on deities, I wouldn't want any incidents."

I tense again, and Alex's arm tightens around my waist. I swallow hard. "No. That would be..." There are no words strong enough. The guys can't grasp the pull of a siren in heat, not that I've experienced it, but my older sisters have explained. It's twisted, inescapable torture. If my sister draws Alex to her? Not likely but... "Let's not find out."

"Did Amah speak to you?" Grace asks.

My face heats. I've never declined a call from Ma. "Um, I didn't answer. Did she talk to you?"

"She did. She said we couldn't see each other."

My mouth gapes. "What? Why?" Alex rubs my back until I settle against him again.

"Heck, if I know, she wouldn't say. Actually, she hit the roof when I told her Alex was helping with a location. She told me to have a cab drop me to a secret cabin in the woods, and lock myself in. That I'd leave at some point, so make sure it was miles away from anyone. And hey, she asked me not to tell you where, because you'd find me."

Amah is right about that. Now that I'm scheduled to see Grace again, I can't imagine not seeing her. She should meet Alex. I think they would get along and I want two people I care about to care about each other too. We've never had that before. Not any of us.

I lock my fingers with Alex's. "Well, until Amah explains herself, we do what we want, and I want to hug my sister."

"I could use a hug," Grace says.

The vulnerability in her voice makes my throat tight. She's had to go through the last twenty-four hours alone and is on the verge of a heat? How much torture does Amah expect her to take?

I swallow hard. "Good. We'll meet in a few minutes, and I'll give you the biggest one ever. Love you, Grace."

"And I, you. Firecracker."

A gasp escapes me. "Well, Ma isn't incapable of sharing!" I told her Alex's nickname for me in passing.

"Bye." She gives a laughing sob and hangs up.

I trail my fingers across Alex's encompassing hold. I wish I could find Venora and Hazel, and hug them, too. Are they in hiding, or trapped by Moros? As if Alex senses the icy knot in my stomach, he slips his hand under my shirt again, caressing away the tension.

"Why would he use Gerty to harm humans?" I ask.

"I've been wondering that myself along with other things. Anice and I work together to lock and unlock between-realm portals, but they're closed. I don't like what his being here may mean, or where the opening is."

I twist to face him. "What could it mean?"

Alex hesitates. "Rath thinks the veil could be weakening, allowing slips between realms. If that's happening, having an open portal is the last of our issues—well, the issue wouldn't matter because the Universe would be kaput."

"Oh, wow, is that all?" I say with an incredulous huff.

Alex wrinkles his nose and reaches to massage my ankle. "Sorry. We shouldn't be talking about this right now. It's—" He cups my cheek and shows me a new emotion I can't decipher. Like pity and question or determination maybe? "Overwhelming."

That ship sailed a while ago. The sirens need more information. "I'd like to know more so I'm able to protect my sisters. They're all I have."

His hand stills. "You have me, Comus, and Rath. Others as well."

I attempt a happy expression. "Thank you."

Alex closes his eyes, jaw firming. "When will you believe that I'd do anything for you?" I remain silent, and he squeezes my ankle.

The slow lapping waves help sort my thoughts. Why would he do anything for me? Sure, he rescued me from the pain of grieving alone, but that was out of pity. He was being nice to someone he's sorta dating. He's also ancient and important. Why would I draw his interest and keep it after the thousands of years he's been worshipped? It doesn't make sense. "Alex, this...relationship isn't something accepted by other deities. There are consequences by being..." I wave my hand between us and sigh. "Whatever we are."

"I don't care about the consequences."

My eyes snap to his. "When it could kill me?"

"We're not having sex. I'm protecting you."

By being an impossible temptation, sleeping in my bed, and letting me taste the impossible. "You could face major problems by *protecting* me the way you do."

"I don't care about me."

"Dammit, I do!" I jerk my head toward the ocean, lock onto the dock, and the birds, though my thoughts stick to Alex. We can't be together, and he's a god—a very kind one who's trying to help an endangered species from going extinct by the hand of another deity. It's his divine duty or something.

He grabs my hips and tugs me to straddle him. I startle from the sudden motion, but he cups my face in both his hands. "Firecracker. *Lula.* I want to be with you. Just you. Do you know why?"

As often as I've studied the thoughts in his eyes, I haven't found an answer that makes sense. "I don't."

"I want to experience every inch of you more than anything. Every mysterious thought, every blush, every eye-roll. I'm choosing you."

My mouth opens even though I haven't a clue what to say, but speech is impossible anyway because he closes the distance and captures my lips. He kisses me with an undeniable passion. Past and future troubles fall away, leaving us to revel in one perfect moment.

Chapter Twenty-Four

ALEX

I haven't a clue what Lula's thinking right now, but she's kissing me like she's happy with my confessions. By her nervous fidgeting, I thought I might have to sprint after her down the beach, but as usual, once we connected, our bodies took over.

This siren had snuffed out whatever sad rendition of passion I sensed with other women. My life is now categorized into before-Lula and after-Lula. After-Lula is my favorite by far. Even with all the shit falling around us, when I'm in her presence, everything's less apocalyptic.

I delve my tongue into her mouth, and she gets a tight grip on my hair. Her moans tighten everything below the belt. Gods, this woman. I need her soft, bare skin pressed against mine. I stand, intent on getting her upstairs when my cell phone goes off.

Lula blinks as if she's coming out of a trance. She drops her head to my shoulder. "This is becoming routine."

We both sigh and I answer. Comus asks, "Are you ready?"

I freeze, trying to remember why we need to be ready. Ah, Grace. "Oh, yeah. What time is it?"

Comus chuckles. "Too busy for saving sirens today, Alex?"

"Kiss my ass. Are *you* ready?"

"It's why I called."

"Hang on," I say, ignoring his sarcasm and glance at Lula, who dials and lifts her phone to her ear.

I squeeze her rear. "Is your sister ready?"

"Hey, Grace, you all set?" She waits a long moment, then mouths, *ready*.

I tell Comus to give me a couple of minutes and hang up. Standing, I place Lula on her feet as she talks to Grace and take a few deep breaths to calm my body.

She smirks. I pinch her side, and she makes a funny *eep* sound and slaps at me. "Sorry Grace, Alex is just being Alex."

I'm relieved that she's acting more like herself after the tragedy of her sister's death. Every curse is unique. I feared she wouldn't be the same if a piece of her soul was taken. Some otherworldlings like werewolves and types of demons bind souls with family or mates. If they live through the death of their bound one, they don't repair. Taking her hand, I lead her to the beach as she talks to her sister.

"I'm sure you're in the right place. Want to describe it to Alex?" Lula eyes me, and I nod. "Okay, see you in a minute."

I take the phone from Lula. "Hi, Grace. This is Alex."

"Oh, Alex!" Her voice is a little higher than Lula's but sweet and melodic. "I've heard so much about you."

"Have you now?" Considering Lula's reluctance to speak about anything involving us, this is surprising news.

"Uh, give me that back," Lula says as her eyes widen, and she tries to snatch the phone.

Putting my finger over my lips, I attempt to quiet Lula as Grace rambles, "Geez, she won't shut up about you. The woman is head over heels—never been happier. I hear it in her voice."

"Never happier, huh?"

Lula's eyes go full-moon, and she leaps to tackle me like a kitten pitted against a lion. "Give it back," she whisper-yells, remaining polite because when someone's on the phone, social etiquette says to remain quiet. Even if that someone is hearing everything they've wanted to know from an enthusiastic, gossipy sister.

Snatching Lula around her thighs, I flop her over my shoulder. Growling my name, she punches me in the back. I ignore her to talk to Grace. "I've never been happier either."

Lula freezes for a moment before doubling her efforts to get free. Her fingers battle mine and her protests get louder, so I tip and catch her around the waist before she hits the sand. I pull her against me, cupping a hand over her mouth while Grace tells me more delightful secrets. Lula licks my palm. I bite her ear, and she growls but also squirms.

Grace continues to ramble. "Oh, wow, you're as sweet as she says you are. I called it from day one. I was telling our sister, Nysa, that Lula was the last one I'd have expected to go all mushy in love on us with how guarded—well, realistic—she is, but sure enough."

The world seems to halt; the waves, the breeze, even Lula stops breathing. She tilts her head back to blink upside down at me.

Interrupting the long pause of silence, Grace adds, "Hey, um, she's told you this, right?"

Lula loves me.

I take a deep breath that I laugh out, turn Lula to face me, and speak to Grace as I stare into vulnerable green eyes. "I'll tell you this, Grace. I'm unsure of Lula's thoughts, but I'm very much in love with her."

I am too. Watching her from afar was near torture and once I stepped into the light and she responded to me the way she did—she let me in and it was even better than I knew it would be. So we have secrets. We will clear those up and soon. She loves me, and I love her, and somehow we will find a way to be together. We'll get Grace settled, then have a deep discussion. She'll forgive me for basically stalking her and I will learn everything about the sirens so we can protect them and get Zeus to see—that won't happen, but we will work through the problems, and go forward together. This is a *good* day.

"Aw, geez. Well, I'm in trouble. And you two are crazy, but I wish you the best, even if some things are impossible." Grace clears her throat and sniffs. "After everything that's happened, I'm glad you're with her. Keep her safe, please. She means so much to us."

"She means everything to me. I'll keep her safe."

Lula's chin trembles, and she bites her lip. Before I drop the phone and take my woman to the sand, I have a job to do. "Grace, look around and tell me what you see."

I step toward Lula, cup my hand against her hair, and tug her against my chest. There's zero resistance as she presses into me and wraps her arms around my waist. I kiss the top of her head as Grace describes the site. "Tall trees. Big pointy cathedral spire. Weird, gray statue in a field—a pig, maybe?"

"Yeah, we have no idea what that thing is either. Great, you're in the right place. I'm going to get a friend, and I'll open a portal near you, then another that will go to the safe house. You'll go there, I'll close you in, then Lula, Prax, and I will head back through the portal to Belize. It shouldn't take long. Are you okay with this? Lula tells us it will be hard for you."

"Yes, I'm okay as long as everyone remains safe. I won't harm anyone if possible. I appreciate everything you've done for us."

"We're glad to help, Grace. See you shortly."

"Hey, Alex?" Her voice turns cold. "Stay as far from me as possible, please."

They really are worried. We're deities though. Otherworldlings don't affect us. "Yes, of course."

We hang up, and I tip Lula's chin up to brush a kiss on her lips. "Grace is my favorite sister." I expect a laugh or to get punched again, but she only blinks watery eyes at me. "We're having a conversation after this."

Lula chews her lips but nods. I swipe my hand through the air.

"A couple of minutes? Brother, that was eight years." Comus strides through the portal with Prax on his heels.

Comus drags Lula into a tight embrace. "Lu, you must stop seducing Alex all the time. The man has a job to do."

She giggles as he releases her. "I'm a siren, Comus. I can't just turn it off."

Comus laughs with her, but she goes silent when she sees Prax. Her eyes widen. I flinch to tackle her to the sand before remembering I'm not a caveman, but I don't like how he's looking at her. His inky hair, dark eyes, and sculpted face have the goddesses swooning when he walks by.

I snag Lula's hip, directing her closer to me, and introduce them. "Lula, this is Praxis, son of Priapus. He's a partner we trust with the sirens' locations. You're safe with him."

He holds a hand out, which she accepts with a smile and shakes. "Nice to meet you."

"Shall we?" I say, raising my hand again.

Lula touches my arm. "Look, I've mentioned it, but if you're affected, don't get near her." Shifting on her feet, she tugs on a curl, then points at Comus. "Don't."

"I'm not going in. Prax is," Comus assures her. "I'm guarding the portal from here."

Lula's face scrunches. "Oh. I wanted you to meet—"

"It's okay," I interrupt, entwining our fingers to redirect her. "Another time. We'll do this fast, alright?"

She blows out a stressed breath. I open the portal and Lula steps through before I can. When I follow, a sweet scent hits me. Trees surround the secluded, grassy area, but details of the scenery take a back seat to the energy soaking into my skin. Every part of me stiffens, including the fists I clench as I try to stay in control.

Prax walks in behind me. "By the gods, what is that?"

I want to taste the air. Desire flows through each cell of my body, synchronizing me for one purpose. Ten feet away, Lula hugs her sister. They sway as they hold each other, grinning widely. Grace is gorgeous with long, straight blonde hair and blue eyes. Her features are delicate like Lula's, yet different. Round, innocent eyes meet mine, compared to her sister's sultry almond shape. She has a sharply sloped nose instead of soft angles. I expected them to look somewhat alike, but while they are both stunning, they bear no resemblance to each other. I'm not sure why that's a shock. Comus described Grace.

Lula faces us in a defensive stance, guarding her sister. I want to tackle her, take her—both of them to the ground. Grace bites her full bottom lip, and Prax breathes out a groan beside me. This is bad.

The women converse, but their words don't register because I'm distracted by the shape of Lula's lips, the curve of her neck. I need to lick her collarbone, trace her hips with my fingers then grip—

"Alex?" Lula's strained voice drags me out of my daydreams. "She's affecting you, isn't she?"

Grace scrunches her nose. "Oh, no. Lula?"

Lula holds Grace's hand and moves backward. "It's okay. Alex, now please."

I walk twenty feet from the Belize entrance and the women, then swipe another portal to the kitchen of the Swiss house. Prax follows me, keeping his eyes on Grace until we pass through. The chalet is small but feels bigger with its open design and exposed rafters. I take a deep breath of the non-pheromone-laden air and chuckle when my mind clears a bit. It smells like plums and the larch wood interiors. I head toward the bedrooms. "Let's check the place fast and get this over with before we get ourselves in trouble."

Prax whistles a short note. "If Lula weren't looking like she'd stab me, I'd already be on Grace. I didn't think otherworldlings affected us?"

"Neither did I. We have research to do." Someone knows something about this species and isn't talking. We can't access the old lore books if they even contain information on sirens. Comus is going to have a fit about this. How do we know so little about them?

"Grace is gorgeous, but whatever's happening feels more powerful than attraction."

"Sirens," I say, throwing a match in the woodstove to light a stack of wood. Grace may be uncomfortable during this time, but she won't be cold. "Let's hurry."

We regroup next to the refrigerator after checking the house when a weird, wavelike sensation prickles my skin. My muscles tighten again as desire pools in my stomach.

Prax exhales as though he's been holding his breath for days. "What was that?"

Muffled, Lula shouts for Comus, and my chest clenches at the panic in her voice. I take a deep drag of air and head back through the portal into the pheromone zone.

Not breathing doesn't help. I want to rip everyone's clothes off and rut in the dirt like an animal. Lula's face is pale, her eyes wide as she whispers to her sister, who seems equally spooked. I should speak, try to figure out what's happening, but visions of the two of them under me invade my mind, and I clench my fists again to keep my hands to myself. Prax paces a line behind me.

Lula yells toward the Belize opening for Comus again. It's going to get awkward if he comes through and Grace recognizes him.

I take a few steps forward. "What's wrong?"

Both women jerk as if a shock of electricity lit them up. They grip each other's hands, grit their teeth, then turn to each other and whisper. Grace's big eyes are even larger.

The impulse to sprint the distance to get to them is getting harder to resist. "Lula?"

Her eyes dart as if the air holds something she's seeking. "This cannot be happening."

"Hey. Talk to me." I want to move forward but am fearful I won't be able to stop myself if I move any closer.

My fists squeeze in rhythm to Lula's rising and falling chest.

She touches her lips, then drops her hand to cover Grace's. "Uh. Pretty sure I'm going into heat."

Chapter Twenty-Five

LULA

Alex's eyes widen. "What? That's not—" He rubs the scruff on his gorgeous face as he looks me over. "Grace. Go through, and I'll shut the portal."

I release Grace's hand in case our touching is causing this phenomenon. Prax stops the pacing that's making Grace shift from foot to foot with each one of his steps. They're syncing.

This is Grace's first heat, so we're unsure if anything happening is normal, especially since neither of us has heard of a siren catching another siren's heat. In theory, we understand the biology and what will occur if we don't get through the portal door. The need to press against Alex's bare skin is overwhelming. Like a string has connected us and is tightening by the second.

"I have to go with her," I say to Alex.

"Absolutely not." Alex puts his hands on his knees. He's fighting it.

I glare at him. "We have a hard enough time staying out of each other's pants. You can't be near us. If I'm going into heat? Alex." I throw him a, *you know this* look.

Prax squeezes Alex's shoulder and heads toward the Belize opening, though he's having difficulty putting space between himself and Grace. "It's amplifying."

I nudge Grace toward the Swiss portal when a jolt shocks us with a pulse of pure lust. My core clenches, tingles, and I swell between my legs. I suck in a sharp breath and attempt to gain control of my body.

"Do we call Amah?" Grace asks.

Amah. I'm so mad at her. "Like she'd say anything helpful. She had to know and had every opportunity to warn us. Not just, 'Hey, stay away from your sister for no apparent reason, la dee fucking-da.'"

"You're right," Grace responds through gritted teeth. "Nysa?"

"Yes. She does the research. Let's get in the house and call her." Grace buckles over and cries out. Prax seems to have given up on exiting and both he and Alex step forward. I drop the bag and raise a palm. "No! Go. Both of you."

Alex and Prax mumble to each other as they prowl back and forth like starving beasts eyeing irresistible meat. Alex pants, open-mouthed. "We won't leave you. Not together, unguarded. The Swiss house is secluded, but no. Not going to happen."

Oh, it's going to happen. I tug at Grace, who stumbles and whines. "Lu. It isn't supposed to progress this quickly. It's unbearable." She moans and runs her hands down her hips, settling them between her thighs. Prax sucks in a breath and gives her the most predatory stare I've ever seen, but Alex shifts his eyes to the sky.

Grabbing Grace's bag, I elbow her once again toward the portal. "Grace, we'll make it. Get through the portal. Their resistance can only last so long." And our willpower slips away each minute. If she's moving into full heat, there's nothing she won't do to make the pain stop. No matter how many humans die or how many deities and sirens get cursed.

Alex groans, drawing my attention to him. My hips roll on their own, and then he's pacing again, running his hands through his hair. His muscles are taut, his jaw clenching. Power radiates from him.

Grace emits a sad whimpering cry, and Prax bolts. Alex catches his arm, swings him around, and talks to him. He lunges again, and Grace takes a quick step away from me.

"Shit!" I snatch Grace, and push her through the opening, then toss her bag in after her. I exchange a final glance with Alex as he holds Prax back with his palms on his friend's chest. The words *I love you* lay on the tip of my tongue, but this moment isn't right. "Close us in." I slip through the portal into a wood-paneled kitchen.

My skin glistens with sweat, but I doubt I'm as heated as Grace. She's flushed and breathing in ragged pants. Her dilated eyes hold wildness on the verge of turning feral. I help her to her feet. Every time we touch, electricity sizzles under my skin and lights up every part of me. Some areas more than others. My thoughts go to Alex, him over me, in me. I almost double over with the realness of it. An angry ache settles between my legs and in my breasts. If this is the beginning, Grace is fighting the good fight.

I point down a hallway. There has to be bedrooms and a cold shower. "Come on." I tug her along. "We've got this."

"I can't, Lu. I need…" Her voice is a whimpering plea and a tear slips down her cheek. "I need him."

"No, sister." How I wish we could though. I watch the portal, waiting for Alex to close it. "We've wanted a sleepover for decades, and here we are, right?"

Grace huffs a laugh and it morphs into a deep reverberating moan. The note strikes a chord in me more profound than the physical plane, and my voice joins hers. It feels good, takes the edge off the growing pain and agitation like the release valve on a pressure cooker. We glance at each other and go quiet.

I move a sweaty lock of blonde off of Grace's forehead so I can see her face. "What the hell was—"

Prax bursts into the kitchen and knocks into a wooden chair that he throws aside. Grace leaps forward, and they meet like two crashing waves. He paws at her, growling against her lips, and she moans in response as they struggle with clothing.

"Wait! Grace—" I move to pull her away, but he's got a firm grip and I have to dance out of their way as they stumble around, grinding in a wild dance. Prax's hand passes by me in a swipe and for a split second, I wish it would catch me because that pressure builds again and calls for release. "Grace? Grace!"

Nothing.

The remaining sheds of Grace's shirt flutter through the air before Prax lowers her to the ground. His hand disappears under the waistband of her pants, and the tension in my body amps up higher. Grace calls out, and my voice joins hers again. I cover my mouth.

Good thing there are no humans here. The destruction would be horrific.

As Grace tugs at his jeans and her bare legs wrap around him, I back away in defeat. I may as well attempt to separate a werewolf from its mate. I have to get out. Not only should I not be watching this, if I stick around the need will consume me as well. There's no stopping this. That's one thing all my older sisters have said, their voices tinged with regret.

Slipping through the portal, I almost knock into Alex's chest. He reaches out for me then jerks away, as though I'll burn him if he touches me.

"It wasn't supposed to be like this," I say, stumbling out of his reach. "What do we do?"

Alex glances through the curtain of the portal. His eyes widen, and he swipes his hand to close the opening. The strain in the air eases, but pheromones still saturate the area.

Alex looks anywhere but at me. "I don't know. Prax is willing to risk it. Couldn't bear hearing her in pain. The Council isn't watching him. Not like me." He takes a step forward, then stops and shakes his head as if trying to clear it. "*Fuck.* Lu, get out of here."

Alex's muscles are straining, and he has that touch of coral in his cheeks that reminds me, unhelpfully, of how sexy he was that morning we got closer than we should have. This is worse. I'd love to say this is a crazy, siren couvade syndrome and everything I'm feeling is an empathetic, but false response to Grace's reproductive cycle, but a moan rides up my throat as if to say, "fake this."

Clamping my mouth shut, I take off in a sprint toward the open Belize portal. I have at least another hundred years until this is supposed to happen to me. Maybe if I escape the lingering pheromones, get to the house, and shower, this will all go away. That's it. We need fresh air.

Alex growls, and footsteps thud behind me.

Grass turns to sand as I leap through the portal and pass Comus without slowing. The last thing I need is for him to also fall under this spell.

"He's affected," I shout over my shoulder.

I run toward the house like my life depends on it, because it does.

Chapter Twenty-Six

ALEX

When I follow Lula through, I nearly take out Comus. He blocks me with a strong shoulder against my chest. "Alex, the portal. You need to close it. Where's Prax?"

Red curls whip in the wind as my obsession runs toward the house. The view brings up some deep-seated impulse. My purpose is to give chase and pin her down. Inside her is where I belong. I pump my fingers as I visualize them on her hips, then press forward, needing to get to what's mine, but Comus shoves me back. "Keep her safe and close it."

Keep her safe. I need to... I swipe the portal closed behind me, sink to my knees, and dig my fingers into the soft sand. With heavy breaths, I try to clear my lungs of siren mojo. It's not working.

Comus squats to observe me. "Your pupils are blown out. Fascinating. Lu wasn't exaggerating. It's affecting me, too." I bare my teeth at him, but he claps my shoulder. "Not at your level, but I shouldn't get close to her. What happened with Prax? Did you open a different portal to send him back to Olympus?"

Struggling, I stumble to my feet. Even though I closed the portal, sweetness lingers in the air. My focus hones on my target. The door slams. Comus's question is sobering. I force my gaze to him. "He stayed with Grace."

Comus's face falls, and he runs a hand over his mouth. He tenses as though he may punch something but places his hands on his hips and stares out at the sea.

My head clears at his pain. "I'm sorry, brother."

"It wouldn't have worked out between us. I cringed every time Grace called me Liam, and it became excruciating to lie to her."

Yeah, I get that. At least Lu knows my name, who I am. Comus went in full-lie with Grace, posed as a human librarian. It's difficult to keep the full truth from Lu but playing a human under the influence of a siren's thrall seems impossible. It was temporary as all siren relationships are, but he got the job done and led us to Lula.

By the way he puffs his cheeks and blows out a breath through tightly drawn lips, it was harder on him than he'd led on. "It's better for her if Prax is there. He'll keep her... safe through this." He crinkles his nose, glancing at the house. "Why does this affect us? The sirens were always tucked away with the major goddesses and Council members. Even getting a glimpse of them was near impossible, but this would have been tough to hide." I shift forward again and Comus steps in front of me, palms to my chest. "Okay, let's deal with this first. What are we going to do about the lingering pheromones in your system?"

"I won't leave her here. There are houses within a mile. What if someone drives up?"

"Send her to Shangri-La, and you stay here."

I pivot and forcefully pace a line. "It's been too long since I've been there. I'm unsure if the area is still clear."

"That place is undevelopable for another hundred years. Besides, Lu's able to take care of anything she comes across, but I'll stay with her. Rath is almost fit to travel, and I'll call in a couple of the others to cover for us."

"You're not getting near her. She thinks she's in heat. Caught it from Grace. I agree."

His head tilts. "Seriously?"

"Oh, yeah. It might go away out of Grace's presence. Maybe." I stare at the bedroom window. "You're right. How did they hide this? Is this a curse too?"

Comus places a hand on my chest and pushes me back. "I'd wager the storytellers and archivists were forbidden to document the species beyond a short description, especially if it's a curse. The old gods either brag in tapestries or hide their shame and never speak of it again."

I swallow hard, attempting to remain sane. "If it doesn't stop, and someone gets within range..." My lower region is throbbing a very pissed-off beat.

Comus glances back at the house. "Shit. She'll take care of them in a much different capacity."

Another wave of lust hits me and, even from this distance, Lu's cry reaches me. I'm wearing a trench in the sand.

Comus gives me a troubled frown. "She sounds like it hurts."

"You should have heard Grace. Not good." I blow out a long breath. "There was this weird force. Hit us like a calling every time she moaned. It's the same with Lu."

Head swiveling from the house to me then to where the portal was open, Comus scratches his beard. "I thought they'd be horny or something. I didn't know it hurt."

"Yeah, and Lu wasn't expecting this. She's scared. I could tell when she was talking to Grace."

"We're not prepared." He chuffs. "How long has it been since we've flown completely blind into a situation?"

Unable to stop moving, I rock from foot to foot. "It's the plan then three backups, always."

The tightness in my body is bordering on torturous. A car engine sounds over the crashing waves, spurring us into action.

We sprint through the sand. Comus points to the house. "Go. Better you than me, but fight it, Alex."

Actually, it may be better in Olympian eyes for him to go to her but it certainly wouldn't be better for any of us. Thoughts of the awkwardness between Dalia, Comus, and me from her unlocking come to mind. If Comus and Lu—best not to think about that in my state.

I veer toward the deck while Comus makes his way to the front. When I breach the doorway into the house, the sweet fragrance amplifies. The stairs seem to have multiplied, the distance stretching with my impatience. I walk through the bedroom. Her scent is everywhere, spurring the memory of her taste, her skin under my fingers. My mouth waters. The shower is running, so I trudge to the bathroom door. "Lula?"

"Go, Alex," she whimpers.

I turn the knob and peek in. "It's not stopping, is it?"

"No, it's not." Behind glass, Lula sits on the tile floor, knees to her chest, fully clothed and shivering as jets of water pelt her. "Nothing is helping. Not cooling, or rinsing, or...touching. You have to get away from me." She grits her teeth and shudders.

The knob may crack under my fingers, but it's anchoring me, keeping me from running to her. "You can't stay here. You'll have visitors."

Her expression morphs from frustration to terror in a heartbeat, and she staggers to her feet. "Alex, send me somewhere. Anywhere, but not here with you or humans. The moans won't stop. Please, get me away from everyone." She runs her hands over her stomach, down between her thighs and hisses through clenched teeth.

If I see her do that again, my fingers will follow. I close the door and rest my head against it. Shifting on my feet, I adjust myself, attempting to relieve the pressure in my pants. "Okay," I call through the wood. "I'm getting you out of here but need to check the location first."

Comus walks up behind me and groans. "It was a woman. She kept going. Damn, that's strong. Hurry, because I'd like to remain friends."

I open the portal to Shangri-La and urge Comus to follow me. Purple flowers dot the knee-high grains of a countryside surrounded by a dense forest of hundred-year-old trees. It's serene, and exactly as I remembered it down to the clean, earthy scent. I listen for anything beyond the breeze dancing through the grass and chattering wildlife.

Comus takes a deep breath. "No one here."

We walk back through the portal, into the bedroom. "Lu. Come out. I'll take you to a place where there are no people for about a ten-mile radius."

The water shuts off, and the glass door squeaks open. Lula emerges from the bathroom, winces, and grips her hips again, face scrunching in pain. "Ow, ow, ow."

I move Comus behind me with an arm and back away though I'd much rather go forward.

She turns toward the portal and stumbles through the opening.

"Stay here," I tell Comus before following.

Lula backs away from me, crushing down a trail in the lush field. "Leave me." Her quiet voice trembles. She runs her hands down her thighs, digging her nails in, and heaves her breath. Each rise and fall of her chest is an absolute fascination for me. I'm drawn to trace the indents she left on her legs with my tongue. She trails her fingers up to squeeze her hips and I know what that feels like under my grip. The texture of her skin is familiar but needs to be tested, tasted, and memorized.

"Go before this gets worse," she whispers.

Worse? I can't imagine anything better. But no. This isn't right. I drag my gaze from her and focus on her safety.

There's nothing here but a silent treeline of thick trunks that stretch skyward to cords of brown vines draped from a deep green canopy. The tops of the trees are so dense, they cover the land like a choppy ocean, consuming a mountain range far in the distance. The only movement is two soaring birds, tiny in a flawless blue sky, and Lula's jerky steps backward as if her body is rejecting her bones. Her teeth chatter.

"I need to stay a few minutes and see if you attract anyone else." And because I don't think my sanity will allow her out of my sight. Forcing my eyes off her is impossible. They just pounce on her half a second later and touch every curve to make sure she's okay. Which she's not.

"Get out of here, Alex. I can't push you away much longer." She sucks in a sharp breath and tugs at her wet shirt, balling it in one small fist. It tightens against her breasts, and I take a step forward.

"Dammit, go!" She reaches down into the grass, searches, then throws a rock at me.

Snatching it from the air, I toss it aside. "I love you, Firecracker." I walk backward toward the portal. My insides lurch as if trying to move me toward her again. Everything in me tells me this is wrong. She can't do this alone. I'm abandoning her when she needs me the most.

Comus waits at the entrance, working his jaw in a fierce rhythm.

"Wait." Lula cries out. She falls to her knees, arms wrapping around herself. "No, go!" She delivers a string of curses that would make a red demon blush.

Every cell in my body struggles against my mind to run to her. The lust wave flows over me and retracts with an undertow designed to drag me where I belong. Her moan—*the* moan—rings through my brain and chastises me for leaving her in this state. She's in pain. She *needs* me.

Comus growls, and I stand still, staring at his intent expression.

"Are we prepared?" I ask, knowing what I'm asking could end us all, and cause the utter downfall of our carefully laid plans.

His eyes stay on Lula. "You mean to stay?" The way he asks isn't accusatory or harsh. He thinks as I do.

I manage a final attempt at rational thought. "What's a worse fate? She said this could last weeks without sex. Do you think she'd make it? She'd find someone if she had to crawl the ten miles. They're not made to do this alone." I lower my voice. "This would accelerate everything to a rate we may not be able to handle but..." Lula whimpers a sob that makes my hair stand on end and I glance behind me. "I won't leave her."

"He'll have to find Lu to curse her, and we won't let that happen." Comus pulls out his phone and backs through the chasm. "I'm calling your brother. He and I will have a meeting. And Rath. He's been itching to move forward."

Lula topples, writhing in the grass. Her deep moan turns into an agonized cry. The sound shakes me to my bones. I raise a palm. "Call together the full group. Alert them to possible conflict. No details."

I close the portal and face my fate.

Lula scrambles backward as I approach. "Alex, no. Please, fight it. Leave me."

I could grab her ankle and drag her to me. My muscles shake from the effort of holding back. She moans again. A note plucked out of the heavens. *Alex*, it says, *take what's yours*. But her worried eyes tell me she's fighting too. She's not ready for any of this. *Me neither, Firecracker.*

"I'm going over there," I say, pointing to a patch of trees. "Staying. Will keep you safe."

Agony rips through me with each step. Away is the last place I need to be. That damn force rolls over me again, tugging my cells closer to hers, screaming at me to ease her pain. I freeze, glaring at the impossibly far away tree line.

Lula's quick footfall approaches. *Thank gods.*

I turn and catch her, then lift her to straddle me. She connects to my lips with harsh force, and I groan, dropping to my knees.

Between hard kisses, Lula whispers, "I'm sorry. I'm so sorry."

"Not your fault." With a monumental effort, I cup her face and move back to look in her eyes. "I'll protect you. You're everything to me."

The small amount of control remaining dies as my hands touch as much skin as possible. I need to taste—*no*—consume her. She presses her hips against me, eager and rolling, and I curse the clothes between us. Grabbing the back of my shirt, I tug it over my head, then throw it. Wet fabric snags against Lula's heated body as I relieve her of her shirt. Lying her back on the grass, I nip her shoulder, to her sternum, to a lace-covered breast, and yank at her pants.

She slides her fingers under her panties and my vision wavers. I growl, angry to part with her for a fraction of a second as I kick off my jeans. I crouch over Lula and rip the lace barrier off. Snatching her hand, I suck her fingers, needing every bit of her, then hold her hips down with my palm.

She frantically flails to wrap her legs around me, more mindless with need than I am. I kiss her hard, and line up with the inferno between her legs. She whimpers and tries to scooch closer, but I've got her pinned. Gritting her teeth, she makes a cadence of growling mumbles and whimpers that would be adorable if not for her panicked, agonized state. She doesn't deserve pain.

Surging forward, I engulf myself until my eyes roll back with a brand of pleasure that is new to me. Lula cries out and slaps the earth behind her, grips grass and tugs, arching.

I was right. Being deep inside Lula is indeed the pinnacle of my divine life. I may be a god, but Lula makes me a lucky one.

Better than any heaven in existence. And she loves me.

Wedging my arm under her, I clutch her ass. Slow and gentle are impossible, and I worry I'm hurting her, but she digs her nails into my back and lifts her hips, sinking me deeper. The pheromone-induced haze has captured us up in the carnal tsunami and demands this fervor.

She moves a rhythm dance with me, little moans falling from her lips. She tries to bite them back but I release her teeth with my thumb and kiss her.

"Let go, baby," I say.

I'm not human. She can't hurt me so there's no reason to fight her nature. The buildup grows strong, tingling my spine. I should slow, be gentler, but Lu's grip on me tightens, and her sweet whimpers turn to a low growl. It brings out an animalistic side I wasn't even sure I possessed. I lick and nip her neck, traveling down. She tilts her head back, an invitation to my sex-focused brain, and I slide my teeth over her until the vibration of her ancient notes tickles my tongue. The moan ebbs and flows with her ragged breathing and syncs with my hard thrusts.

She drops her knees wide and I release her neck as I slam to the hilt. Getting close, I inhale her breath. The world pauses, everything tense and frantic, silent and overwhelming. She tightens around me, and eyes pleading before she cries out, loud and long.

My body obeys, whipping passion down my spine.

I push up on straight arms, bellowing to the universe as we ride out pulse after intense pulse in a release that seems like it was pent up for millennia.

Everything I am belongs to her. She can have it.

Have everything.

The world beyond Lula creeps back in slow silence. The sun heats my back as flawless, stark-white clouds move against the bluest sky I ever remember seeing. Leaves and grass restart their gentle rustling.

Lula trembles under me, wide-eyed and rapid breaths racing with mine. "I love you." She loops an arm around my neck, pulls herself up, and kisses me hard. She's still frantic, but the pain has left her eyes, and the tight lines holding her mouth in a grimace have melted away. "I love you so much, Alex. And I need you again."

So much for an afterglow. "Love you, too."

There's no pause in how my body responds to the mystic pheromones and I'm glad I stayed. I get it now. This was a curse aimed to demean the sirens. What purpose would it serve other than to torture them with killing human after human in an unstoppable death orgy? It was probably delivered by a jealous goddess who better have left in an exodus because she will not want to be in the universe when I find her. Sirens are meant to be with gods during this time, not humans. And this siren is meant to be with me.

I move back to kneel, holding her upright, tight against me as I try to regain my lost composure. Lula's flushed, her lips kiss swollen and red. Her curls are everywhere, still damp from the shower. Tangled in them are a few stray flowers. I pluck a small, purple one and toss it over my shoulder. Big green eyes gaze at me, so full of love and hope, the emotion threatens to strangle me, but then she rolls her hips.

Reaching down, I give her something to squirm about and she moans. She pushes closer against my fingers then tries to scoot away as if embarrassed. The pink highlighting her cheeks confirms her expression. Palming her backside, I keep her in place and grin. *No, Firecracker. This is mine now.*

I had contemplated if being with Lula on a sexual level would change the magnetism between us.

It has.

I want to possess her as she has me. Her body against me every day for the rest of eternity wouldn't be enough. I'll learn everything about her to a basal level and vice versa. Take her again and again until another being grows from our love and there's no dispute that we belong to each other.

I'm torn between the dozens of ways to savor her, but each idea revolves around claiming her. Filling her with my seed and having it take root. It's a new feeling I'm a bit shocked to experience. Is this part of the pheromones?

"Alex, please."

Her pained whimper spurs me into action and I surge further into the heat of her. Her lips part and she arches, one hand clutched around my neck and the other flat over my heart. When she moans that note again, I thrust to capacity and groan along with her.

Leaning forward, I nip her chin to get her attention. "How do you like it?"

Her eyes roll back and close as she moves her hips with me. "No words. 'Best ever' doesn't quite cover this."

She's right but now that the initial demand for release is slightly sated, I want to please her beyond comprehension. "No, Firecracker. How do you want me?"

"I want you. No commands. Do as you will. Yours."

I raise my eyebrows. She squeaks as I tip her back down to the grass and take her again, probably too hard, but she doesn't seem to mind. The release is impossibly strong, definitely mystical. Recovery time isn't only a human trait.

Her breathing calms, and she focuses on me. I touch her face, kiss her, and she reciprocates, her breath fluttering over my skin, causing chills. She smiles up at me, her eyes trailing over my face as if she's trying to memorize this moment. I roll, taking her with me, and run my fingers through her tousled mane as my mind pieces itself back together. Us ending up here was inevitable, though I couldn't have predicted siren heat being the method of our tumble.

The Council will find out. Dionysus told Comus that my grandfather is watching me for this exact thing. If they know about the sirens, they will understand. I will make them understand.

Lula palms my chest and pushes herself up. The call of lust laps at me again and all thought but our connection grows fuzzy. There's nothing more stunning than her working herself over me. She nibbles her lip and stares down at me like I created the universe.

I could live for a thousand years under her and never want for anything.

Now, we need to change the world to make that possible.

Chapter Twenty-Seven

LULA

There's no real concept of time, just the setting and rising sun, and the frenzied times Alex and I have been at each other. Twelve, maybe? Well, I wanted him, and he has delivered over and over again. Not that either of us had much choice in the matter.

I'm so glad it was him. He's saved me from excruciating pain, and from mental anguish that brings tears to my eyes when I consider what could have happened other than this. It's hard enough to kill someone who's trying to kill me or others. If innocent humans would have been around instead of Alex, I'm not sure how I'd cope after that.

I'd imagined being with him a hundred times, but I still wasn't prepared. Alex fills every centimeter of my needy body, the depths of my soul, the seconds of my life. He's everywhere.

One strong hand grips my hip, and the other gallivants down my spine, mixing up my brain with how hard and gentle he can be at the same time. He thrusts again, desperate and demanding. "Beautiful," he leans to whisper in my ear.

This is the greatest day.

Peeking back at him, I moan in response, gripping the pummeled grass. The pulse of the siren jolts through me.

He presses a kiss on my shoulder and bares his teeth against my skin. His sexy grunts make another wave hit me, and my sore insides clench, frantic for what he can give me. The tension may rip me apart, and just when I can't take anymore, my body sets into another hard orgasm as Alex holds himself deep within me and growls a final, long groan. His warmth spills, calming me from the inside out. One by one, my muscles unclench. I sigh long at the moment of peace.

Alex drops his forehead to my back, short puffs of laughter tickling my skin. He slides his arm around my waist, kissing over my shoulders as he guides me to the ground. We both hiss as he slips out. Turning me to face him, he lies on top of me. As we catch our breath, he holds my cheeks and presses soft kisses to my cheeks, nose, chin, then, at last, my lips.

"I wasn't too rough, was I? Are you okay?" His dilated eyes fill with concern.

"I'm great," I say, sliding my hands over his heated skin. "Tired and sore, but great."

He nuzzles against me. "I never want to hurt you, Lula. I love you."

This isn't real. I'll wake up any minute from this heaven, but when I test that theory, closing my eyes tight then opening them a couple of times, Alex still stares down at me in amusement.

"You're here," I say.

"Good of you to notice."

He's warm and heavy and very, very real. Gently kissing my sore lips, he makes comforting little "hmms." I want this to last forever—for him to be mine, and me to be his. To experience this with him every day without threat or consequence would be the greatest gift. However, there will be consequences.

What is our future going to bring? I swallow hard and tell him the truth. "No matter what happens, Alex, I appreciate you so much."

His eyes glass over as he clutches me to him, kissing my tender lips until I believe we could be together, that this will work out for us. It has to because it's *us* now. Our life.

"Tell me again," he whispers.

"I'm yours, Alex. I love you."

His grin blazes bright. I beam and wrap my legs around his waist, threading my fingers into his hair. I allow myself to picture a future with him while he makes love to me again. Sharing a home, being wrapped in Alex's arms every night, and having a green-eyed little girl with curls and a mission of doing right by others. I see her running in as the sun comes up and jumping on us until we get up and make breakfast together. I want it all.

As the day progresses, my temperature lowers, and the pulses subside. Alex's touch rarely leaves me. I wrap myself around him. "This is the happiest I've ever been."

He kisses my forehead. "Me too."

We lie naked on the soft ground. The grass is flat beneath us from our numerous romps. I run my fingers over Alex's chest and bask in his warmth, taking in every inch of his body in the setting sun. "Where are we?"

"Asia. A place I call Shangri-La. I discovered it hundreds of years ago and sometimes I visit to ponder in peace. It hasn't changed since I found it."

Though preoccupied, the rolling fields, dark green trees, and array of colorful flowers did catch my eye. It's silent except for a few bird songs and the swish of the warm breeze rustling the long grass. "It's gorgeous."

"You're more gorgeous." He shifts to nuzzle his face in my hair. "You didn't know you would go into heat, did you?"

"No. Neither did Grace. Amah should have told us."

"She knew?" At my *yes, absolutely* expression, he continues. "Is that why you're angry with her?"

"Yes. Well, it's the last straw. Why won't she talk about what we are? It's important." I huff. "She said not to get near Grace. She and Gerty fought to make sure we were always alone in the world. She knew. How does it even work? According to our records, it takes weeks to build to the peak, but it took hours and it's apparently contagious. There are eight."

Alex moves to look at me when I pause.

I clear my throat. "Seven. There are seven of us now, and Amah's keeping secrets that would help us understand our race better. I'm the closest one to her and she won't tell me shit. Who does that?"

Alex strokes my face. "She doesn't want you near me."

"No, she doesn't. We argued on the phone. Amah won't trust

anyone, but she was flat-out pissed I was with you and allowing you to help. Why wouldn't I? Although..." I signal to our state of nudity. "She wasn't entirely wrong on that account." I sigh. "What will happen, Alex?"

"Whatever happens, I'll protect you. You're mine, Firecracker. We'll change the world and be together. No boundaries."

I want to roll my eyes or scoff but only stare at Alex and hope he has a solution. He seems so determined as if he understands how everything will play out. But— "How?"

Alex holds my face in his hands. His concerned expression pops the peaceful bubble that's been encasing us all afternoon. "Lula." He swallows hard, and my stomach lurches. "I'm going to tell you something and—"

"Alexiares?"

I gasp and cower as Alex shields me with his body. He glares over his shoulder at the sound of the voice. His tense body relaxes. "Anice. Hey, brother. Want to turn around for Lu's sake?"

My eyes widen as I peek over Alex's shoulder. It's surreal looking at his twin as Alex holds his bare skin against mine. Anice waves and gives me a tight smile. He's Alex's corporate version with his shaven face, short hair, polo shirt, and khakis. He sets a white paper bag and a black duffle down in the grass and turns away. "I brought food and clothes. I'm going. Come back when you can."

"Anything we need to worry about yet?" Alex asks, holding me a little tighter to him.

"Not yet. Just...updates. Rath has joined us at the house. Prax is uh, his senses are regaining, so I thought it may be okay to come here." Anice stiffly moves toward the rip in the air and gives a glance over his shoulder. "And now I have."

"Okay. Thanks, brother."

"Yep. Hurry, if you can. We have lots to talk about." Anice disappears into the portal.

When it closes, Alex rolls on top of me and kisses me. "Your pheromones are still present."

"I see that," I say. "I'm starving. When did we last eat?"

Alex stands, and roots around in the large bag. He tugs out two bottles of water and lobs one to me. "Lunch yesterday. We've been distracted."

I chug the bottle, not realizing how thirsty I was. A notebook would be handy right now so I can report all of this to the other sirens. As he brings forth white boxes, his furrowed brow confuses me. I place a hand on his arm. "Hey, what's wrong?"

He grumbles something unintelligible to himself, then cups my face and kisses me. "Nothing that can't wait yet another day."

"You sure?"

Alex opens a container of fried white meat doused in cream. He stabs it with a fork and offers me a bite. The moment I get a taste, hunger pangs hit me as fiercely as my heat. It's melt-in-your-mouth fish, cooked in a rich buttery lemon sauce I'd eat with a spoon. Alex hands over the box with a smile and grabs another.

We ravish the boxes, but by the time I take my first bite of chocolate torte, Alex's hands are on my hips, and he's dragging me to him. This romp is purely for us though. The crazed need has lessened to gently lapping waves, and I now want to be close to Alex, enjoying every second of this new freedom I never believed I'd experience.

IN THE DARK, AMONG CHIRPING BUGS AND LATE-NIGHT BIRDS, I'M tucked into Alex's side, sated and happy. "I don't want this to end." I sit up and flinch at the soreness in my muscles. "But I need to find my sisters."

Alex looks over my bare body, gives a disgruntled sigh, and lifts up my crumpled, grass-stained shirt. "This isn't going to do." He pulls a tee out of the bag and hands that over instead. "We'll find them. Plus, the sooner we figure out how to handle what Zeus could throw at us, the better."

He doesn't bother with clothes, but grabs the bags, and opens a portal. We step onto dark bathroom tile. "I'm not risking walking you through the house with the guys until we've showered," he says, flipping on the water.

Alex washes with speed, then attacks my hair with shampoo and wild fingers until I slap them away, laughing. "Go talk. It will take a few minutes to detach the flora from these curls."

"Are you sure? I don't want to leave you."

I brush my fingertips against his scruff and kiss him. "Yes. Go ahead. I'll be down in a few."

His arms surround me. He holds me tight for a long moment, letting the jets run over us, before leaving me to the warm water. My jasmine soap has nothing on the scent of Shangri-La.

Sore and shaky, I pick flowers and grass stalks out of my hair, smiling as I remember how they got there. I'm exhausted, yet energetic. There's a warmth within, and I place a palm on my belly. It could happen but isn't likely. Not on the first heat.

It's for the better. We don't need evidence of our illegal actions—still, my hand circles. How is Grace? What thoughts are running through her mind right now?

With my hair in order and the dirt scrubbed away, I step from the shower. Comus and Alex are in a muffled argument downstairs. Rath's voice joins in. Thank goodness he's okay. My relief is short-lived, as a loud thunk shakes the floor, and the quarrel escalates to yelling. I jerk a shirt over my head, hop to pull on my pants, and sprint the stairs to the ruckus.

"What's going on?" I ask, eyeing the guys. Alex's face holds a rage I haven't seen as Rath stands between him and Comus, who grips his hips and turns toward the window.

All conversation stops. Alex shoves out of Rath's grasp and covers the distance between us in a few long strides, pulling me to him.

I peek over his shoulder at Rath. He stands by the door beside the couch, which is now askew, and stares out at the ocean while rubbing his neck. The skin underneath his fingers is dark.

Kissing Alex's cheek, I shimmy out of his hold to cross the room to Rath, wrapping my arms around him. "Are you okay?"

He hugs me back with near-crushing fervor. "I'll make it."

I catch the expression on Comus's face, which is all tension. "What's going on?" I repeat.

Rath releases me as Alex grumbles, "Nothing."

Comus's eyes narrow.

The air is thick with male dominance. This has to stop. "Well, I call shenanigans."

Comus clears his throat. "Alex and I need to leave for a few. Rath will stay with you."

"I'm not leaving." Alex moves to stand beside me, shooting daggers at Comus.

I grab Alex's hand and squeeze. "What's wrong?"

After a moment of contemplation, Alex sighs a deep breath. "War call. Anice already left. He and...the others will handle it."

"Moros?"

He chews his cheek while eyeing Comus. So, yes then.

"How long have you been feeling it? Is it strong?"

"Right before we came back. Yes, it's underway."

That's probably what he wanted to talk about. A dark and chilly tremor runs through me. "You're going to portal to him like last time?"

"No. I'm not leaving you."

Easy fix. "No problem. I'm coming with you."

The room erupts with protests.

"Absolutely not." *Comus.*

"No way. No." *Alex.*

"Over my dead body." *And Rath.*

"Moros likely has my missing sisters. I've already lost one of them because of this bastard, and I don't intend to lose another."

"Lula, you can't." Alex shakes his head.

I glare at him. *Watch me.* Why is he acting as if me wanting to get to my sisters is some crazy idea? It's not, and I'm going. I turn to Comus. "Anice is there? Get him on the phone, and I'll talk to him." And get him back here by portal, then I'll go through.

Comus snorts. "No, Lula. Alex and I need to go alone. Moros easily kills gods with zero remorse. You have no power over him. We know how to treat him and can stay relatively safe around him, but if he thinks you're involved with Alex, things will turn disastrous."

They have history? I give Alex a questioning glance.

"I locked him in a hell realm," he says with nonchalance. "He's got a bit of a grudge."

"I can help," I say. Their silence and shifty glances at each other make me growl. "If Moros has one or both of my missing sisters, and tries to make them sing, we will beat him at his own game. I'll control the crowd." If my past when Lena was around is any indication, my thrall may overpower theirs. "I'll force them to run away—save them even if she commands them. If possible, I'll talk to her and see if he has Hazel as well. You *need* me. I'm going."

"What if he doesn't have them?" Alex asks. "What if he sees his opportunity to have another siren and takes you? I can't, Lula. You don't understand how much I just can't."

His eyes are glassy and wild and it takes me a moment to wrap my head around the emotion on his face. Protective, determined, and scared. I don't like it. I don't like any of this.

Rath approaches, his voice low. "If he has your sisters, and I'm able to get close enough, I can get them out of there."

"You can?"

He bobs his head. "Absolutely."

"Great." I snatch Alex's fingers in mine while I wait for him to open the portal. We'll stay far enough away from the psycho. Four of us are better than two, and against one old god? We can do this.

Rath approaches. "Let me show you how I'll get your sister out."

I watch in puzzlement as he slowly reaches for my free hand and slips my fingers into his. How is this going to help my sisters?

Alex kisses my head. "It's too risky, Lu. Zeus is there. I'm sorry."

My grip on Alex falters at the sound of Zeus's name. He jerks his hand from mine just as Rath tugs and spins me, wrapping his arms around me. Backed into him, I struggle, but his grip is iron.

Numb dizziness overtakes me in waves. I raise my fingers and watch them turn ashen then disappear in wisps of smoke. "Rath? No! Alex! No, no, no—"

Alex grimaces as I fight against Rath, screaming a garbled mix of obscenities until everything goes dark gray.

Chapter Twenty-Eight

ALEX

Comus and I sprint out the door to the shoreline. Once there, I close my eyes and grasp at the location we need to be, but my thoughts are elsewhere.

I didn't expect Lula to insist on coming with me, but I have every intention of keeping her from ever being face-to-face with Zeus. Her curses echo through my head. Images of her struggling, face taut with insulted disbelief, haunt me. Fading doesn't hurt, and if any danger shows up at the house, Rath can hide her faster than I can. Still, it was torture to watch.

"Focus, Alex. You're going to need every bit of concentration to get us there and deal with this shit storm. If we stop Moros now, that's one less thing in our way."

Our conversation from a couple of days ago comes to memory. "We could use him. He could be an excuse for more darklings to cross." He found out how to return. We could pin our plan on him and keep Lula out of it until she walks in to save the day. She'll be the hero, and Moros will still be a monster.

"Rath doesn't even agree with that method," Comus says. "And he's the radical one. Moros is uncontrollable. The only being qualified to control the darklings is stuck in the shadows for the next minute, and if she finds you before we get to Moros, we'll never leave. Zeus will find out about your indiscretion faster because you were a no show after being summoned and Moros will harm another sister or two after he uses them to wipe out the humans little by little. We have to stop him now, then get Lula on board."

My stomach churns at the thought of the conversation I'll have with Lula. "I couldn't tell her earlier. I tried, failed, and I've waited too long. The day I came back from meeting with Ichnaea should have been the moment I confessed everything."

"Lula will understand what you had to do, and why. She's strong, and damn near fearless when it comes to helping others. Keep on the path by sharing little, and slowly bring her into this. That's the plan."

"Yeah, but how would you explain? We've studied Lu and her sisters like a new-found specimen because Olympus hid information on them. She's been my test subject. How would you take the news if you were in her shoes? She's going to walk away, and she should. Gods, this is so screwed up."

"Alex, let's address this later. If we don't go now, Zeus or Moros will find Lula, and you won't get the chance to tell her. For the love of Hera, focus."

He's right. I inhale a deep breath of ocean air and search. Finally, my attribute breaks through, and I pinpoint the location. Comus keeps his attention on the house, watching for Lula, as I slice my hand through the air, and peek inside the portal.

The vegetation in this area looks similar to the place we saw Moros last time, but this group of humans is alive and twice as numerous.

Just as planned, Anice stands next to our grandfather. They've brought along Apollo, Dionysus, Deimos, Ares, Athena, and some demigod guards as well. I would like to have seen Hermes but Zeus probably thought Hermes wouldn't come back to Olympus if he saw humans at this point.

The thought that we're exposing the sirens sits like a heavy ball in my gut, but if we stop Moros right now with the other deities and return him to the hell realm, everyone will be safe. We'll adjust our plan to fit the situation. It might even help our cause.

I close the portal and weave through the humans with Comus following me. We halt beside Anice. Twenty feet away, Moros has a brunette at his side, her upper arm tight in his grasp. I don't recognize her, though she is gorgeous. Another siren?

"I take it he's not surrendering?" I whisper to Anice.

Tight-lipped, he shakes his head.

"You two again?" Moros grins. "So lovely for you to join our...discussion. Where's your comrade? Were his wounds too much for him?" The bastard smiles as if awaiting marvelous news. "It's a hard death, isn't it?"

He wants us scared and angry, like my grandfather, who's darkening the sky with speeding, black clouds. Zeus can't do anything to Moros but punch him and he's giving away his mood. His emotions are too much to control but why? Yeah, we need to deal with Moros again, but Zeus was calmer a couple of hundred years ago when he tasked Anice and me with booting the God of Doom from the realm. Moros had defied law, went to Earth through an open emergency portal in the Council's chambers, and created a plague. This is Zeus's first walk among the mortals since then, and he needs to work on his poker face.

"Death? We wouldn't know." I smile wide for Moros and use an amused tone. He hates it when I act like him. "Rath is fine. Shrugged your evil right off. Now, let the woman go." I move forward, and Anice and Comus sync with me. "Keep away from his hands," I whisper to the surrounding gods. "Break his arms at the elbows if you can."

"Or get his shoulders out of joint," Comus adds, tilting his head until his neck cracks.

"That too. Wait until there's a distraction, then we move. Have patience." This time is different. We warred with him for a mere hour last time, but he killed so many, and now he has a probable-siren in his clutches.

Moros takes a step back, but we follow as a unit. Thunder rumbles around us. He gives the woman a shake. "Sing, little bird."

She whimpers, and I lock eyes with her, noticing they are the same shade of green as Lula's. I stumble to a halt. She'd mentioned Venora and Hazel shared the rare eye color with her. I need to get this siren away from him and take a chance on her name. "Venora?"

Moros's smile fades and he looks back and forth between us.

Her eyes widen, confused but hopeful. She nods as Zeus booms, "Moros, this has gone on long enough. Unhand the daughter of Aglaope and surrender."

I exchange a glance with Comus. Zeus knows the sirens—the original mothers. The skies darken, showing my grandfather's foul mood. This situation could get worse with a quickness.

"How does it feel to set eyes on one of Agie's blood again?" Moros continues back through the human crowd, which parts for him and his captive but closes for us, making keeping up with them difficult. "Does it hurt that I've had her daughters and you haven't? They are so similar with their hair and eyes." He tilts Venora's head back and forth and she gives a choked gasp.

Comus and I share a look. I mouth, *Agie?* There's an old, undocumented story between them and I'm itching to understand it.

"Where is your wife?" Moros says, looking around. "I was hoping she'd appear for a chat. It has been so long." His voice is slow and chiding.

Lightning cracks a half-mile off, twin bolts that make the humans flinch and move closer together. He's playing a game with my grandfather and winning.

"Careful, Moros," Zeus growls.

"We could have had a delicious battle with the right players." As we shoulder through, Moros jerks Venora again, harder this time. "Sing or give me the information I seek."

"First let Hazel go," she says. "Please."

"You're not in any position to negotiate, pet." Moros chuckles as he drags her even faster through the crowd. "Tell me. Now."

"Moros!" Zeus booms. "Flank him," he says to Ares.

The red-eyed god smiles and he and Deimos slide out and run along the edge of the humans. Two guards mumble to each other before one breaks from us as well.

"I don't know!" she chokes and begins to weep. "She's missing. Please, you don't need Hazel."

Moros shakes her once again, jostling her back and forth so hard, I'm afraid her slender arm will pop out of joint. The shirt she's wearing swings around her, too big. Has she been eating? Her profile reminds me of Lula's and rage surges through me. This is her sister, her line. This could be Lula, now or next.

I shove through a group of humans, who stay on their feet, but barely. "She won't go far if you break her, Moros."

He sneers. "Oh child, are you attached to this rare species? Are you already bored with your bride, and following right in your bloodline's path?"

Lightning hits too close to Venora, who screeches, making the human crowd jerk as one.

I turn my head to my grandfather. "Stop." Lighting will do nothing but harm Venora and humans, possibly us as well.

His jaw flexes. "You know nothing, Moros."

Moros watches Deimos and Ares out of the side of his eye. Did Deimos nod at him? He blocks Ares from moving forward with his arm.

Moros looks back at me. "I know much." I step within reach, but he pulls Venora close, hand around her throat, and kisses her jaw. She cringes. "Especially about sirens. They have their advantages. You know all about that, do you not, King?" He spits 'King' as if it's a curse, as he eyes Zeus. "Show them, Venora. Show them the power they exiled. Sing for the crowd. Now." His tone is defensive, which perks my attention, but then he whispers something in her ear. She pales further before his expression hardens to one he has aimed at me far too many times. *Watch this*, it says.

Venora trembles, face crumpled in anguish. Furious, I struggle for composure, afraid the wrong move could end her. "What is it you want, Moros?" I step sideways, waiting for that split-second opportunity. Comus follows and Athena crowds my back.

"I told you last time, stupid boy. I want the world—my world in its perfect state." He eyes Zeus with a scowl. "You should not have kept us apart."

"She was not yours." Zeus throws three humans aside and they crash into others, spurring a line to fall like dominoes. Dammit, not what we need. He doesn't seem to notice. "Anicetus, Alexiares, create the portal. It is time to return to the hell realm, Moros."

Moros tightens his grip on Venora's neck and gives a wry smile. "Now."

A tension fills the air and humans start shuffling. Breathing comes in pants for some, and others cover their ears and whimper. One breaks into a run and smashes into another, who also takes off, creating chaos. This is an attribute of fear. *Deimos.*

Venora's voice trumpets out the beautiful notes I dread to hear. The silent, confused crowd comes to attention, turning toward the siren.

"Venora, no!" I shout, and spring, but Moros whips back as well, whispering in Venora's ear, and a guard launches in front of us.

There's a scuffle close by but I can't get a visual of anything as the guard drags a sword from the golden sheath hanging at his side. Athena leaps in front of me, dagger in her hand. People no longer scatter, but they move toward Venora, acting as an unknowing barricade.

Moros laughs, but Venora stops her song and points at us. "Stop them!" she commands. "Don't harm them but stop them." When the humans careen at us, Venora yells, "Hazel's at six-hundred fi—"

Moros roars and covers Venora's mouth as the crowd engulfs us. He backhands her, then tosses her slumped form over his shoulder as the bodies close in and block my vision. I struggle to reach them, now pushing people out of the way, but as a swarm of ants overpowers a hornet, humans overtake me, pinning me beneath a mountain of bodies. I can't get out without injuring the people stacked on me, though some already groan or cry out with the weight. Comus yells, muffled but close. I find an opening as hands grip my legs and arms, but they can't hold me back as I drag myself from the pile just to see a car fly down a road, kicking up dust as it goes.

The ground rumbles and a lightning strike rips through all other sounds like gunfire. Screams sound along with the rumbling creation from my grandfather and the load on top of me lightens.

When I'm able to rise from the tangle of squirming people, chaos meets me. Humans cower and run in every direction. Lightning flashes around like disco lights and thunder reverberates through my chest as a heavy bass would in a nightclub. My grandfather stands in the center of a downed group.

Moros and Venora are gone, as is Deimos, and one of the guards. Athena has the other guard on the ground, her dagger lodged an inch below his chest plate. Dionysus kneels beside them, talking to the guard. Zeus wears a mask of utter rage, yelling at Apollo, who strides to Ares. The God of War writhes on the ground with his own spear through his side. What the hell?

My first instinct is to sprint in the direction of the car but the drop my stomach prevents my feet from moving as Anice and Comus sidle up to me and we survey the horrid scene before us.

Direct strike. Twenty bodies scattered, singed skin and burnt hair are pungent on the breeze. I move to the nearest victim to begin CPR. "Why would you do this?"

Comus drops to his knees to help another victim, a child with a dark red lighting burn on her face, while my brother and Dionysus observe. Anice springs into action as the young woman I'm working on gasps a breath of air.

"What are you doing?" Zeus asks.

I move to another human, a man who looks to be in his mid-fifties. "Cardiopulmonary Resuscitation. CPR. Electrocution victims have an excellent chance of survival if you restart their heart." I glare at my grandfather as I start chest compressions. "I can't believe you did this."

His stony face remains apathetic.

The child Comus has been helping twitches awake and cries. It's a refreshing sound, and I breathe a little easier.

"Apollo," I yell. "We need you here."

"He's assisting Ares," Zeus says as if I didn't have eyes.

"Ares is moving and immortal. He'll be fine in an hour." *Unfortunately.* "*Our* people need help." There are too many bodies still on the ground, too many unmoving.

Apollo looks to Zeus, who doesn't say a thing. The God of Healing tugs the spear from Ares, ignoring the god's pained cry, hands it to him and rushes to a man gasping for air after his heart restarted.

"Where are we?" Comus asks as he moves to work on someone else, a woman that may be the child's mother.

I continue to pump the middle-aged man's chest and take a quick look around. A group of wide-eyed humans has come out of their stupor now that their purpose has been served and survey the catastrophic scene.

I call out to them. "Where are we?"

"I'm a nurse." A woman hurries over, dropping beside me to check the man's vitals. "What happened?"

German. "Lightning strike," I answer, also in German. "Where's the nearest hospital?"

She glances around. "I... don't know. I'm not sure where we are."

"It's okay. We need help."

That gets her on track and she checks the pulse of my victim. "Keep going." She moves to the next person and shouts orders at a few other people standing around, who jump into action.

Zeus snorts, but I ignore him. The nurse studies his grand robes as she pulls out her phone and dials. The man I'm working on heaves for air and rolls over to vomit. I move to the next and notice Anice is aiding a teenage boy. My twin is pale and stressed. The boy's face is ashen.

"Anice, switch with me."

He keeps his eyes down. "No."

The nurse takes over for me, and I run and kneel beside Anice to scrutinize the boy. He's not older than fifteen, and there's no pulse on his floppy, pale wrist. Primary flaccidity has already occurred. "Anice, he's gone."

I'm not sure when Anice last interacted with a human, but determination lights his eyes, and he resumes chest compressions. I lay a hand on his shoulder, but he shrugs it off.

The nurse joins us and takes the teen's wrist. "I'm sorry," she says, squeezing Anice's arm. With a final glance at the boy, she rushes off to help those still in need of saving.

Humans run back and forth shouting questions and directions in ordered chaos. They touch each other and hold the hands of scared survivors, their voices reassuring strangers. Zeus watches, silent and unmoving. He hasn't seen the humans in hundreds of years. Hasn't visited his charges to see how they've progressed, nor accepted that they've influenced us too. He cut us off from them, but our language has changed, following the mortal's lingo and we haven't had a death since the hybrids. They calm and change us but could do more if we reconnected. We're not meant to be this way, our realms should be *our* world.

My anger boils over like a geyser. "Do you see what they do? How they care for each other even though they've never met. When was the last time you saw a group work together so well, and with such compassion? This happens every day on Earth."

His eyes narrow. "Careful Alexiares. The Council works together every day."

"You're wrong," Anice says. I turn to see him glaring at our grandfather with wet eyes. To my dismay, he pumps the boy's chest again.

Zeus frowns. "Anicetus, what do you mean?"

I pat my brother's cheek. "Anice. Stop. There's nothing more to be done. Humans are fragile. You tried."

"No," he says, but slows. Finally, he gives up, but his attention remains on the boy. His eyes lift to our grandfather, harden, and turn murderous. Then, he's up and slamming his fist into Zeus's surprised face.

A moment too late, I grab Anice and pull him back. He's shaking. "You're as bad as Moros," he snaps. "Why would you let loose a bolt in the crowd like that?"

Our grandfather rubs his bearded jaw, his cold eyes studying my brother. "They should not have held me back."

"They were enthralled!" Anice starts for him again, but I manage to hold him with Comus's help. "You killed them!"

"Shh, brother," I whisper to him.

Thunder rumbles and another lightning strike hits the ground a couple of feet away. Several humans screech, and Apollo stands. Athena and Dionysus slip between Zeus and us, dragging the guard with them.

"We need to go," I calmly address Zeus over Dionysus's shoulder. "Or we'll cause hysteria. You don't want that, and it appears we have some things to work out." I signal to the guard.

Anice relaxes under my grip and gazes at the teenager again.

"What has happened to you, Anicetus?" Zeus asks, inflection as hard as the thunder.

Ambulance sirens sound in the distance.

"You happened," Anice says. "I see how you've lost whatever humanity you may have had."

"*Humanity?*" Zeus spits the word on the ground. "We are not human." His careless shrug makes me want to launch at him myself. He looks to Council members as if they're in on a joke, but the others are busy surveying the humans. Their shoulders are slumped and faces drawn in frowns.

Anice strides away toward a thick patch of trees. We follow and once out of sight, he opens a portal. "They are better than us and far better than you."

"Anicetus," Zeus growls as my brother strides into Olympus.

I block the passage. "Give him a moment."

Zeus needs to leave him alone. When Anice gets riled up, no one should approach. He's the undefeatable deity and while it takes a lot to push him to this level, he's there and looking for a fight. We need peace, not another war. That's the tried-and-unsure divine method and it's time we turned to a better age and worked out our issues instead of stabbing those who don't agree with us.

Ares limps over, scowling, his red gaze on the guard. Some demons have his eyes, but he won't confess to having made them that way. "We have a problem." His grumble is mournful in nature.

No way. Comus runs his hand over his mouth and looks at me with wide eyes.

"Tell me where Deimos is," Zeus says, looking around. His eyes pause on Ares's robes as if he's only now noticing he's coated in blood. "Explain."

I whip my head to the path the ambulances are coming in as if I'll see the car Moros took out of here. They're long gone. Back in the dark ages, Moros had followers, but Deimos? Sure, he's an asshole, but he's also a Council member. The wheels spin, smoky and flaming behind Comus's eyes.

"There has been a deception," Ares says.

Oh, hell. I don't know whether to punch the air or kick dirt. The Council is fucked if Deimos spills their secrets to the God of Doom, but the world may be as well. Doom and terror now walk the Earth. And they have Lula's sisters and an Olympian guard.

I turn and walk into the portal as Zeus roars. I don't flinch, nor does Comus, who steps in line with me. We follow the walkway of Olympus' Grand Hall.

"That will change a few things," I whisper to Comus.

He pulls his phone out and sends a text to Rath. "Maybe for the better. Maybe not."

He usually has an idea and pitches it at me to mull over. This doesn't bode well. "You asked about Firecracker, right?" I won't say her name in this palace of marble and enemies.

His phone buzzes. He flips the phone over and breaks out in a relaxed laugh. The sound lowers my bunched shoulders an inch. "She's fine, though you're not when she sees you again. Game plan?"

Works for me. I deserve it. "Humans and sirens need protection," I say, stating the obvious. None of this is their fault. At Comus's nod, I add, "Surreptitiously find out what Zeus knows about the sirens and see if Deimos and the guard can be tracked."

"Definitely." Comus peeks over his shoulder and speeds his steps, loafers quiet on the walkway.

"New priority one: find Deimos, Moros, get Venora back and end this. We will need help. We need to work together."

"That would be ideal and take a certain spotlight off you, which is necessary, and vying for priority one."

I need to get back to Lula, now more than ever. "Want to take bets on how long this meeting will take?" Maybe we'll actually learn something this time.

"Four hours and two tantrums." Comus holds a hand out.

"Two hours. The third tantrum and a storm out will cut us off early."

We shake and step into the Council room.

Chapter Twenty-Nine

LULA

"You're such an ass!" I yell at Rath.

He folds his arms behind his head and shifts deeper into the mudroom's loveseat. "Hey, I can't help it if you clump all your battleships together and I take out your entire fleet in record time. You are a shitty strategist, Lu."

"I am not." Actually, I'm not sure I've ever had to strategize anything beyond an evening out, but even then, it's not like I followed the plan. I stick to rules; don't enthrall unless necessary, don't go looking for trouble, stay away from crowds—okay, so one out of three isn't terrible, right? I *am* a shitty strategist.

"Are too," he says as if this is common knowledge between us.

"What are you, five? 'Are too.'" This conversation is getting more immature by the second, but something about Rath brings out a sassy preteen vibe I've watched actors harness on sitcoms.

"I'm older than you." He rolls the sleeves of his charcoal gray Henley. "B7."

I flop on the couch and sigh to the ceiling. "You sank my battleship."

"Yeah, I did." He unfolds himself from the loveseat and reaches for the ceiling.

"Cheater."

"You take that back, woman, and admit that Battleship just isn't your forte."

Rath returns my glare with practiced ease. I stand and walk past him, showing him my teeth in contempt. He arches a brow. "Where are you off to?"

"To drown my sorrows in ice cream."

There are only a few spoonfuls of chocolate left and if Alex thinks I'm leaving them for him, he's so wrong. We both check off chocolate as our favorite dessert, but he stranded me here with no explanation or way to know what's happening. Comus sent a text message Rath will only describe as 'We lived, details later.'

Now, I wait.

As soon as I reach the kitchen, Rath appears in front of the fridge, snags the container from the freezer, and grabs a spoon from the drawer.

I point my finger. "Don't you dare." I need that.

He raises his eyebrow again and passes it over with no attempt to keep it away.

I twist my lips and drum the cardboard top with the spoon. "Thank you."

Rath is like a cat. He'll rub against your leg one second and bite you the next. Although his nips seem more teasing in nature as if he's asking a question that can only be answered with immature banter stemmed from rage. Annoying but effective.

In a yelling match, I told him about how pissed off I am at Amah because I can't trust her anymore, and Alex has ruined my chance to find my sisters, but he better be okay too. With more poking of the right buttons, Rath had me admitting that I'm terrified of Zeus, Moros, the other gods, and of getting pregnant, which I shouldn't be. He had me explaining the history of our siren cycle to him, if any of that is true—I honestly don't know anymore—and then I was back on being mad at Amah all over again.

It was an impressive rant that should have never happened, but when I ran out of steam, Rath squeezed my shoulder and made me a sandwich. Somehow that made everything better and I think we may be good friends now.

He leaves to make another sweep of the house. At least there's more time between his scans.

Entering the shadow realm was by far the oddest thing I've ever experienced. Rath's attribute reduced me to nothing but my mind, which lay suspended in the dark points of the house. He dragged me to the dark attic, which was empty, but also bright because I wasn't trapped in a shadow. I *was* the shadow. If he hadn't anchored me, I would have explored—wandered off on a reverse light beam.

Once I solidified in the empty mudroom, I cursed him, Alex, and Comus to the fiery hell realms, then laid into Grace for turning off her phone, then Rath directed my rage into the massive info share.

After that, he moved through the house, examining every nook and cranny with me following along, eating my BLT.

Ten minutes later, he made the same sweep, then again another ten after that. I calmed with time, and understand my guys are trying to keep me safe. Still, Alex will be in the doghouse when he returns, but my remaining anger is giving way to concern for Rath.

His casual demeanor doesn't hide the fact he's a nervous wreck underneath, and it's distracting me from my fury. His eyes flick in the direction of normal house sounds—the icemaker turning on, a creak of settling floorboards, a bird caw from the deck. He won't let me go to the bathroom without standing guard by the door.

He fingers over the dark spot on his neck, and I don't like it, so I'm making it my job to distract him with riveting games of Battleship and checkers. He excels at both and has bested me each time.

A growing concern for Alex and Comus competes with my worry for Rath. It's been a half-hour since the text. How long will they be? Suspecting that Rath is nervous for them as well makes it worse. He says they're fine now, but his jaw is tight and he smiles at me often, as if easing my mind is his job, but his eyes tell me he'd rather kick a wall, cross his arms, and pout until they return because he should be there with them. As should I.

Rath returns to the kitchen, and I take the last bite of ice cream, scraping the bottom of the cardboard container. I'll make Alex and the guys brownies. "They'll be okay?"

His attention wavers from the windows to me and he drops his hand from his neck. He smiles. "They will. Hey, let's watch a movie."

I'm not reassured. "How long will they be?"

"As long as it takes. What do you like to watch?" His curt answer tells me I won't get much out of him.

"I don't know. What do you have here?"

His lips twitch up in a half-smile. "A bunch of stuff I doubt you will like."

What kind of television do deities watch? Maybe they sit together on Saturdays, a mythological documentary playing, yelling about how inaccurate the human's myths are and throw popcorn at the screen. "Lead the way." Does Alex have a favorite movie?

We head into a room I haven't explored yet. Four large armchairs face a huge screen. "Ah, so here is the bachelor portion of the house. I was getting worried."

Rath chuckles, probably remembering an earlier conversation we had on men who like to lavish. He denied ever taking a bubble bath, but I bet he's lying. He seems like the kind of guy who will pamper himself. Opening a cabinet, he sweeps his arm at an extensive collection of movies from the decades.

My breath hitches at the variety of titles. I've watched most, laughing and crying along at the gift humans brought to me with the invention. They let me in. Gave me a million windows I could peek in to view a slice of humanity that someone created and shared willingly.

A touch to my arm brings me out of a fog of dramatic plotlines and tension-filled kisses. My heart squeezes tight. I've experienced these things now. Not all, but a sweet, fulfilling taste.

I beam at Rath. "These are good titles." I tip an old literary masterpiece from the shelf so he can see the title. "This is your favorite, isn't it?"

He scratches his neck. "That's not mine."

"Mmhmm. Sure it isn't."

He leaps into action, bumping me out of the way with his hip, he jerks it from its location to pop into the DVD player. "It's not. Comus likes anything historical. I was hoping you'd pick something more explosive." His words are playful but the tone is concerned. He doesn't seem to like it when I'm upset but doesn't realize that I'm overwhelmed in a good way.

"We can watch exploding things."

"No, Lu. If you want to watch this one, we'll watch this one."

"Aw, be careful, Rath. I can see your sweet side." I pat his cheek and speak in a singsong voice. "What an angel." The scowl is more natural on his face.

"Don't make me regret being nice," he says. "I will fade you to the arctic if you don't stop."

"I hate the cold," I say, wrinkling my nose and poking his side. "Do you threaten your woman like that?"

"She'd use me for target practice." His eyes stay adhered to the wall. He means that?

The legends of the gods are twisted with occasional bouts of mercy and obsession. I'm so curious about how Olympian relationships work. Is there room for Alex and me in their world?

I open my mouth to dive in, but Rath waves me off. "Nope. No way. Not getting into that." He sprawls his long frame into a chair and pushes play on the movie.

Looks like I hit a sore point. I'll have to explore that. He's so playful. Is his goddess? Not if she would shoot him for teasing.

I do my best to lose myself in the movie, but my mind is everywhere it shouldn't be. Is Rath's goddess young too? How many others are his age and what do they do for the world? I have a library of divine knowledge beside me, and we're watching something I've seen ten times. Alex and Comus understand even more. How much do they remember of the old ways, and is that how things still are?

Halfway through, I pause, making an excuse for snacks, but I haven't been watching for at least fifteen minutes. Where are they?

Rath is up and stalking around the house as soon as I stand. When he comes into the kitchen, he stares out the window with that unsettled expression again. For the thousandth time, images of the guys fighting and losing run through my troubled mind. What if Zeus already knows what happened with my heat? Moros could have both my sisters and be planning something huge? What if Zeus and Moros have my sisters as well as Alex, and they are on their way here to murder us all. *Okay, that's too far.* Comus texted and said they were fine. That was also an hour and a half ago.

I snag pretzels, toss the unopened bag on the small side table between our seats and curl back into the comfy chair, leaving the movie frozen on the screen. "I'm worried about my sisters, Alex and Comus...you."

His expression tightens, and he plops down as well. "They'll be back soon."

"You don't know that."

"We have to believe it." He rubs his neck. "We must believe everything will work out because if we don't, it won't. If we give up, everything falls apart."

I didn't peg him as an optimist. "Okay, so everything will work out. Excellent. What's the plan?" He eyes me warily and tilts his head, so I add, "I mean, we can't just sit, right? What happens if they don't come back soon? I need to find my sisters, and I can't do that from this chair."

An expression passes over Rath's face that I think is relief or at least understanding—like he sighed on the inside. "We sit, for now, then we plan and move forward." There's a faint smile on his lips as he looks at the television.

"Yeah, but how? Alex seems to have a game plan of some kind, but he's vague and..." I trail off, considering. My golden god is always thinking. He's so forthright with certain information, throwing it out there like these Olympian secrets are common knowledge, but they aren't. He's shared so much with me but I think I told Rath more about my life today than I have Alex. That makes me scrunch my nose. "He's told me some, but it's not connecting. He seems involved in Olympus." He's dragged away all the time for meetings and attribute calls.

"He is heavily involved and as for plans, it's complicated and alters daily. It seems disconnected because there's no way to pin down an exact path. He'll explain when he can."

When he can? Rath can tell me Alex is wrapped up with Olympian duties but as he reaches for the remote, doesn't seem keen on offering more. I glare and block his hand. "You don't trust me?"

"Sure we—I do, Lula, but certain information will put you in danger. Make you a target."

I give off a short, painful laugh. "As if I'm not in danger already. My sisters are missing." Rath goes to open his mouth, but I hold up a finger and raise my voice. "We've been in hiding, which isn't unusual.

We don't see each other, we don't settle. Well, my sisters don't." I can't handle moving every six months as Amah does, and she hates that about me. "I'll get cursed before this is over and you know it. I've brought hell down on my sisters and I'm not happy that Olympus is the threat. That crushes more than a few fairy tales for me."

Rath purses his lips and taps the arm of the chair with a long finger. "You're protected. Zeus would have to find you first and touch you to curse you. We're not going to let him get close to you. We'll bring you into this, but one thing at a time. Progress comes with a sheer ton of patience. Alex needs you to be understanding with him."

"But—"

"Lula. Patience. Can you do that?"

I growl and flop my legs over the armchair. "Fine. Truth or dare?"

"You have got to be kidding me."

"Nope, not joking. Unless you care to talk about what Alex and Comus are doing instead, ponder their whereabouts, plan my revenge for cutting me off from my sisters."

"Keeping you safe, you mean." He makes a disgruntled groan. "This is going to go south. Truth."

"Who is she?"

His eyes narrow. "What are you talking about?"

"You called out my feelings about Alex because you understood. Who is your goddess?"

"Dare."

Oh no. That's not how the game is played. "Too late. Let the cat out of the bag, Rath. It's good for you."

"Not this cat."

I wait, unmoving in a silent standoff until Rath leans forward, resting his elbows on his knees and linking his fingers. "I can't believe I'm telling you this." He waits so long to speak again, I have time to shift in my seat, sit up, cross my legs, and clear my throat. "Artemis."

I squeak with shock and clamp my lips together, biting them shut. Artemis? Like *the* Artemis? "Oh."

"Just say it." He rolls his hand through the air. "Tell me how ridiculous it is that she has worship altars, books written about her, statues, even companies in this age named after her and she's seeing—sneaking around with a shunned, no-name god of the newest generation. As if I don't know." He swirls a long finger through the air. "That's not even starting with the virgin-for-eternity issue."

"Is that true?" I ask, wide-eyed. Alex and I lasted a whole two months. How long has Rath been with Artemis and not had sex?

He shoots me a dirty look. "Have I told you how much I hate truth or dare?"

"Have you played truth or dare?"

"No." He leans back, crossing his arms.

"Then how can you hate it?" I smile wide at him. "Is she pretty?"

"Gorgeous." He closes his eyes for a long moment. "And tough as nails, but fragile too."

"How long have you been with her?"

"That's all you are getting. Truth or dare?"

I wonder how many people he shares with. I reach over and squeeze his arm. "For what it's worth, I don't think it's ridiculous. You're a catch, Rath."

Rath pats my hand but he doesn't really react. Only stares ahead. "Truth or Dare?"

This should get interesting. "Dare."

Rath stands and walks out of the room. He returns with a lemon and tips his head toward the hallway. "We're going to want to be in the kitchen for this."

Chapter Thirty

ALEX

Zeus pauses inside the Council room door, turning to me. His drawn face is red with rage. "We meet about Moros. Now."

Why does he think I'm still here? I walk beside him, deeper into the Council Room, and join the Council members. I haven't seen them look so distraught since this happened last time. There's no trace of smugness as they take their thrones. Ares won't look up from the floor, but with the blow he received today, he will tuck his tail for a week.

Four seats are now empty, and it takes all my willpower not to point and say, 'I told you so.' Deimos is evil, and I don't like that he's on Earth, but I don't like Deimos anywhere. How many times did I try to deter my grandfather from letting him sit on the Council? I've lost count.

Comus stands tall beside me and Zeus glares, his expression disapproving. Per the plan, Comus has become more outspoken in the last few weeks, and as we expected, Zeus and the other Council members are grumbling. The calmer, rational members on one side, the hate-filled warmongers on another, and a few split between, delightfully unsure of which way to turn. They divide at the slightest diversion, and another point in the plan's timeline comes to fruition.

What will they do with the Moros issue, and the information bomb I've laid out and am set to detonate?

Zeus will side with the bigger group and bully the others into submission. He's a politician that way. He opens his mouth, and I know exactly what he's going to say.

"Comus needs to be here," I interrupt before he tells me my friend can't open portals, therefore it's not his business.

"Alexiares—"

"I would tell him and Rath, anyway." I've gone through this moment a thousand times in my head. There are outcomes, two likely, six possible, two outliers. They run the gamut from making my grandfather amused, to one of us getting bolted, but it's time to move forward, for humans, for Lula, and for Olympus. "You've listened in on our phone calls enough to understand that."

Boom.

The room holds a collective breath. Zeus spins to face me, puffing up like a disdainful peacock. "Tell me how you—"

"How do I know you're listening to our conversations? Because we handed you the technology. We understand how it works. Do you enjoy what humans invented?" I smile, though no one else is. "It's great, isn't it? Our humans have done incredible things." The Council has listened in on our selected conversations for so long, I doubt they'd know what to do if they stopped. Which is exactly what we've been hoping for.

Zeus exchanges a glance with Dionysus, who then eyes Comus with a loud warning only a father can pull off without words.

"Moros has returned," Dionysus says quietly, facing Zeus again.

Instead of listening to his most trusted friend and advisor and taking the hint to address the primary agenda item, Zeus stands tall and stares me down. "Tell me what you are up to, Alexiares."

"You first," I state slow and clear. If he's smart, he won't open this line of conversation with me.

"Answer me," he says, tone cold. He's not smart. And here we go.

"I'm trying to figure out what purpose you think I will serve for you. Why you continue to force Ichnaea and me together when neither of us approves, then try to breed us as if we were livestock, when there's a two-thousand-year-old law forbidding birth." I ball my fists, words coming fast and hard through tight vocal cords and tense muscles. "Why you shun purebred, gifted gods like Rath, and why you keep us from *our* humans when we're meant to be—"

"Silence!" His bellow echoes off the marble like a crack of lightning.

I flinch, preparing for the sting, the burn of electricity, the scent of ozone and burnt flesh. Lula will be angry if he singes off my hair again. As will I. I like her fingers there, gripping hard while she moans for me. When I get back to her, hair or not, I'll own every sound she makes whether it's screaming at me, or for me.

"Not anymore," I calmly say, though my heart may thump itself out of my chest. "Why won't you share *your* plans with anyone, not even Council members?" Keeping my focus on him and not checking the reactions of the others sends dry, painful stabs to my eyes. Comus will see everything. He always does. "We all deserve to kno—"

"I told you to be silent, boy!" His voice booms through the vast room in an echo of thunder. He strides to his throne and sits with effortless elegance—an inherent part of his godliness. I'm staring at the flesh and blood version of the statues mortal sculptures were once so fond of making. "You will demand nothing of me," he sneers. "I have grown tired of your games with the non-deities and must determine whether you will continue your observations."

"Of course I will continue my observations," I say. "It would be better if all of us visited the Earth regularly, even if you already know much of the otherworldlings. They've changed in our absence. We should discuss the differences from the last time you...interacted with them and the present day." *Tell me everything about the sirens.*

He holds up a hand. "We *shall* speak of Moros."

Comus clears his throat. "Then let's speak of Moros. He's returned."

I'd like to continue the other line of conversation with Zeus but Comus must see that the king is at the end of his rope.

I didn't realize throwing that information out there would be so refreshing, but we've kept secrets for so long, they've festered. We've had to for the greater good, but the expense has been sleepless nights, stress that has resided in my gut for so long that it owns property, and lies that have blown over to every aspect of my life. I don't want to keep them anymore. Not from the Council, or Olympus, and not from Lula.

Maybe freedom starts with the truth.

Zeus blows a long breath from his nostrils because of his tightly locked jaw. He focuses back on me. "Did you bring the God of Doom here?"

"No." His accusation makes me huff in disbelief. "He killed nine deities when we escorted him from the realm last time. He nearly murdered Rath when we found him this time. You're looking at me after what just occurred on Earth?" I motion to Deimos's empty throne.

The obvious choice to anyone who didn't know him would be Hermes. He sits across the room from Deimos, and he can move through the realm veils with passengers, though I don't believe he travels unless requested. He's pro-human, always has been, and fought hard to prevent the separation. It almost lost him his seat on the Council. He will have a hard enough time defending himself without me pointing a finger at him.

Zeus ignores my suggestion. "Did Anicetus?"

"I didn't," Anice replies from the doorway. His eyes are red and vacant. "I would never bring that monster back."

"Then how did he return?" Zeus doesn't seem shocked by the appearance of my brother, though the other Council members keep their squinting eyes on him.

There are incalculable ways this conversation could go. Perhaps, my grandfather will remember the bond we used to have back in the ages when he had complimented my determination for the truth and wellbeing of our universe. He's not immune to reason. My mother and father once dragged it from him so they could be together.

Comus bobs his head in encouragement.

I turn to face my fate. "We have a theory." With Rath's new way of thinking, we've speculated in excess, but one hypothesis stands above the others, not only because it may be correct, but because it would help get us exactly where we need to be—reconnected with the

Earth realm. I clear my throat. "We believe the realm's stability is off because Olympus is disconnected from Earth."

Murmuring erupts in the room. What I've just told them is that their King broke the realm because he was afraid of someone else taking over Olympus. At least, I hope they picked up on that.

They were there, they know.

The humans weren't always worshipful, and the otherworldlings have talents sometimes beyond Olympian gods. Sometimes the beings on Earth were downright murderous, but Moros was around, pumping his negative influence into the realm along with others. He wouldn't leave during the exodus, unlike his siblings who recognized that the time to move on was upon them. Their power was waning and another universe called for creation. Probably. Long ago, I read about that phenomenon—when the universe calls for an exodus—but no one talks about it because… Olympus.

Zeus had War, Terror, and the vengeful virgin Huntress helping Olympus guide the mortals. Was he expecting worldwide peace and harmony? Sure, he has Athena and Hermes as balancers, but they are the peacemakers and keep quiet. The only time I've seen Ares silent is today when shame overshadows any dickish inclinations. Dionysus and Apollo have come a long way in millennia, but they're loyal to their king.

To give Zeus credit, he's not pitching the fit I thought he would. He's quiet, eyes on me, but he's listening to the murmurs of his Council, holding his poker face close. Has he realized the gravity of this theory if it's correct?

The group settles, buzz fading as they realize the King hasn't yet weighed in on my words.

"You believe the separation that keeps both our realms safe has created a portal in the hell realm?" Zeus's face says that idea is possibly the stupidest thing he's ever heard. He has a slight smirk and laughter in his eye.

"Not a portal, a rip, but yes," Comus says, challenge clear. "The separation caused a rift in our relationship with humans and otherworldlings. Influence is less potent, and some deities haven't used their attributes in a century. Olympus is full of unfulfilled deities and

Earth holds lost otherworldlings and humans who need guidance while they progress."

Zeus's eyes widen. "Who is unfulfilled? Name them."

Yes, sure. Here's a list. "Everyone," I say. "There is not a deity in Olympus who uses their attributes to their full potential anymore."

His eyes narrow. "And what about you, Alexiares? Are you not fulfilled?"

I bite back a smile. He never sees the moves ahead or considers his words before he speaks. He blurts out what he thinks the loudest of his people want to hear. I mill everything over a thousand times before I utter a word because if I say the wrong thing and send Zeus or others on a path I shouldn't, I risk lives.

In this situation, I set him up four moves ago. I love it when he delivers my punchline.

"I use my attributes and feel the full extent of my influence every time I'm with the humans. Each conversation is a dose of energy—an exchange I've missed every day since you had the connection to Earth broken and the portals closed. Do you remember what it was like to walk among them?" I'm getting to the Council. Athena wears a forlorn frown, and Dionysus licks his lips. Comus told him about the new grape strains the humans created, and the hundred types of wine his influence inspired. Even Artemis digs her nails into the antlers carved in her throne as if the wind touches her cheeks during a thrilling chase. "Yes, gods yes, I am fulfilled. Because I walk the Earth."

Zeus shoots to his feet. "I do not believe this for a moment—"

"Sire," Dionysus says, eyeing the ground. "This will take research and advisement, however—"

"Yes, yes," Zeus grumbles, wafting his hand through the air. He sits again, steepling his fingers in front of his lips. After a long stint of silence, he drops his hands to the throne's carved arms. "You will not speak of this...theory—" He crinkles his nose as if scenting something foul. "With anyone outside this room. I shall involve Pythia and discuss it further with the Council."

Out of the corner of my eye, Comus winces, but I clear my throat in warning for him to remain calm. Moros is back and as much as my grandfather probably wants to discuss my sex life to understand my reluctance to commune with Ichnaea, the God of Doom is the priority and hopefully will give us extra time.

"We would appreciate that and—as always—will lend our assistance to Olympus as necessary."

"Since you have so many theories," he says with a sneer. "You must have an idea on how to stop Moros and the sirens from creating more chaos on Earth. Tell us how you would approach his recapture."

He wants my opinion now? The lines of exhaustion are even more prominent around his lips and the dip in his chin from his frown. He's angry and scared, but there's more. Today blindsided him. I recall his expression when Moros brought up Aglaope. That shocked him, and there was pain there. He knew her well. Probably kept her like he does his pets—no that's not right. The pets are cursed infertile, and the sirens reproduced when they came to Earth, but not in Olympus. Why? Maybe they were testers for the birth-control elixir.

I'll get answers eventually, but with caution and tact. Not now, when whirlwinds of emotions threaten to become a tornado at the slightest temperature change.

I straighten under the scrutiny of the room and hope this is the right path. "We need to bring the sirens to Olympus and keep them under our protection before Moros harms them further. Then we will find him and send him back—" A thought sparks like a puzzle piece bursting from thin air. If we could take the Council to the hell realm and they see that the darklings need their brand of violent influence, we may not need to endanger the humans to get the Council out of Olympus, and Lula may not have to be involved at all. "After the gods do a thorough check of the stability of the hell realm."

Comus makes a little hum of consideration and Zeus's thick brows furrow. "Why would we bring otherworldlings into Olympus?"

"Because Moros is using them as a weapon."

"Sire, if I may..." Dionysus interrupts, finger raised in the air and a deep furrow to his brow. I steal a glance at Comus who appears as perplexed as I am.

"You may not," Zeus snaps. "Alexiares, Anicetus, and Comus, you are dismissed. The Council meets now about enforcing a bounty on the sirens."

The world goes off-kilter, and I'm frozen speechless.

"A bounty?" Comus takes a step forward. "This is not their fault."

And this is not the way we want the deities to visit the Earth. They will wreck the world beyond repair if they appear in himations, swords raised and attributes flying. All I see is chaos, news spewing panic about the Armageddon, and bombs exploding everything.

"They are dangerous," Zeus replies, his eyes fixed to a point over our heads.

What is going on?

Anice moves up beside me. "They are not dangerous. Moros is using them, taking advantage of their meek demeanor. Besides, you don't even care if humans die. You force deadly events on them all the time to gain worship and control."

Some would call Anice diplomatic, and for the most part, he is, but once he chooses a side, there's little he will hold back to make his point. I admire that but as the air tenses, charged with electricity, I step in front of my brother as I'm less likely to get fried than he is at the moment.

"I have made my decision." Zeus's only movement is his tapping finger against the marble forehead of the right eagle on his throne. "We will leave Moros with no weapons."

As soon as I open the portal and we step into the mudroom, Lula screams bloody murder from somewhere in the house.

"Lula!" My heart is in my throat as I sprint the hallway with Comus on my heels.

"Don't do it," Rath yells over Lula's shrieks. "You have ten more seconds."

We breach the kitchen to find Lula hopping around pinching at her t-shirt. "Oh my god," she says. "This is fucking torture! I hate you. I officially hate you, Rathbarth Shadowkeeper."

Did she call him by his given name? I'm shocked he isn't killing her, and even more surprised that he's laughing in keeled-over guffaws. It's been a hell of a long time since I've seen Rath like this, and he was falling-down drunk at the time.

I try to calm my speeding heart with slow breaths.

Comus says precisely what in my mind. "What the fuck?"

"Time," Rath says. "Hey," he says, lifting his chin at us but keeping beaming eyes on Lula.

With a final screech, Lula jerks her tucked t-shirt out of her pants, and a couple of dozen ice cubes drop to the floor. She's puffing like she just ran a race and holds her shirt away from her skin. Her eyes meet mine and widen as her cheeks pinken. My gaze lands on the drawn-on handlebar mustache she's sporting before moving to her red curls, adorned by a splayed banana peel, pinned on like a quirky fascinator.

Rath snaps to and wipes bright red lipstick off his mouth with the back of his hand. He leaves the hearts drawn on both cheeks in the same color. He's wearing what looks like a himation made out of toilet paper.

"Tell me you're drunk," Comus says. "Like super fucking blitzed out of your skulls right now."

Lula, face as red as Rath's lipstick, stoops to gather ice cubes. "Dammit, we forgot to drink."

"That would have been an excellent excuse for this." Rath tries to run his hand through his hair, but it gets stuck on the two blond pigtails pointing straight up into the air. His eyes close as he groans and yanks the hair bands out then musses up his mane.

Comus nudges me. "Are they high?"

"I have no idea."

Lula comes over to me but stops short of grabbing distance. "Tell me what happened."

"There's a banana on your head, Firecracker."

She jerks at it, hisses as the pins hold fast, finally detaches it, and tosses it in the trash. "Okay, and—"

"And you have a mustache."

She huffs a frustrated sound and glares back at Rath. "It had to be a permanent marker?' Is there any rubbing alcohol?"

"Hey, you're the one who wanted something worth two dares so you could ask *the big question*," Rath says, retrieving the first aid kit from underneath the sink. "The housekeeper leaves this here."

Lula snatches an alcohol pad from the kit and starts rubbing furiously at her drawn on-mustache until only faint lines remain against red skin, then heads over to Rath.

"The big question?"

"None of your business," Rath grumbles, standing patiently while Lula rubs the lipstick off his face.

My vision flits between Lula and Rath. "You were playing truth or dare?"

Lula's attention remains on her task. "Yep. Rath had to entertain me since you left me behind. I was a nervous wreck, you know. Ass." I wish like hell I didn't have to tell her everything that just went down. After a moment of uncomfortable silence, she glances at me and must read the stress on my face because she frowns and comes closer. "What happened?"

I swallow, dreading this. I need her in my arms, against me, her curves in my hands so I know she's real and safe and mine.

Rath turns, and swishes closer as well, pausing to curse and rip off his toilet paper skirt. "Did he hurt anyone?"

"No, but Zeus did." I lock eyes with Lula. "Moros has Venora and Hazel."

Lula covers her mouth with both hands, her eyes angling to anguish I've seen entirely too much to have known her so short a time. I make her a silent promise: next decade will be nothing but smiles and sex.

I approach as I would a wild creature harboring unknown intentions, and cautiously trail my fingers against her hip. She slides into my grip and wraps herself around me, letting me get lost in her scent as I hold her tight, palm splayed on her back feeling every breath she makes.

"I'm sorry, Lu," I say. "We will do everything we can. Are your other sisters in safe places? Hidden?"

"Yes," she says, voice muffled against my neck.

"We should move Grace to be on the safe side," Comus says.

Rath narrows his eyes and mouths, *Council?* Comus nods, frowning. Rath bares his teeth in a frustrated grimace. Sometimes I think he understands the Council better than we do. He knows and predicts their moves far faster than I can.

"Okay," I say. "We have a lot to talk about."

My Song's Curse

LAST NIGHT WAS ANOTHER TESTAMENT TO HOW WELL LULA AND I match.

We laid out the bad news but offered no plans of attack or further conversation due to Rath's warning glares. I wouldn't have taken the conversation further anyways until I talked everything out with the guys. Lula set her jaw. Her determination matches ours, she's part of us.

A call from Grace interrupted the silent aftermath of the recap, and Lula snuck up to our room to talk to her sister.

While she was upstairs, Rath told me to keep quiet about studying her. He had gotten her to spill about her sisters. I knew she was mad at Amah but it's more than that. She feels betrayed because Amah kept information she needs. That hit home like a missile strike. I wanted to march upstairs and confess everything, but Rath said it will break her.

Little at a time, or, as suggested, not at all.

That doesn't sit well with me, even if the next conversation goes as planned. We're not humans, but Lula lives among them, acting like them, and she's a siren—a walking lie detector. She's not used to deceit like the Olympians live with daily, and she shouldn't have anything but all of me.

This lie is part of me.

It's how we came to be, why I stepped from the light and kissed her like I'd known her for years. Well, one year.

But I haven't said anything. Not yet.

When she returned, she let us know that Prax returned to Olympus with my brother's help. I assume they didn't hit it off well. The last few hours without Lula were painful. Maybe that's pheromones, or maybe it's how deep we are. Lula says Grace is fine but embarrassed about it all. Coupling during a siren heat would have been an odd experience for strangers.

Then, Lula gave me a vulnerable, lip-biting look and blushed.

It took me thirty seconds to get her upstairs.

It took her thirty seconds to have me half-naked and sprawled across the bed, staring up at her in awe.

The light settles firmly in the sky, lighting our room. I've waited for her to wake for an hour—watched the way her lips twitch in her sleep and the exact rhythm of her breath when her body decides it's really going to get up this time. Like now.

Lula blinks open her gorgeous eyes, focuses on me, and smiles.

If there is justice in this world, I will have this moment every day.

Chapter Thirty-One

LULA

Alex stops tracing the pattern he was drawing on my hip when he peeks over my shoulder to see Amah's name on my phone. He kisses my neck as I shift my weight and detach myself from him and the couch we've been melted into all morning.

"Hi," I answer, walking up the stairs.

"Hi, Lula," Amah says, mouse quiet.

The silence lingers between us as I pass rooms and take the door at the end of the hall, leading out to the upper deck. Comus and Rath sit on the dock, bare feet dropped in the water. I lean on the rail and inhale salt and seaside nature, absorb the bright, cloudlessly breathtaking day.

Alex walks out, hands shoved in his pockets, and hair waving in the breeze. Could anything on Earth be so perfect? He glances back as if he can feel my eyes travel his broad shoulders and godly backside. Finding me on the upper deck, he winks and keeps moving toward his friends. Our friends.

"Lula?"

"I'm here."

"I'm sorry."

She should be. I could have prepared, understood more. Things didn't happen for me like they did Grace. Her nails hardened to sharp points and she craved Prax's blood. Not all of it—she didn't go fangs and vampire queen or anything, but she accidentally clawed him in the moment and…tasted it. The need to be near and drink water was strong for her as well. She said she's still cleaning up the mess they made.

I could have cared less about anything but Alex and me being as close as possible, everything else shut down, but I remember Nysa telling me she laid down in a river during her last heat because she needed to drink and wash the blood away. I need to talk to the others and compare notes, see if there are other discrepancies.

"Sorry?" I say in a huff. "Amah, I can't even put into words how unprepared I was for any of this."

Yet, I'm not exactly regretful. I'm one step from terrified, yes, but Alex and I feel real now. Rath and Comus treat me like a long-lost sister and I'm happy as I can be with everything falling apart. The three of them sit on a dock in paradise, talking to each other and occasionally glancing up at me, waiting for me to get off the phone so I can join them because I belong with them.

I'm so damn happy.

"I know, Lula, but I couldn't talk about it." Amah sniffles. "Are you okay? Feeling anything yet?"

Sirens know quickly if they're pregnant. If the pregnancy takes, within a week we go on a food bender, then sleep for days.

"No. Nothing. Why couldn't you? What on Earth is keeping you from telling me—us things we need to know."

Amah breaths out a long breath. "I just—"

"Here we go. You just can't. Why? Because you want to hold all the secrets?" I pace the upper deck, ten steps, and turn.

"No, no that's not—"

Ten steps and turn. "Because I'm not trustworthy enough to—"

"Because Hera swore us to secrecy!" There's a little gasp, then Amah groans.

"Hera?" Like Zeus's wife Hera? Queen of Olympus, Grandmother of Alex. "Okay, you can't be silent now. You told me you'd never met a god." The thought that this woman who I've always considered to be my mother has lied to me my whole life brings a scratchy ache to my throat. I sit on the deck. Plop down right in the center and rub my forehead. "You lied."

"I—" Her voice breaks. "I've never met a god. Only a goddess."

Oh, she's being technical, is she? "The Queen of Olympus, Amah. A divine being. I can't believe this. When? What?"

"Lula, when the goddess Queen tells you and your two sisters to stay far from each other and never ever speak to anyone about your existence, even the children you haven't yet had, you do as she says. We were sixteen."

They were the same age. "Your sisters? My mother and… Gerty?"

The original three had a heat like Grace and I did. Comus was right, it was the first Punic War battle when a *storm* caught the Roman fleet and took out a hundred thousand. It was three sirens in the throes of a combined heat. They were a pheromone hurricane. The first generation was born right after, over two-thousand years ago. It's why Amah won't tell me about my mother, and why Gerty and Amah wouldn't say their ages, only an estimate because 'keeping time was different,' or 'we're too old to think about such things.' They knew exactly. She understood what would happen if we got near each other when one was in heat.

"We were born on the same day, Petra, Gerty, and I. We grew up together, then Hera…" She trails off as if realizing she's speaking this for the first time.

Unless I'm the only one on the out. That sends a chill down my spine. My sisters have always treated me differently. Not Lena or Hazel, but the others. Even Grace, who I'm closest with next to Amah seems to avoid history conversations with me. I assumed it was to avoid painful conversations about my mother but it always irked the hell out of me. Maybe that's why I'm so intent to know more about us.

"Keep talking," I say, rolling a finger through the air as if she can see me.

She clears her throat in her polite, 'ahem,' manner. "Hera came and told us to say goodbye to our mothers, that they had to leave to stay safe and to never return to Greece. We scattered, meeting once a century, each time a little farther from the Olympians as we explored the worlds. Our daughters were born, they left us as well, but we met when we felt it was safe. We finally made it to America and thought we could see each other more frequently. The portals were scarce, and in the new world, the talk of gods gave way to other conversations. We were wrong."

"Why? What happened?"

"Lula." Her voice is a sobbing cry and I clutch at my chest. "I can't. Not like this. You need to get away from them. Then we will talk. Leave, hide, and I will speak to you, face to face. I've missed you so much, Lula."

"Leave? You want me to leave someone who is honest with me so you can make amends for lying to me?" The door clicks closed behind me, and Alex stares down at me with furrowed brows, thick arms crossed over his defined chest. I should be in those arms, kissing that chest. I focus back on the call. "So you can what? Feed me more half-truths?"

"I wouldn't Lula, I won't. Please, just get away from the gods first."

"I won't leave him. I trust him, Amah. He's helping us, even though it's putting him in danger. I—" His expression is pained as I glance over my shoulder at him. "I love him, and I won't give him up. I'm so mad at you for asking this of me."

"Lula, you can't—"

Stabbing the call button, I hang up. Guilt floods my mind, suffocating me with realization.

I just chose.

Alex kneels in front of me and he drags me against him as I cover my face with both hands. "What if something happens and that's the last thing I said to her? I'm so angry, but I love her. I don't know what to do."

"Hey," he coos. "She worries about you. She can't understand this because she's never experienced what we have."

"Are you sure?" I ask, wrapping my arms around his neck. I trail my fingers over his eyebrow, temple, down his cheekbone, and let the tickle of scruff light up my nerves. "Because I'm not. She's been lying or withholding the truth. She—" I don't know what stops me from telling him about Hera. Maybe it's Alex's uncomfortable expression. Poor guy had no idea he was inheriting a flock of drama when he met me. He has enough to worry about and I don't trust her words. Maybe I'm not ready to share this huge secret Amah has kept from me all my life. If it's true, why? What happened in Olympus that made Hera hide the original sirens and where did she take them?

He strokes my back. "Come on. We need to talk about some things."

The tension point in my throat drops to my stomach but Alex stands, taking me with him. We head through the house, out the doors, walking across the warm sand, our fingers linked tight. It's so natural, that I can't imagine my hand not being in his. I haven't bothered to put on shoes since I've been here, so I sit next to Rath and stick my feet in the cool, lapping waves.

Rath watches me and tilts his head. "Talk to Amah?"

I nod, and he grimaces, giving the back of my neck a squeeze.

Everyone is oddly quiet as Alex takes his place beside me.

Comus clears his throat. "As I was saying, I think it's time for a new Council."

"You're suggesting a coup," Alex says, his finger tapping a rapid beat on the dock boards. His eyes are tired, void of enthusiasm.

"Yeah," Comus says. "We won't continue to live like this. Just as we're wondering what other crazy shit the Council will pull, they put a bounty on an innocent race. They're reckless, power-hungry, destroying the realm, and someone must stop them right now." He exhales long and loud. "It's time to assemble and plan."

"Zeus will take his revenge, and put more people in danger," Alex says as he fidgets with the hem of his shirt. I take his hand and look at him in question but he keeps his eyes on the sea.

"He will try." Comus looks at me with a clenched jaw. "The Council will handle any perceived threat or misunderstanding in the same manner as the sirens. They blindly lash out because they feel their people slipping into a new mindset. They're losing their realm."

"They deserve to lose it," Alex growls. "They need to step down and allow the younger deities to influence the realm. It's time. I'm not sure how we are going to convince them to do that beside forcing an exodus, but we must try." His words are choppy as though they've been scripted, and I wonder how many times he's thought of this and held back from sharing it.

Comus and Alex look to Rath, and ideas spin behind his eyes. "An exodus is a good place to start but we will need to be quiet about it. If we assemble, and have the numbers to overthrow the current Council, but don't do it secretly, they may strike out and start a war of gods. On top of that, if more darklings follow Moros away from hell, we may not have a realm to influence. We need help."

The gods resume their looks of deep concentration.

Maybe I could help? Me and my sist—maybe not my sisters. How would I be able to do anything for the gods though?

I have so many questions, and for once, I ask them.

We talk about the first exodus and how the titans left after a bloody war. Zeus killed anyone who questioned his self-proclaimed royal title when the realm was vulnerable, and somehow Moros allowed it, though he's more powerful and unkillable.

Alex explained how Zeus separated Olympus from the Earth with mystic witches and a theory that actually worked, though settling the divine buildings, landscape, and deities back down to overlap Greece may or may not be possible again ever. It angered so many gods that a huge number left in another exodus and threw the world into the dark ages. Moros stayed for a while before defying law and disappearing to Earth for hundreds of years in silence, then started killing humans, making it blend in with plagues but Alex and Comus recognized the wounds. They locked him in the hell realm, and don't know how he returned.

I'm enraptured and appalled. Alex comes out of the odd funk he was in and they take turns explaining Olympus in this amazing way that reminds me of harmonies in a song. Each understands the exact place to weave in and when to allow the spotlight to go to another. They're so close and my heart warms to think they've allowed me into their inner circle, made me part of them.

The information they share though is terrifying. The younger generations are basically slaves to the older and while no one says it outright, I can tell Rath hasn't had an easy time. My protective instincts flare like wildfire and I glare up at the sky as if the older gods could look down and see my disapproval of them.

The energy in Olympus is tense, the mystical timeline of the universe may be asking for another exodus, but the guys hope to avoid violence. That's the old way and they're ready to move to a strategy based on humanity and reason. Conflict may be able to be settled peacefully if everything lines up like fate. I could hug each of them because peace is my wheelhouse whenever possible.

When the conversation wanes, my skin is pink from the lateday sun, and we sit again in silence.

The concentration and nervous energy rolling off the gods gives me anxiety. "I'll be right back," I say and take my antsy legs into the house for drinks. I peek back to see them talking, but Alex lies back on the wood, arms crossed over his face. He's so stressed and I hope my being here, possibly pregnant with a bounty on my head and missing sisters that are causing havoc on Earth isn't too much. Who am I kidding? Of course, it is.

I find a decent assortment of alcohol, bar glasses, and a vintage cocktail shaker in a tall cabinet, and clap my hands when I realize there are ingredients for a sidecar. There's even a lemon already cut since Rath made me eat half for truth or dare so he could make fun of my sour-face.

The shape of the cold metal shaker between my hands has me longing for my old cigarette-girl dress. That was a fun time. Maybe if the Council had come down to Earth during the Jazz Age, we wouldn't be in this situation.

I'm as rattled as the cubes in the shaker, and so sad I'm nearly sick about my sisters. My chest is tight with worry for them that it may cave in, but I have Alex, Rath, and Comus. It sounds as if we have some very capable gods on our side too, Prax and Anice. I'm sure there are others. In times of possible war, lines are drawn and sides are taken.

I blow out a long breath and begin pouring with shaking hands.

This quiet beach house is something else. Even empty, it breathes with life and divine energy. I'm not alone here. Maybe everything will work out, and I can fill the blank walls in the upper hallway with some choice pictures. The rooster would fit on that empty space above the cabinets. Yes, I think we could make a life here if things were different.

I butt the door open on my way outside and walk back to the dock. Holding up the tray of drinks, I cock my hip, and in my best twenties accent announce, "Come get 'em, boys. Let's get zozzled and save the world."

I break character to wince. That was so cheesy, but I get three smiles, and they stand to take the glasses. We settle back down again in the same places, Alex, me, Rath, then Comus. It feels right and normal. If Grace were here too, she'd wedge herself between Rath and Comus and toss her blonde hair over her shoulders, face up to the sun. They would love her. My other sisters too. Even Amah, if she ever gets over that fear-the-gods thing. We'd have to prepare for our contagious heats.

Wow, I've been in the sun too long.

We've been separated for thousands of years and here I am daydreaming of beach cookouts. Our situation isn't going to change overnight, and there will be no rest until Ven and Hazel are safe.

Alex nudges me. "So about saving the world. You in?"

I want to kiss that vulnerable, questioning pout right off his lips. I lean and do just that. "I don't know how helpful I can be next to your attributes and—" I wave my hand through the air. "Divineness. But Olympus needs to change. My sisters need help and I'll do whatever I can for them, and for you. Obviously, I'm in."

Alex's chest rises and falls as if he'd been holding his breath. He gives a definitive, exalted bob of his head.

Comus raises his drink. "To peace, and sirens, and saving the godsdammed world."

We collectively blow out lengthy breaths as we clink glasses.

Rath sips with an appreciative eyebrow raise, then downs the martini. "Food." He kisses my head and wisps away, leaving a gap between Comus and me.

"I'll set the table." Comus grins and stands up. He kneels to give me a one-armed hug from behind because the other holds half a martini. "We'll yell when it's ready."

Alex watches the ocean, sips, then turns his eyes on me and leans close. "I would have loved you in the twenties."

I grin. "You would have loved me more in the sixties. I loved clothing in that decade. I had some extremely short shorts."

"Mmm. I'd love you in any decade." His jesting tone turns serious.

I turn my head to taste the liquor on his lips, then part from him only far enough to breathe the words, "Thank you." He tilts his head, so I clarify. "Thank you for everything you've done to keep my sisters and me safe."

Instead of relief, concern slides over his features. "I've only wanted to protect you."

"I know," I whisper and run my knuckles over his jaw. "You're so good to me."

Alex sets our glasses down and drags me to straddle him. He cups my face with both hands. "I'm sorry you're stuck in this, Lu. We'll do everything possible to get your sisters back. The sirens *are* under our protection. I won't let anyone hurt you. I'm...Lu..." He trails off, gives a long exhale, and touches his forehead to mine.

In my wildest dreams, I never expected to meet a god, much less fall in love with one. "I'm in love with you. So much." Gripping his shirt, I pull him close to brush my lips against his. He tightens his grip on my face and connects with sweet urgency before he pulls away and hugs me close. "I love you, Firecracker. Whatever happens, we stick together, alright?"

No matter what, this god is mine, and I am his.

I place my palm on his chest, feeling his mighty heart thump under my palm. Of all the things out of our control, *we* are not a problem. "Of course, Alex. I'm yours."

THE END

Thank you for reading! Did you enjoy?

Please Add Your Review! You can sign up for the City Owl Press newsletter to receive notice of all book releases!

And don't miss more paranormal romance like **BLOOD ROGUE** by City Owl Author, Linda J. Parisi. Turn the page for a sneak peek!

Sneak Peek of Blood Rogue

BY LINDA J. PARISI

Every city has a pulse, a vibration, a sound. Take New York City, for instance. The city that never sleeps; it's unstoppable, frenetic, and definitely treble. Then there's the *new* New York. Hoboken, New Jersey, the land of thirty-something's tired of living four to a one-bedroom apartment, the city across the Hudson, anchored in the bedrock of the Palisades. Hoboken pounded out bass, slow, deep, rhythmic, and solid, like the beat of a human heart, the one organ a nine-hundred-year-old vampire would never take for granted.

Charles Tower, Chaz to those who knew him best, stood in *Beans* — his guilty pleasure. He stared at the rows of jars with black beans, brown beans, beige beans, appreciating that in his human life, coffee would have been as foreign to him as a heavy metal band. As a human born in the year 1094AD, he would always wonder what the brew tasted like. He hoped it would be as heavenly as the aroma permeating the store, sweet, earthy, and pungent. He inhaled deeply and exhaled slowly, feeling a little bit like an addict.

Yes, he knew all about that word, as well as need and cravings, the likes of which a human could never understand. There was the blood, and there could only ever be the blood, even when he tried to enjoy something as simple as a coffee shop.

What the hell is wrong with me?

Would there ever be a time when he could step up to a cash register and pay for a bag of Arabica that he'd give away, without thinking about the river of life? Maybe he'd be better off thinking of the rogues, the out of control vampires that he'd had to kill too often lately.

Frowning, he turned, left the store, and stepped out onto the sidewalk. Mayhem assailed with a cacophony of sound. The blare of a car horn, the rumble of a truck over uneven pavement, to the thoughts of the hundreds of people he didn't want to listen to. He tried to block out the sounds, to no avail. He stepped right into the path of three lovely women who parted like the Red Sea then came back together again as they passed. One, the blonde with the ponytail, looked back over her shoulder.

Chaz stilled. Her round face could've used more chin and less cheekbone. She had dark brows and even darker rimmed glasses. But, there was something about the beautiful eyes behind the lenses. Bright, the color of a midday sky, filled with energy and curiosity and such life. God, he could drown in that gaze, never surface, and remain happy forever.

Except for the blood.

She turned to her friends, and the moment died the way moments like this do, except he heard her say, "Oh my God. I just saw the most gorgeous guy."

"What?" asked the tallest of the three. "Stacy? Stacy Ann Morgan? The geek-cop? Noticing—oh-my-goodness—" She placed a hand against her chest. "—a man?" Her tone oozed attitude.

"Ease up, Kels."

Stacy. He liked that name. Curiosity piqued, and the irrational need see those eyes again had Chaz wanting to hear more. He turned and followed them at a safe distance.

"No way. This is simply too delicious. Maybe Stace'll try and dissect him first. Wait. No. She'll run a two-week background check on him right down to his seventh cousin's middle name."

"Low blow, Kels," the woman on her right said. Her shoulders drooped a little, then her back straightened. "You do realize she carries a gun, don't you?"

"Ladies…stop! I'm right here you know."

Yes, indeed, he thought.

She walked with a long determined stride and had a trim, athletic body. She seemed to assess everyone and everything around her as she walked. Was that out of curiosity or protectiveness? By blocking out the myriad of voices around him, he also blocked out hers, so he'd have to find out.

"Of course you are," continued the one they called Kels. "But we know all about you quiet ones, don't we? You may act shy around the opposite sex, but still, waters run deep and all, right?"

They walked a few steps into *Adrian's*. Chaz continued down the block. Sometimes prudence really was better. But then he pivoted, turning back. This time, not for the blood but for the want of simple human contact. Stopping in front of the steps, he hesitated again. There would only be one winner tonight, the blood, and for a moment that made him sad. He shook that off and walked through the door. They were standing in front of the bar like they were waiting for a table to the restaurant.

He walked over and ordered a glass of Cabernet and leaned on the wood as he took a small sip. He watched Stacy's gaze soften as she leaned toward the sad woman.

"How are you holding up, Tori?"

A woman wearing expensive-smelling perfume approached him, and he tore his gaze away. Every pore on her face was filled with artifice, and he shook his head, making it clear he didn't want to be picked up. Her lips thinned at the rebuff, but she turned around and went back to her friends while he focused on the conversation he wanted to hear.

"They say time heals. Some days it's almost bearable. Some aren't."

He watched Stacy reach out and hug her friend, wishing he had someone that deeply invested in his well-being, someone close. Vampires were singular and very territorial. They had to be to survive.

While Stacy and the one she called Tori spoke together, the woman they called Kels turned to stare at him. Her brow lifted, her hips shifted so that the line of her leg drew his gaze. He palmed his chest and mouthed, "Who, me?"

She nodded, offering a sly, knowing smile. He took his time

pushing off the wood of the bar and sauntered up to her, already feeling her claws dig deep. She entwined her arm with his, but Chaz had no interest and extricated himself with deft precision. He ignored her pout and flashed them all a huge grin.

"Good evening, ladies. I know this is incredibly forward of me, but might I buy you all a round while you wait? Charles Tower at your service." He bowed, gracing them with the manners which had been proper in his time, and they hemmed and hawed, all except *her*. Stacy simply stared at him, assessing, head slightly cocked as she made her judgment. Funny, for the first time in just over a century, he didn't want to be found lacking.

You can service me anytime.

How…unexpected. He nearly grinned. Then he heard, *Where the hell did that come from?* He wanted to ask the same question. Too bad this night was about need and not pleasure.

Kels, the dark-haired one who was all talk licked her lips like he was some kind of treat. She turned him off, much too full of herself to be inviting. Tori, the sad one, frowned and eyed him up and down a couple of times, her gaze filled with mistrust. He let her see what she wanted to see, someone normal, someone human, and she nodded slightly. Then he claimed the prize, sinking into that incredible crystalline blue gaze once more, made even more delectable by the doubts she expressed.

"Sir? What can I get you?"

He started and looked up, indicating that the ladies each give their order to the bartender. "Put it on my tab."

Kels refused to give up, wedging her body into the tight space between the other women so that she separated him from her friends. Chaz steeled his features, daring her to touch him again. Her human instinct warned her, and she stepped back, allowing him to reach out and move Stacy away from getting stepped on. He trailed a light finger across Stacy's skin as he let go, pleased to see her skin bead from his touch.

"Do you come here often?" She winced, and he held up his hand, feeling a touch of dismay. "I know. Lousy pick-up line, right?"

He cocked his head, gave her a rueful lift of the corner of his mouth, and let the truth ring through his words. "But I've been so overwhelmed by your presence that I don't know what to say."

She didn't answer.

"Okay, that came out a bit too much, didn't it?"

She nodded, and he drowned in her killer blues, which was hard to do for one already dead. "Shall I rephrase?"

She stared, disbelief filling her gaze as she shouted her thoughts. *Make that more than once.*

Outwardly determined and in control, that was very evident. But inside? How fascinating. "Perhaps I should start over?"

She still didn't answer.

"You don't talk very much, do you?"

Her gaze flitted from her hands to his chest and then after a deep breath, made eye contact. But at that moment, her shoulders squared and she gazed at him openly.

Her cheeks bloomed pink. "I work in a lab." She half laughed. "The extent of my conversations run from who took an evidence bag to why the damned mass spec is down again."

She tightened her fingers around her glass and stared down at her drink again. *Is this really happening?*

Now he couldn't help himself as he grinned.

Look at the simple curl of his lip—the arch of his brow.

"Perhaps we could start with your name?"

Her heart sped up, and he could hear the rush of her blood in her veins. His mouth watered. Chaz swallowed, hating his reaction to her. She seemed nice, too nice to simply be used.

"Sorry." Again, twin spots of pink tinged her cheeks. "Stacy. Stacy Morgan." *Nice going, dumb head. Probably thinks I'm sixteen now.*

Actually, Chaz found the combination of her boldness and insecurity intriguing and decided to reassure her.

"I'm a bit rusty in the world of social gatherings myself," he said.

She certainly made for an interesting combination. Supposedly she was some kind of scientist, her friends called her a cop, but she carried an innocence about her he hadn't encountered in a very long time.

The bright light in her gaze dimmed with uncertainty. Chaz might be considered more human than his fellow vampires, but make no mistake, this moment was all about the blood and only could be about the blood.

"Me too. Umm, let me introduce you. This is Kelly." Chaz wondered if his message had been clear enough. She shook his hand and let go quickly. "And this is Tori." Her sad friend was much more reserved and much less trusting.

"Ladies? A pleasure to meet you both." He inclined his head with a slight smile and leaned against the bar again. He picked up his glass, his gaze studying them over the rim. "This place is really busy tonight."

Kelly agreed. "More than usual."

Tori didn't answer.

He turned his attention back to Stacy. "I gather you're here to celebrate? Special occasion?"

"No," she answered. "We try to meet up when we can."

"Then I wouldn't be tearing you away from your friends if I asked."

Her nose scrunched up, making her glasses fall. She pushed them up with her finger. "Asked what?"

"Would you like to get out of here? Grab a bite?"

She gulped a deep draught of her drink then put her glass on the bar. He followed with his glass, still holding onto the bag of coffee. She seemed caught as she hesitated.

"Somewhere quieter? I can hardly hear myself think."

Her heart began to flutter. "I'd like that."

With a nod, the bartender came over, and he handed the young man a hundred-dollar bill. "For the tab and anything else they want."

"Ladies? Again, a pleasure to meet you. I've given the bartender enough to cover your drinks and perhaps more. Stacy's agreed to have dinner with me. So if you'll excuse us?"

Are you kidding me? For real? Kelly practically shouted.

Tori was much more skeptical and cautious. She threw Stacy a look. He couldn't help but hear her shout. *If I don't get a text from the restaurant, I'm calling the cavalry.*

She had good friends. "Stacy, you won't forget to send a text, will you? To let everyone know you're safe?"

"Of course," she answered, nodding, looking ready to roll her eyes, so Chaz led the way outside, blowing out a deep breath before he gave her a smile.

"Much quieter."

She didn't answer.

"You have some very good friends."

"Sometimes they forget I can take care of myself." A wisp of hair had loosened from her ponytail to frame her face. She blew it off her cheek with a sideways breath.

"I'm sure you can, but they also care about you."

"A little too much, but I guess I shouldn't complain. Certainly not to someone I've just met."

He dipped his head, lifted a brow, and smiled. "Let's make this a special occasion then. Our first meeting. The Chart House?"

She shifted her pocketbook strap on her shoulder, and some of the tension in her shoulders eased. "I've been there. That would be lovely."

He inclined his head but drew his brows together as if he had a problem. "I have a favor to ask. Would you mind driving? My car is in the garage of my building. We'd have to walk a ways to get it. Or Uber."

"Sure." She turned, and Chaz followed, admiring the view before falling into step next to her. That long stride of hers nearly matched his. "You had everyone going, you know."

"Excuse me?"

"My friends. They're not exactly subtle."

He lifted his eyebrows, hoping he appeared ignorant or innocent, but she didn't seem to buy it.

"Come on. You mean you didn't see the drool all over the floor? Kelly tried to chain you to her."

"That's why I stood next to you. I'm not interested in the obvious."

"Okay. So if I'm not obvious?" she asked, heading down another block. "What exactly am I?" She stopped next to a beat-up Jeep.

A word popped into his head, and he hated it immediately. "Intelligent. Strong. Beautiful."

She tipped her chin, head tilted, eyes widened, and huffed. "Really?"

"Really," he repeated. He climbed in the passenger side while she got in behind the steering wheel. As she put the key in the ignition, he covered her hand with his. Her gaze lifted, filled with confusion, anticipation, and a bit of curiosity. He leaned in and breathed in her scent, a heady mixture of expensive perfume and hormones. Her skin pebbled as he blew lightly on her cheek. Chaz heard the distinct rhythm of her heart as it hammered in her chest, which rose and fell with short rapid breaths.

His incisors grew, and he swiped a taste of her neck. Perfect.

She moaned as he bit down. *God, she tasted sweet.* Much more like dessert than a meal. He sucked and swallowed, sucked and swallowed, and her heart slowed, pounding in his ears to the same rhythm as the city.

Chaz.

He reared back away from her neck. Had he taken too much? Horror filled his gut. No, her flesh was still warm, pulse low and steady, eyes closed.

Thank God.

He leaned over again and bit down, but this time it was to give her the Lethe, the drug that would make her forget he ever existed. He admired her beauty one last time, then reached in her purse and found her driver's license, committing her address to memory. *Shouldn't have done that, Charles.* He climbed out of the car and placed the bag of coffee in the crook of her arm. She would wake up in about an hour or so and not remember a thing.

Damn. That sucked.

Chaz walked home deep in thought. He couldn't get Stacy out of his head. He replayed every moment they spent together, and then he remembered a small detail he must have disregarded. She was a scientist *and* a cop? What if she could help him understand what was happening to his people, why there were more rogues now than he'd seen in the last three hundred years? The idea tantalized. Then his stomach hollowed. He'd be putting her in grave danger. The Council would never allow a human to know about them.

But she was strong. A police officer. She'd be able to stand up to The Council.

And if they decided to end her life anyway?

Chaz shuddered. Then his cell phone buzzed. He stared at the number and smiled. "Pitch?"

"Charles Tower, as I live and breathe."

"You don't."

"Semantics."

"Captain Pritchard. To what do I owe this pleasure?"

"I'm at your place. Apparently, you're not."

Chaz smiled. "I will be in two or three minutes. It's been a long time. You slumming?"

"Uh, no." Pitch hesitated.

"What's going on?"

"When you get here, Chaz. When you get here."

Pitch wanted to talk in private? His stomach clenched. He walked as fast as he dared without attracting too much attention and made it home in two minutes.

With the sun having set, a chill breeze picked up, adding to his unease. A police siren sounded in the distance, reminding him of his duty to protect, making him wonder if there was another rogue they needed to put down. Pitch pushed off the wall and stepped out of the shadows when he arrived at his building. Black hair pulled into a knot at the nape of his neck, slight of build, but with a wiry strength and determination that just wouldn't quit, Pitch was the one vampire Chaz would always want guarding his back.

He clapped his friend on the shoulder, gave him a quick hug, and opened the door. "Smells like you just fed."

Her address was a burned tattoo inside his brain. "I did. Do you need to go out and come back?"

"Nah. If I leave, I'm not planning on coming back. You feel me, bro?"

Chaz winced. There was something out and out wrong about a Colonial Army Captain trying to mimic modern slang. He stepped into the elevator, and Pitch followed. Still curious and out of sorts from wishing he was with Stacy and not Pitch, he didn't say anything. He opened the door to his loft and walked up to a credenza, opened a drawer, and pulled out a key, which he threw to his friend. "In case you need a place to crash."

"Thanks."

Turning, he pinned his friend with a stern stare. "Okay. So what's going on?"

Pitch rubbed the back of his neck and started to pace. "You're gonna think I'm crazy, but I'm worried about Mick."

Chaz snorted then let out the laughter he tried to hold in.

"I know. I know," Pitch answered. "I'm crazy, right? But I'm really worried about him." Pitch stopped pacing, and his brows drew together and two creases furrowed his forehead. "I've been trying to get a hold of him for two weeks. He's not answering my calls or texts. So I went by his place. Doesn't look like he's been there in a while."

"He's been off the grid before."

"Yeah, but if I'm a real pain in the ass, he'll answer. Eventually. Not only have I tried him like three or four times a night, I even checked out his cottage up in Vermont. No sign of him."

A chill crept down Chaz's neck. He dismissed it immediately, as the idea of the three laws and that robot movie filled his head. Vampires had their three laws also.

Vampire rule number one stated a vampire may drink but were forbidden to drain a human to death. Rule two: humans must never know vampires exist, and every human must be given Lethe, so they never remember anything after a vampire has fed. Included in this rule was an edict that, unless a vampire was willing to put his life on the line to defend his actions, he dared not turn a human into a vampire. A long time ago, Chaz figured that was because there weren't that many humans walking the earth. Now he figured this was to continue to safeguard their anonymity.

The final rule, the most important, Chaz believed, was that a vampire should not drink from another vampire. *Ever.* Drinking from another vampire created a connection for as long as their eternity lasted. Before Pitch was born, Chaz and Mick had been forced to drink from each other to stay alive. Chaz would've known if Mick was in trouble.

A chill settled on the back of his neck anyway. "Mick is a big boy.

He's been taking care of himself way longer than we've been around."

Pitch waved his hand, dismissing Chaz's explanation. "I know. But this…this feels different."

"What do you mean, different?"

"Well, for one," he paused, glancing at the bottles of wine in the rack. "You gonna offer me a drink?"

Chaz walked over to his bar and poured them both a small glass of wine. Pitch chugged his. That chill on his neck turned ice cold. "The last time I talked to Mick, he sounded, well, I know you're not going to believe it, but he sounded concerned. Anxious, even. And we both know that's just not Mick."

What? How was that possible? Why didn't he know? Oh shit. What the hell was going on? Chaz sipped on his wine to cover his angst. "Did he say why?"

Pitch stared down at his glass like he wanted ten more. Chaz knew what kind of pain that caused. "Got mad and told me to quit bugging him, that I'd know what was going on when I needed to."

Chaz nodded. "Well, that sounds like Mick, doesn't it?"

"Yeah. Except that was the last time I talked to him. Over two weeks ago."

When Chaz clapped his friend on the shoulder, Pitch looked up. His gaze was filled with worry. "Listen. You need to feed. I'll check around. Try and find him, although we both know if Mick doesn't want to be found…"

Pitch nodded.

"Let's touch base tomorrow night, okay?"

"Hey, look," Pitch said. "Maybe I'm just being paranoid. But he's like a father to me."

"To us all."

He walked Pitch to the front door and gave his friend a quick hug. "He's probably doing it on purpose 'cause you've been bugging him."

"God, I hope so." He punched Chaz in the shoulder and straightened as if the weight on his back lessened. "Thanks, man."

"And not a word to Ozzie or the others yet."

Pitch nodded. "No need worrying them."

"Agreed." Chaz smiled. "Next time, let's go hunting together. Like the old days."

"I'd like that."

"Good. I'm glad you stopped by." But as Chaz shut the door, he knew he was lying. Mick had sent him a file a couple of days ago that made no sense. Pictures of an abandoned estate up in New York. No message. Just the pictures.

What the hell are you doing, Mick? And why aren't you talking to me?

A few hours later, Chaz was still trying to figure out what was going on when his phone buzzed. He read the number, and relief flooded his veins. "What the hell, Mick? You've had Pitch going crazy. Even had me worried."

Silence. Then a voice whispered. "Help me."

Don't stop now. Keep reading with your copy of BLOOD ROGUE by City Owl Author, Linda J. Parisi.

And find more from Poppy Minnix at www.poppyminnix.com

Want even more paranormal romance? Try BLOOD ROGUE by City Owl Author, Linda J. Parisi, and find more from Poppy Minnix at www.poppyminnix.com

---

Ultimate control has its downside, especially when There is the blood and can only ever be the blood. So, how will love survive in a world of pain?

Vampire Charles Tower never knew anything sweeter than the taste of Stacy Morgan's lips.

He never imagined anything crueler than her being marked for death by the only father he's ever known.

Mikhail reared him. Taught him how to survive. Now he's gone rogue and it's up to Charles to put the man down.

But can he convince himself, and Stacy, that love between them is impossible?

That's hard to do with a woman like her, especially when she offers herself up as bait.

Now they must fight against the centuries-old customs that bar them from being together and the rogue vampire who wants every last drop of Stacy's blood.

Please sign up for the City Owl Press newsletter for chances to win special subscriber-only contests and giveaways as well as receiving information on upcoming releases and special excerpts.

All reviews are **welcome** and **appreciated**. Please consider leaving one on your favorite social media and book buying sites.

For books in the world of romance and speculative fiction that embody Innovation, Creativity, and Affordability, check out City Owl Press at www.cityowlpress.com.

Acknowledgments

To the City Owl staff who saw what My Song's Curse could be, thank you. You've prepped it into this lovely thing, and I appreciate every step you've taken to send this novel out into the world. It's been a sweet process.

My kind, encouraging friends, Shirley and Nadean, deserve a medal. They read the first draft and actually kinda liked it. You are by far the bravest souls with love-goggles on, and I appreciate the hell out of you, as do Alex and Lu because without your "I LOVE THIS, PUBLISH IT!" pep talks, they may have stayed in their short story.

Thank you, gremlins. You let me write in twenty-minute bursts and only complained sometimes, which was completely valid because Candyland is an awesome game. I will probably forever be in your memory as holding up my finger as I wrote just one more paragraph with the other hand. I love you to pieces, my tiny distracting rockstars.

Hey, hubs. Yeah, you got the dedication as well, but I should still say how incredibly awesome you are, because you truly are. Thank you for letting me stay up late to finish a scene, letting me zone into my writing with no guilt, and always being on my side. I am yours, and you are mine, and we are so lucky.

My brainstorming/crit group DEF ladies Lourdes, Jackie, Jaycee, PM, Raisa, and Cassandra are the best writer buds a girl could have. I adore you all. Thank you for the motivation, critiques, and help figuring out what the heck happens next and how to make the bad guy badder. You all are amazing, talented writers, and I'm glad we're a thing.

Ah, my critter friends Davis, Morgan, Barbara, Bigga, Owen, and Lori. You have poked and prodded this novel into working order. Thank you so much for the feedback on everything from dude voice to my thousand incorrect uses of a comma.

Cassandra! Thank you, my lovely friend, for letting me talk your ear off during edits. You met every brainstorm with more questions to build the world and soothed every panicked I-don't-know-what-I'm-doing moment with your stoic, "You've got this." If all writers had a writer friend like you, we'd have more beautiful books in this world.

Immy, you write more bravely than anyone I know. You're a constant inspiration to push the line and let an honest voice fly free.

Thank you, Nicole, for being on my team from chapter one. You opened doors and were my first breath of this industry. I'm so glad to have met you.

Tee, thank you for teaching me how to make My Song's Curse sing. Your honest but needed direction has been crucial in making this into a novel I love and am proud of.

About the Author

POPPY MINNIX is an award-winning paranormal romance and urban fantasy novelist living in Maryland. When she's not writing, she's chasing after two young kids, reading, playing board games with her hubs, or plotting her next writing project. She has a love for powerful men and women who are already exceptional but find that together they can conquer their inner demons—or actual demons.

www.poppyminnix.com

twitter.com/PoppyMinnix
instagram.com/poppyminnix
facebook.com/poppymwrites
goodreads.com/poppyminnix

About the Publisher

City Owl Press is a cutting edge indie publishing company, bringing the world of romance and speculative fiction to discerning readers.

www.cityowlpress.com

Made in the USA
Middletown, DE
17 April 2024